SHIELD'S LADY

AMANDA GLASS

POPULAR LIBRARY

An Imprint of Warner Books, Inc.

A Warner Communications Company

"I need you, Sariana. In ways you can't even guess at yet."

Sariana tried to free herself, but she was suddenly caged between Gryph's hands. "Gryph, please listen to me. You have a fever, probably brought on by your wound. You need rest."

He shook his head slowly. "No. All I need is you. I'll show you." He lowered his head and took her mouth once more with devastating force. Sariana responded even as she tried to tell herself she should get out of the bed. But when he pressed himself along the length of her, letting her feel the rock hard strength of him, her own body grew warm again with passion. Tentatively she put her arms around him and stroked the hard, muscled strength of his shoulders.

"That's it, my Shield Lady," he said in aching relief. His mouth moved across hers and down the column of her throat. He buried his lips in the curve of her shoulder and breathed deeply of her fragrance. "That's what I want from you. Touch me. Give yourself to me..."

SHIELD'S LADY

Chapter
1

THE unconscious man stirred slightly and groaned. He did not open his eyes and therefore was unable to appreciate the flamboyant luxury that surrounded him.

He lay on the polished marble floor of an ornately appointed room. A high, heavily embossed ceiling arched overhead. The golden glow of the vapor lamps filtered through intricately beveled glass fixtures. A long, narrow table of polished black stone dominated the small chamber. The table was curved, forming a semicircle.

Five people sat around the table. Two of them, the older man and woman, were obviously the matriarch and patriarch of the clan. The other two, a handsome young man and an equally attractive young woman, were clearly sister and brother. The distinctive combination of silvery blond hair and night-dark eyes that marked the father also characterized his offspring. The mother was also blond and dark-eyed, although her coloring came from a different set of genes. None of the four could be described as petite. The

Avylyns were a tall, well-built clan, the men broad-shouldered and the women full-bodied.

The fifth person present was another young woman. She was quite slender and far more delicately built than the others; she also lacked their regal height, much to her private disgust. There were times when she would have found the sheer presence that being tall and statuesque conveyed very useful. She had, however, found ways to compensate.

Her neatly arranged brown-gold hair and wide, hazel eyes also set her apart. But even if her looks and coloring had not been radically different, her attire would have made it clear she was not a member of the Avylyn Clan.

Sariana Dayne was discreetly dressed in a conservative, dark green outfit that featured a strictly tailored jacket and a simple, flared skirt that ended just above her ankles. The snug little jacket emphasized her slenderness and its crisp, high collar framed her throat. Beneath the hem of the skirt dark stockings and low-heeled slippers of soft leather were visible. She wore no jewelry.

The other two women at the table were wearing modishly cut, low-necked gowns in vivid gemstone hues with billowing sleeves and full skirts draped over large bustles. Their high-heeled slippers were made of heavily embroidered satin and their hair was arranged in towering confections of cascading curls.

The women's jewelry was magnificent. The Avylyns were, after all, a clan of jewelers. Fragile links of gold set with colorful stones were entwined in their hair. Several pairs of earrings vied for space on each pair of earlobes. The Avylyn women had their ears pierced in so many places Sariana had often thought it remarkable that there was any skin left there at all. Their ample bosoms were adorned with wide collars fashioned of gold and silver and two kinds of rare quartz. They had rings on almost every finger.

The men were equally gaudy in appearance. They wore brightly colored doublets, scarlet tights and shirts with enough fabric in the slashed sleeves to set a ship asail. They wore nearly as many jewels as the Avylyn women.

Sariana had noticed lately that Bryer, the handsome eldest son, had adopted the new fashion of wearing a vividly decorated codpiece. He had one on tonight. The truth was, she probably couldn't have failed to notice it if she'd tried. Codpieces were not easily overlooked, especially ones set with semiprecious stones.

The Avylyns had flair, Sariana observed once again with secret amusement. There was not a dull one in the bunch.

The members of the Avylyn Clan tended toward the dramatic in their choice of clothing just as they did in everything else. After a year of living in the household, Sariana was accustomed to her employers' dazzling attire and volatile ways. She had even grown quite fond of them, much to her surprise. They could be exasperating but they were also rather fascinating, just like everything else here in the western provinces.

The man on the floor groaned again, interrupting Sariana's thoughts. One booted foot shifted slightly on the marble.

"Excellent," Sariana said as she looked down at the man sprawled on the floor. "We're in luck. He's not dead." She kept her voice light and cheerful, trying not to show the relief she felt. Never let the client know you were nervous was one of her mottoes. She sent up a silent thank you to whatever unseen forces looked out for business consultants. At least she wasn't going to have to worry about explaining a dead man to the authorities. Her palms were still damp from the anxiety she had been hiding.

"Might be better for all of us if he were dead," Bryer Avylyn said gloomily. "He's going to be very angry when he wakes up."

Sariana glared at the striking scion of the Avylyn Clan. "Don't be ridiculous. What happened was an accident. I'm sure this Shield person, or whatever it is you call him, will understand that when we explain what happened. How could we know that your Aunt Perla's recipe for a mild hypnotic drug would have this reaction on him? It should have done nothing more than put him into a light trance. It was supposed to make him friendly and amenable. It wasn't supposed to make him pass out."

Bryer lifted his head to meet Sariana's eyes. A lock of his brilliantly blond hair fell across his brow. Sariana knew that the charmingly sexy style in which Bryer's hair arranged itself had been precisely calculated by a very fashionable hairdresser. The style highlighted Bryer's dark eyes, making the contrast to his gilded hair that much stronger.

"Sariana, you don't understand," Bryer informed her with deep foreboding. "Shields are not known for their understanding and patience. You don't seem to grasp the fact that this man is potentially very dangerous. He was raised on the frontier. He makes his living fighting the border bandits. He is not going to take kindly to what we have done. I'm telling you we should never have tried this trick. We should never have listened to you in the first place."

Bryer's mother, who was sitting at the other end of the glistening black stone table spoke firmly. "That's enough, Bryer. This was a family decision. We all agreed with Sariana that getting a Shield to help us was our only chance."

Indina Avylyn glanced at her husband who sat at the opposite end of the semicircular table. "Isn't that right, Jasso? You yourself said it. We're all in this together. We had no choice. We must go through with this wild plan for the sake of the Clan of Avylyn."

Sariana couldn't help but admire the stirring quality Lady Avylyn had infused into those last words. Lady Avylyn had descended from a clan of dramatists. Even though she had married into a jewelsmith clan, she had never quite abandoned her origins.

Lord Jasso Avylyn shook his graying blond head uncertainly as he stared down at the man sprawled on the floor. "I fear we have no choice now but to go forward with Sariana's plan. We can only hope this Shield doesn't wake up in such a towering rage that he decides to kill us all before he even listens to our proposal."

"Father, he wouldn't do that!" Mara, the Avylyns' only daughter, sprang to her feet in an impassioned movement.

She had inherited some of her mother's talent. The skirts of her long, deep blue gown swirled around her delicate high-heeled slippers. Her chest, a great deal of which was exposed by the elegant gown, heaved dramatically. The motion of her chest caused the beautiful jeweled collar around her neck to shimmer. "I spoke to him last night, remember? I had a chance to talk to him in the tavern before I put Aunt Perla's medicine into his ale. Admittedly he was somewhat drunk, but he certainly didn't seem violently inclined."

Bryer gave his sister a disgusted look. "Of course he didn't seem violently inclined. He was trying to seduce you. And you were enjoying playing the role of loose woman, weren't you? I'll wager the only thing you talked about with him was sex. The last thing he was likely to do was show you his violent side when he was trying to talk you into bed. But he's a Shield, Mara, never forget that. You have heard the legends about Shields. Violence is bred in their bones."

"So is honor!" Mara was incensed. She whirled to confront her brother, her dark eyes flashing. "By the blood of the Ship's Captain, Bryer Avylyn, don't you dare call me names. I was playing the role I was assigned to play. No more, no less. This was all Sariana's idea, remember? She's the one who suggested I portray a tavern wench looking for a good time."

"Children, please," Jasso said anxiously. "This is no time to quarrel. Our goal is to regain the prisma cutter from the hands of those thieving Nosorians. We've gone too far to back out now."

"But, Father . . ."

Sariana decided to intervene before the situation got completely out of hand. A family quarrel was in the making and she had neither the time nor the patience to weather one tonight. All of the blond, handsome Avylyns had strong tendencies toward melodrama. In that respect they were typical of most of the inhabitants of the western provinces. Give any one of them a convenient stage, Sariana had learned, and one could expect an outrageous display of dramatic fireworks. Not to mention a lot of noise.

Sometimes the noise of the Avylyn Clan was too much for her. Sariana had been brought up in a far more civilized household. But the elegant, sophisticated, well-managed home of the Dayne Clan lay halfway around the planet of Windarra on the eastern continent. A year earlier Sariana had made the wrenching decision to leave her clan and journey across the seas to the wilds of the western continent. There was not only an ocean between her parents' home in Rendezvous and her new home in the town of Serendipity; there was also a gaping abyss in terms of lifestyle. Sariana was still working on the problem of culture shock.

The artisans, craftsmen, designers and gemologists of the Avylyn Clan were technically Sariana's clients. Officially she was their business manager. Although she was only a couple years older than Mara, there were times when Sariana felt more like a nanny than a business manager.

She coughed gently and tapped the table with the heel of the small fan she carried. The fan was a western affectation she had somehow acquired. It had its uses.

"If I may have your attention, please." Sternly she regarded each member of the Avylyn Clan present at the midnight meeting.

The need for secrecy had led Lord Jasso, the patriarch, to ordain that only the oldest and most immediate members of the Prime Family be present tonight. Even Luri, the youngest son, was not here. Needless to say, no one beyond the Prime Family had been notified of either the loss of the valuable prisma cutter or the plan for recovering it. Aunts, uncles, distant cousins and other assorted Avylyns were being kept in blissful ignorance, as were all business rivals. The responsibility for protecting the cutter was, after all, the task of the Prime Family of the Clan. Now that it had been stolen, Jasso's duty was clear. He had to get it back, even if it meant dealing with a dangerous Shield.

In practical terms that meant Sariana had to find a way to retrieve the cutter. A business manager's lot was often a difficult one.

"We are committed now," Sariana said coolly. "There is no turning back. Granted, the fact that the drug didn't work as it was supposed to has made things slightly more difficult, but we can adapt to the situation."

"It's because they're different," Lady Avylyn said with a sigh.

Sariana glanced at her, impatient with the interruption. "I beg your pardon, Lady Avylyn? What are different?"

"Shields. The members of the Shield clans are different," Lady Avylyn explained gravely. "That difference is more than just a matter of customs and dress and manners. It goes all the way to the bone."

Sariana blinked in astonishment. "I'm afraid I don't understand, Lady Avylyn."

It was Lord Avylyn who tried hurriedly to explain. "It's part of the legend, you know. Shields are—well, not quite like the rest of us. It's difficult for you to understand because you don't have any equivalent to the Shield class in the eastern provinces. Here the Shields occupy a special niche in society. They are living legends."

Sariana glanced at the man on the floor with a mildly derisive expression. "That's a living legend? He looks more like a frontier bandit who wandered into town and got drunk."

Lady Avylyn was horrified. "Don't ever call him a bandit, Sariana. Shields are very proud. They spend their time getting rid of bandits. You should hear some of the tales of frontier battles."

"No offense," Sariana said briskly, "but in my opinion, you westerners give entirely too much credence to your legends and tales."

"Just because you easterners have forgotten all your First Generation tales doesn't mean we have ignored our own history," Mara exclaimed.

Sariana was annoyed. "The fact that we easterners didn't bother to immortalize our history in a lot of silly ballads

and plays doesn't mean we have forgotten that history."
She resented the implication that the descendants of the
colony ship *The Rendezvous* had not protected their history
as well as the descendants of *The Serendipity* had.

"The descendants of the First Generation colonists from
The Rendezvous," she continued, "may have lost most of
their technology and some of their records in the struggle
to survive on Windarra just as your people did, but we
didn't invent a lot of wild tales to fill in the gaps. This is
not, however, the time to be arguing over which group of
colonists kept the best track of their history."

"That much is true," Lady Avylyn said and then dramatically lowered her voice. "But whether or not you choose to
believe our legends, Sariana, please be careful when dealing with them. Especially this particular legend." She indicated the man on the floor. "There aren't many Shields.
Never were. Their birthrate is very low and the offspring
are always male which sometimes makes for some, uh,
difficulties . . . "

"I don't see why," Sariana said with a frown. "Oh, you
mean there aren't any women in their social class except
those who marry into it?"

"Their marriage customs are rather odd," Lady Avylyn
began awkwardly. "You see, they—" She stopped as the
other members of the family stared at her. She cleared her
throat and waved her fan in a gesture of impatient dis-
missal. "Never mind," she went on hurriedly. "It's rather
complicated. Just take our word for it. Shields can be difficult. The last thing one wishes to do is antagonize them."

"Shouldn't you have mentioned that fact when you first
told me a Shield might be able to help us get back the
prisma cutter?" Sariana retorted.

"We did tell you that Shields are different," Jasso reminded her. He sounded resentful and with good reason.
When the plan to engage a Shield had first been proposed,
Sariana hadn't paid much attention to warnings of potential
difficulties. "We explained they walk their own paths and
tend to stay on the outskirts of society. They live on the

frontiers for the most part. One doesn't run into one in town very often. Fortunately."

Bryer looked speculatively at the man on the floor. "But occasionally one finds a Shield useful."

"Useful as a mercenary," Sariana clarified dryly. "Let's all stop snapping at each other. For better or worse, we've got our Shield and we managed not to kill him in the process. Barely. We must go forward from here. Our first priority is getting back that prisma cutter, and from everything you have told me, hiring a Shield is our best bet."

"I'm not sure he's going to consider this a valid employment contract," Jasso said skeptically. "I wonder why he passed out from that tiny drop of hypnotic drug Mara gave him?"

"Because Shields are different," Lady Avylyn said firmly. "I told you that."

Sariana was amused more than alarmed by the Avylyns' conviction that the man on the floor was somehow fundamentally different from other people.

Sariana eyed her captive. He certainly dressed differently than the members of most of the other social classes she had encountered in Serendipity. The truth was, she found his strictly styled, close fitting dark trousers and unadorned long-sleeved shirt something of a relief from all the showy fashions that were popular in the capital city of the western provinces.

He had on a severely cut waist-length jacket instead of the more popular flowing cape, and his boots and belt were made of untooled leather. There was nothing outrageous or ornate about his attire. No gems set in the heels of his boots or tracings of silver on the collar and cuffs of his shirt.

And no codpiece, Sariana noted with a flash of humor. She found that fact oddly reassuring.

The only item of the Shield's apparel that could be called decorative was the black leather pouch he wore attached to his belt. The pouch itself was made of the practically indestructible hide of the legendary snake cat. Sariana had never actually seen a snake cat, but Luri, the Avylyns' youngest, had regaled her with hair raising tales of the beasts. Apparently they favored swamplands and could swallow a man in one gulp.

Sariana had no idea how accurate such tales were, but on the whole she was happy to forego the experience of encountering a live specimen. She wondered if the man on the floor had actually hunted for the leather to be used in his pouch or if he'd bought it.

It was the clasp on the leather pouch that constituted the man's one item of adornment. But that single item was a major exception. The pouch was sealed and locked with an intricate mechanism fashioned from pure prisma.

Sariana had learned enough about the jewelry business from the Avylyns to recognize the strange silvery crystal when she saw it. She had also learned something of its value. The clasp on the pouch was worth a fortune. Prisma was the rarest and most expensive of all jewels. The man sprawled on the floor did not look as if he could afford such an expensive closure for his pouch. Perhaps he'd stolen it.

"My apologies if I offend the Clan," Sariana said firmly, "but to be honest, the man does not appear to be all that dangerous. That's the problem when one puts too much credence in First Generation myths and legends. One forgets to deal in facts. I see no reason why we can't continue with our plan just as soon as he wakes up."

Lord Avylyn was troubled. "Do you really think you can deal with him, Sariana? How are we going to explain what happened in the tavern?"

"Don't worry," she assured him confidently. "I'll do the talking." She glanced again at the black leather kit attached to the Shield's belt. Something made her very curious about it. On impulse she rose to her feet and strode briskly around the table to where the man lay motionless.

"Sariana!" Lady Avylyn gasped. "What are you doing? Don't touch that."

"Nonsense. It might be useful to know what the Shield considers valuable enough to decorate with prisma."

Sariana knelt down beside the man and examined the

leather strap that held the pouch to the belt. She put out her hand to undo the fastening and then paused uncertainly. Behind her she could practically hear the others holding their collective breath.

Up close like this, the Shield appeared larger and infinitely more solid than he had looked from across the room. A man lying sprawled on his back fooled the eye slightly and looked smaller than he actually was. But now that she was kneeling beside him, Sariana got a whole new perspective. She began to sense why the Avylyns were so wary of the Shield they had captured.

There was a smooth, well-muscled strength in his shoulders and the lines of his thighs were sleek and powerful. He was lean and tough looking, and the arrogant set of his features—even when unconscious—only served to emphasize his other hard qualities.

Sariana realized she was forgetting to breathe. She found herself inexplicably and acutely aware of the man in a way she couldn't explain. She was suddenly, intensely interested in him. No, it was beyond that. She realized that for some reason she was fascinated by him. If she had any faith in western tales of goblins and fairies, she might have believed she was under a small spell. But that was a crazy notion.

Her fingers hovered above the fastening that held the leather pouch to the Shield's belt, but she didn't quite touch the object. Instead she found herself examining the man's face more closely.

His hair was black, as dark as a midnight sky. He wore it much shorter than the fashionable men in town. Sariana's gaze moved quickly over his closed eyes. She speculated briefly about their color and decided they would probably be dark. Dark eyes were common on the western continent. Then her gaze went to his sharp nose, took in the well etched but grim shape of his mouth and went on to the hard lines of his jaw.

The Shield could not be deemed handsome, but Sariana knew with a sense of shock that this man would never need to trade on his looks. It was clear to her that he would make his way in the world on his own terms, even though he moved on the fringes of respectable society.

A tiny shiver went through Sariana as she crouched, gazing down at the man on the floor. She realized that she had been staring at him much too long. She had to break the strange sense of enthrallment.

Angry at the effect the unconscious Shield had had on her, she quickly jerked open the leather catch that held the pouch to the belt.

Lady Avylyn took a deep, shaky breath and Mara gave a soft cry as Sariana lifted the pouch free. Jasso and Bryer just groaned.

In that instant the Shield lifted his dark lashes without any warning and Sariana had the answer to her earlier question about the shade of his eyes. They were an unfamiliar blue-green. She had never seen eyes quite that color before in her life. They locked immediately on her face. Sariana was gripped by the unnerving conviction that she suddenly knew far too much about him.

He could be dangerous.

An implacable enemy.

He would be a fiercely possessive lover.

Sariana felt the breath catch in her throat at that last, unbidden thought. For a few shocking seconds she questioned the fundamental intelligence behind the plan she had initiated and talked the Avylyns into accepting. She wondered if she had just made the biggest mistake of her short career as a business manager.

But as she had told her clients, there was no turning back.

Gryph Chassyn focused painfully on the woman standing above him, the one who had had the breathtaking arrogance to actually separate him from his weapon kit. No sane westerner would have risked such an act, unless the fool was looking to get his or her throat slit.

The woman was still standing because Gryph sensed that she did not realize the significance of what she had done. There were others in the room who did realize it, but he ignored them. The woman was the one who held his kit. She was the one he watched. She fascinated him.

Gryph's first coherent thought after he concluded she was not an enemy was that he wanted her. Badly. A ravenous hunger was pouring through his veins. It was unlike anything he had ever experienced around a woman. It left him feeling disoriented, frustrated, and shaking with a strange tension.

He forced himself to focus all his attention on regaining his control.

Gryph moved carefully, levering himself up on one elbow. His eyes never left the woman who held his kit. He had been fighting his way up through the hazy, drugged fog inside his head for several minutes, listening half consciously to the voices of the five people in the chamber. Having the weapon kit taken from him had instantly jerked him back to full awareness.

"Return the kit to me," he ordered calmly. He held out his hand with a casual imperiousness he hoped would do the trick.

But the woman actually clutched the leather pouch more tightly and took a quick step backward. She managed a surprisingly brilliant smile. Gryph decided that under normal circumstances he would probably find himself responding to that smile. But whatever had happened to him at the tavern was not normal.

"I'm so glad you're awake at last," the woman said easily. She walked briskly back to her place at the table where the others sat stupefied by the small scene that had just taken place. As she sat down, she put Gryph's weapon kit on the polished black stone in front of her. "I'm Sariana Dayne. I am the business manager for the others here with me tonight. They form the Prime Family of the Avylyn Clan. Well, most of the Prime Family. Luri isn't with us. He's a bit too young for this sort of thing."

"I think I'm a bit too old for this sort of thing," Gryph said, feeling the need to stop her lightly tumbling words.

He recognized her accent now. She was from the eastern continent. Had to be. That explained her recklessness regarding his weapon kit. Gryph forced himself to draw a deep, slow breath while he tried to sort out the various elements of the bizarre situation in which he found himself. It was difficult to think with a raging headache and a body that seemed far too heavy and awkward. At least he had the rush of lust back under control. At this point he was grateful for small favors.

The woman's smile became even more brilliant. "I'm sure you have a number of questions and you don't look as if you're feeling very well, but I assure you I can explain everything."

"An excellent idea." He rubbed the back of his neck. "Why don't you tell me what this is all about?"

It was an order, not a polite request, and he saw that Sariana understood that at once. The others appeared almost mesmerized with anxiety. That was good. Gryph was not unfamiliar with the response. It left him free to concentrate on Sariana. He had already decided that she was the most dangerous one in the group.

Sariana cleared her throat with a small, discreet cough and managed to keep the smile in place. "We have a business proposition to put to you, Shield."

"My name is Chassyn," he replied through set teeth. "Gryph Chassyn." Sariana's subtle air of feminine challenge set off immediate responses in his system. He did not like his present position in front of her. He needed a little more advantage. With great effort he rose from the cold marble floor, disgusted to find his legs were decidedly unsteady. It took nearly all his strength and willpower just to stay on his feet. He hoped the Dayne woman didn't notice the effort it cost him.

"Gryph Chassyn," Sariana repeated thoughtfully, as if tasting the name. "Well, Gryph, let me tell you about the business deal we would like to present to you."

Gryph winced as pain shot through his head. He made his way slowly over to the center of the curving stone table so that he was directly opposite Sariana. Then he braced himself with one hand on the polished surface. He tried to make the movement nonchalant, but the truth was he was afraid he would wind up back on the floor if he didn't use the table for support. He looked steadily at Sariana who was sitting just out of reach. His weapon kit was sitting just out of reach, also.

"First tell me what you put in my ale."

Before Sariana could open her mouth to answer, another voice spoke up. A small, miserable, infinitely contrite little voice.

"It was a mistake," the young Avylyn female cried. "It wasn't my idea. I certainly didn't mean to hurt you. Aunt Perla's concoction was only supposed to, uh, relax you slightly."

Slowly Gryph turned his head and glanced at the young woman. For the first time he focused on the other people at the table. His eyes narrowed with lazy menace as he recognized the beautiful blond who was gazing at him with such a stricken expression.

"Ah, yes," he said blandly, "the tavern wench. I seem to recall your name was Mara. I owe this headache to you?"

"It was all her idea," Mara blurted, pointing the tip of her jeweled fan at Sariana.

Gryph nodded and turned back to face Sariana. "Somehow that doesn't surprise me." He drummed his fingers lightly on the tabletop in a gesture of barely suppressed annoyance. "My own fault," he muttered. "I must have seen the bottom of too many ale glasses by the time Mara the sexy tavern wench sat down at my table. I was careless."

"About our business proposition," Sariana continued in a brisk tone.

"What about it?" Gryph eyed his weapon kit and wondered if he was up to making a quick grab for it. The heaviness that gripped his muscles was fading, but not very rapidly. Whatever had been put into his ale had probably mixed with the alcohol already in his bloodstream and created a strong drugging effect. Given the small differences between a Shield's physical reactions and those of other people, it was predictable that the drug hadn't worked quite as planned.

Sariana spoke quickly. "A certain valuable object has been stolen from the Avylyns. We wish to engage you to get it back for us."

Gryph glanced at her, considering. "Why didn't you just ask me straight out if I wanted a job? Why the drug routine?"

Sariana sighed. There was regret in her eyes but her voice didn't falter. "We sent three messages to the apartments you are renting. You chose to ignore all three."

"You were behind those stupid little notes requesting a business meeting?" he asked in astonishment. If he'd known she'd been the author of those very formal, very elegant, very arrogant notes he would have been at the Avylyns' front door immediately.

"Yes, as a matter of fact, I was," Sariana replied. "Now, as I was saying, if you hadn't ignored them—"

"I ignored them," Gryph said calmly, "because I'm not looking for a job at the moment."

Bryer spoke up, his curiosity getting the better of his nervousness. "Then why are you here? Shields rarely spend much time in Serendipity or any other town unless they're looking for a job."

"Or a wife," Gryph reminded him.

The Avylyns stared at him.

"I wondered if that might be your reason," Lady Avylyn said quietly. She looked uneasily at her daughter.

Gryph could have told her not to worry about her precious Mara. He had absolutely no interest in the young woman. She might have made an amusing bed partner for one night, but she was not a potential Shieldmate. He had known that as soon as she had sat down across from him and asked him to buy her a glass of ale. He'd already had a fair amount to drink and he had given up his search for the evening. Under such circumstances, Mara had appeared temporarily interesting.

Sariana was paying no attention to the undercurrents in the room. She seemed unaware of the Avylyns' new source of anxiety as she plunged ahead with her business proposition. Gryph had to admire her perseverance. And her tongue. The latter never seemed to be still for long. He leaned on his hand and fantasized briefly about shutting her up with a kiss. It would be interesting to see how much longer she could continue to chatter once he had his tongue inside her mouth.

"When you proved unwilling to meet with us," Sariana was saying crisply, "I made the decision to use a mild hypnotic in the hopes that it would put you into a more, shall we say, receptive state of mind while we negotiated. I realize that probably strikes you as somewhat bold, but under the circumstances I felt I had no other option."

"Bold?" Gryph examined the word. "No, I wouldn't say it was bold. Dumb, perhaps. Stupid, maybe. But I don't think bold quite captures the spirit of such a piece of idiocy."

Sariana's brows came together in a quelling expression. "Look, I have apologized for the inconvenience you have experienced. Believe me, I would not have attempted such a thing if we had not been quite desperate."

"*Inconvenience*? Is that how you describe what you did to me? You have an interesting way with words, lady."

"I am trying to explain to you exactly what happened so that we may proceed in a rational manner to conclude a perfectly reasonable business deal," Sariana said with obviously forced patience.

"Plan A has obviously failed. Have you got a Plan B?" Gryph told himself that if he weren't feeling so rotten he might almost be enjoying himself. The lady was amusing, as well as a challenge.

And she still had her small, silvered fingertips around his weapon kit. He knew she sensed its importance to him and he also knew she was frantically trying to figure out how to use the kit to get what she wanted. It would be interesting to see what she did next.

Sariana Dayne was no great beauty, Gryph decided objectively. But her sleekly styled hair and quietly refined clothing made her stand out in comparison to the vivid Avylyns. He liked the sparkling intelligence in her hazel eyes, her small tilted nose and the fullness of her lower lip.

She had vital, appealing features. She was the kind of woman who drew a man with more subtle lures than those used by giggling, fluff-headed beauties such as Mara Avylyn.

"We don't have what you might call a Plan B," Sariana said slowly, tapping her silver nails absently against the black kit under her hand. "But I would like you to listen to our original proposal."

"Did anyone warn you that a Shield's services don't come cheap?"

Sariana rallied to the challenge as if she thrived on this sort of encounter. Her smile was more dazzling than ever. "I was told such services are quite expensive, when they can be purchased at all. I understand you usually spend your days chasing bandits, but that you will occasionally take on private commissions."

"Occasionally." Gryph tried a smile of his own. One that showed plenty of teeth. "For a price."

"Yes, well, I should make it clear right from the start that the Avylyns have something of a cash flow problem at the moment."

"A cash flow problem," Gryph repeated blankly.

"Just a small one," Sariana assured him breezily. "Nothing that won't be under control within the next few months. It means, of course, that you would have to be willing to accept your payment at a later date than you might under most circumstances, but that shouldn't be a major hurdle in our negotiations."

Gryph held up a palm in an effort to slow her down. He was finding it difficult to follow the conversation. "Wait a minute. You mean you want me to do the job now and then sit around and wait a few months for my pay?"

Sariana lifted her chin. "I assure you, the Avylyns' cash flow problem will be under control very soon."

Gryph glanced around at the elegantly dressed women of the clan. They stared back anxiously. "There's enough jewelry hanging around the ladies' necks to finance several weeks or even months of my services. Assuming I'm willing to go to work for you."

"Most of that lovely jewelry is in hock to the bank, I'm afraid," Sariana retorted cheerfully, as if it were a minor detail. "Collateral, you know. We needed to raise vast sums to revive the business. It's necessary that the Avylyns' continue to keep up appearances in the meantime, of course. They must continue to dress and entertain according to their social status. But I'm afraid there's no cash to spare from the personal accounts. And even if we could find a way to sell off some of the jewelry from the Avylyns' private collection, we would be highly reluctant to do so. The sort of gossip that would start would be devastating to the Clan at this juncture."

"What made you think," Gryph asked with grave interest, "that I'd be willing to wait for my payment?"

Sariana drew a breath. Her small, sweetly rounded breasts rose behind the green fabric of her gown. Gryph found himself watching the movement instead of paying attention to what Sariana was saying. She had very nice breasts, he decided. Nice waist, too. A man could lie on his back, put his hands around that waist and lift Sariana up and over himself so that she straddled his thighs. Then he could ease her down onto his shaft until he filled her completely. Gryph decided he would like to see the expression in those hazel eyes if he did exactly that. His mind was so engrossed with the image he had created for himself that he caught only bits and pieces of what Sariana was saying.

"Regarding your request for assurance that you will be paid," Sariana went on, "I want you to know that the Avylyns and I have considered the matter carefully. We understand that you, like the bank, need some form of collateral. Lady Avylyn suggested a rather unusual idea. She said you might be willing to postpone taking your pay if, in the meantime, she offered to introduce you socially. She seems to think you might have an eye toward marriage and that you would welcome the opportunity to meet socially acceptable young ladies. Marriage is always an important decision and if you are presently considering it, then you might be interested in Lady Avylyn's kind offer. If, however, that doesn't appeal, I have another suggestion."

Out of the flow of words pouring so earnestly from Sariana's mouth, Gryph caught the one that mattered most. He nearly lost his balance. He gripped the edge of the stone table with far more force than was necessary.

"Marriage," he repeated, his tongue thick in his mouth. He raised his eyes to Sariana's politely composed face. "To you?"

"Oh, no, not to me," Sariana said with a light laugh. "I'm afraid you weren't listening. I said the Avylyns have agreed to introduce you socially to their friends and relatives. I understand that it is somewhat difficult for a Shield to meet suitable young women. Probably has something to do with spending too much of your time chasing bandits on the frontiers. Be that as it may, if you are agreeable to our offer, I see no reason why we can't conclude our deal this evening. You would start work in the morning. What do you say?"

"I say you have the fast tongue of a Rendezvous lawyer."

"It seems to me that the Avylyns are prepared to be quite generous," Sariana said. "Given the limitations of your present social status, I should think you would be grateful for their offer. That is, if you are, indeed, in the market for a wife."

Gryph experienced a sudden, nearly overwhelming desire to reach across the table, drag Sariana out of her chair and carry her out of the chamber. He knew what he would do with her as soon as he had her alone in his own bed chamber, he told himself. He knew *exactly* what he would do with her.

"Listen, lady Business Manager," he said grimly. "I don't know where or how you did your social research, but I can guarantee that the last thing I'd sell my services for is a little help in finding a wife. I've been desperate, but never that desperate. *I'm a Shield, damn it*. I'll do my own wife hunting."

There was a collective gasp of anguish from the assembled Avylyns, but Gryph ignored them. His attention was on Sariana. She did not gasp or cry out in horror. She merely blinked, her long lashes momentarily veiling the speculative intelligence in her eyes.

Without a word she moved the weapon kit a little farther out of his reach. Gryph abruptly decided he'd had enough of her little games. He gathered himself for a quick, determined swipe at the kit.

Just as his hand came out, however, Sariana released the kit and it sank instantly out of sight. Gryph watched in shock as his precious weapon kit vanished into a concealed opening in the stone. The opening was already sealing shut. There was not even a line to mark where the trap door existed. Westerners loved such gadgets.

Impatience, irritation and the indulgent curiosity that Gryph had been experiencing up to that point disappeared in an instant. Fury engulfed him. The hand Gryph had been extending to grasp his kit locked around Sariana's small wrist instead. He yanked her forward until her upper body was sprawled across the table. Her eyes widened and he realized he was finally seeing genuine alarm in her gaze. It was about time, he decided.

"Get it back." Each word he spoke fell like a stone into the appalled silence that had seized the chamber. "Now."

"Please," she whispered, "just listen to me. That's all I'm asking. Let me tell you the whole story of the prisma cutter. We need your help."

"Get back my kit or I'll find a way to make you vanish just as easily as you made it disappear. Understood?"

"You've made yourself quite clear," she replied in a shaky voice.

She was finally scared, but her eyes still met his with steady determination. In spite of his raw mood, Gryph felt a reluctant surge of admiration for Sariana's daring. He knew of no other woman in Serendipity or the outlying provinces who would have taken such a risk.

"Give it to him, Sariana," Jasso hissed. "Quickly."

"Hurry, before he kills us all," Lady Avylyn pleaded.

Bryer and Mara sat staring at Sariana, panic in their expressions.

"What will it cost us to get your help?" Sariana whispered, her eyes huge.

Gryph was amazed. "You're still trying to negotiate a deal, lady?"

"We need your help," she repeated doggedly. "If you won't accept the offer of being introduced socially while you wait for your payment, what kind of a deal will you accept? Name your price."

Gryph looked down at her. "Tell me who needs my help."

"I've just told you. The Avylyn Clan."

He shook his head, knowing suddenly what he wanted from her. "No. Not the Avylyns. They would be long gone by now if it wasn't for you. Tell me who really needs my services. Tell me who will pay whatever she has to pay in order to get them."

Sariana stared at him, confused. Gryph waited, willing her to understand what he wanted from her. Then he saw the knowledge dawn in her large eyes.

"I need your help," Sariana said quietly.

"Say it again."

She set her teeth. "I need your help."

Gryph nodded, satisfied. "That's right. You. Not the Avylyns." He released her. Sariana sat back in her seat, massaging her wrist unobtrusively. She regarded him with wary, smoldering eyes.

"Get my weapon kit out of that stone table," Gryph ordered calmly.

Sariana pressed a hidden button under the table and a section of the polished stone surface silently slid open. She reached inside and retrieved the kit.

"I only wanted to make you listen to my proposition," she said, handing the kit to him. "I just wanted to get your attention long enough to convince you that you won't lose in this deal."

"You've taken more risks tonight than you even realize,

Sariana Dayne," Gryph remarked as he quickly fastened the weapon kit back on his belt. "But you're in luck. I've decided I need the work after all. I'll take the job provided you can afford daily expenses. I'll let you know later what my final fee will be."

Chapter
2

SARIANA was awake very early the next morning. As usual, she had dressed and breakfasted long before the rest of the household. Soon after her arrival in the western provinces she had discovered that the locals tended not to worry very much about such things as punctuality or disciplined work hours. .

Lady Avylyn had admonished Sariana more than once for what she perceived as a lack of proper priorities. "Really, my dear," the matriarch of the Avylyn Clan had declared, "you work much too hard. You must learn to play a bit more or you will run the risk of turning into a very dull little old lady."

"I think the results of too much play and too little work are quite obvious in the present financial status of your clan, Lady Avylyn," Sariana had retorted. "Only a lot of hard work is going to salvage the situation now."

"Yes, well, I'm sure you have a point, Sariana, but it does seem a pity for you to miss so many lovely parties. Life is short, my dear."

"I am well aware of that, madam. And because of that fact, I cannot waste a moment of my time here in the western provinces. The sooner I accomplish my professional goals, the sooner I can go home."

"Yes, yes, I quite understand. But to be truthful, I cannot comprehend why anyone would want to return to the east. Such a dull, dreary place."

Sariana had gritted her teeth, knowing Lady Avylyn had never been to the eastern continent. But westerners had a definite image of the foreign lands of the east and that image was of a grim, gray, humorless place where no sensible person would want to live.

The westerner's failure to appreciate the hard working, sober, disciplined ways of her homeland was a constant source of irritation to Sariana. She was fiercely determined not to lower her own personal standards in such matters while she was in exile. It was one of many small battles she waged here in the west.

Sariana was dressed this morning in one of the elegantly restrained business gowns she'd had made at a local clothing design shop. The owner of the shop, a short, stout woman who prided herself on introducing the latest styles to her customers, had been most upset by the order for a simple fitted jacket and long, narrow skirt in a subdued shade of gray.

"Too dull, much too dull for you," the shop owner had protested when Sariana had given her the order. "You are living in Serendipity, the fashion capital of the western continent. Even the people in the smallest towns of the farthest provinces wear more stylish garments than the sort you wish to order. Bustles are in style but you don't want one. Slashed sleeves are in vogue but you don't want them, either. Look here, you haven't even asked for any ribbon trim. I could do so much more, even with this simple design, if you would just let me choose the color and add some trim."

"I'm a businesswoman," Sariana had explained, not for the first time. "I prefer more restrained styles."

"Ha. We have plenty of business people here in Seren-

dipity," the woman had shot back. "None of them has anything against a little style and color. That's the problem
with you eastern folks. You're much too dull and sober and
tiresomely strict. No fun at all. Remember, you're not living in Rendezvous now, my dear. You're living in Serendipity. Here we have color and light and contrast and lots
and lots of style." The woman had waved one hand in a
sweeping gesture that included all of Serendipity, the surrounding province of Pallisar and the whole western continent.

It hadn't been easy, but Sariana had finally gotten her
way with the shop owner. The small confrontation had
been typical of the sort she endured on a daily basis in
Serendipity. Sometimes it was tiring to hold her ground,
but she usually managed to prevail. It was amazing how
effective persistence and rational determination could be
against the flamboyant, emotional and melodramatic ways
of the locals.

The expansive Avylyn household consisted of three long
wings of chambers, gardens and halls that radiated out
from a central core structure in the manner of spokes on a
wheel. Sariana's suite of apartments was situated in the
spoke farthest away from the Avylyns' private chambers
and Sariana liked it that way.

The location of her rooms gave her a sense of privacy
and some necessary distance from the ceaseless uproar that
seemed to be the normal mode of communication for the
Avylyns and everyone else in Serendipity. Nobody did
things in a quiet, reflective, composed manner. Everyone
looked for and found the most dramatic and extreme reactions to any given situation. Tears flowed, anger exploded
and laughter sang out, all with just the slightest provoca-
tion. No one worried much about self-restraint.

It seemed to Sariana that normal day-to-day life provided plenty of opportunity for westerners to indulge their
tastes for the extreme, but she had quickly learned that
when a real excuse came around—weddings, funerals, or
births, for example—all the stops were pulled and the
moon was the limit.

The walk to her office, which was in the middle spoke on the floor above the jewelry design rooms, normally took Sariana through a long, glass hall full of exotic plants and flowers and into the luxurious central hub building with its spacious showrooms, ballrooms and reception areas. This morning Sariana took a short cut outside through the gardens.

It was another brilliant morning, of course. All the mornings were brilliant during the summer. Afternoon rainstorms were also typical of the season. Such storms were filled with lightning, thunder and torrents of water. Fall, winter and spring would bring their own kinds of brilliance and spectacle. Leaves of unbelievable hues in the fall; dazzling snows that made the ground look as if it were covered in prisma arrived in the middle of winter; a riot of new color and rich greenery would herald the Spring. Nature was as vivid and cheerfully temperamental in the western provinces as the people themselves. It was all so radically different from the moderate climate and serene tones of her homeland. Sariana sighed softly, thinking about it.

She would sometimes awaken in the middle of the night with a familiar nightmare. The dream was a strange one, appearing in a variety of guises, but it always had its roots in the same underlying fear. It was a fear that she would somehow become so entangled in the chaos and color of the western continent that she would never be able to return to Rendezvous.

Lying in her bed after one of those disturbing dreams, Sariana would stare into the darkness and do battle with a homesickness that was so strong and so deep that she sometimes gave into tears.

The Avylyns would have been shocked to know the depths of her loneliness. They had done their exuberant best to make her welcome. But if they had known about the tears, they would undoubtedly have been relieved by the knowledge that their calm, practical and restrained business manager was, indeed, capable of some strong emotion.

At least she hadn't awakened with an attack of homesickness last night, Sariana thought wryly as she hurried through the gardens and into a wide hall. She'd had too much else on her mind to allow herself the indulgence of self-pity.

Disaster had come within a footstep of her and the Avylyns last night. She knew that now. She had known it when the Shield had grabbed her wrist and looked down at her with eyes that held the lethal allure of a bottomless sea. The memory made her shiver even now in the bright light of day.

Perhaps she should have paid more attention to her clients' nervous fears about using a Shield. But it was too late to go back now. What was done was done. They now had a Shield working for them, whether or not they wanted him.

The middle wing of chambers was always humming with activity, even at this time of day. The Avylyns employed many people, most of whom were related to the Clan. The basic social structure of class and clan was similar to a guild system. A person who could not claim a proper social class or clan family was a true outlaw. He was also usually unemployed.

As she hurried into her office, Sariana nodded absently at a household attendant and requested a large pot of strong laceleaf tea. She needed it this morning. When the tea arrived she took it with a word of thanks and firmly closed the door.

With a sigh of relief, Sariana walked across the white marble floor to the circle of black stone that was her desk. In the center was a cushioned chair suspended from the ceiling that rotated easily in a complete circle to follow the curve of the desk.

She pressed the hidden mechanism that opened one section of the desk, stepped through into the inner circle and assumed her seat. The desk closed soundlessly behind her. It would take an expert's eye to find the seam.

The surface of the stone desk was completely bare except for the tea tray. Sariana touched another hidden device and a section of the polished surface opened to reveal a pile of business papers. She stared at them morosely. The last thing she felt like doing this morning was going over the deplorable state of the Avylyns' finances. She had been doing little else every workday for the past year. At times the task of saving the financial life of the Avylyn Clan had appeared hopeless. But now she knew she was well on the way to salvaging the Avylyns' fortunes and with them, her own.

Sariana knew that her hopes of future success and her chances of returning to her homeland were inextricably tied to the Avylyns' success. She would do just about anything to ensure both. The thought of being stranded in the western provinces for the rest of her life was enough of a spur to make her take risks she would never have taken under normal circumstances.

It even made her willing to deal with a Shield.

Sariana stabbed the closure device on the desk and watched with morbid satisfaction as the financial papers sank instantly out of sight.

The cleverly designed tables and desks in the Avylyn household were not the only interesting discoveries Sariana had made since her arrival in Serendipity. The people of the western continent were an inventive lot with a definite flair for the cunning and the bizarre. They loved gadgets.

Her own people were a far more serious and sophisticated crowd, skilled in matters of business, finance, education and trade. Occasionally Sariana wondered if the people of the two continents had gone in opposite directions because of the different environments each group of colonists had faced or because of the arrangement of the social classes on board the original colony ships.

It was never intended that the settlers on board *The Serendipity* and *The Rendezvous* be separated. The two ships were meant to land near each other. The resulting colony would thus have started out with a full compliment of all the social groups deemed necessary for survival and progress in the new world.

At least, that was the original plan of the radical group

of social philosophers who had set out to colonize the planet of Windarra a few hundred years before. Most of the clans of the various business and educational classes had been on board *The Rendezvous*. Nearly all of the artistic, craft and design clans had boarded *The Serendipity*.

Each ship had been given an equal share of representatives from the medical and social philosopher classes. The ships' officers and crew had formed a social class of their own. It had been decided that after the landing, the members of that particular class would be adopted into the clans of their choice. The theory was that they would no longer be needed as a separate and unique class. The starships were not designed to make a return trip to the home planets.

Unfortunately, the original plans for the expedition were never realized. Shipboard emergencies had struck both colony ships almost simultaneously as they prepared to approach Windarra. Huge explosions of light and energy had nearly engulfed both.

The starships had managed to limp down through the atmosphere and each had made barely controlled crash landings, but those landings had been on separate continents. The communication facilities and a great deal of technology had been destroyed. Many lives were lost. Each group of colonists had assumed the other group had perished in the strange explosions.

The colonists from each ship who had lived through the crash had been faced with the task of surviving without the assistance of the social classes that had been on board the other ship. The result had been some radical changes in the original plans of the philosophers, but the basic outlines of the class and clan system still held on both continents.

Sariana had learned, however, that those outlines had held much more firmly in the eastern provinces. In the west the social structure had shifted and changed to a major extent. The lines between clans and classes were becoming quite blurred, although the general system was still in place.

Sariana wrinkled her nose in disapproval as she reminded herself that in the west matters had actually gotten to the point where marriages across class lines were common. Romantic liaisons and outright illicit affairs between people of different social classes were even more common. Sariana could only shake her head over the faltering social structure.

It wasn't that her own people were so much more virtuous. They weren't. But they had the good sense and the social awareness to keep their affairs, like their marriages, within class boundaries.

The changes in the social system on the western continent had come as quite a shock to the easterners when both groups had finally rediscovered each other a few years before.

It was ironic that it had been a western invention, the fast, sleek windrigger sailing ships, that had made that rediscovery possible. Contact between the descendants of the original colonists was finally reestablished, but things had changed.

Each group had managed to survive without the other. That was a lesson that would not soon be forgotten by either contingent. It was clear to the people of each continent that, contrary to the predictions of the social philosophers, they really didn't need each other. Both groups tended to be equally arrogant and regard the other group as slightly less advanced and certainly less sophisticated than itself. Trade had been established but socially there was still very little mingling.

It was one thing for a member of an eastern continent clan to trade with someone from a western clan, quite another to contemplate marriage into that clan. One had to maintain one's social standards, even if one occasionally found the clever little gadgets devised by the westerners useful or intriguing.

It was amazing how little easterners knew about westerners, Sariana thought. Take this business of the west having created a whole new social class called Shields. It was a typical piece of western inventiveness. The original social philosophers would have been appalled.

Sariana stared gloomily out the high arched windows that opened onto a garden of vivid flowers, wondering how she had gotten herself into such a predicament.

She was still contemplating her fate when the door to her office swung open without any warning. Sariana didn't swivel around in her chair to see who was standing in the doorway. Her instincts already told her. A ripple of awareness went through her nerve endings and she gritted her teeth.

"The luck of the day to you, Gryph Chassyn," she murmured. Ritualistic greetings and manners were useful to fall back on when one was faced with potential disaster, she decided. Above all else, she must maintain control of this situation.

"Luck to you, lady," Gryph said carelessly.

He came silently into the room, the heels of his boots making absolutely no noise on the marble floor. It was a neat trick.

"You might as well turn around and face me," he added dryly. "I've come to talk business with you. Business is your specialty, I'm told. I believe we have a few matters to discuss before I undertake the task of finding the Avylyns' precious prisma cutter. I decided it would be much easier if you and I talked about those matters without any Avylyns present."

Sariana took a firm grip on herself and bravely swung around to confront him. The morning light streaming through the large, arching windows did not alter the impressions she had gotten the night before. If anything the Shield appeared more formidable than he had the previous evening. Of course, she reminded herself, he was also no longer suffering from the effects of Aunt Perla's hypnotic drug.

"How are you feeling?" Sariana inquired politely.

Gryph's blue-green eyes flashed with an unreadable expression that was quickly veiled. "Like I've spent the night refighting the fire on board *The Serendipity*." He smiled mockingly. "Kind of you to ask, lady. Especially considering the fact that you're the one responsible for my condition last night."

That stung. "You very obligingly got drunk all on your own and made an attempt to pick up the first attractive woman who happened to sit down at your table," Sariana said in clipped tones, telling herself sternly that she should not allow him to bait her this way. "The Avylyns and I merely took advantage of the situation."

"Is that right?" Gryph threw himself down onto a long, cushioned bench in front of one window. He sat with his back to the light, his legs spread apart, and leaned forward, resting his elbows on his knees. He regarded Sariana with an assessing gaze. "How did you know I'd be in that particular tavern at that particular time?"

Sariana attempted a modest shrug. "I've had Bryer watching the most likely taverns on a regular basis for the past couple of weeks. Once we learned there was a real live Shield in town it wasn't hard to find out where he was hanging out."

"I wasn't trying to hide. Did it ever occur to you to try walking into that tavern yourself last night, sitting down across from me and making your offer in the normal fashion?"

"Of course not. You had already turned down three polite invitations to do business. There was no reason to think you wouldn't turn down the fourth," she said. "I was forced to take desperate measures. It wasn't as if there was a lot of choice. You Shields seem to have a monopoly on this sort of private mercenary work."

He gave her a brief, predatory grin. "No other social classes have shown any desire or ability to go into business against us."

"That I can believe. Even members of the town guards don't take on private investigative assignments. Something tells me you Shields discourage competition." Sariana sat forward, folding her elbows on the polished desk. "On the other hand, what respectable clan would want its sons growing up to be professional mercenaries? It wasn't just your price that traumatized the Avylyns. They were actually afraid of you."

"A Shield's reputation is his stock in trade," Gryph said with patently false modesty. "But last night I got the impression that you were trying your hand at the intimidation and extortion business yourself. Do they teach you things like that in those fancy business universities in Rendezvous?"

Sariana felt the heat rise in her cheeks. For a few seconds she couldn't quite meet his eyes. "I'm learning here in Serendipity that one must occasionally make certain concessions to the local way of doing things if one wants to get anything done."

"What a load of keenshee bird guano," Gryph retorted pleasantly. "No sane westerner, especially not a respectable clan like the Avylyns, would have dared tried the game you played with me last night. Not unless someone with an incredibly persuasive tongue talked them into it. It would take a real eastern sales exec to do that. You have my full and unreserved admiration."

"Thank you."

"I always admire professionalism when I see it. Tell me, what were you going to do with my weapon kit?"

Sariana's gaze jerked back to his. "I don't know," she said honestly. "I didn't even know what it was, just that it was apparently very important to you."

"Oh, it is that," Gryph assured her far too smoothly. "Very important. Did you think you could hold it or its contents for ransom? Use it to get me to agree to what you wanted?"

Sariana's flush deepened. "I was getting desperate," she mumbled. "Nothing seemed to be going the way I had planned. You hadn't responded to my requests for a private meeting. The drug hadn't worked the way it was supposed to. You weren't being at all cooperative. You even turned down the Avylyns' offer of social introductions. You'll never know what it cost them to agree to such an offer, by the way."

"I can guess. Fancy clans like the Avylyns sometimes

find Shields useful, but they sure as hell wouldn't want their daughter marrying one. I agree with you. The Avylyns were desperate. But they wouldn't have had the guts to try drugging me and then stealing my kit."

Sariana winced. "As I said, nothing seemed to be working properly last night. I was afraid you would walk out on us as soon as you regained consciousness. But when I touched that pouch I got the feeling you wouldn't leave the room without it." She glanced at the leather kit on his belt. The prisma in the lock shimmered slightly, reflecting color from every range of the light spectrum. It drew her, made her want to touch the valuable crystal. Sariana had to force herself to look away from it. "I just wanted to make you calm down and negotiate with me. You were behaving very arrogantly, you know."

His eyes gleamed briefly with a combination of amusement and amazement. "And you weren't?"

"Definitely not. I was simply trying to forge a business arrangement."

Gryph's teeth flashed again in a smile that held as much menace as humor. Sariana shifted uneasily beneath that smile. She had never met someone who could convey both threat and amusement simultaneously. It was unsettling. Gryph Chassyn was just one more glaring example of the bizarre twist fate and civilization had taken in this wild land.

"I think we'll discuss that statement later," Gryph murmured. "Right now we'd better get down to business."

Sariana eyed him warily. "You really are going to work for us?"

"For you. I thought I made that clear last night."

"But it's the Avylyns who want your services," Sariana protested.

"I didn't hear them asking last night. All I heard was your voice asking for my help. No mistaking that eastern, upper class accent, lady. It was you."

"This is ridiculous. What difference does it make whether you work for the Avylyns or for me? The goal is the same." Sariana hid her flash of anger by reaching for the teapot and pouring herself a second cup. She must stay in control, she reminded herself.

"The goal might be the same, but there will be one hell of a difference at the end of the job when it comes to collecting my fee."

Sariana's hand trembled and laceleaf tea slopped onto the desk top. Her gaze collided with Gryph's. "What sort of game are you playing?" she bit out.

"I haven't decided yet." Gryph shifted his position, leaning back against the wide window frame and propping one knee up in front of himself. For the first time he looked away from Sariana, focusing on the brilliant flowers in the garden outside. "Tell me about the prisma cutter."

Sariana bit her lip, disconcerted. Then common sense told her she was probably better off letting him change the subject. This man could be very unnerving.

"You know what a prisma cutter is?"

"Sure. The only kind of gadget that can cut, shape and polish prisma crystal." Gryph spoke casually.

"You seem to know more about it than I do," Sariana said in businesslike tones. "I'd never even heard of prisma, let alone a prisma cutter until I came to Serendipity. At any rate, this cutting tool is vital to the status and prestige of the Avylyn Clan. They've held it in trust for each generation from the days of the First Generation. They're very attached to it. The Avylyns are quite emotional about such things. Given their present precarious financial situation, I'm inclined to agree with them in this instance. They cannot afford to have it known that they have lost the symbol of their leadership in the field of the jewelers' arts. It must be retrieved at all costs."

"Where do you think it went?"

Sariana hesitated. "The Avylyns suspect it was stolen by a rival clan in the same field. Jasso thinks someone in the Nosorian Clan may be responsible. Apparently they're a bunch of hotheads over there," Sariana added wryly. "It's amusing to hear an Avylyn labeling someone else a hothead. Everyone in the province seems to be hotheaded and emotional."

Gryph eyed her. "Maybe you'll learn something while you're living among us."

"I have already learned a great deal, I assure you," she retorted. "None of it particularly comforting. Now about this cutter—"

"You said you don't know much about prisma," Gryph interrupted thoughtfully.

"We don't have such a crystaline substance on the eastern continent."

"Your people were fortunate. You didn't find any of the ships in your lands, apparently. Or maybe I should say you haven't found any yet. They're usually well hidden. If someone doesn't accidentally trigger one, it can stay buried for years."

Sariana frowned in confusion. "What ships?"

"The prisma crystal ships." Gryph turned his head to give her an impatient glance. "Didn't the Avylyns tell you about them?"

"All I know is that the prisma is extremely rare and extremely valuable. According to the Avylyns there hasn't been a new deposit of it found in the past fifty years or so."

"That's because there hasn't been a crystal ship found in fifty years. Prisma is the material the crystal ships and their weapons are made from. It's rare and almost indestructible. You only get a new supply if you locate a crystal ship. The only thing that can cut prisma is a special cutting tool. Only a few of those tools were ever found inside the ships. No one's ever discovered a way to cut prisma without one. That makes the tools as valuable as the prisma. By the Lightstorm, lady, you sure are ignorant, aren't you?"

Sariana drew a deep breath and spoke through her teeth. Her voice was a little too sweet, but she doubted if Gryph would notice the sarcasm. "I have only been here for a year," she said. "I am attempting to learn as quickly as I can. You will understand the problems involved, I'm sure, when you stop and think about the rather exotic, not to say bizarre, customs and legends I am forced to deal with on a daily basis here. Kindly tell me a little more about the prisma ships."

"Well, well," Gryph said with great interest, "you have a temper in the mornings, don't you?"

"I'm surprised you noticed." Her voice was sweeter than ever.

"Oh, I noticed, all right," he replied. "It's reassuring to know that being born and bred on the eastern continent didn't strip you of all of the more interesting emotions. You want to know about crystal ships? I'll tell you about them."

"You know a lot about them?"

"I exist because of them."

Sariana's eyes widened. "What is that supposed to mean?" she asked in amazement.

Gryph transferred his gaze back to the gardens. "The Shield class was created to deal with the prisma ships. There haven't been any ships found for fifty years, so there hasn't been much need for the Shields' special talents lately. Fortunately, we're versatile. We've made ourselves useful in other areas. We excel at bandit hunting, for example. A useful craft as far as the other social classes are concerned."

"But who makes these prisma crystal ships?"

Gryph shrugged. "No one knows. They were here on Windarra when the First Generation arrived."

"That's ridiculous," Sariana scoffed. "I've never heard of such a thing."

"Only because your people didn't run into any of the ships on the eastern continent."

"And there haven't been any such ships discovered on the western continent since the descendants of *The Serendipity* and *The Rendezvous* rediscovered each other," Sariana concluded knowingly. "How very convenient. The legend lives on and no one has to provide any proof. Sounds like a typical western fairy tale to me."

"You don't believe in legends?" Gryph sounded more amused than surprised.

"I prefer to put my belief in balance sheets, checking accounts and taxes. Legends and ballads are for children."

"Maybe the right legend could make you change your mind," Gryph suggested softly.

"I doubt it," she answered firmly. "But I can see that the legend of the crystal ships might serve a useful purpose for your social class. The tales undoubtedly help ensure that the other classes show you some respect. The Avylyns tell me there aren't many of you Shields. Apparently your limited numbers enable you to keep your prices high. I always admire that sort of sound business planning."

Gryph swung his head around to stare at her and Sariana wondered if she'd gone too far. Normally her quick tongue was an asset, but there were times around this man when she got the impression it could get her into trouble. She sat very still for a long moment, waiting for the glitter in his eyes to cool. The tension in the room was breathtaking.

When Gryph spoke Sariana remembered to breathe again.

"You have no idea of the risks you're running around me, do you?" he asked in a voice that was terrifyingly casual.

The fury was fading rapidly from his eyes. Sariana recovered herself quickly and put the awkward moment behind her. She could handle this man. She could handle anyone from the west if she just put her mind to it. Cool intelligence always had the edge over extravagant emotional indulgence. She just had to concentrate on keeping calm and staying in charge. And talking fast.

"I wasn't aware that I was taking any particular risks. I was simply making a business observation. And as for your legend about prisma crystal ships—"

"You don't believe it."

"I'm afraid not." Sariana tapped one silvered nail on the desk top. "Have you, yourself, ever seen one?"

"No."

"I rest my case."

"If the ships don't exist, how do you account for the existence of prisma?" Gryph asked softly.

"I'm sure it's simply a natural, rather rare substance found here on the western continent," she told him loftily.

"And the prisma cutters?"

"Probably a piece of technology left over from the days of the First Generation. A certain amount was salvaged from *The Serendipity* after the crash, just as some things were rescued from *The Rendezvous*. Both groups were fortunate. Without that minimal amount of technology and knowledge, especially medical knowledge, those first colonists would probably not have survived at all. Things were hard enough as it was from all accounts."

"You think you've got an answer for everything, don't you?" Gryph asked.

"Not for everything. Not yet. But just give me a little time," she tossed back smoothly.

"Time? Why should I give you time?"

Without any warning Gryph got to his feet and crossed the white marble floor with long, sure strides until he was standing on the opposite side of the desk. He planted both hands, palms flat, on top of the polished surface and leaned forward to confront her.

"I don't owe you time or anything else, Lady Sariana Dayne. Just the opposite. Because of that trick you played last night, you owe me. I'll give you a word of warning because I know for a fact you won't listen."

"What word of warning is that?" she retorted tightly.

"I always collect what's owed to me."

Adrenalin and awareness coursed through Sariana's system. She shot to her feet and opened her mouth to tell Gryph Chassyn what he could do with his warnings.

But her words were never vocalized. Instead Sariana felt herself trapped as Gryph caught her face between two surprisingly rough, strong palms. An instant later his mouth covered hers in a kiss that shocked her to the toes of her soft leather slippers.

Sariana had rarely been kissed and certainly never like that. For all her education and worldly upbringing, she had been a protected clan lady. In addition, the unrelenting pressures of the educational system back in Rendezvous had ensured that there was very little time left to students for such frivolities as sexual experimentation.

The one year of her life that might have been considered free was this past year. But during the whole time she had been in Serendipity Sariana had felt like a stranger in a strange land. She had preferred to feel that way. The last thing she had wanted to do was engage in a sexual relationship with one of the locals. She wanted nothing that would tie her to the west, even temporarily. Besides, she had her standards.

The only man she had even begun to consider in a faintly romantic light was halfway across town waiting for her to join him for lunch. And it was a fact that Etion Rakken had never had the unmitigated gall to kiss her in this manner.

Gryph's embrace was rough, hungry and passionate. It was also astonishingly arrogant and forceful, as if he were stealing something he was fairly certain he wouldn't be able to get by asking.

It was as if he were staking a claim.

The kiss, Sariana knew somewhere in the depths of her being, was meant to be a small, symbolic act of masculine aggression. And when Gryph boldly parted her lips and thrust his tongue briefly and forcefully into the soft, intimate warmth of her mouth, she knew it was symbolic of the more intimate act of sex as well. Lack of personal experience in such matters did not imply lack of knowledge.

Sariana tried to jerk free of the embrace but something was happening to her, something she did not understand.

A waterfall of sensation was suddenly pouring over her, leaving her dazed and vaguely frantic. She did not recognize some of these emotions. They were oddly alien, as if they came from someone else. Then she realized abruptly why they seemed so strange. These emotions were masculine, not feminine.

There was hunger, irritation, need, aggression, passion, arrogance and, swamping all the others, sheer, unadulterated male possessiveness.

It was impossible, Sariana thought desperately. She was imagining things. Nevertheless she had the disorienting feeling that she was actually tapping into some of Gryph's feelings. She raised her hands and pushed futilely against his shoulders. He held the kiss a few seconds longer, just long enough to let her know that she could not force him to halt the embrace. It would end when he wanted it to end.

And then, without any warning, it was over. Sariana was set free as abruptly as she had been taken captive. She caught hold of the edge of the desk for balance and stared at Gryph. She was far more shaken than she wanted to admit. She hastily used the only defense she had, her quick tongue.

"I'm sure you already know your manners are utterly abominable," Sariana managed with a smooth sarcasm that she hoped masked her inner turmoil and rage. "So I won't bother to give you a lecture about them. I doubt if you're capable of learning much on the subject of manners, anyway. I have it on good authority that you were raised on the frontier, far from proper society. You'll be interested to know your lack of breeding shows. And because you are ill-bred, you probably don't mind that it shows." She turned away to open a section of the desk. "You might not believe it, but I do have better things to do this morning than fight off the advances of an over-priced mercenary whose social class is obviously disintegrating even as we speak. Please leave."

There was a stunned silence from behind her. Gryph didn't move.

"We have a lot more to discuss," he finally got out. His voice sounded surprisingly thick and ragged.

"We have nothing more to discuss." She kept her rigid back to him as she riffled the papers in front of her. "If you have accepted a contract to recover the missing cutter, as you claim you have, I would appreciate it if you would get started on the project. As I mentioned last night, complete secrecy is required for the sake of the Clan. Your cover story is that you have been hired by the Avylyns to ensure the safety of their jewelry collection on the night of their annual costume ball. Your presence in the household will appear normal until then. It will be expected that you need to make proper security arrangements. After the ball, if you still haven't found the cutter, we will need to invent another cover story. Or find another Shield."

"Lady Sariana, we have to talk," Gryph said heavily.

She whirled to face him. "I do hope that in the matter of secrecy you can be trusted."

He stared at her as if she had gone crazy. "*I'm a Shield*. Don't you know what that means? My word is better than prisma."

"One hopes that, while you may not have a decent set of manners, you do have some business ethics. You do, after all, belong to some sort of accepted social class, even if that class does choose to reside on the frontier for the most part. You are not a complete outlaw. Now, I have work to do. Please leave."

"Lady, if you think you can just casually toss me out of your office like this, I've got news for you."

Whatever Gryph would have said next was lost as the door to Sariana's office opened again to admit Indina Avylyn. She came into the room like a ship in full sail, her towering hairdo barely clearing the door.

"Oh, here you are, Sariana," she said in tones of tremendous relief. "I've been looking for you. I have the menus for the food we will be serving for the costume ball. Now I know I have specified some rather expensive items, but I've already explained that this is one area in which the Avylyns must not stint. The Clan has been giving this ball for nearly seventy years. People expect the best from us. If we cut corners this year they will suspect that all is not well with us. We mustn't allow that to happen." She stopped short as she realized someone else was in the room. Mild alarm dashed some of the enthusiasm from her eyes. "Lord Chassyn. The luck of the day to you, sir. Please pardon me if I'm intruding on a business conference, but this is terribly important. I must have Sariana's approval of these expenses."

"Luck to you, Lady Avylyn," Gryph said. He inclined his head with a graceful degree of polish that belied the accusations Sariana had just made concerning his manners. "I understand the importance of your situation. Sariana and I can continue our discussion after she's looked at your menus."

Sariana stabbed at the mechanism that opened a complete section of the black stone desk. "I'm afraid Sariana is going to be unavailable for any further discussions of any sort this morning. I have a business appointment. Lady Avylyn, I will be happy to approve your menus this afternoon. Lord Chassyn," she added with a mocking emphasis on the title, "I'm sure you'll understand if I dash off. Pressing business I'm afraid."

Sariana practically fled from the room.

Gryph gazed thoughtfully at the empty doorway. "Pressing business?"

"Oh, she probably has an appointment with her friend at the bank," Indina Avylyn explained.

"She has a friend in banking? A male friend?"

"Etion Rakken," Indina said hurriedly as she gathered up her menus. "He's also from Rendezvous. Came over a number of years ago and never went back. I think he and Sariana feel they must cling to each other while they reside here in the west. There are so few people from the eastern continent who actually live here, you know. Perfectly natural that Sariana and Etion should stick together. Sariana is so lonely. She hides it well, of course. You know how those easterners are about showing emotion. But we all know she's homesick. Etion always has a cheering effect on her, though. She'll be fine this afternoon after she's had lunch with him. You'll see."

Gryph could still taste Sariana's mouth. His body was still pulsing painfully with the instant response he had experienced when he'd caught hold of her and kissed her. For a moment during the embrace he had known without a doubt that he had touched her in ways that were not just physical in nature. And she had responded.

Shieldmate.

He was certain of that now. He had found a potential Shieldmate. A woman he could make his true wife. A woman who could give him a son. The knowledge dazed him. The thought of her going off to spend the warm, lazy morning with another man sent a rush of frustrated heat and rage through his veins.

The realization that the other male was undoubtedly far more socially acceptable to Sariana than Gryph would ever be was enough to ruin the rest of the day for him.

Chapter
3

TWO days later, Sariana left for another engagement with Etion Rakken. This time she was meeting him for late morning tea. Such outings were always welcomed by her. Lately, however, with the pressures of dealing with the Shield, the Avylyns' upcoming ball, as well as the demands of her normal schedule, Sariana was more grateful than ever for the brief moments of escape.

The early summer sunshine warmed the wide stone sidewalks and the cobbled streets of downtown Serendipity. Sariana was accustomed to the boisterous, outrageously dressed crowds that thronged the squares and avenues of the capital. In her elegantly restrained attire she was the one who stood out.

Pausing near one of the many sparkling fountains that graced virtually every corner of the city, Sariana prepared to cross the street. She was getting better at the deceptively simple task but she still exercised caution. Lifting her skirts she stepped off the sidewalk.

And was nearly run down by a dragonpony being ridden at full speed.

"By the Captain's Blood, lady, watch where you're going," the pony rider yelled cheerfully as he thundered past. The pony's clawed feet scraped on the stones mere inches from Sariana's boots.

"Here, now. Where did you come from?" shouted a wagonmaster as he sawed at the reins. The wagon swerved around Sariana with a dramatic flourish.

Sariana lifted her chin and ignored both close calls. She had learned that only cool arrogance, a fine disdain for danger and the ability to calculate distances with great precision guaranteed a safe crossing. Carriage drivers and riders tended to view the contest between themselves and pedestrians as a glorious, endless game.

Sariana prided herself on not having yet sunk to the point of swearing at the flamboyant drivers and riders who challenged her right to cross the streets. There were times, however, when she wondered how much longer she could restrain herself under the trying conditions. She had lived in the Avylyn household long enough to acquire a wide assortment of colorful phrases.

She dreaded the day she would start using those phrases because it would mean she had allowed herself to be dragged one step deeper into this crazy culture.

She made it across the street, narrowly avoiding being trampled by a teenager on a high spirited dragonpony, and saw with relief that Etion Rakken was waiting for her in the usual spot. His deep red hair shone in the sun and his dark eyes regarded her with genuine appreciation as she walked toward him. He was sitting under an awning at a popular sidewalk cafe.

Rakken was wearing a version of the local masculine fashion. It wasn't quite as colorful as the attire of the males around him, but neither was it as severely tailored as what he would have worn back in Rendezvous. Etion liked to say he had adapted to the local culture. Sariana sometimes feared the changes in him had gone even deeper. Etion had given up all thought of going home.

Today he had on a dark brown frockcoat, a beribboned white shirt and yellow breeches and hose. Sariana risked a discreet glance downward to see if Etion had taken to wearing a codpiece yet. She was relieved to discover he had not. There was still hope for him, she thought with wry humor.

Sariana smiled brilliantly for the first time that day as she exchanged greetings and took the seat beside Etion. He had already ordered tea and a plate of pretty little cakes for her. She couldn't help but notice, however, that he was on his second mug of ale. A year ago he had kept his drinking limited to the evenings. But sometime during the past few months he had started ordering ale at luncheon. Now he was starting in on the ale at mid-morning tea. The knowledge disturbed her. Etion was changing. To take her mind off that unhappy thought she picked up her teapot and examined it with an admiring eye.

It seemed to Sariana that nothing in the western provinces was ever plain or merely functional. The westerners loved decoration, the more elaborate, the better. The tea Etion had requested had arrived in a beautiful little pot designed to look like a wedding coach, and every centimeter of the cakes on her plate was frosted with fancy swirls and patterns.

"You look most charming today, Sariana. A very elegant, cool and serene little lightbird among all these mad, fluttering, squawking keenshees. How are you?"

"A bit frazzled to tell you the truth." Sariana wished very badly that she could confide completely in Etion. He already knew just about everything there was to know about the Avylyn family finances. He might as well know about the missing prisma cutter and the hired Shield, too.

But she couldn't betray the Avylyns' confidence. They were frantic about getting the cutter back. They were also adamant that no one outside the immediate family know the scandalous truth. The hiring of Gryph Chassyn and the reason why were to remain dark secrets within the household.

"You don't know how good it is to see you today, Etion.

It's been the usual madhouse at the Avylyns for the past few days, especially with the annual costume ball coming up soon. I had no idea of the enormity of the event when I agreed to budget for it."

"I warned you. Nobody here entertains in a casual fashion. I suppose Lady Avylyn wants to spend three times as much as you have allowed?"

"At least. Etion, nobody in that family has any concept of economy or financial prudence. It's a wonder the Clan has survived this long."

Etion grinned cheerfully, his handsome face crinkling into fine lines at the corners of his eyes. Rakken was several years older than Sariana. There was a touch of distinguished gray in his red hair. He had been one of the first people from the eastern continent to make the trip across the ocean when contact had been reestablished between the two groups of colonists. He had arrived nearly five years earlier and had stayed.

Rakken's prowess in banking and his sophisticated business education had given him a strong edge over the local competition, most of whom had only a primitive concept of economics and finance. There had been no business clans on board *The Serendipity*. The descendants of those first colonists had been improvising ever since. Rakken was making a lot of money showing the locals how the banking game was played by professionals.

"Are you going to hold me responsible after all for getting you into that situation?" Etion asked humorously.

Sariana flashed him a quick, laughing smile. "Are you kidding? I may complain from time to time, but you know perfectly well I'm grateful to you. If I manage to rescue the Avylyns a lot of things could change in my life."

The amusement in Etion's eyes faded and a bitterness that was usually well-concealed briefly took its place. He took a long swallow from his mug. "You still think that if you prove yourself here you'll be able to go home to Rendezvous and take your place among the rest of your Clan as if nothing had ever happened? You think the folks back home will accept success here in the benighted western provinces as real success? Don't set yourself up for a fall, Sariana. Don't feed yourself a lot of false hopes."

She poured the tea with a steady hand, refusing to let Etion's warnings get to her. "I've decided to reapply to the academy, Etion."

"Nobody gets a second chance at the Academy of Business," Etion said very softly. "No matter how well he does once he's left Rendezvous. As far as the academy is concerned, failure to matriculate directly out of the university levels means it's all over for you. Remember that, Sariana. Accept the fact that you're here in Serendipity for good and learn to live your life as if this was home. Stop dreaming."

"My dreams are all that keep me from going crazy at times, Etion." Sariana sipped her tea and gazed out across the square. "My dreams and your friendship." Determined to change the subject, she indicated one small building across the street. "I think I know where the pastry chef got her ideas for decorating these little cakes. Look at that shop over there. Doesn't the trim on the windows and roof look exactly like the trim on these cakes?"

Etion hesitated and then gave up the lecture he had tried to deliver. His mouth curved as he followed her glance but his eyes were bleak. "You're right. The chef probably looked out the window this morning when she was getting ready to decorate the cakes. Any westerner will tell you that artistic inspiration can come from any source."

Sariana's gaze moved consideringly over the other buildings in the square. "I'll have to admit that the local architecture was somewhat startling at first, but I think I'm almost getting used to it. There is a certain experimental zest to the local buildings and the design of towns. Oh, most of the time it looks overdone," she added quickly. "Too much ornamentation. Too many flowing staircases, too many overwrought facades, too many grand galleries and gardens. But lately I've decided it all has a crazy kind of charm. Back home everything is designed to be functional and utilitarian and dignified. At least the local architecture is never dull."

Etion watched her face as he sipped his ale. "A people's

architecture reflect something of their nature. The same applies to clothing, I imagine."

"I know, and I sometimes get exhausted just looking at all the incredible costumes as well as the amazing architecture," Sariana said with a small laugh. "But at other times it occurs to me that Rendezvous could benefit from a small infusion of design from the western provinces." Her eyes sparkled for an instant. "And the west could certainly learn something from us."

"It will be interesting to see where we all are in five or ten or twenty years," Etion remarked.

"Well, I for one plan to be back home in Rendezvous managing my clan's trade interests," Sariana said with conviction. "It's what I was meant to do from the day I was born. What about you, Etion? Will you ever go home?"

"It's too late for me, Sariana," he reminded her with soft bitterness. "I've told you that. I'm good at what I do, but nothing will ever make my clan or my business associates back in Rendezvous forget that financial scandal five years ago. I'm just damn lucky contact with the western provinces had been established by then or I would have had no place to run."

"I suppose I'm lucky, too," Sariana mused. "A few years ago failure to matriculate to the academy would have been the end of the line for me. I would have had to accept a low level position within my own clan or marry into a less important business clan. Last year when everything collapsed around me I needed a place to run, also."

"The difference between us is that I've accepted my fate. You have yet to come to terms with yours." Etion leaned forward with uncharacteristic intensity. "Remember, Sariana, when you finally do realize that it's better to be a success here than a failure back home, I'll be waiting. You and I have a lot in common. Our skills and training compliment each other perfectly. Together we could become very successful here in Serendipity. We would make a good team. Think about it."

Sariana sat very still. Etion's words would have constituted a marriage proposal back home and they both knew it. She inclined her head in a formal, gracious response. "You honor me, Etion."

"Think about it," he repeated. "That's all I'm asking." He sat back and picked up his mug. He smiled but his dark eyes remained curiously remote. "I know you have to satisfy yourself first. You have to find out if there is any way you can ever go back to Rendezvous on your own terms. I wasted my first three years here trying to find a way back. But while you search for your own magic ticket, think about the possibilities of a future here with me. We could accomplish a great deal together."

"Thank you, Etion," Sariana said gently. "You are very kind."

He grinned unexpectedly. "I'm desperate. If you leave where will I find a sane, intelligent, rational woman with whom I can communicate?"

Sariana laughed and changed the subject.

Thirty minutes later Sariana finished her tea and smiled regretfully. "I must be getting back. I have to see how much further into bankruptcy Lady Avylyn is going to take the Clan with her plans for the ball. Thank you for the tea, Etion. You'll never know how much I needed the break." She got to her feet. "You will be coming to the Avylyns' party, won't you?"

"Wouldn't miss it. You're sure the Avylyns' won't mind?"

"Of course not. They've convinced everyone that having an eastern business manager and an association with a bank run by a financial genius from Rendezvous is very trendy. It puts them at the forefront of fashion and they love it. They've also hinted to everyone that it's a brilliant financial maneuver. Their friends and rivals are all talking about hiring easterners, too. Who knows, Etion? We may be opening up new careers for all the academy rejects from our homeland."

"An interesting thought. The luck of the day to you, Sariana. I'll see you at the ball."

"Luck to you, Etion, and thank you very much for your

gracious proposal. I give you my word I will think about it."

"Do that, Sariana."

Sariana turned away with a last smile and found herself doing exactly as Etion had asked. She thought about his businesslike, practical and eminently rational proposal for a marriage alliance. He was right, she knew. If she was fated to be stranded in this strange land for the rest of her life, Etion would make a most suitable marriage partner for her. They had a great deal in common—including their exile.

Strangely enough, she found herself more disturbed by Rakken's proposal than she ought to have been. Not because accepting it would mean giving up on her dreams to go home, but precisely because it had been such a businesslike, practical and reasonable offer of marriage.

It was ridiculous, but she found herself wishing there had been a little more emotion attached to Etion's offer. She would like to have felt he wanted her for more personal reasons than because they had business interests in common.

Sariana sighed. She had definitely been living in Serendipity too long if she was starting to think along such lines. Every young woman of a high ranking eastern clan in any social class knew that marriage was not a matter of emotion. It was first and foremost a business arrangement.

Even as Sariana administered the brisk little lecture to herself the bright morning sky suddenly clouded over. Lightning flared and thunder rolled. The warm summer shower caught her three blocks from the Avylyns' front door.

Sariana shook her head philosophically as the rain drenched her hair and clothing. The shower was typical of life in Serendipity. Unpredictable.

Gryph Chassyn closed the door of his new sleeping chamber and started down the long hall that led toward the central hub of the Avylyns' villa. His new quarters were definitely a cut above his old ones which were located in a far less affluent part of town. He decided the fringe benefits of this new job were going to be pleasant.

He wondered what Lady Sariana Dayne would say when she found out he had just been assigned a suite near her own apartments. Gryph had a hunch she would not be pleased. Lucky for him Lord and Lady Avylyn were far more intimidated by a Shield than they were of their business manager. That morning Gryph had asked for the rooms and he had gotten them, no questions asked.

He emerged from the long wing into the central hall of the villa just as a young blond-haired boy came racing into the hall from the workshop wing. Gryph didn't need to see the boy's dark eyes to know he was about to meet the Avylyns' youngest son.

Luri Avylyn was clutching a small cage of elaborately designed gold wire as he dashed across the wide, circular hall. His attention was focused on the small creature inside the cage and he almost collided with Gryph. Less than a meter away he came to an abrupt halt and automatically began a proper, if hasty, apology without looking up. He was too obviously fascinated by the contents of the cage.

"Your pardon, sir, I was on my way into the guest wing. I didn't see you."

"No harm done," Gryph said easily. "What have you got in the cage?"

Luri raised his head excitedly. "It's a present for Lady Sariana. Do you know her?" Then his dark Avylyn eyes grew very wide as he realized who was standing in front of him. "You're the Shield, aren't you? Bryer said one had been hired to protect the jewelry that will be on display the night of the ball. I'm Luri."

Gryph nodded and crouched down in front of the boy to examine the cage. "The luck of the day to you, Luri. You say this is to be a present for Sariana? It's a scarlet-toe, isn't it?"

"That's right. Do you think she'll like it? It took me days and days to catch one. I finally found this one in the gardens down by the river."

Luri held out the gold filigree cage. The small, brilliant red lizard inside blinked its scarlet eyes at Gryph.

"That's a very handsome scarlet-toe," Gryph said as he admired the lizard. "Uh, do you happen to know whether or not Sariana likes lizards?"

Luri shook his head impatiently. "She's never had one. In fact, I don't think she's ever had any pets. The people of the eastern provinces are quite strange, you know."

"So I've heard." Gryph grinned at the boy.

Luri automatically responded with a wide smile and then curiosity got the better of him. "Are you really a Shield?"

"I'm a Shield in the same way that you are a Jeweler."

Luri's chin lifted slightly with pride. "My specialty is going to be gemology. When I'm grown up I will be in charge of buying the uncut stones our craftsmen use in their work."

"Sounds like a good profession," Gryph said seriously.

"Bryer's an expert in fine metals."

Gryph nodded as he studied the scarlet lizard.

Luri shifted from one foot to the other, still clutching the cage carefully. His eyes darted down to the weapon kit attached to Gryph's belt. Then he drew a deep breath and blurted out his next question.

"Is it true that no one can open a Shield's weapon kit except the Shield himself?"

Gryph glanced up and saw the breathless fascination in the boy's eyes. "That's not quite true," he explained quietly. "There is one other person who can open a Shield's kit."

Luri's dark eyes grew wider. "Who?"

"A Shield's lady can open the kit. She is the only other person on the face of the planet who can unseal the prisma lock."

"Do you have a lady?" Luri demanded.

Gryph shook his head. "Not yet."

"Are you going to get one?"

"If my luck holds."

Luri chewed on his lower lip. "Are you sure you couldn't teach me how to open the kit?"

Gryph laughed and rose to his feet. He ruffled the boy's bright blond hair with a friendly hand. "I'm afraid not."

"But if you can't teach me or anyone else how to do it, how will you teach a wife?"

"Every social class has its secrets, Luri. You know that. The way we teach our wives to open our weapon kits is a Shield secret."

Luri nodded seriously, well aware of the inviolable laws that protected such secrets. He sought for a way around the problem. "Can you show me what's inside?"

"Maybe," Gryph said thoughtfully. "Maybe I will do that one of these days when the time is right."

"Why does the time have to be right?"

"It just does. That's all."

"Oh." Luri considered his words and then decided to try another angle. "If you won't show me what's inside the weapon kit will you at least tell me some good tales of bandit fighting?"

Gryph gave that some thought. "I suppose I've got time for a quick one. Do you know the story of Targyn and the cutthroats of the Cretlin Mountains?"

"I've never heard that one. Who was Targyn?"

"He was a very strong and clever Shield," Gryph began with proper gravity. "He killed his first bandit when he was just a little older than you are."

"All by himself?"

Gryph nodded. "So the story goes. At any rate, as the years went by he spent more and more time in the mountains hunting bandits who attacked the traders and miners who use the mountain passes. His name became a legend. The bandits got together one day and decided they had to find a way to get rid of him. Since Targyn almost always hunted alone, they figured they could lure him into a special dead end canyon and trap him there."

"Did it work? Was Targyn trapped?"

"He let them think he was," Gryph said. "But Targyn was very clever. Much too clever for the bandits." He went on to explain exactly how Targyn had escaped the trap and lived to fight another day.

"What finally happened to Targyn?" Luri asked breathlessly. "Is he still alive?"

"No," Gryph said soberly. "Targyn finally got himself killed up in the mountains. He took many bandits with him when he died, but in the end he was pushed off a high cliff. He fell into a deep mountain lake and was drowned. His body was never recovered."

Gryph decided not to mention the more mundane fact that many Shields had been privately relieved to learn that the valiant Targyn had met his end in a suitably noble fashion. Had he lived, it was felt, Targyn might have proved to be a problem. The man had not been completely sane. Gryph was more relieved than most when Targyn met his glorious end. He'd had a sneaking hunch that the Council of the Shields was seriously considering sending him out to get rid of Targyn. But there was no need to mess up the great legend Gryph was relating to Luri with that minor detail.

"Tell me about his last battle," Luri urged. But the boy's plea was cut off as the grand doors of the main hall were opened by a household attendant in response to thundering chimes.

A drenched Sariana stood on the doorstep, futilely trying to wring out the hem of her long narrow skirt. Her clothes were plastered to her, revealing the soft, gentle curves of her slender frame. She looked up apologetically as the attendant exclaimed in dismay and urged her into the hall.

"My fault, Letta. I misjudged the weather again."

"My Lady, you're drenched." The stout, older woman fussed around Sariana, getting her inside and shutting the doors behind her. Then Letta turned to regard Sariana with an admonishing expression. "When will you learn that you must always take a rainscreen with you during the summer months in Serendipity? By the Lightstorm, just look at you. You're soaked to the skin. You must go and change immediately."

"Yes, Letta, I think I'll do exactly that." Sariana started quickly across the wide hall, peeling off her tight jacket as she went. "You'd think I'd have learned my lesson about trusting the weather around here months ago," she added just under her breath.

Gryph heard the remark. "What's the matter, Sariana?" he asked as she strode, dripping, toward where he stood with Luri. "Still having trouble with a few of the local customs? Isn't our weather tame enough for you?"

"No, it is not," Sariana snapped, clearly annoyed at finding him in her path. She glowered at him as she pushed wet hair back off her face. "Your weather is frequently as outrageous, unpredictable and contrary as—" She saw Luri and stopped talking immediately.

"As the people who live here?" Gryph finished helpfully. "You'll have to forgive us. Sometimes it's hard to figure out exactly what an easterner wants, let alone what she needs."

He kept his voice pleasant so as not to upset Luri, but he knew Sariana was well aware of the expression in his eyes. He also knew it alarmed her slightly. He nodded, satisfied. At this point he would settle for making any impression at all on her, even if it wasn't the best. She had been going out of her way to avoid him for the past two days. It irked Gryph, because he had made up his mind to be on his best behavior around her. She seemed determined not to give him any chance at all to impress her. It was impossible to court a woman who went down another hallway in order to avoid greeting him.

"Don't waste your valuable time trying to figure out what I want or what I need, Shield," Sariana advised as she made to step around him. "We're not paying you for that particular service. Speaking of your services," she added firmly, "I will expect a progress report from you tomorrow morning. Meet me in my office after breakfast."

"You do have a way of putting a man in his place, Sariana," Gryph made himself say smoothly.

"Some men need to have their proper place explained to them. Now if you will excuse me, I would like to go to my rooms." She glanced down and her voice softened miraculously. She broke into a dazzling smile. "Why, hello, Luri. What have you got there?"

Luri thrust the golden cage toward her. "It's a present for you, Sariana. A scarlet-toe lizard of your very own. It will keep you company at night."

Sariana's expression was a mixture of puzzlement and delight. "What a beautiful little cage. I'll bet your cousin Moris did this, didn't he? It looks like his work." Automatically Sariana reached out to take the cage from Luri's hands. "Is the lizard Moris' work, too? I thought it was Tarla who liked to design reptile brooches. What a beautiful piece of work. I don't recognize the gems. I've never seen such glowing red stones before." Then she got her first good look at the creature inside the gold filigree. "It's alive!"

"Of course it's alive," Luri said. "Who wants a fake lizard?"

"Or a dead one," Gryph added thoughtfully. He smiled at Sariana when her eyes flashed briefly to his face. Then she looked again at the creature in the cage.

Gryph had to hand it to her. Sariana barely flinched. Her brilliant smile stayed in place and she never missed a beat as she said to Luri, "What a fabulous lizard. It's so beautiful it looks as though it had been made in an Avylyn workshop. Why, it's even got red eyes."

Luri was pleased with her response. "It took me a long time to catch it. I had to get up before dawn every morning and go out into the gardens. You have to have just the right bait to catch a scarlet-toe, you see. They only eat certain kinds of leaves. You have to be very quick to get one."

Sariana gave Luri an appraising look. "Maybe its wrong to keep it in a cage, Luri. A little creature like this should be free, don't you think?"

"Oh, in a few days he'll bond to you and then you won't have to keep him in a cage," Luri explained. "They make great pets for ladies."

Sariana turned a helpless, beseeching gaze on Gryph.

He took the opportunity to step in with more helpful

information. "They have an affinity for females just as krellcats have an affinity for males."

"You've seen my krellcat," Luri reminded her. "This scarlet-toe will want to hang around you the same way my krellcat is always hanging around me."

"I see," Sariana's voice was very faint. "Uh, where is your krellcat this morning?"

"I left him in my room. I was afraid he might eat the scarlet-toe."

"I see," Sariana said again weakly. "Is this business of keeping krellcats and scarlet-toes for pets an old western custom?"

"It's not a very old custom," Gryph said easily. "It's only been in the past few years that anyone discovered what great pets they make."

"Oh," she said a little too cheerfully, "what an odd coincidence. Recently in my homeland a few people have started keeping odd pets, too. They seem quite attached to them. I never had time for a pet, what with my studies and all."

Gryph watched her standing there, wet and bedraggled from the storm with a caged lizard she didn't want in her hands and he didn't know whether to laugh or offer comfort. He had the feeling she would be infuriated by either approach.

"There's an old Serendipity saying that fits occasions such as this," Gryph finally said blandly.

"What's that?" she asked with deep suspicion.

"Take what you can get when you can get it. Life doesn't come with any guarantees."

"Sayings like that cover a lot of territory, don't they?" she retorted.

"Do you really like the lizard, Sariana?" Luri asked, eager for more enthusiastic appreciation of his gift.

"It's beautiful," she said with an obvious sincerity that surprised Gryph. "The most beautiful lizard I've ever seen."

Luri looked bashfully pleased. "I'm glad you like it. Now you'll have to think of a name for it."

"I think I'll call it Lucky Break," Sariana said, slanting Gryph a dangerous look from the corner of her eye. "Lucky for short. Thank you, Luri. Now I think I'd better go and change my clothes. I'll see you at dinner."

"I'll bring a supply of leaves to your room so you can feed Lucky," Luri promised.

"Thank you."

"Luck of the day, Sariana," Gryph said cheerfully as she turned to go.

"Thank you, Lord Chassyn." She didn't glance back but her tone was excruciatingly formal. "If my luck gets any better than it is already, I may have to consider increasing my insurance coverage." She vanished down the hall in a swish of wet, gray skirts. Her hands were filled with scarlet and gold.

When she had gone, Luri turned back to Gryph, his expression delighted. "I think the scarlet-toe will make her less homesick, don't you? Especially at night."

"What makes you think she's especially homesick at night?" Gryph asked curiously.

Luri shrugged. "A couple of times I've seen her walking in the conservatory after everyone else has gone to bed. I sneak out of my room sometimes to check the pond for baby moonfish. When they're small, they only come out from under the rocks at night, you know. Anyhow, as I was going by the conservatory hall I saw Sariana. The first time I saw her I thought she was a ghost. I was almost scared."

"What made you think she was a ghost?"

"She was wearing a white night robe and she was just sort of drifting through the plants and trees. She didn't make a sound. It was the only time I've ever seen her with her hair down. She looked a little sad. I almost went in and spoke to her, but I was afraid she would be embarrassed. Mother says easterners don't like to have other people see them when they're sad."

"Your mother is probably right. Easterners like to pretend they don't have emotions like the rest of us."

"Why?"

Gryph shrugged. "Maybe it makes them feel superior."

Luri lost interest in that subject. "Well, now she'll have the scarlet-toe to keep her company at night."

"I'm sure she'll enjoy it, Luri." Gryph's mouth curved faintly. "I just hope the scarlet-toe realizes how lucky it is."

Chapter
4

AT midnight that night, Gryph stood silently beneath the fronds of a huge, sprawling hydra palm and watched the white-robed figure glide soundlessly through the conservatory.

Luri was right, Sariana did look a little like a ghost. But this was no creature made of transparent, untouchable vapor. Gryph knew the lady moving toward him on velvet slippered feet would probably resist the touch of his calloused hand, but that didn't mean she couldn't be grasped and held.

He had given the matter a great deal of thought since his first encounter with Sariana and he knew he had reached a turning point in his life. In courting Sariana he would be seeking to alter his own future and hers. Not an easy task.

It would be more of a hunt than a courtship, he figured; the most demanding kind of hunting he had ever done. Chasing bandits was much simpler than courting Sariana was going to be. Everything was against him. He was from the wrong continent and the wrong social class. On top of that he got the impression she didn't even like him very much. Oh, she was aware of him, all right. He was sure of that. But that didn't mean she liked him. Dealing with him was a necessary bit of unpleasantness she was willing to endure in order to reach her goal.

But every time he saw her a jolt of shuddering awareness went through him. The sensation was nothing as simple and straightforward as lust. That he could have handled one way or another. Instead, it was an acute, indescribable hunger that poured through his entire body like hot rain. It was different from normal sexual desire, more powerful, more complex and, therefore, more dangerous.

The driving need had been born within him the night he had awakened, mind spinning from the drug, and focused on the woman who had dared to touch his weapon kit. Even unmated and unlinked with him, she'd had the power to reach him in some manner. She hadn't even been aware of what was happening. It had all taken place on a very subtle level. An untuned mind such as Sariana's would not have understood the tendrils of awareness that had pulled him out of his drugged haze.

The powerful emotions that had been incited in that moment had been steadily gaining strength since then. Kissing Sariana two mornings ago had done nothing to alleviate the growing need within Gryph. It had only fed it, making it more powerful and demanding.

Now a restless, driving energy pervaded his bloodstream. Soon the demand for release would become much more fierce. Gryph knew deep in his guts that there was only one way to satisfy the hunger within himself. He needed Sariana Dayne in a way that was unique to his kind.

He had never felt these volatile sensations before in his life. He had known there was a chance he might escape coming under the sway of their compelling power. Not every Shield was lucky enough to find a true Shieldmate.

But he was prepared for the violent sensations. At least, he decided wryly, he was as prepared as a man could be for such an onslaught. His father, like his father before him, had tried to explain the uniqueness of a Shield's hunger when he found a woman with whom he could link and mate. A Shield could satisfy the appetites of the body with any woman who appealed on a physical basis. But finding a Shieldmate was another matter altogether.

It wasn't a matter of love or even of passion. It was a matter of survival. Only a true Shieldmate could give a Shield a son.

Shield marriages were different in some fundamental ways from the normal alliances of men and women. The people of the western provinces knew that. The special laws, social structures and customs that pertained only to the Shield clans respected that difference.

Gryph wondered how far he'd get if he tried to explain all that to Sariana. He had the distinct impression she would not take pity on him and offer herself in total surrender.

Gryph stood very still in the deep shadows of the palm and went over his options. At this point he only had two. The first was to leave the Avylyn household at once. Preferably tonight. There was still time to get away and put an end to this whole business. He suspected that, once out of sight of Sariana, the powerful forces simmering in him would eventually fade. They had to be channeled and focused before they could grow much stronger. They were not completely ungovernable, at least not if he halted things at this stage. A strong, willful man could handle them.

The second option was to complete the channeling and focusing of the fierce desire within him. To do that he would have to take Sariana Dayne to bed. There he could forge the bond between them in the ancient way of the Shields. Once the link was established, she would be married to him by Shield law. Then she could give him a son.

Two options and two options only.

There was no middle ground. A brief affair was out of the question. A man didn't have affairs with potential Shieldmates. When he was lucky enough to find a mate, he grabbed her and held on with all his strength. When the future of a clan was at stake, a man did not fool around with one night stands.

Sariana was almost within reach. She still hadn't seen him. The golden light of Windarra's summer moon bathed her in a pale glow, turning her into a creature of magic.

He still had the option of leaving, Gryph reminded himself. He could step farther back into the shadows and she would pass by without seeing him. Then he could leave this household forever. He nearly smiled at the ludicrous notion. As if he could walk now.

Gryph made his choice. He took a deep breath and sealed his own destiny by staying where he was.

Then she saw him. Her soft mouth parted in startled surprise and her eyes drank in the sight of him as if he were something more than a man.

"The luck of the evening to you, Sariana," he said quietly. "And to me. I think we're both going to need it."

She recovered herself quickly. "You startled me. What are you doing here, Gryph?"

"My job. I'm in charge of security around here, remember?"

She frowned. "You're in charge of finding that damn prisma cutter. The business of protecting the jewels the night of the ball is simply your cover story, an excuse to explain your presence in the house. What do you think you're doing strolling around in the middle of the night?"

He smiled, understanding the defensiveness in her voice. "I have as much right to be here as you do."

"I suppose you know you have a way of making people extremely nervous."

He shrugged. "I can't help the way others react."

"Ha. You deliberately provoke uneasy reactions. You like making people nervous."

"At the moment I'm not trying to make you nervous, Sariana. Don't be afraid of me."

Her chin came up proudly and her eyes were deep pools of feminine mystery in the golden moonlight. "I am not afraid of you."

"Excellent." Gryph took her arm in a proper, gentlemanly grip and urged her along the conservatory path. "Then let's continue our midnight stroll together."

"I was just about to go back to my room."

She tried to politely disengage herself from his grasp as they walked down the path. Gryph pretended not to notice. It was good to touch her like this; good to be close. She was warm and soft and very feminine. Her hair was streaming down her back, falling around her shoulders in inviting waves. Gryph inhaled deeply, bathing his senses in the sweet herbal scent of it. He shuddered slightly in reaction.

There was another scent mingled with the sweet herbs. It was the subtle fragrance of Sariana herself, and it disturbed Gryph's senses on every level. His body was responding to it, growing hard and tense and ready. He willed himself to relax. He had made his decision. Now he could afford to bide his time. He wanted to do this properly. After all, he was the son of a Prime Family, and Sariana deserved a proper courtship. He sought for words with which to soothe and calm her. The ones he found surprised him.

"It's all right, Sariana, you're not the only one who occasionally gets lonely."

She flashed him a surprised glance, her lashes concealing the expression almost immediately. "What makes you think I'm lonely? This household is filled with noise and activity all day long."

"But it's not home," he pointed out.

Some of the wary tension faded within her. Gryph could feel it dissolving and hoped it was because Sariana was finally relaxing.

"No, it's not home," Sariana said quietly.

"Why are you in Serendipity?" Gryph asked curiously. "Very few people from the eastern provinces come to the west to live."

"I'm here because I failed to make the cut at the Academy of Business," she told him. "When I failed to do that, I automatically failed to accomplish a lot of other important things."

"Such as?" Gryph prompted.

She hesitated. "Why do you want to hear about me?"

He considered telling her the truth; that he wanted to know all there was to know about her because soon he would be taking her as his Shieldmate. She would be linked to him with bonds neither of them had ever experienced before in their lives. She would belong to him completely. She would be the mother of his son, if his luck held.

Common sense told him now was not the time to try to explain any of that.

"I think," Gryph said carefully, "that I would like to hear about you because it's midnight and we're alone and sometimes it helps to talk."

She softened under his hand, her eyes curious now. "You surprise, me, Shield. I would not have thought you were the type who ever needed to talk at midnight."

"Maybe you shouldn't make a practice of jumping to conclusions. The world is full of surprises," he said. "What happened when you failed to get into this academy you mentioned?"

She lifted one shoulder. "I failed to fulfill the destiny for which I had been groomed since the day I was born. Without academy training I was not eligible to take over an executive position within my clan. My family was horrified. I had shown such talent and such promise. Every waking moment had been spent preparing me for the role I was to play. When the news came that my career was being cut off at the university level, my marriage was canceled."

Gryph felt a knife twist in his stomach. His fingers tightened on her arm. "You were going to be married?"

"You're hurting me," Sariana said politely.

"Sorry." He forced himself to loosen his grip. "Tell me about your marriage plans."

"There's not much to tell. My parents had arranged the marriage when I entered the university."

"To whom?" Gryph thought he was going to explode if he didn't get all the answers quickly. It was all he could do to keep his voice neutral.

"To the oldest son of another important clan in my social

class, of course." Sariana gave him an odd glance. "Are you all right?"

"I'm fine," he declared between his teeth. "This man you were to marry—did you love him very much?"

She flinched beneath his hand as if his question had truly startled her.

"I barely knew him. I only met him on a few social occasions. He seemed quite admirable."

"Admirable?"

"He was a year ahead of me at the university and showing tremendous potential. He was training to take control of his family's legal interests. His family was one of the Prime Families in our social class, naturally."

"Naturally."

Sariana eyed him warily. "Are you being sarcastic?"

"Not at all." Gryph swallowed to clear his throat. "I take it this very admirable person made it into the academy?"

"Yes."

"And when you didn't, his family went looking elsewhere for a suitable bride."

"That's about it," she agreed with a sigh. "I was so shamed by my failure. I could hardly face my family."

"Why did you fail?"

Sariana's mouth tightened. "The academy board said my test scores revealed too much of a tendency toward experimentation and innovation and not enough grounding in the fundamentals. The best I could hope for at that point was an insignificant position in my family's business and, eventually, an insignificant marriage to some other academy failure. Not exactly an inspiring future. I had to get away. Had to prove myself."

"So you came to Serendipity. How will you prove yourself here, Sariana?"

"I'm hoping to prove my potential by making a reputation for myself as a business manager who can rescue clans such as the Avylyns that are in real financial trouble." Sariana looked up at him with a shy eagerness. "I'm going to reapply to the academy and ask for permission to retake the entrance exams."

"Will that be allowed?"

"It's highly unusual, but under special circumstances the academy members will allow it. My goal is to give a graphic demonstration of my abilities here in Serendipity and use that to persuade the academy to give me another chance. I'm very close to pulling the Avylyns out of the red, you know. In a few more months, if all goes well, they should be back on their feet financially."

"If the academy members agree to give you another chance," Gryph said slowly, "you'll go back to Rendezvous?"

She smiled. "You'd better believe it. I'll be on the next available windrigger home. How else could I finish my education and take my proper place in society?"

Gryph had to fight to control the frustrated rage that shot through him in that moment. Deliberately he subdued it. He must take this slowly and carefully.

"What will you do if the academy is not willing to relent?" he asked.

Her smile vanished into a rather grim line. "Then I'll be trapped here in Serendipity. I have thought about it a great deal and I've decided Etion Rakken is right. It would be better to stay here if I can't take my rightful place back home."

"This Rakken," Gryph said, "he's already made such a decision for himself?"

Sariana nodded. "He has resigned himself to his exile. He is very successful here and he takes what consolation and satisfaction he can from that. If I am forced to stay, I'll probably marry him."

Gryph reached out reflexively with his free hand and snagged a huge whispflower. His fingers closed around it, plucking it from its stem and crushing it into a pulpy mass in the blink of an eye. Sariana stared in shock.

"What are you doing? Those are Lady Avylyn's prize whispflowers! She's planning to enter them in an exhibition next week."

Gryph opened his hand and looked down at the smashed petals. "Accidents will happen."

"That was no accident. You did that deliberately," Sariana accused.

Gryph shoved the evidence into his jacket pocket. "Maybe Lady Avylyn won't notice if one of her precious flowers is missing."

"If she does notice, I'm certainly going to tell her who is responsible," Sariana threatened.

Gryph laughed softly. "Little tattletale. You'd inform on me?"

"In a flash."

He shook his head, still grinning. "What? No loyalty at all to your poor, underpaid employee?"

"What has my poor, underpaid employee accomplished since he started this job?" she demanded.

Gryph was slightly taken back by the way she had switched the topic. "As a matter of fact, I've subcontracted out some work to an informer. A man named Brinton. He's one of those very useful people who knows every back alley in Serendipity. And he makes a living selling information to those who are willing to pay to know some of the things that go on in those alleys."

"A clanless man?" Sariana asked, obviously appalled. "A criminal?"

"Not everyone has the advantages of belonging to a respectable clan, Sariana. In spite of the social philosophers' fine plans, society is a long way from being perfectly structured. Here in the west the rules get bent a lot. You know that. I doubt we're all that unique. Don't you have any clanless people in the eastern provinces?"

"Well, yes, but to actually deal with such a person . . . "

"You're not dealing with him. I am. To tell you the truth, Brinton's not such a bad sort. His information is usually highly reliable. If a rival clan hired someone to steal the Avylyns' prisma cutter, the chances are good one of Brinton's many sources will have heard some rumors to that effect."

"I don't like it," Sariana stated.

"You don't have to like it or dislike it. It's done."

She chewed on that for a moment. "When will you hear from this Brinton?" she finally asked.

Gryph smiled grimly. "I'm glad you have enough common sense to be able to accept the inevitable. At heart you're a practical woman. That's a useful trait. As far as your question goes, I'm not sure when I'll hear from Brinton. He does things in his own way and in his own time. It shouldn't take him long to find out if there are any rumors going around about the cutter, though."

"I'd like to get this matter settled as soon as possible."

"I'm aware of that fact, lady. But you're going to have to be patient." Gryph paused until he had her full attention. "Unless you'd like to fire me and continue the investigation yourself?"

"Don't be ridiculous. I wouldn't know how to conduct such an investigation and I can hardly go to the town guards with this."

"Not if you want to keep the matter quiet," Gryph agreed blandly.

Silence settled on Sariana for a long moment. Gryph could practically hear the thoughts churning in her head. But when she spoke she surprised him with her question.

"Why did Lady Avylyn address you as Lord Chassyn the other morning in my office?"

"The title is mine by right. I'm a direct descendant of a Prime Family of the Shield class. Our class may be an insignificant one in your eyes, with no equivalent in the east, but it is a legitimate class here in the west."

She looked at him curiously. "I didn't mean to offend you."

"Didn't you?" Sometimes, Gryph reflected, his future Shieldmate displayed a most amazing talent for annoying him.

Sariana appeared uncharacteristically contrite. Her apology was gracious and formal. "I'm sorry if I have offended you or your social class. Please forgive me. All social classes are deserving of respect and equality, just as the social philosophers decreed when they created them. I have been under a certain amount of strain lately. Sometimes I speak before I think."

"You ought to watch that, Sariana," Gryph couldn't resist saying.

She frowned. "Watch what?"

"Speaking before you think. That's a western habit. We tend to get emotional about things, you see."

To his surprise she took the comment seriously. "I have noticed the tendency."

"I'll bet you have. You couldn't have lived here for a year and not seen a lot of examples of that *tendency*. We're a little hot-blooded here in the west. Also occasionally rash, passionate, and amazingly reckless at times."

Sariana grinned unexpectedly. "The Avylyns call it artistic temperament. They seem to think it was inevitable, given the fact that most of the social classes on board *The Serendipity* had an artistic orientation. Sometimes I've wondered if it might be caused partly by your environment. Everything seems very strongly stated here in the west. The climate, the landscape, the plants and animals. Nothing is dull or colorless." She glanced at the huge conservatory clock and gave a start. "I'd better get back to my suite. It's very late."

"I'll walk you back."

"No, no, that's quite all right," she protested quickly. "I wouldn't want you to go out of your way."

"It's not out of my way. My suite is in the same wing as yours. Lady Avylyn graciously assigned it to me this morning."

"Oh."

Gryph took some satisfaction from the fact that she couldn't find anything else to say to that. Sariana, he was learning, was rarely at a loss for words.

They walked in silence down the long gallery of the wing in which their chambers were located. At Sariana's door they came to a halt and Gryph reached down to touch the hidden spring mechanism. The door opened on its silent hinges and Sariana stepped inside. She started to turn, a polite farewell on her lips, then stopped abruptly as her attention was caught by something inside the room.

"Oh, no!"

Gryph was inside the room at once, scanning the interior with a practiced eye. "What's wrong?"

"The scarlet-toe. It's out of its cage." Sariana hurried forward to examine the empty gold cage. The tiny door stood open. "How could it have gotten out? I'll have to find it. I can't possibly go to sleep knowing there's a lizard running around my room."

"Scarlet-toes are very clever," Gryph remarked. The alert tension that had gripped him when Sariana had cried out in dismay vanished. He took a good look around the room while Sariana darted about anxiously looking in corners and under chairs.

The ornate bed was suspended from the ceiling by four heavy chains in the typical western fashion. It hung a half meter above the floor, but it was impossible to see under it because of the bed drapes.

The walls were painted a warm yellow, the elaborate architectural details picked out in white and gilt. High, arched windows looked out over the gardens toward the river. There was a fine cabinet finished in black enamel and decorated with a flower motif. A couple of suspended chairs and a writing desk completed the basic furnishings. A doorway on the other side of the room led into what Gryph knew would be an ornate bathroom. Westerners loved ornate bathrooms. The wealthier the family, the more exotic the household baths.

"We've got to find it," Sariana said, glancing inside an empty vase. "I can't go to sleep in here unless I know it's back in its cage. Here, Lucky. Where are you, Lucky?"

"Scarlet-toes are harmless, Sariana. You don't have to worry if we don't find it."

"Easy for you to say," she muttered as she began to check all the tiny drawers of the writing desk. "You're not the one who has to sleep in a room with a lizard."

"The real danger is to the scarlet-toe," Gryph pointed out as he went down on one knee beside the bed and swept aside the drapery. You might accidentally step on it when you got out of bed in the morning."

Sariana groaned and opened another drawer. "What a horrible thought."

"Yeah. Especially for Lucky." Gryph bent down to look beneath the bed and saw the flash of red gems in the shadows. "Ah, here we are."

Sariana slammed a drawer shut and hurried across the room. "You found it?"

Gryph settled back on his heel. "It will be easier for you to catch it than it will be for me. I told you this morning, they like females."

"You're serious, aren't you?" Sariana looked ruefully resigned.

"I'm afraid so." He waited, curious to see what she would do.

"Well, I can't leave it where it is. It will drive me crazy all night wondering if it's sneaking around my bed somewhere." She dropped to her knees and peered under the bed.

"Don't make any sudden moves. It's still quite wild. But it will be curious about you. Put out your hand very slowly."

"What if it bites me?" Sariana hissed. She went down on her stomach and slithered halfway under the bed. She disappeared from the waist up, leaving Gryph with a view of her charming rear.

"It won't bite." Gryph stayed where he was, enjoying the soft curves of her buttocks and thighs as they were revealed by the shifting folds of her robe. "Don't worry, Sariana. All it secretly wants to do is curl up in your palm and warm itself against your skin."

"I hope you know what I'm doing." She wriggled a little farther under the bed.

Gryph fought the almost overpowering urge to shape his hand to the lush curve of her hips. "Just trust me, Sariana. It doesn't want to hurt you. It wants to be held and touched and petted by you. At this point it just isn't quite certain how to approach you, that's all. You need to show it that you want it."

"I hate to break this to her, Gryph," her voice was muffled, "but I don't particularly want a lizard for a pet. I just didn't know how to tell Luri that."

"You can't really know how you feel about it until you've held it close," Gryph said softly, still studying the gentle mounds that were so close to his hand. "Don't make snap judgments."

"It's not a snap judgment. I've never been fond of lizards. I don't know many people who are."

"The scarlet-toe seems strange and alien to you now. You're wary of it because it's unfamiliar to you. Just as I am."

Her wriggling body went still. Then Sariana said tartly, "I hadn't thought of you and the scarlet-toe as having all that much in common."

"We're both from the west," Gryph noted in soft amusement.

"And you both have teeth."

Gryph blinked, unsure how to interpret that. "Sariana . . ."

"Ah! Got 'em." Her body snapped forward quickly and an instant later she was sliding back out from beneath the bed. She sat up, triumphantly holding her captive. "Here it is. Get the cage."

Gryph studied the careful way she was clasping the small red lizard. "It's not necessary to keep a scarlet-toe in a cage. Not after it gets to know you."

"This one will very definitely stay in a cage." Sariana stated firmly. "I'm not taking any chances with something that has as many teeth as this thing does." She got to her feet and went quickly across the room to deposit the small lizard inside its gold filigree home. Then she latched the cage door shut. "There we are. Safe and sound. In the morning I'll try to convince Luri that his gift would much rather be free to romp along the riverbank."

Gryph rose slowly, watching Sariana as she bent over the gold cage. "I don't think it will want to be free in the morning, Sariana. I think the bonding has already started. Lucky won't want to leave you."

"Nonsense. Any wild creature would rather be free."

"There are exceptions to every rule."

Sariana grinned as she turned around to confront him. "Not in the eastern provinces, there aren't. We don't bend the rules very much where I come from, let alone make exceptions."

"You're not at home," Gryph reminded her. He went slowly forward, approaching her as she had approached the scarlet-toe. "Things are different here."

She didn't move, but some of her amusement faded. She seemed to realize finally that there was more going on in the room than the successful capture of a scarlet lizard. She searched his face, her eyes wide and questioning. "Gryph?"

"Don't be afraid of the differences between us." He moved a little closer, pleased that she still wasn't trying to dodge his slow, careful advance. In another step or two, he could touch her. He wanted that. Wanted it very badly.

"I'm not afraid of you, Gryph."

He smiled faintly, pleased by the words. "I think it would take a lot to frighten you. A nervous little coward would not have made the voyage to the western provinces when things went wrong at home."

Sariana shook her head slightly, her mouth trembling between a smile and uncertainty. "I didn't have much choice."

"You had a choice. You took the one that held the most promise, but also the one that held the most risk. With a temperament like that, you might be more at home here in Serendipity than you would be in Rendezvous. Have you ever thought of that?"

"No," she said flatly, "I haven't."

Gryph took a chance. He put out his hand and touched the fold of her robe where it fell just below her shoulder. The soft thrust of her breasts was only a few centimeters from his palm. He sensed her catching her breath and he sought desperately for a way to calm her again.

"You're a woman who's not afraid to take risks," he

whispered, his voice rough and husky with need. His fingers trembled on the fabric of her robe. "Will you take a risk with me?"

"I don't know what you mean. I'm already taking a tremendous risk just by hiring you."

He brushed that aside, impatient with her small attempt to sidestep the issue. "I'm talking about another kind of risk and I think you know it."

A frantic protest mingled with anger leaped into her wide eyes. "You ask too much, Shield!"

"And I overstep myself, don't I?" he taunted gently. "I go too far, reach too high, dare too much, demand more than I have any right to expect."

"I see you understand your situation perfectly," she muttered. Her lashes came down to veil her eyes. "Gryph, please, it's very late. You must leave. Don't embarrass both of us by going any farther with this."

"I can give you a little time, Sariana. Not much, but a little. Would that help? I want to do this right."

She trembled. He could feel the small shiver that went through her and he knew with absolute certainty that it was caused by excitement as well as feminine wariness. He could make her want him. He was sure of it. He just had to give her time.

"Time?" she breathed. Her eyes were luminous pools. Emotions moved just beneath the surface of those pools, sending tremors through her whole body.

"Would that make it easier for you?"

"I don't know," she gasped. "I don't know. Please, Gryph, I can't think."

"I want you."

"You hardly know me." Her eyes were pleading with him now, pleading for understanding and reassurance. But he saw the passionate curiosity in them, too, and he aimed for that.

"I know you better than you think." He leaned down to brush her mouth with his own. Relief and triumph swept through him when she didn't instantly pull away.

Deliberately he kept the kiss gentle and undemanding. He would not make the mistake of overwhelming her as he had the last time he had kissed her. He didn't want her to be frightened of him. His whole body was clamoring for release, but he could control himself tonight. He would give Sariana the time she needed.

Sariana stood very still beneath his kiss. Then her lips parted slightly. Gryph took the invitation at once, sliding his tongue deeply into her warm mouth. His hand moved down from her shoulder to the curve of her breast. When he felt her nipple hardening beneath the fabric of her robe he thought he would go out of his mind. He held the kiss as long as he dared, held it until he felt the stirring of a new kind of tension in her and then he reluctantly broke the intimate contact.

"Sariana, Sariana," he muttered against her lips. "Tell me that all you need is time. I can wait if I must."

"I don't understand any of this," she whispered. "What are you doing to me?"

"There's no point in fighting it. I don't think either of us has much choice." He brought his other hand up to cup her face between his palms. Somehow he had to impress upon her the inevitability of their union. It would be simpler and far less difficult for her to accept that union if she came of her own volition to understand there was no real choice. "I'll try not to rush you."

"Gryph . . ."

"I'll give you some time, just as I promised. But please, for both our sakes, don't make me wait too long."

"No man has ever asked me to have an affair with him." Her words trembled in the air between them. "I'm not sure I want one. Not now. Not with someone I hardly know . . ."

He dared not tell her that what he was asking involved far more than a short-term arrangement. She would almost certainly panic if he did. But it was possible he could convince her to enter into what she thought would be a brief affair. She was a young woman of passion, although she did not yet fully comprehend that. She was far from the constraints of home and she found herself alone and lonely in a foreign land. The thought of having an affair might be very tempting to her.

"I told you earlier that you are not the only one who is familiar with loneliness," he reminded her softly.

She nodded slowly. "The Avylyns explained that the Shields number very few and that most of you walk alone for the most part. You live on the fringes of society."

"In a sense you and I are both strangers in this land."

Her small fingers closed around his wrist. "Is it very difficult for you, Gryph? Being a Shield, I mean?"

"No more difficult than your chosen exile is for you."

A wealth of gentle sympathy was mirrored in her eyes. "I think I understand."

"Thank you, Sariana." He brushed her mouth once more and then he made himself release her.

Without a word he turned and walked to the door. But just as he was about to leave he looked back over his shoulder. She was standing where he had left her beside the golden cage, her eyes full of aching, unasked questions.

"Time," Gryph said distinctly. "I can grant you a little time. The luck of the night to you, Sariana." He stepped outside into the hall and shut the door firmly behind him.

Halfway down the corridor to his room he remembered the crushed flower in the pocket of his jacket. He removed it and stared at the broken petals for a moment.

Then Gryph smiled to himself and tossed the flower into a nearby trash receptacle discreetly disguised as a vase.

The nice thing about dealing with Sariana was knowing that she was not weak and fragile like that flower. She would not get crushed if the wooing got a little rough.

The lady was a potential Shieldmate and such women were not fluffy, delicate or weak, in spite of their outward appearances. He would give her time because that was the courteous thing to do and he was, after all, a lord of a Prime Family. He could do the gentlemanly thing when it was required. Besides, he wanted to impress Sariana with his proud manners.

But in the end, whether he used the courteous approach or some more direct means, Sariana would belong to him. The decision had been made.

Chapter
5

THE message from Brinton arrived the night of the Avylyns' costume ball.

It couldn't have come at a more inopportune time as far as Gryph was concerned. He'd had plans for the evening. Plans that revolved around showing Sariana he knew how to conduct himself on a dance floor.

But instead of gliding around a ballroom with Sariana in his arms, Gryph moved soundlessly through the dank, twisted streets of Serendipity's lower quarters. He was headed toward the rendezvous point and enroute he brooded about his annoyingly bad luck. Brinton might be an excellent source of information in certain subjects, but his timing could be miserable.

Dancing with Sariana and showing off his best manners hadn't been Gryph's only goal for the evening. He'd also wanted to get a good look at Etion Rakken. He was curious about his competition.

Instead, here he was wandering through garbage strewn alleys dressed in a new shirt of black linen, his boots polished until they gleamed, his gray jacket and trousers perfectly pressed. There hadn't even been time to change his clothes. The message that had arrived at one of the Avylyns' back doors a short time ago had been carried by a small, grimy, barefooted boy. It had been terse and cryptic.

Gryph had sensed the urgency behind it at once. Brinton was an old hand at this kind of thing. He wouldn't panic easily. His uncanny nose for underground gossip must have turned up something very interesting.

Gryph made his way unobtrusively along a back street the town council considered so unimportant it had decided not to waste money illuminating it with vapor lamps. There wasn't even much moonlight tonight. The roiling clouds of another summer storm were quickly obscuring the night sky.

If Brinton was at the rendezvous point as he had said he would be, Gryph reflected, there would still be plenty of time to get back to the ball before it concluded with the late night buffet. It had been a long time since he had danced. He sincerely hoped it was like riding a dragonpony in that once you learned how, you never forgot.

His best hope for not making a complete fool of himself lay in the fact that he suspected Sariana probably wasn't much of a dancer herself. He had a hunch she'd spent a lot more time in the classroom and library than she had in a ballroom.

That was Sariana's problem, Gryph decided. She hadn't spent much time in fun and games. She'd been too focused on the entwined paths of a successful career and a marriage that was intended to be a business alliance, not a passionate relationship. But Gryph was confident he could fix all that for her.

All he had to do was get her attention long enough to convince her she was working toward the wrong destiny.

Getting her attention was not, however, proving as easy as he had thought after that midnight encounter in the conservatory. Gryph had seen very little of Sariana for the past three days. She seemed to be always either buried in paperwork, in conference with Lord and Lady Avylyn, or on her way to another "luncheon meeting" with Etion Rakken.

Every time he had managed to find Sariana alone, he had been treated to a long string of pointed inquiries about the progress of his assignment. He was beginning to wonder if it might not be wisest to find the damned prisma cutter just so that Sariana would be forced to shut up on the subject.

The lady had a way of keeping a man at bay. Gryph smiled in spite of his mood. She was invariably self-possessed, self-assured and self-confident when she was discussing business. When she wasn't discussing business she managed to keep the conversation focused squarely on the unimportant or the trivial.

The woman could certainly talk, Gryph reflected.

But Gryph was certain he could sense the passion that was locked away in her. The need to be the one who unlocked it was fast becoming an all-consuming need.

Gryph turned a corner and started down a narrow brick path that didn't warrant the title of street. He pushed all stray thoughts of Sariana and the ball temporarily aside as a prickle of heightened awareness went down his spine. He was getting close to the meeting point stipulated in Brinton's message. He started counting the yawning black mouths that were alleys leading off of the path. When he reached the third one he stopped. Brinton should be waiting nearby.

Gryph stood motionless against the wall, letting the darkness swallow him. There was no sound or movement in the shadows around him. The distant rattle of a carriage floated down the street behind him and was soon gone. No intelligent carriage driver would hang around this part of town for long.

Then he heard the faint groan from the end of the alley and Gryph knew that Brinton's career as an informer had just hit a snag.

Gryph's fingers played lightly over the prisma lock of his weapon kit. The leather pouch opened. He reached inside and withdrew the small vapor light. He thumbed the mechanism that released a spark into the vapor and instantly a faint beam revealed a portion of the littered alley.

It was empty except for what appeared to be a pile of old clothes at the far end. Gryph hesitated, all his trained senses protesting his decision to enter what could easily become a trap. The alley only had one exit.

But Gryph was grimly certain that it was Brinton who lay in a crumpled heap at the base of the brick wall. And there was no getting around the fact that he probably wouldn't have been there if he hadn't been working for Gryph. Brinton might have been lying in some other dark alley, waiting for some other customer, if he hadn't taken this particular job, but that was beside the point. With a last glance up and down the path to ensure he was alone, Gryph entered the alley.

A few seconds later he crouched beside the fallen man, reached out to touch him and knew there was no hope.

"Brinton?"

The man didn't move, but there was another low groan. Brinton was barely breathing. The tiny vapor lamp revealed a dark, widening stain on the man's shirt.

"Hang on, pal. I'll get you out of here." Gryph knew from the size of the stain and the feel of Brinton's skin that there wasn't much point in trying to get him to a medic, but there was little else that could be done. There were better places to die than in an alley.

"Shield." The single word was little more than a breath between Brinton's bloodied lips.

"Yes," Gryph said, as he pushed a hand under Brinton's shirt to see if he could slow the bleeding before he tried to move the man. "It's me. By the Lightstorm, I'm sorry, Brinton. I swear I had no way of knowing things were this serious."

"No! Not you. Another Shield." Brinton's eyes opened slightly and he tried to focus on Gryph's face. His words were thick and heavy in his mouth. "I didn't find out who has the cutter."

"It doesn't matter, Brinton. Take it easy, man. I'm going to get you to a medic." Gryph felt blood and torn flesh beneath his hand. Quickly he worked to tighten Brinton's shirt into a makeshift bandage. Brinton slapped restlessly at his hand.

"No time. Get away, Chassyn. Get away."

"I'm going to put you over my shoulder," Gryph said, bracing himself to lift the smaller man.

"No . . . point. Listen to me. You always paid on time. Good client. Reliable. I owe you for . . . you helped me a few years back."

"You don't owe me anything."

Brinton shook his head and blood trickled down his chin. "Not true. I owe you. Going to pay you back. To-night. Only way I can. Information. Didn't find the cutter, but something more important. There's another Shield out there who doesn't want it found. You hear me, Chassyn? *Another Shield.* I don't know who . . . he's responsible for the missing cutter."

Gryph went still. "A Shield did this to you?"

"No. I'm not worth a Shield's time. But he probably sent the ones who got me. I heard . . ." Brinton coughed again. "I heard something about the thieves taking the cutter to Little Chance. You paid for this information. Take it and use it. But be careful. The cutter's not worth your life." Brinton began to gasp painfully.

Gryph waited no longer. He had done the best he could for the bleeding. He leaned down and maneuvered Brinton over his shoulder. The man was unconscious now. It was just as well.

Gryph started toward the alley entrance, balancing the dying man's weight with one hand and holding the small vapor lamp with the other.

He was only half out of the walled trap when the caped figure with the blade bow in his hand stepped into the alley. The vapor lamp's slender ray picked him out just as he raised his arm to fire the bow.

Gryph's reaction was reflexive. He shut his eyes and flicked a second switch on the small hand lamp. The narrow beam became a short-lived, blinding flare of light that filled the alley. An instant later it vanished completely leaving everything in utter darkness. The capped figure shouted in anger as he was temporarily blinded. The bow zinged softly.

Gryph was already throwing himself to one side and groping for a throwing blade, but the weight of Brinton's body made the maneuver uncharacteristically and dangerously awkward. He felt the impact of the stranger's blade as it sliced through his jacket and across his shoulder. Then he felt the pain.

He staggered and opened his eyes as Brinton's body slid to the bricks beside him. There was no sound from the informer. Gryph thought he was probably already dead.

The man with the blade bow was gone. Gryph knew from experience that it would take a couple of minutes for the effects of the brilliant flash of vapor light to wear off. His assailant was probably reeling blindly down the street, searching for a place to hide until he regained his sight.

Gryph leaped for the alley entrance. His vapor lamp was useless now. It could only be used once in such a maneuver and then it had to be recharged with vapor. Gryph's eyes were functioning normally because he'd closed them during the burst of flaring vapor. There was enough illumination from scattered starlight to search the street outside the alley.

But even as he reached the street he heard the sound of dragonpony hooves on pavement. Not one pony, but two. The man with the blade bow had brought a backup. In the dim light Gryph watched in frustrated fury as two dragonponies galloped out of sight around a corner. The man on the first pony was leading the second animal. The slumped figure on the second pony was undoubtedly the man with the bow.

"Damn it to the heart of the Lightstorm," Gryph hissed, swearing futilely at his own stupidity, slowness and bad timing.

He turned back into the alley and felt for Brinton's pulse. The man was dead.

Gryph clamped a hand around his bleeding shoulder and started back toward the Avylyns' section of town. On the way he thought he'd better stop at the home of a medic he happened to know. A man who could keep his mouth shut.

The Avylyns' annual ball was an enormous success. Sariana stood in the shelter of a bay window and sipped a glass of wine-spiked punch while she watched the dancers. She was glad to find herself alone for a few minutes. The ballroom was vibrant with color and laughter and music. The room was a showcase for the most fantastic fashions tonight. Each costume was more outrageous and overdone than the last.

Her own gown was simple and quite plain in comparison to those around her, although it was certainly dramatic by her personal standards. When she had dressed earlier that evening Sariana had been mildly shocked by the low, off-the-shoulder neckline, the tight bodice and the frothy, side-split skirts. The gown was a shimmering emerald green trimmed with gold. When she walked or danced it revealed a great deal of her legs. It was supposed to represent the costume of a farmer's daughter, but Sariana seriously doubted any farmer's daughter had swept out a stable while wearing such a daringly cut dress.

Lady Avylyn and her daughter had selected the gown for Sariana, having decided on their own that she could not be trusted to come up with something suitable.

They were right, Sariana reflected in amusement as she glanced down at her outfit. Never in a million years would she have chosen anything such as this.

But there was no denying the fact that the moment she had put it on she had begun wondering if it would appeal to Gryph.

She could stop wondering about that. Gryph was nowhere around. She hadn't seen him since the afternoon. Perhaps he was taking seriously his cover job of guarding the Avylyn jewelry collection.

If that were the case, however, he should be somewhere in the room. Most of the best Avylyn pieces were being worn by members of the family tonight. The others were on display in locked cases.

"There you are, Sariana. I've been looking for you. Whatever are you doing in here? I hope you are enjoying yourself. Everything has turned out just splendidly, hasn't it?" Lady Avylyn spoke excitedly as she swept into Sariana's small hiding place. As she entered the alcove the enormous skirts of her golden velvet gown took up most of the available room. A magnificent assortment of jewelry was draped on every portion of her figure revealed by the dress. Pendant earrings, acres of bracelets and a necklace that could have sunk a ship glittered in the light.

"I was just taking a break," Sariana explained. "I'm afraid I'm not accustomed to this much exercise."

Lady Avylyn beamed, fluttering her gilded fan. "I saw you dancing earlier with Etion Rakken. Such a nice man. Where is he?"

"Dancing with Lady Tarlana. A duty dance, he said."

"Ah, yes, Lady Tarlana's clan does business with Etion's bank, too, I believe. I do hope Etion will continue to be discreet."

"Believe me, the last thing Etion would ever do is discuss one client's finances with another. Not a word of the Avylyn financial situation has leaked out for the past few months, has it? All the gossip that was starting to grow when I arrived on the scene has been squelched. You can have complete faith in Etion's discretion."

Lady Avylyn smiled brightly, too pleased with the success of the evening to spend much time worrying about anything as mundane as the Avylyns' financial situation. "Yes, of course we can. It appears we are going to survive our unfortunate situation and as Jasso was saying just the other day, we owe it all to you, my dear. Without you I dread to think where we would be by now. If only we could conclude this nasty business with the prisma cutter."

"I think you can trust Gryph to get it back for you."

"I hope so." Lady Avylyn cocked a gilded brow in a sly expression. "Do you know, I believe the Shield is quite fascinated by you, Sariana."

Sariana felt oddly flustered. "Not at all, Lady Avylyn. I'm sure you're wrong."

"Trust me. I am more familiar with the many interesting manifestations of romantic attraction than you are, Sariana. I hate to say this, but in some areas your education has been lamentably weak."

Sariana grinned. "You needn't name the areas of concern, my lady."

"Very well, I won't. But I still think you should be made aware of the fact that the Shield is attracted to you." The older woman's dark eyes grew momentarily more serious. "If all he wants is an affair, that is one thing. It would probably be good for you to engage in a wild, passionate fling with a man, any man. We have all been hoping that you and Etion might—"

"Lady Avylyn!"

"Never mind," Lady Avylyn said hastily. "I just wanted to warn you that if you should decide to become involved with the Shield, you ought to know that they are—well, different. I think I said something to that effect once before. They have their own rules and customs, as I've tried to explain."

"They conduct their love affairs differently than other men?" Sariana asked dryly.

"Well, no, not their love affairs. In that regard, they are quite, uh, normal, I imagine. That is, I have never heard anything to the contrary."

"Lady Avylyn," Sariana finally said, amused and exasperated, "what exactly are you trying to warn me about?"

The older woman drew herself up to her most noble height. "Marriage," she said darkly.

"Marriage!" Sariana felt herself flushing furiously. The knowledge was maddening. "I assure you, marriage is the very last thing on my mind at the moment. And I would certainly have little interest in forming an alliance with a Shield, of all people. Why, Gryph isn't even of the same social class as myself. We have absolutely nothing in common. The whole notion is quite out of the question." Sariana knew her own clan would be shocked at the idea.

Lady Avylyn brightened, obviously relieved. "Just as well. Just as well. Shield marriages are, well, never mind.

It's difficult to explain and I'm not sure anybody except a Shield and his mate really understand the relationship, anyway. It's just that since you weren't raised here, you don't know much about Shields and I felt it my duty to warn you that . . . Never mind. No warnings are necessary as long as you are quite certain that both of you are only interested in having a fling."

"I'll tell you a secret, madam. I don't know what I want."

"Then my advice is to throw yourself into an affair." Lady Avylyn tapped Sariana's wrist with her folded fan. "Indulge yourself in some fun, my dear. It would do you a great deal of good, I'm sure. See you at the buffet."

Lady Avylyn swung around in a whirl of golden skirts and sailed out of the alcove.

Sariana stared after her. Lady Avylyn was right. The only sort of relationship Sariana could possibly have with Gryph was an affair, and she had been toying with the mildly scandalous, wholly fascinating idea since the night he had found her in the conservatory.

Things were different in the western provinces. One could be a bit reckless and daring and no one would think twice about it. One could even have an affair that crossed class lines and the most anyone would do was smile.

For the past three days Sariana had been mulling the matter over. She had deliberately evaded Gryph while she tried to sort out her own confused feelings on the subject. In the end, she had sat down at her desk and resorted to the management tool of composing a neat little matrix of positives and negatives.

On the positive side, she was unmarried and she was old enough to conduct an affair. She was wise enough to handle it discreetly, which would have been the main requirement back home. She wasn't sure discretion was terribly important here in the western provinces unless one or both members of the couple were married.

The truth was, she probably wouldn't have to worry all that much about discretion. She had written that fact into the decision matrix, too. It seemed important. She was an ocean away from her homeland where such things were valued and she was unlikely to ever see anyone here again if she managed to return east next year.

Also on the positive side had been a reluctant admission that she was attracted to Gryph Chassyn in a way she had never known with any other man. She was uncertain about the wisdom of satisfying the compelling curiosity that was growing within her. Yet she thought that, on the whole, it might be better to test its depths. It was always better to confront the unknown and deal with it.

She had added that sensible note to the positive side of the matrix, too. The longer she sat at her desk, the longer the list of positives got.

In the end, the negative side of the matrix had contained only one entry; a worrisome note reminding herself that she really had nothing in common with a Shield. The only thing he could possibly want from her was a sexual liaison.

Of course, she told herself now as she watched the couples circle the glittering ballroom, a sexual liaison was all she was looking for too.

Something seemed to be missing in the equation, however. She was afraid to ask what that something might be.

Sariana sipped her punch and wished desperately she knew more about sex and men in general. She had the vague but disturbing sensation that she was standing on the brink of a very sheer cliff.

A faint tapping on the window made Sariana spin around. The diaphanous skirts of her gown swirled weightlessly. She barely stifled a scream when she saw the dark figure on the opposite side of the glass. Then his eyes met hers.

"Gryph!" She saw the way he was clutching one shoulder and a frantic sense of panic set in. He was hurt.

Having got her attention, Gryph stepped back into the shadows of the garden. Sariana didn't hesitate. She caught up her skirts in one hand and slipped quickly out of the alcove. She passed unnoticed through a tangle of laughing guests and a moment later she was safely out of the ballroom. Once she was clear of the hall, Sariana broke into a run.

A short time later she was on the path that would bring her to the gardens directly outside the alcove. The glow of light through the windows guided her. She was almost on top of Gryph when he materialized out of the shadows. His eyes were silvery pools shimmering with an emotion that might have been pain or lust. Sariana assumed it was pain.

"About time you got here," he muttered. He was still clutching his shoulder and swaying slightly on his feet. He looked somewhat the way he had the night he'd been drugged with Aunt Perla's hypnotic potion. "I'm going to need a little help and I didn't want to startle any of the household attendants."

"You're bleeding. There's blood all over you."

"Not all of it's mine. Help me get to my chambers, Sariana."

Sariana carefully took his uninjured arm and started down the garden path toward the wing of the house that contained their suites. "I'll send one of the attendants for a medic."

"No." Gryph drew a deep breath. "I've already been to one. He closed the shoulder and put something on the wound for the pain before I could stop him."

"Why would you want to stop him from giving you a painkiller?" Sariana demanded.

"I'm a Shield."

Sariana was incensed. "What difference does that make? Do Shields have to go around proving their bravery by refusing painkillers when they've been hurt?"

"Has anyone ever told you that you have all the makings of a scold?" Gryph retorted. "With very little effort you could turn into a complete nag."

"With you for inspiration, I'm willing to make the effort," she snapped. "Now tell me what's going on here. Why didn't you want a painkiller?"

"Some kinds of drugs don't work on a Shield the same way they do on other people. Remember the night you knocked me unconscious with that mild hypnotic you had

Mara slip into my ale?" His words sounded increasingly slurred.

Sariana was stricken with guilt. "I didn't realize it would affect you that way. I was assured it wouldn't combine with the alcohol into anything more potent than what it already was."

"It wouldn't in most people. It does in a Shield. The painkiller the medic used tonight is having a similar effect."

"You mean you're about to faint?"

"Not if I can help it," he told her grimly.

"Gryph, tell me what happened."

"I got hurt."

"I can see that! How?"

"Sheer stupidity. Stupidity will do it every time."

"Does this have anything to do with that missing prisma cutter?" Sariana demanded with sudden intuition.

"It does."

"I was afraid of that! I had no idea this business was going to become dangerous. We'll have to go to the town guards after all."

"No, we will not go to the guards." The words were carefully and deliberately spaced, each one an immovable block of stone.

"We most certainly will," Sariana declared. "I don't want anyone else hurt just to protect the Avylyns' reputation. I'm in charge of this matter and I will make the decisions."

"You," Gryph informed her, voice blurred but no less resolute for that, "are no longer in charge. I am."

Sariana stared up at him. "Never. Why would you want to be in charge, anyway? You've never been particularly enthused about the task of getting back the cutter."

"Things have changed."

"What's changed?" She pushed open a side door and guided Gryph into the hall that led to his suite.

"I'll explain it all later. Right now I just want some

sleep. Do me a favor, Sariana, stop snapping at me and put me to bed. Please."

She gave up and did exactly that.

Three hours later when Gryph awoke from a restless sleep he was immediately aware of three things. The first was that his shoulder ached. The second was that the chamber seemed much too warm.

The third was that he was not alone in the darkened room. Sariana was curled up in the depths of an armchair beside the bed, sound asleep. It was the first time he had ever seen her in repose. There was a gentle vulnerability about her that made him want to reach out and gather her into the protection of his arms. It had stopped raining and a watery golden moonlight revealed the green satin slippers on the floor beneath the suspended chair. The frothy skirts of her gown formed a pool of gilded green on the cushions. The toes of her stockinged feet poked out from beneath a fold.

An overwhelming wave of desire and longing swept through Gryph. He was in no condition tonight to control it.

Sariana's lashes stirred and lifted as she sensed his awakening. Her eyes met his and Gryph's body sang an ancient song as he saw the shy, tremulous, sleepy desire in her gaze. She wanted him.

Without a word he held out his hand. If she came to him now she would be his. He knew that with a triumphant certainty.

Sariana's gaze drifted down to the hand he had extended across the quilt and then lifted again to his face. He saw the questions and the uncertainty and the feminine caution in her. All his instincts urged him not to hesitate. He should reach out and take hold of her before she lost her nerve and turned to flee.

But another part of him said that all he had to do was wait. It was like catching a scarlet-toe. The victim was her own worst enemy. Sariana was not going to run from him tonight.

Sariana uncurled herself slowly and it was easy to see that she was poised between the urge to flee and the need to stay and learn the secrets of the attraction she was experiencing. Then she got to her feet and walked slowly over to the bed. She reached down and touched Gryph's fingers wonderingly.

He closed his hand around hers and tugged her down onto the gently swinging bed.

Chapter
6

S ARIANA had made her decision as she sat watching
him sleep. Gryph was sprawled on top of the rheenfeather quilt, his smoothly muscled body bare from
the waist up. Earlier, when she had helped him into bed,
Sariana had tried to persuade him to slide beneath the covers
but he had refused. He had stripped off his jacket and shirt
and dropped, clearly exhausted, on top of the bed.

She had sat watching him until she, too, had fallen
asleep. She wasn't sure what had awakened her a moment
ago, but she had been vibrantly aware that she had reached
her decision.

Now Sariana allowed herself to be pulled down onto the
gently swinging bed without a murmur of protest. This was
what she wanted. She knew it in the depths of her being.
She was going to take Lady Avylyn's advice and fling herself headlong into an experience that would be unlike anything she had ever known. Sariana was excited and
shocked at her own recklessness, but the reaction only
served to heighten her awareness.

Gryph's eyes were holding hers with unrelenting intensity as he pulled her down to lie beside him. The gleam of moonlight was reflected in his blue-green gaze, creating a thousand tiny shards of light between his black lashes. There was a compelling promise in that gaze, one Sariana could no longer ignore.

This was the man with whom she would explore the boundaries of her own sexuality. She wanted to learn what it would be like to please him and to be pleased in return. She had waited long enough. It was time.

Her senses were filled with wonder and excitement and delight as he settled her beside him on top of the quilt. She was lightheaded with the thrill of it all. Only one thing worried her now.

"Gryph, your shoulder. I don't want you to hurt yourself."

"Forget my shoulder. I can barely feel it. All I want to feel now is you. By the Ship's Fire, Sariana, I've waited too long for this night. Too long for you."

"It's only been a few days, Gryph. We still hardly even know each other." Her fingers drifted curiously across his chest, stirring the crisp hair that angled down to a point that disappeared beneath the waistband of his trousers. He shuddered and she was enthralled. There was a heady sense of purely female power in knowing she could make him respond like this. She touched him again, this time gently grazing his flat nipple with the tip of her silvered nail. Gryph drew in his breath and his hand tightened on her wrist.

"You don't understand and I can't explain it to you now," he said roughly. "In the morning you will know what tonight means. Come closer, Sariana."

She obeyed with a shy eagerness, the skirts of her gown flowing across the bed as she nestled against his side and put her head tentatively on his uninjured shoulder. His hand twisted urgently into her hair, loosening the brown-gold mass until it was free of the sleek style in which it had been bound.

"So warm and soft and mysterious." Gryph lifted a

handful of her hair and inhaled deeply. "I want to know all your secrets, Sariana."

Sariana felt his hard, muscled tension, felt the heat of his body reaching out to envelop her. "You're the one who is mysterious, Gryph. I don't know you very well and I'm not at all certain I understand you."

"But you want me," he stated.

"I . . . I think this is what I want. Gryph, this is all so new to me." She felt a faint twinge of uncertainty that momentarily interfered with the wonderful sense of discovery and excitement.

"We have much to learn about each other, lady, but the learning starts with this."

He caught her mouth with his own and Sariana gasped at the urgency of his kiss. Behind it lay an unfathomable pool of dark isolation and aloneness, a bottomless spring of masculine need. It blotted out everything, including the flash of uncertainty she had felt moments earlier. Now all that mattered was bringing light into that darkness. The only light she had to give him was herself. Sariana trembled but she didn't pull away as Gryph deepened the kiss.

She was still adjusting physically and emotionally to the compelling feel of his mouth when she felt his hands on the fastenings of her gown. She flinched when he began to undo them impatiently. Some of Sariana's growing desire was again halted by a tingle of confused uncertainty. Somehow, in the fantasies she had been indulging of late, she had imagined a slower, more sensual prelude.

"Be careful," she whispered softly. "You'll ruin the dress." She didn't care about the dress, but his implacable intensity was a bit unnerving. She wanted to slow him down.

"To the Lightstorm with the dress. Do you think it matters?" He tugged at the bodice and it came free to her waist. The finely woven chemise she was wearing beneath the gown was revealed. Her flowering nipples pushed upward against the thin fabric.

Gryph groaned and rolled onto his side. He eased Sariana onto her back and stripped the gown completely off her in one swift movement. Then he pushed up the hem of her chemise and peeled off her stockings. His calloused hands were rough on the soft skin of her thighs.

A moment later Gryph yanked the chemise up over her head and Sariana was suddenly nude. He stared down at her, drinking in the sight of her small, full breasts as he ran his hand along the curve of her thigh.

It was all happening too quickly. A belated sense of caution was mingling with her growing confusion and Sariana began to doubt the wisdom of her earlier decision.

"Gryph, wait. You go too fast for me. I need time. Please."

His eyes were wild, tormented seas in the shadows of the room. "I wanted to give you time but I can't. Don't you understand, Sariana?"

She shook her head slightly, wondering at the desperation she thought she heard in his voice. It was hard to imagine this strong, controlled man being desperate about anything, let alone the beginning of a brief romantic affair.

"No, I don't understand," she admitted. "Please don't ruin this for me."

"*Sariana.*" He made a strangled sound under his breath, a shattered exclamation that was half curse and half plea. It seemed to contain as much anguish as desire, and Sariana was instantly seized with a powerful need to soothe and comfort him. She touched his shoulder, not in a sexual manner, but in the same way she would stroke an injured creature. He shivered under her fingers.

She could feel him controlling himself with an intense willpower. His eyes closed tightly and his hand flexed into a fist. Sariana became aware of the heat of his skin and she grew worried. Surely he was too warm, she thought. Could sexual need bring on this kind of heat in a man?

Gryph was indeed in the grip of a fever, but she began to doubt that it was a fever brought on by passion. More likely it was the result of his wound. Her own budding sense of desire was rapidly changing into deep concern.

"Gryph, you're ill," she said, trying to sit up.

He opened his eyes, his expression stark in the shadows. "No. Not ill. Not the way you mean. I need you."

She touched his forehead and found it damp. "Later," she assured him gently. "There's plenty of time for us to get to know each other in this way. Right now you need sleep."

"Touch me," he commanded thickly.

"I am touching you and you're burning up with fever."

"Touch me," he repeated as he grabbed her wrist. He dragged her hand down his body to where his trousers were stretched tight across his heavy, throbbing manhood. When he heard Sariana catch her breath in reaction to this graphic demonstration of his desire, Gryph nodded savagely. "Now do you understand? I need you. I won't force you. I can't. It doesn't work that way. But I *need* you. In ways you can't even guess at yet."

He was rambling, Sariana thought worriedly. She tried to free herself but she was suddenly caged between his hands. Anxiously she searched his face. "Let me get you something for the fever."

"No."

"I'll be right back," she assured him. "I won't leave you alone."

"No."

"Gryph, please listen to me. You have a fever. Probably brought on by your wound. You need rest."

He shook his head slowly. "No. All I need is you. I'll show you."

He lowered his head and took her mouth once more with devastating force. Sariana responded even as she tried to tell herself she should get out of the bed. But when he pressed himself beside her, letting her feel his hard strength, she felt her resolve slipping.

He did want her. She was amazed that such demanding desire could coexist with the feverish heat from his wound, but she was forced to accept it. The truth was, her own body was growing warm with passion. Tentatively she put her arms around him and stroked his hard, muscled shoulders. Her knee flexed inward, touching his leg intimately.

"That's it, my Shield Lady," he said in aching relief. His mouth moved across hers and down her throat. He buried his lips in the curve of her shoulder and breathed deeply of her fragrance. "That's what I want from you. Touch me. Give yourself to me. Link with me."

She told herself he was rambling again. But this time she couldn't find the will to try to stop him. She was captivated by the depths of his demanding desire and enthralled by the discovery of her own response. She was being gathered into the center of a storm and with every minute that passed her chances of escape grew slimmer. There was a light in the center of that storm—many lights. Fractured, glittering pieces of a rainbow formed a thousand splinters of color. It was like looking into prisma and watching the light that reflected from it transform itself into something more than light.

Colors that moved through the spectrum and beyond danced in her head. They were rays of light so exotic she could not put a name to them.

Caught up in the lure of such a shimmering chaos of light, Sariana no longer thought of escape. She longed only to share the glittering waterfall with Gryph. She knew in the deepest reaches of her senses that he was the only one who could lead her safely through it just as she was the only one who could take him into the heart of the rainbow.

They needed each other.

"It's going to be all right, Sariana. It's going to be all right. This is the way it was meant to be for both of us."

His hand went to his belt and he tore off the remainder of his clothing. In the pale light Sariana saw the full, hard length of his manhood and she shivered. He was taut and heavy with need and her own body responded to it even as she watched him with an awed, questioning gaze.

Gryph saw the expression in her eyes as she lay looking up at him. He lowered himself quickly back down beside her.

"You must not fear me, Shield Lady. You and I are right

for each other. I have never been where I am going to take you right now, but I've heard others describe it. It will seem strange at first. I am told there is some discomfort, but we'll face it together. Do you understand?"

Sariana was feeling oddly dizzy. For a moment she wasn't certain if she heard him say the words or if she only imagined the reassuring sentences inside her head. Then she brushed aside the odd sensation and smiled at him with a tenderness that seemed to dazzle him. His confession was sweet and kind and endeared him to her as nothing else could have done in that moment.

"You've never done this before, either?" she asked softly.

He shook his head, his eyes never leaving hers. His rough hand slid over her breasts. Her already aroused nipples became firm, tight, incredibly sensitive.

"Never," Gryph admitted. "I had almost decided it would never happen for me."

"Oh, Gryph, I'm so glad." Sariana hugged him quickly, her delighted words spilling out in a rush. "I'm so glad this is all new to you, too, although I would never have guessed. You seem so sure of yourself. I can't imagine a man your age and with your obvious . . . your very bold . . ." She paused to find the words, "I wouldn't have thought that a man with your impressive physical attributes would have denied himself the pleasures of sex all these years. Men are usually so eager for that kind of thing. Even in the eastern provinces where people are so much more self-controlled it would be unusual for a man to remain celibate this long. Is it the custom in your class for the men to remain virgin until they reach your age?"

Gryph blinked as if he were having trouble following the conversation. His hand stilled on her breast.

"Uh, Sariana, I don't think you quite understand what I'm trying to explain."

"It's all right," she reassured him quickly. She could guess the cause of his awkwardness. His male ego was probably already berating him for the confession. "I do understand. Men hate to admit they have little or no sexual experience. But I want you to know I'm very touched that we can explore this and learn about it together. You've made me very happy. Now I know I won't have to feel like the only novice in this bed. We'll be true equals. It's such a relief to know we're starting out together."

A look that might have been either frustration or anguish tightened Gryph's already stark features. "Sariana—"

"Don't worry, I would never have guessed that you lack experience," she said hastily. "You're doing beautifully."

"Thank you," he muttered tightly.

"I guess you have good instincts," she went on encouragingly. "You seem to know exactly where and how to touch me. You're moving a little too quickly, but I understand why now. All the same, let's slow down a little. I'm afraid I'm not nearly as adept as you at figuring all this out. But I want to do the right things, too. Tell me where you want me to touch you." Experimentally she trailed her fingertips down over the hard planes of his buttocks. "Do you like that?"

"Sariana, you're doing great. But would you mind very much just closing your mouth?"

Her delighted enthusiasm faded. She looked up at Gryph uncertainly, her eyes widening with hurt.

He groaned and brushed her lips with his own. "I'm sorry, Shield Lady. I didn't mean to offend you. Hell, I'm going to make a mess of this yet if I don't close my own mouth."

She sensed his genuine contrition and her feelings were instantly mended. She brushed her fingers gently through his hair, aware that he was very tense.

"Don't worry about it," she said soothingly. "I'm sure it's perfectly natural for you to be suffering a certain amount of performance anxiety. After all, this is your first time, too. You mustn't expect too much of yourself."

He made a slight choking sound. "Do you ever run out of words, Sariana?"

She smiled mistily. "Am I chattering? Maybe it's because I'm nervous."

"I think you're right," he announced gravely. "We're

both nervous. The only solution is to get it over with," he said harshly, decisively. He moved his hand down her silken stomach to the triangle of hair above her thighs.

Sariana stirred beneath the exciting touch. The urgency that was controlling Gryph seemed to have gotten a grip on her, too. She could feel the driving force in him and knew an answering force within herself. When his hand went lower still, she cried out softly. Instinctively she pressed her thighs together.

"Let me touch you, Shield Lady," Gryph said against her mouth. "Open your legs for me and let mc feel your warmth. I want to be sure you're ready for me so that I can claim my rights as your true mate."

She did as he asked and then trembled in excitement as he found the soft skin of her inner thighs.

"*Gryph.*"

Gryph drank his name from her lips. His body trembled against hers as he slipped his rough fingertips into the delicate, hidden folds between her lcgs. Sariana knew she was dampening his hand. She hoped he didn't mind.

"You're as hot as I am," he muttered in husky wonderment. "I can feel your heat. You're wet and warm and you want me, don't you?"

"Yes, oh, yes, Gryph." She twisted against his hand. She wondered if she should be embarrassed by her body's ungoverned response, but then she realized Gryph was glorying in it. He was taut with his own reaction to her.

"Sariana," he began thickly, "listen to me carefully. I have to ask you something and you must answer truthfully. Do you understand? I'm honor bound to put these questions to you."

Sariana moved her head restlessly on the pillow. "I swear I have no diseases and . . . and I don't think I'm likely to get pregnant. Earlier this evening I was figuring out the timing of my monthly cycles and I'm sure I'm safe tonight. I've discussed such things with other women and I've heard that as long as I—"

"*Sariana.*"

She opened her eyes, startled by his impatience. "Yes, Gryph?"

"One of these days we're going to have to do something about your unfortunate tendency to talk at the wrong times," Gryph said explosively. "I'm sure you're in excellent health. So am I. And as for your getting pregnant—"

"Don't worry about it," she said quickly.

He groaned, clearly frustrated, and kissed her back into silence. Then he trapped her face between his rough palms and lifted his mouth only a centimeter or two above hers. Sariana thought she would drown in the brilliance of his eyes.

"Sariana," he said very carefully, very distinctly, "nothing on this planet would give me as much pleasure as getting you pregnant."

"But, Gryph—"

"That is not, however, what I want to discuss with you tonight. Now hush up and listen to me and then answer truthfully."

"Yes, Gryph."

"Do you give yourself willingly to me, Sariana? Do you choose to link with me?"

She had never heard the expression "linking" before and could only assume it was a Shield term for what they were about to do together, a euphemism for sexual intercourse.

"Yes," she whispered.

"Say the words, Sariana," he ordered. "I want the words."

She could no more have resisted his hoarse, urgent command than she could have stopped the rising sun. Out of nowhere the proper response came to her. She didn't stop to question the words. They appeared in her head and she used them instinctively. She was in too much of a rush to satisfy Gryph's request to bother questioning the odd phrases.

"I willingly give myself to you, Shield Lord. I choose to link myself with you."

"There is no going back," he warned.

Again, Sariana wasn't sure what he meant, but she was

in no mood to press the issue. Desire was sweeping through her, hotter and sweeter than anything she had ever experienced in her life.

Gryph moved, shifting slightly, and the bed swayed gently on its ornate chains. Sariana couldn't see what he was doing, but before she could ask Gryph was back. He loomed over her, his broad shoulders blocking the light from the window.

"Give me your hand, Sariana."

"Another Shield custom, Gryph?" Suddenly she was no longer feeling quite so joyous and lighthearted with the bubbling effects of desire. A new, strangely powerful mood was beginning to grip her, a mood she seemed to be picking up from him. It was odd to realize that somehow she was aware of his emotions through all this. It was disorienting. She remembered that same disorientation had washed over her when he had kissed her the other morning in her office.

"Yes, Sariana," he said as he took her hand in his own. "Another Shield custom."

He laced his fingers through hers and then he lowered himself between her legs. His hair-roughened skin was exquisitely exciting against the softness of her inner thighs. She became intensely aware of how big he was. His weight pressed down on her. Gryph's eyes were moonlit seas as he slowly eased himself to the damp, warm entrance of her body.

"Gryph?"

"Just keep holding my hand, Shield Lady. Remember, we go through this together."

She nodded, her breath growing fast and shallow with excitement. She felt his wide, blunt shaft probe her tender folds of flesh and she flinched.

"Hold me, Shield Lady. Put your free arm around me and hold me as tight as you can. Don't let go, whatever happens. Just remember I'll be with you all the way."

His mouth covered hers. She could feel the throbbing tension in him. It was as if he had braced himself for a trip into strange, unknown territory. His fingers tightened around hers and he moved their clasped hands a short distance across the quilt until Sariana realized they were touching an object.

Belatedly she recognized the leather of his weapon kit beneath her palm. Then she was touching the cool prisma of the lock. Gryph was holding her hand flat against the crystal now. A part of her wanted to question the strange action, but the rest of her was too caught up in the gathering storm that was about to break.

Rainbow gems glittered in the swirling heart of the whirlwind. Gryph was going to run with her into the center of the storm and catch flashing prisma jewels with her.

"Now," Gryph said against her mouth.

"Yes, now, *please*." Sariana clutched him more tightly with her free hand. His muscles bunched, strong and powerful, under her palm. He was rigid with desire.

Gryph gathered himself and then, without any further warning, thrust deeply into her.

Prisma crystal shattered into a million jagged jewels. Hot, sharp, glittering rain showered down over Sariana. She gave a choked cry as the sensation poured through her. She heard an answering, guttural shout as Gryph sank himself to the hilt within her small, velvet channel. Sariana's body convulsed around him. Small, delicate muscles clenched in a resistance that was too little, too late.

Some discomfort, Sariana remembered Gryph had said. *I have heard there is some discomfort*. She nearly screamed in rage and pain.

He had lied to her. All the books she had ever read on the subject had lied. Everyone had lied.

This was not the small, momentary discomfort she had been expecting. This was agony. Something was wildly, incredibly wrong. Her whole body was in chaos.

The pain came not just from the soft, tender, bruised flesh between her thighs, though that was bad enough, it also came from her shoulder.

Her shoulder. No. It was impossible. Sariana was stunned by the dull, throbbing ache that was suddenly and inexplicably occupying that portion of her anatomy. But that wasn't the worst of it.

The worst part was the white, burning sensation in her hand where Gryph held her fingers to the prisma lock of his weapon kit.

But even that was not the end of it. On top of everything else, her body felt hot and feverish.

Sariana's eyes flashed open in bewildered accusation. Her body stiffened in reaction to the trauma. She found Gryph staring down at her, the lines of his hard face drawn taut in an agony that clearly matched her own.

"Gryph, stop. Something's wrong. Something is wrong."

"Hang onto me, Sariana. It will pass. Just hold on to me."

She heard the words, but she could have sworn he hadn't spoken aloud. She couldn't be sure of that, however. Everything seemed to be spinning chaotically around her. Nothing was real or stable or solid except Gryph. He was the source of all this pain and agony, but she sensed he was also her only salvation.

And then, in a blinding flash of intuition, she knew beyond a doubt that he was feeling everything she was feeling, including the pain he had caused her by his sensual intrusion into her body. Sariana wondered dazedly how such a distinctly feminine anguish was being translated by his own masculine nerve endings.

Perhaps in the same way her uninjured shoulder was throbbing with the ache of an unclosed blade wound.

Perhaps in the same way both of them felt the prisma burning an invisible brand into their palms.

Perhaps, just perhaps, in the same way she was painfully, violently aware of his blazing masculine need. None of that fierce desire was diminished by the accompanying pain. Her senses were shocked by the depths of that masculine need. She felt it as intensely as if it were her own.

"You are my Shield Lady. We are bound together until death."

The words vibrated inside her head. Sariana closed her

eyes, unable to question this new, strange manner of hearing. She understood nothing in this moment except the feeling of being completely and totally possessed. Even that sensation seemed to be working the same way as the shared pain, she realized. It reverberated between herself and Gryph. They were like mirrors for each other. Sensation bounced back and forth, growing more intense with each reflection. The light from that mirror scattered into countless rays.

Sariana not only felt herself possessed, she was somehow also the possessor. She held Gryph just as he held her.

Time hung still for an endless moment in the darkened bed chamber.

Then, with agonizing slowness, the savagely disorienting sensations calmed. The unnatural pain faded and took on more normal dimensions, as if she and Gryph were each reclaiming that which was legitimately their own discomfort and freeing the other of the added burden. Even the branding sensation in Sariana's palm began to disappear.

"It's going to be all right, Shield Lady. The worst is over." Gryph pulled her hand away from the weapon kit and folded her throbbing palm within his. Then he kissed her trembling fingers. "I swear to you, Sariana, I had no idea it would be that violent. The link between us must be very, very strong. I've never heard of a mating such as this one."

"Gryph, I don't understand any of this." Sariana's mouth was so dry she could hardly get the words out. The initial, painful sensations that had gripped her were almost gone, but the sense of disorientation was taking longer to fade. And one particular focus of discomfort had not yet returned to normal. Gryph was still sheathed deeply within her body and she was intensely aware of every centimeter of his invading shaft. Her body felt unbearably tight and stretched as it sought to accommodate his.

"I know, my sweet." Gryph was trying to speak soothingly, but his voice was still tight from his unreleased sexual tension. "I know. It's over now. I'll explain everything to you in the morning. But now you and I have some unfinished business."

Sariana winced as he began to move within her. The pain had diminished, but she still felt overly sensitized.

"Gryph, I don't want—"

"Hush, Sariana. No more words. Not now." He continued to stroke gently in and out of her warmth. "Let yourself relax and respond. There is so much passion waiting to be released within you. I think the linking was all the more painful partly because of that passion. We are going to be very good together, you and I. Damn good."

Sariana was not so certain of that, but her body seemed to be accepting him now, albeit somewhat unwillingly. She still felt stretched far too tightly, but the sensation was not as uncomfortable as it had been. In fact, it was oddly exciting. She tightened her hold on Gryph, preparing to let herself explore this new, more pleasant feeling. Her legs wrapped around his waist in an unconscious need to get closer to him.

Her sensual movements had a totally unexpected effect on him. Gryph lost his control.

"Sariana."

He arched forward, surging deeply into her as his whole body went taut. Gryph stifled a shout of triumphant release and then he shuddered and collapsed on top of Sariana.

Minutes passed and Gryph did not move. Sariana stroked his warm back slowly, not certain what to do next. He seemed to be in a deep sleep. Then she became aware once more of the heat in him. He was still feverish.

Slowly, carefully she wriggled out from under Gryph's heavy body. He didn't stir. She slid toward the edge of the bed. Her hand brushed the weapon kit as she did so. She jerked her fingers back reflexively and then realized there was no longer any burning sensation coming from the prisma lock.

Sariana got to her feet and nearly fell over. She was weak and dizzy and every muscle in her body seemed to have turned to liquid. Turning, she glanced down at the bed. Gryph would be cold by morning. She fumbled with the quilt and managed to cover him with it. Then she checked his wound to make certain it had not started bleeding. The bandages appeared clean.

Sariana quietly picked up her clothes and pulled them on. It was fortunate that the hallway outside would probably be empty. She could make it to her own suite without being seen. She opened the door and let herself out of the room. A moment later she was safely in her own chambers.

As she closed the door behind her a small, slithering sound made her look down. The scarlet-toe was making its way toward her across the floor.

Sariana laughed shakily and bent down to scoop it up. "I don't know why I bother to keep you in a cage, Lucky. It's obvious you're too smart to stay trapped in one. Are you sure you wouldn't like to be free?"

The scarlet-toe leaped from her hand to her shoulder and curled happily into her warmth. Sariana looked at her bedraggled reflection in the mirror. Her gown was drooping, her hair was tangled and her eyes were huge and shadowed. The lizard looked like a brilliant scarlet jewel on her shoulder.

"Maybe it's too late for you to be free, just as Gryph said," Sariana whispered. But it was her own reflection she was studying as she spoke, not the lizard's.

For better or worse, she seemed to have embarked on an affair with the Shield lord. She wondered if it might be better to limit the event to a one-night stand.

Sariana wasn't sure she could survive another night in Gryph's arms.

Chapter
7

THE vivid dawn light awakened Gryph the next morning. He lay still for a moment absorbing the knowledge that he was alone in his bed. Then he sat up slowly, wincing at the ache in his shoulder.

All things considered, he was not particularly surprised to find Sariana gone.

As a wedding night, last night had bordered on being a complete disaster. The groom had been clumsy from beginning to end and had fallen asleep immediately after the main event. The bride had undoubtedly been traumatized by the pain for which she had been totally unprepared. She certainly had not gotten any satisfaction from the encounter. On top of everything else, Gryph suspected Sariana didn't even realize she was married. He'd been too groggy from the medic's painkiller to explain the law of the First Generation Pact to her.

He made his way into the antechamber that held a huge sunken tub, a sink and other assorted necessities. He needed several of those necessities this morning.

The tub in Gryph's chamber was fashioned to resemble a grotto, complete with its own waterfall and a collection of vivid green plants. He turned the bird-headed spigot that set the waterfall in action and then stepped underneath the hot water. Deep in the basement of the Avylyn household vapor heaters kept plenty of hot water available at all times.

As he stood there contemplating the imitation rock wall in front of him Gryph tried to decide how best to approach Sariana this morning. It was not an easy decision. When all was said and done, he did not know a lot about women. No man did. The fact that this particular female was from the eastern provinces further complicated the matter.

She had lived in Serendipity for a year, but it was clear she did not yet know all the local customs and laws. If she had known them, she would have stayed in Gryph's bed last night. Any western woman would have recognized the full significance of what had happened.

Gryph was faced with the task of explaining everything to Sariana this morning. He turned off the waterfall and reached for a thick towel. He did not look forward to the coming encounter. Something told him his new bride was not going to enjoy learning of her status. He had really botched this business of wooing a Shieldmate. Gryph damned the medic's painkiller and damned his own impatience.

There was nothing to do but go forward and finish the business. He tossed aside the towel and went back into the main chamber to dress.

He did so carefully, pulling on a clean shirt, trousers that had recently been pressed by one of the household attendants and his best jacket. Then he spent several minutes cleaning mud off his boots.

When he was finished he critically examined his image in the gilded mirror. He looked reasonably neat and clean, but that was about all that could be said for him. Nothing he did was going to make himself look handsome by city standards. It was difficult to turn a warrior into a man of fashion.

Gryph turned away from the mirror, his mouth hardening into a determined line. Sariana had started all this, whether she realized it or not. She would have to take the consequences. Gryph just wished he had a little more time in which to ease her into a willing acceptance of the situation.

Gryph stood thinking for a moment, remembering what had happened the night before in that filthy alley. Because of those events he knew he could not grant Sariana any time at all. Everything had changed now. There were more dangerous matters to be handled than a wife who did not yet realize she was a wife.

Gryph walked out of the chamber and down the hall to Sariana's room. There was no point in postponing the inevitable. The sooner he got this part over the better, as far as he was concerned. He was a Shield, the only son of a proud family, raised on the frontier, a man trained to hunt other men, but he was, in the end, only a man. When it came to dealing with a woman he was as easily baffled and as thoroughly cautious as the next man.

He halted in front of Sariana's door and pulled the cord that rang the soft chimes inside her room. As he waited for a response he glanced down and saw that he'd missed a scuff mark on the toe of one boot. Irritated, he quickly rubbed it against his trouser leg. The door opened just as he was checking to be sure he'd removed the mark.

Gryph's head snapped up, his senses leaping in anticipation even though he knew a difficult time lay ahead.

For a few seconds he just stared at Sariana. She was smiling hesitantly at him. The morning light poured into the room behind her, highlighting the gold in her sleekly coiffed brown hair. Her eyes were nearly gold, too, the expression in them feminine and mysterious and shy and questioning. The buff colored suit she wore fit her very snugly, emphasizing her small waist and the proud tilt of her gently curving breasts. A flash of crimson drew Gryph's eye. The scarlet-toe was clinging possessively to its perch on Sariana's shoulder. It regarded Gryph with an unblinking gaze.

Gryph found himself smiling slightly as he looked at the lizard. Then he met Sariana's eyes again and it hit him full force. This was his Shieldmate, he thought dazedly. He had done it. He had found a woman with whom he could link. The always precarious future of his clan had been provided with one more chance at survival. He had taken the first major step toward fulfilling his primary duty to his clan and at the same time he had found himself a true mate.

Gryph wanted to shout his triumphant joy until the elegant corridors of the Avylyn household rang with the news of what had happened between him and Sariana. He wanted to take his Shieldmate back to his clan house and parade her in front of his parents and his friends.

But most of all he wanted to sweep Sariana off her feet, carry her into the bed chamber and lay her down on the swinging bed. He wanted to make love to her properly this time. He wanted to watch her respond to him, hear her cries of pleasure and satisfaction, see the full knowledge of their relationship blaze in her gentle eyes.

Instead of all that, Gryph inclined his head in a formal greeting and said, "I bid you the luck of the day, Sariana."

She returned the polite greeting, her tremulous smile growing more confident. "Luck to you, Gryph. I thought perhaps you would want to sleep in this morning. How is your shoulder?"

He smiled crookedly, memories of the night shimmering through his head. "You will be happy to hear that it feels a great deal better than it did last night."

Sariana's own smile slipped a little and Gryph saw the memories in her eyes. "I'm glad. It must have been quite . . . quite uncomfortable for you."

"You know exactly how uncomfortable it was for me, don't you, Sariana?" Gryph watched her closely, wondering how much she would admit to remembering. He drew in a deep breath and prepared to make his apologies. He certainly owed her a few. "And I know how unpleasant parts of last night were for you," he added quickly. "In addition to your own personal feelings, you were being bombarded with a lot of what I was feeling. I sincerely regret the pain you experienced last night."

"I'm not sure I want to talk about this, Gryph. I've been thinking, and I've decided that some things are better left undiscussed. I'd had several glasses of punch last night by the time you showed up and I'm afraid I may have been a little drunk when you—"

He interrupted her, intent on completing his formal apology. "I was not in full control, as I should have been. My only excuse is that, as I told you, such a linking as we shared was as unfamiliar to me as it was to you. I didn't realize how much you would pick up on what I was feeling. No one ever warned me the bonding would be that strong. I wasn't prepared for it myself so I couldn't prepare you. If you're worrying about it, I can promise you that next time neither of us will be so jolted by the experience. Our senses will quickly adjust and become attuned. We will learn to filter out the discomforts of a linking and focus instead on the, uh, more pleasant aspects . . . " Gryph felt himself redden slightly as he ran out of words. For the life of him he couldn't tell what Sariana was thinking.

She looked up at him, her expression unfathomable. He wondered how she could still be such a mystery to him after what they had been through together last night. Then he remembered his father once telling him that the mystery of a woman, even a Shieldmate, was never completely solved. Gryph waited in an agony of suspense for Sariana to acknowledge the link that had been forged between them. When she did, he would explain her new status to her.

"Last night was something of an experience for both of us, wasn't it?" Sariana observed with astonishing calm. She absently touched the scarlet-toe on her shoulder. The creature's tongue lanced out and briefly touched her palm. Sariana lowered her hand and smiled a little too brilliantly at Gryph. "I think we were both a little out of control. You were obviously reacting strongly to the anesthetic the medic gave you for your shoulder and I was reacting to the Avylyns' punch. I am still not completely accustomed to the clever concoctions you westerners create with alcohol. In the east we stick to wine and beer. I should know by now that any punch served at a party here is bound to be quite strong. But I'm glad to hear you're feeling better this morning. So am I."

Gryph stared at her, at a loss for words. He had been prepared for hurt accusations, a host of questions and a great deal of confusion on Sariana's part. There was much, after all, that needed to be explained. The one thing he had not expected was a complete denial of the whole experience. He remembered belatedly that the lady had a way with words.

"Sariana," he finally said quietly, "there's no point in denying what happened last night. You were not under the influence of too much punch and I was fully aware of what I was doing, even if I was a little groggy from the anesthetic." His mouth curved faintly. "You, of all people, know the anesthetic wasn't working very well, anyway."

Sariana's fingers tightened on the door. "Why don't we meet in my office after breakfast, Gryph? We have a lot to discuss. I want a full report of what happened last night when you went to meet your informant. Then we can make plans for the next step in this matter of retrieving the prisma cutter."

"Don't think you can retreat behind a wall of words and a business discussion," he muttered. "Listen, Sariana, I don't want to put this off until after breakfast. I think we should discuss it now. You have to understand a few things."

She nodded quickly. "Yes, I know. I have a whole list of questions."

Gryph relaxed slightly. "I thought you might."

"To begin with, I want to hear every detail about the meeting with your informer last night. I want to know exactly what happened so we can make plans. I still think we may have to call in the town guards. But we must try to think of some way to protect the Avylyns' reputation. If you're to continue on this assignment, we'll have to concoct a new excuse for your presence in the household. I've been giving that some thought this morning and I've come up with a couple of ideas that might work."

Gryph stared at her, realizing he hadn't made any headway at all. Sariana was prepared to ignore the whole experience. He could hardly believe it. He stepped through the doorway, forcing her back a pace. From its perch on Sariana's shoulder the scarlet-toe watched Gryph and bared its tiny teeth. Gryph paid no attention to the lizard. His attention was focused on Sariana.

"You don't seem to understand what's going on here, Sariana," he began with as much patience as he could muster. "I realize you're confused. I'm prepared to explain everything to you. But this is between you and me. I am not particularly interested in the Avylyns' problem at the moment."

Sariana's smile vanished. "I am sorry to hear that, Gryph, because you were hired precisely for the purpose of interesting yourself in the Avylyns' problems. Are you telling me I am not going to get my money's worth out of you?"

"What money's worth?" he exploded. "So far I haven't received a single trell note from you. Forget the money, we've got more important things to discuss and not a whole lot of time in which to discuss them."

Her chin lifted challengingly. "You're going somewhere?"

"*We* are going somewhere. You and I. From now on, Sariana, we will be doing most things together."

Sariana drew herself up to her full height which put her somewhere in the neighborhood of Gryph's shoulder.

"I was not aware you were going to be so possessive," she stated. "Just because we were, well, involved for one night, does not mean you have any claim on me."

"No claim on you! Have you lost your senses, lady?"

"You westerners are all alike." Sariana glared at him. "High-strung and emotional. If you're going to insist on conducting a temperamental scene over the subject of our relationship, I would prefer to do so later in my office.

After we have analyzed what you found out about the missing cutter last night."

"I'll just bet you would prefer to hold our discussion in your office where you can hide behind that black stone desk of yours and give lectures on the emotional nature of westerners. But I'll be damned if I'm going to let you get away with that." Gryph paused to take a grip on his temper. Patience, he reminded himself. This was a time for patience. He was dealing with a strong-willed, proud young woman who had been through a very disorienting experience. Her first sexual encounter with a man had not been anything close to what she had probably been expecting. She was only trying to cope with something that must seem very alien to her. "Sariana, I want to explain a few things to you."

"Such as?"

"Such as the laws of the land," he retorted gently. "You've been living with the Avylyns for several months. Hasn't anyone ever mentioned the First Generation Pact to you?"

"No. And I really don't have time for a history lesson. Nor do I feel like listening to any legends right now. I'm on my way to breakfast."

She walked straight past him into the gallery and closed the door behind her. The scarlet-toe on her shoulder showed its teeth again in what Gryph decided was a very superior attitude for a lizard. It was an attitude the creature had clearly adopted from its new owner.

Sariana made her way briskly along the gallery, the hem of her gown snapping at her ankles. Gryph watched her for a moment, absorbing the tilt of her proudly carried head, the straight line of her gracefully shaped back and the no-nonsense sway of her hips.

It occurred to him then that his new Shieldmate had a full measure of pride as well as courage. She was trying very hard to pretend that nothing unusual had happened, but beneath that sweetly arrogant pose was a young woman trying to grapple with what must have been a very unsettling mix of emotions.

Obviously she had decided on the approach she was going to use to deal with her problem. She was going to try to pretend nothing had happened. Gryph admired her spirit even while he was forced to struggle with his own temper.

Automatically he touched the lock on his weapon kit, remembering the passion and pain and the unbreakable bond that had been forged during the night. Then he thought about Brinton dying in that alley because another Shield wanted the prisma cutter. Gryph had no choice. There was no time to continue the wooing process. He could not afford to wait on the convenience of his nervous bride. If she thought she could interview him later in her office and discuss their *relationship* at some unspecified time in the future, she had a surprise coming.

He had tried to do this quietly and in private, but she had refused to listen to him. She was bent, as usual, on having everything her own way. To that end she was endeavoring to use her first major line of defense, her glib tongue. Her lack of fear of him was almost laughable. She still had no idea how indulgent he was being with her. She still did not know that under the law, her fate had been sealed last night.

Gryph did not like untenable, unresolved situations. It was his nature to face matters and settle them.

Perhaps the easiest, fastest and surest method of handling this situation was to force Sariana to face reality.

Sariana swept into the breakfast room and realized just how late she was running when she saw the Avylyns already gathered for the meal. Five silvery blond heads turned toward her and five pairs of dark eyes took in the grim look on the face of the man striding through the doorway behind her.

"The luck of the day to all of you," Sariana said with all the cheerfulness she could manage. No one in the room could imagine how much effort it took. Her normally strong self-control was very shaky. She didn't quite trust any of her emotions or feelings. She had known the mo-

ment she opened her door and found Gryph on the other
side that life had suddenly become precarious.

The only positive thing she could find in the situation
was that she was becoming accustomed to the unpredict-
ability of her life these days. Nothing had been straightforward or predictable since the day she had learned she had
failed to make the cut at the academy. The only thing she
could do was hold on to her self-control. At times it
seemed that it was all she had left.

The Avylyns made the proper greetings and then burst
into exuberant chatter as they discussed the success of their
annual ball.

"It came off superbly," Lady Avylyn chortled with great
delight. "I was just telling Jasso that we were right not to
stint this year. Not a soul suspected that we might be having a few trifling financial problems."

Lord Jasso nodded his head in satisfaction. "Quite so.
You were right, my dear. Everyone was most impressed,
I'm sure."

"Well I, for one, had a wonderful time," Mara pro-
claimed, her eyes darting to Gryph's face as if to be certain
he had registered her comment. Sariana realized the
younger woman was slightly miffed about Gryph's lack of
interest in being socially introduced to her friends and acquaintances. Sariana also suspected that Mara had developed a rather deep curiosity about the Shield.

"You always have a good time as long as you dance
every dance," Bryer told his sister.

"I didn't see you sitting on the sidelines," his mother
said with a complacent smile. "You did a turn with every
young lady in the room."

Bryer grinned. "What did you expect? I was merely fulfilling my responsibilities as a host."

Luri spoke up. "I don't see what's so great about dancing. Waste of time if you ask me."

The yellow-eyed krellcat, Luri's constant companion,
yawned in agreement and tucked its furry, sinuous body
into a more comfortable position on the boy's arm. The
small creature eyed Lucky with surreptitious interest, but

apparently decided hunting would not be permitted at the breakfast table. The cat went back to dozing.

"Give yourself a few more years, Luri. You'll change your mind," his brother said.

Luri opened his mouth to respond, but his attention was distracted by the lizard on Sariana's shoulder. "Hey, you really like the scarlet-toe, huh, Sariana? I knew you would once you got to know it better. I told you they make great pets."

"Lucky seems to have adopted me," Sariana said, examining the contents of the serving dishes. "I feel guilty leaving it in the cage now. The poor thing always looks so forlorn when I leave it behind." She helped herself to a cup of tea and a breakfast muffin and politely ignored Gryph when he sat down across from her.

"Did you have a good time last night, Sariana?" Mara asked with a direct look. "I saw you earlier in the evening but lost track of you later."

"You know I tend to keep earlier hours than the rest of you," Sariana said. She sipped tea with careful restraint, aware that Gryph was helping himself to large portions from each of the bowls.

"Sariana!" Lady Avylyn gave her a scolding glance. "You don't mean to tell me you went to bed early last night? What about your friend Etion Rakken? He was looking forward to dancing with you again."

"I doubt that Rakken knew what he was missing," Jasso said with a knowing smirk. "The banker was as drunk as a keenshee bird in a gullberry patch by the time the ball ended."

"As it happens I had business to attend to last night," Sariana said. "Business I think we should discuss right after breakfast. If you would all be so kind as to come to my office as soon as we finish here, I would appreciate it."

"Business," Mara repeated with a groan. "Who wants to talk about business this morning? I want to talk about the ball."

Lord Avylyn gave his business manager a sharp look. "Does this concern the cutter?"

Gryph answered before Sariana could speak. "The prisma cutter has become Shield business."

Everyone turned to stare at him, including Sariana who didn't have the least idea of what he was talking about. It was obvious his words meant something to the Avylyns. They looked distinctly startled.

"Shield business?" Jasso exclaimed. "But how? Why? I don't understand. That cutter has always belonged to the Avylyns. Our family has held it since the first crystal was sold to us."

"Calm yourself, Lord Avylyn," Gryph said. "When the cutter is found, it will be returned to your family. I meant only that locating the cutter is now a Shield matter. I will pursue it for Shield purposes and when I find it, I will give it to you. I just want it clear that there is no longer any question of my working for anyone else in this matter."

Jasso was stunned. "You're going to look for it for free?" he finally got out.

Gryph glanced at Sariana and then gave his attention to his food. "Let's just say that my fee has been paid in full."

Sariana suddenly realized that everyone in the room except Gryph was now staring at her. She sat tensely in her chair and stared back in bewilderment.

"Is something wrong?" she finally asked in irritation.

"Nothing is wrong," Gryph stated. "Eat your breakfast. You wanted a conference in your office after the meal? All right, you'll have your conference."

Sariana bristled. "There is no need to take that tone with me. You may have decided for some obscure reason that you are no longer working for the Avylyns, but—"

"I never was working for the Avylyns, remember? I was working for you. And you have paid me well."

Across the table Gryph's eyes clashed with hers and Sariana felt herself turning pink. She was suddenly aware of the conclusions the Avylyns must be rapidly drawing from this small scene. Gryph was as good as implying that she had paid his fee last night while everyone else had been noticing Sariana's absence from the ballroom. The implication was obvious. A flare of temper pulled her to her feet.

"If you will excuse me," Sariana said through her teeth, "I will go to work. When you are finished, please join me in my office."

She was halfway to the door, her attention riveted on escape, when she struck something with the toe of her slipper. Automatically she glanced down and saw that the object on the floor was Gryph's weapon kit.

"You appear to have dropped something, Gryph," she remarked icily as she bent over to pick it up.

"Thank you," he said with unexpected tenderness. He stayed where he was and gave her a curious smile. "I'm glad you found it. I hadn't noticed it was missing from my belt."

"That's hard to believe," she retorted, remembering how he had awakened from unconsciousness the night she had detached the kit from his belt. "Here, you'd better take it. I certainly don't want to be responsible for it."

Gryph started to hold out his arm but then he winced painfully and lowered it again.

"Oh, your shoulder. I almost forgot." Sariana was flooded with remorse as she recalled vividly just how much his shoulder had pained him the night before. For all she knew he was in much greater pain now that the light anaesthetic had worn off. "Are you all right? You shouldn't stretch it that way. You should take it easy."

"What's wrong with his shoulder?" Luri asked with great interest.

"Nothing that won't heal in time," Gryph explained. His gaze was still on Sariana. "If you would bring the kit over to me, I would appreciate it."

"Of course." She moved toward him, aware of the cool prisma lock under her fingers. Last night that lock had burned itself into her palm, or so she had imagined. The punch served at the ball had certainly had a strange effect on her senses. Everything had seemed so incredibly intense. It was amazing what tricks the night could play on a woman's senses. Wordlessly she held the kit out to Gryph.

"Would you open it for me, Sariana?" he asked quietly.

The silence in the room was almost overpowering. Sariana was aware that the Avylyns seemed frozen in their seats. Their attention was focused completely on the small scene being played out in front of them. In fact, they all appeared mesmerized by it.

Sariana glanced down at the weapon kit and frowned. "Open it? But why?"

"I need something inside and I would appreciate it if you would open the kit for me," Gryph said, still speaking in that unnaturally soft voice.

"Can't you open it?"

"My shoulder," he said half-apologetically. "The pain seems to be radiating down into my hand."

"Maybe you should see another medic," Sariana said quickly. "The wound might have become infected during the night. What about the fever? Has it gone completely?"

"Hush, Sariana. I swear I'll be fine. In the meantime, if you would just open the kit for me, I would appreciate it more than I can say."

She looked at the lock. "I don't know how to open it."

"Just touch it, Sariana. Touch it the way you did last night and think of it as being open."

Sariana was suddenly overcome with the compelling urge to do as he asked. She had been curious about this strange pouch since the night she had taken it from his unconscious body. Now was her chance to see just what was inside. She was actually being invited to do so. She couldn't wait.

Eagerly she explored the lock with her fingers, finding no obvious mechanism. She looked up. "I don't see how it works, Gryph."

"I told you how it works. Just touch it and think of the kit as being open."

He was speaking the words, Sariana realized, but his soft, dark voice seemed to be coming from somewhere inside her head, just as it had at times last night. She wondered if she was still suffering from the effects of the punch.

"Open it, Sariana."

Instinctively Sariana obeyed. She touched the lock and pictured the weapon kit as being open.

An instant later it was open. She stared down into the dark interior of the pouch, trying to see what lay inside. But before she could investigate further, Gryph reached out easily with his injured arm and plucked the kit out of her grasp.

"My thanks, Shield Lady," he said.

Sariana frowned and started to ask him why he called her that, but she got no chance to do so. All five of the Avylyns, as well as two attendants who had entered the room to refill the teapots, were on their feet, talking and exclaiming at once.

"Sariana," Lady Avylyn said in loud accents that managed to float above the other voices in the room, "why didn't you tell me, my dear? Last night when we talked you implied you were merely thinking of having an affair. You said nothing about marriage. I distinctly asked you if marriage had been mentioned."

Sariana swung around, her mouth open with astonishment. "Marriage? What are you talking about, Lady Avylyn?"

"You opened his weapon kit," Mara said in awed tones. "You opened a Shield's weapon kit. He has chosen you for his bride."

Luri was bouncing up and down with excitement. "He told me only his Shieldmate would be able to open the kit. And you did it, Sariana. You really did it."

"Who would have guessed our little business manager would make a suitable bride for a Shield?" Bryer asked with a quick grin.

Lord Avylyn waved his hand for silence and then inclined his head very formally toward Sariana. "On behalf of my clan I extend our best wishes and congratulations."

"By the Lightstorm," Bryer said, "this is sure a surprise. Wait until your folks hear about this, huh, Sariana? I bet they'll be stunned. They don't even know about Shields, do they?"

"What's in the kit?" Luri demanded eagerly. "Did you get a chance to see what's inside? I've always wanted to get a good look inside a Shield's weapon kit."

Sariana turned her appalled gaze back to Gryph. He was calmly sipping tea. His eyes met hers over the edge of his cup but he said nothing. She scanned the faces of the Avylyns. "Have you all gone crazy? What is this nonsense about marriage?"

Jasso's brows came together. "You must know that under the laws set down in the First Generation Pact you have allowed this Shield to claim you for his bride."

"I know nothing of the kind!" Sariana heard her voice rising to a shriek and frantically worked to control it. She never shrieked. "What are you talking about?"

Lady Avylyn glanced doubtfully at her. Then she narrowed her eyes thoughtfully. "The Pact was made between the First Generation social classes of *The Serendipity* and the Shields. A Shield is entitled to search for a mate in any social class he wishes. But he cannot take you by force, Sariana. It is clearly stated in the Pact that the woman must be willing. Did Gryph rape you last night?"

The beautiful little tea cup cracked and disintegrated between Gryph's fingers. He didn't move from his chair but his eyes were suddenly dangerous.

"By the Lightstorm, I have done nothing against the Pact. I am a Shield. By definition that means I have obeyed the laws governing my marriage rights. Ask her."

"Ask me what?" Sariana was tense with a strange panic. "Will somebody please tell me what is going on here?"

"*Ask her*," Gryph ordered.

Lord Avylyn turned to Sariana. "Sariana, you must tell me the truth. Did you give yourself willingly to this man?"

Sariana was mortified. "How dare you ask such things in public or even in private. I know you westerners are far more liberal about—this sort of thing than those of us from the east, but surely you have some respect for a woman's privacy."

Lord Jasso waved that aside. "This is no time for false modesty. Sariana, you are living in my household. As a member of it you are entitled to my protection." He shot a defiant glance at Gryph who ignored it. "But if no law has been broken, then I must assume that you are, indeed, married to this Shield. Did you go with him willingly last night or did he take you by force?"

Sariana wanted to scream. She felt as if she were caught in a nightmare. She jerked her gaze from Jasso's concerned expression to Gryph's implacable face.

"Answer him, Sariana. But see to it that you answer him honestly," Gryph said calmly. "Because if you try to lie, I will force the truth out of you. Believe me, I can do it."

Sariana took a step back toward the door. "You have all gone out of your minds. I don't understand any of this."

Lady Avylyn looked at her with compassion. "Just tell us the truth, Sariana. It is very important."

"He did not rape me, if that's what you want to know." Sariana put a hand to her throat, wondering if she was losing her voice. It sounded so faint. "But I never agreed to marry him."

Lord Avylyn shook his head helplessly. "Don't you see, Sariana? You already are married to him. You proved it a few moments ago when you opened his weapon kit. Everyone knows that only a true Shieldmate can open her lord's weapon kit. The prisma locks are sealed to everyone else. A Shield gives the secret to his wife on their wedding night. It is the proof of their bond when she opens the kit the next morning in front of witnesses. Under Pact law, you are married."

"No," Sariana said, feeling as though the walls were closing in around her. "This Pact law, whatever it is, is a western law. I am an easterner. Do you understand? *I am an easterner.*"

Lord Avylyn looked at her sorrowfully. "I am sorry, my dear. But as long as you are living with us, you are subject to our laws and ways. You know that."

Sariana whirled around and fled as if all the terrors of the western frontiers were at her heels.

Chapter
8

S ARIANA ran toward the only source of comfort and rationality she knew in a world that seemed to be turning upside down. By the time she reached the wide, carved doors of Etion's bank, she was breathing hard. Before going in she forced herself to stop and draw several deep breaths.

No one had much noticed a harried looking woman making her way through the streets of Serendipity, but once inside the bank she would draw unwanted attention to herself if she didn't calm down and appear a little less frantic. The last thing Sariana wanted to do was embarrass herself or Etion. When she had caught her breath, she swept through the doors and into the building.

The people of Serendipity carried on their banking with the same loud enthusiasm they applied to nearly every other activity. Rakken's bank was no staid, solemn hall where business was conducted in hushed, reverent tones as would have been the case in the eastern provinces. Instead the building was full of lively, surprisingly organized employees who gossiped, argued and joked with their clients. As usual, there was color and drama everywhere, from the outrageous styles in clothing to the rather loud confrontations taking place at the loan desks.

One of the secrets of Rakken's success was that, unlike other easterners who had tried to conduct business in the west, he hadn't attempted to impose eastern ways on his employees or his clients. As Etion had once explained to a newly arrived and thoroughly bewildered Sariana, one had to adapt in order to survive. For Etion, Sariana knew, there was no hope of going home. He had to make it here in Serendipity. He had adapted. Perhaps a little too much so judging by the way he had gone through the punch the night before.

But then, she was in no position to make accusations in that regard, she reminded herself grimly. Just see where the indulgence in punch had landed her.

She pushed her way through the mix of fashionably dressed people, her attention focused on reaching Etion's office at the far end of the hall. He saw her through the glass windows that separated him from the activity on the floor and rose to greet her as Sariana walked purposefully past the receptionist.

"Sariana. This is certainly a surprise. The luck of the day to you." He examined her with a concerned frown. "Am I late for an appointment? If so, I sincerely apologize. I've been fighting the most nagging headache this morning."

Sariana stripped off her gloves and flung herself down into the nearest chair. "No, you have not missed an appointment. And don't bother wishing me the luck of the day. This is very definitely not my lucky day."

Etion sat down slowly, as if he were afraid to move too quickly for fear of breaking some portion of his anatomy. He stared at her shoulder. "I see. Something is wrong, I gather? More trouble with the wild Avylyns?"

"More trouble than I could ever have imagined," Sariana said bitterly. "Etion, I need help and advice and I need both quickly."

"Of course. But Sariana, what have you got on your shoulder? It looks like a lizard."

Sariana glanced at the scarlet-toe. "It is. I forgot all about Lucky. Poor thing. It's a wonder it didn't fall off my shoulder while I was running through the streets. Never mind the lizard, Etion. It's just a pet. Believe me, it's the least of my problems."

Etion smiled gamely as he leaned back in his chair and steepled his fingers. "Calm down. I don't think I've ever seen you look so agitated, Sariana."

She flushed with embarrassment and made another bid for self-possession. "Please forgive me. I've just been through a very harrowing experience."

"Obviously. Suppose you tell me everything in slow, graphic sentences."

"It's not funny, Etion. In fact, it could be a major disaster for me. It could ruin everything, including my future." Unable to sit still, Sariana jumped to her feet and paced to the window. She stared unseeingly at the street outside. "Tell me something, Etion."

"Anything."

"What do you know about the Shield class?"

He was silent for so long that Sariana finally glanced over her shoulder. Etion was staring at her in astonishment.

"Well?" she prompted uneasily.

He drew a breath and shrugged. "Not much, I'm afraid. It's my understanding that there aren't many Shields and that most of them live in the frontier provinces."

"What else do you know?"

"I told you. Not much. The locals seem somewhat in awe of them. Very respectful. But they don't discuss them very much. And Shields tend to keep to themselves for the most part. They're not what you'd call gossipy. All I know is that they form a unique social class. One that operates under its own rules in certain regards. The other social classes appear willing to respect those rules. Something to do with a pact made during the First Generation. It's all mixed up with a crazy western legend, I believe."

Sariana realized she was chewing on her lower lip, ready

to burst into tears. Stay in control, she admonished herself. If she wasn't very careful she would humiliate herself in front of Etion. She paced across the room and stared out the other window.

"What do you know about this pact?"

Etion sighed. "Again, not much. The locals don't talk about it very much, but they seem to take it for granted. For a long time after I first heard about it I thought it was probably just another of their precious First Generation legends. You know how fond they are of them."

"I know," Sariana said tightly. "Go on, Etion. Do you still think this business with the First Generation Pact is only a legend?"

"If it is, it has the weight of law," he said simply.

"Law." Sariana closed her eyes, fighting back panic. All her life she had been a law abiding citizen.

"Sariana," Etion said gently, "what kind of trouble have you gotten yourself into?"

"The Avylyns tell me I have gotten myself married to a Shield," she admitted starkly.

"*Married*." Etion snapped to his feet behind the desk. He winced and massaged his head. "Married? To a Shield?"

Sariana couldn't bring herself to turn around and meet his gaze. Humiliation warred with desperation. "Etion, I am so horribly embarrassed. I should never have come here, but I didn't know where else to go."

"Calm yourself, my dear." He came up behind her and started to put his hands on her shoulders in a comforting grip. There was a small hiss and a rather nasty display of teeth from the scarlet-toe. Etion dropped his hands quickly. "Tell me exactly what has happened."

Sariana curled her fingers into small fists at her sides. She was on the verge of blurting out every last detail—including how and why she had hired a Shield for the Avylyns—but at the last instant she changed her mind. Etion didn't need to know all the facts, only the most crucial ones.

"It is all terribly simple. I . . . I had a little too much

punch to drink at the Avylyns' party last night and I wound up in bed with a Shield. This morning in front of the Prime Family of the Avylyn Clan he claimed I was his wife. They believed him."

"Prisma and light," Etion swore heavily, his voice hoarse and startled.

"I know." She spun around, searching his face wildly for some sign of hope. "Is that really the way the law works here, Etion? Have I actually married the man?"

Etion stared at her for a long moment. Then he moved away. He sank down onto the edge of his desk and picked up the beautifully chased little arithmograph he used for making calculations. His fingers absently played with the keys.

"It's possible," Etion said at last.

Sariana felt her last hope dissolving. She clung to her composure with all her waning strength. "Tell me what you know about this stupid pact."

"I've told you, I know very little about it. It's unusual to run afoul of it. The Shields keep to themselves for the most part, but they apparently have a few unquestioned privileges. One of them is the right to seek a wife when and where they choose. They are not bound by traditional social class customs or laws when it comes to selecting their mates. The only rule I've ever heard, and that one's rather fuzzy, is that the woman in question must be willing."

"But I am not willing."

Etion hesitated and then asked bluntly, "Not this morning, perhaps, but what about last night?"

Sariana felt the jaws of a huge trap closing on her. "I didn't realize what I was getting into. I thought I was getting involved in an affair, not marriage."

Etion was silent for another long moment. "It seems to me that there is something about the Shield having to provide proof of the marriage. Something to do with opening his weapon kit in front of witnesses."

Sariana winced. A stinging sensation in her palm made her realize she was digging her nails into her hand. "Yes."

"You did that, Sariana? You opened a Shield's kit in front of witnesses?"

"The entire assembled multitude of the Avylyn Prime Family."

"You have a problem, Sariana."

She whirled around to confront him. "I know that. The question is, how serious is it and how do I solve it?"

Etion looked at her helplessly. He rubbed his temples again. "I don't know. I just don't know. As long as you are living in the west, you must abide by local law. You know that as well as I do."

"I'll have to leave." Sariana began to pace the room. "I'll have to go home."

"Home to what?" Etion asked bluntly. "There's nothing for you at home except a dead-end career and a marriage that offers considerably less potential than this one does."

Sariana's head turned sharply. "Are you implying that my . . . my association with this Shield might have some potential?"

"Who knows? The Shields are unique. They have a certain degree of power here in the west or they wouldn't be allowed to live by their own laws. You know as well as I do that the original social philosophers were adamant about the laws applying equally to all social classes. With the exception of the Shields, the westerners have abided by that philosophy, just as we in the east have followed it. Think about it, Sariana. The Shields must have wielded some fairly impressive authority in order to get themselves exempted from the laws everyone else abides by. I've told you I don't know much about them, but it seems to me it might be worth your while to explore your new situation before you give up entirely."

"I can't think straight." Sariana stared at the ornate facade of the building across the street. "My mind is in chaos."

"Not surprising under the circumstances. But panic will do you no good, Sariana. What's done is done. You must find a way to make things work in your favor."

"All of my plans are going up in smoke before my eyes," she whispered.

"Then you must make new ones," Etion said reasonably.

"I know you're right, Etion, but I'm having a hard time dealing with this. Who are they?"

"The Shields? I'm not sure."

"They must have their roots in one of the original social classes that arrived on *The Serendipity*. Perhaps the crew of the ship? It was intended by the philosophers that the crew members would be absorbed into the established social classes after the landing. But what if they refused to be adopted into the other classes? It's possible they invented a whole new class."

"It's possible," Etion said quietly. "Your explanation is a reasonable one, although it doesn't explain how they managed to convince the other classes to grant them certain exemptions from the laws. But it might interest you to know that according to local legend, the Shields were not on board *The Serendipity*."

"What?" Sariana was so stunned she nearly lost her balance when she spun around to confront Etion. "Not on board? But that's impossible."

"I know. I'm only telling you what scraps of the legend I've picked up during the past few years."

"Do you realize what that legend implies? It would mean that the Shields were already on Windarra before *The Rendezvous* and *The Serendipity* arrived. It would mean they didn't descend from the original colonists. It would mean they weren't ... aren't ... human." Sariana floundered at the enormity of the implications involved.

Etion looked at her. "It's only a legend, Sariana."

"But it's so wild, so ridiculous. The westerners have a dramatic bent, everyone knows that, but to invent a legend like that is too much, even for them. If the Shields weren't among the original colonists, where could they have come from?"

"Sariana, calm down." For the first time Etion's voice held a harder edge. "We've agreed, it's only a legend. The point is that, for whatever reason, the locals have granted the Shields certain privileges as a social class. You, apparently, have just married into that class. You would do well to study your new status before you panic. Use the training you were given in dealing with problems, Sariana. You've had a fine education, even if you didn't make it into the academy. Stop and think. You might be able to use your new situation to some advantage."

Sariana tried to absorb Etion's logic, but she seemed incapable of putting aside her agitated emotions long enough to think clearly. "I need time," she murmured. "I've got to think this through. It's all so crazy." She looked at Rakken and admitted the harsh truth. "I'm scared, Etion. I'm more frightened now than I was the day I found out I failed the academy entrance exams. What am I going to do?"

Etion moved toward her, his hands outstretched to take her into his arms. "I don't know, Sariana. But I do know that nothing will be accomplished with panic. Sariana, my dear Sariana, if only you had accepted my proposal the other day."

"Oh, Etion, I've been so stupid." Tears burned in Sariana's eyes. At any other time she would have been appalled at the public display of such emotion, but right now she needed comfort as she had never needed it before in her life and Etion Rakken was the only one who could understand what she was going through. She moved blindly toward Etion's arms.

The scarlet-toe hissed angrily as Etion started to put his hands around Sariana's waist. The lizard bared its small teeth and eyed the man with a menacing, jeweled gaze.

Sariana paid no attention to the lizard. She was too intent on accepting Etion's comfort. Etion's hand rose to flick the scarlet-toe off of her shoulder and out of the way, but before either he or the lizard could act the door to the office slammed open with sufficient force to rattle the tiny panes of glass in the windows.

"Touch my wife and I'll slit your throat," Gryph said calmly from the doorway. His hand rested lightly on the weapon kit at his belt.

Etion's hands fell away from Sariana as he jerked around to confront the intruder in his office. Sariana spun around, too, appalled.

"Gryph! What are you doing here?"

"That's obvious, isn't it? I'm retrieving my possession before she strays too far. Let's go, Sariana, you have caused enough scenes this morning."

For some reason that accusation was just too much. Fury began to replace the desperation and panic she had been experiencing. It was an emotion unlike any she had ever felt before in her life. It raged through her, threatening to take control of her the same way passion had taken control of her last night.

"Scenes? You've got the nerve to imply that I'm responsible for these scenes in which I find myself? Of all the arrogant, outrageous, disgusting things to say. How dare you, Gryph Chassyn? How do you dare to say such things after what you have done to me?"

His sea green eyes flicked from Etion's face to hers. Sariana was dumbfounded to see the flare of warmth that lit his gaze when he looked at her. Nothing altered the hard, taut lines of his face, however. He held out his hand arrogantly.

"Let's go back to the Avylyn villa, Sariana. I'm sure you would prefer to scream at me in private. When you're finished and you've had a chance to calm down you will thank me for depriving you of an audience."

"I'm not going anywhere with you!"

"Come now, Sariana," he said with a gentle understanding that further infuriated her. "It would be one thing to indulge your temper in front of a westerner who accepts such behavior as normal. But it would be another matter altogether to do it in front of one of your countrymen. Think how embarrassed you would be afterward."

Sariana was growing lightheaded with her anger. She was so outraged she couldn't even speak. She looked into Gryph's eyes and it dawned on her with alarming clarity that he was right. She couldn't throw a tantrum in front of

Etion. It was unthinkable. She had to get out of this office and the only way out was with Gryph.

The only way out was with Gryph.

Where had she gotten that notion? she wondered. It had just popped into her head. It reminded her of the way other words and sensations had jumped, unbidden, into her head the previous night as she lay in Gryph's arms. Perhaps she was on the edge of some sort of emotional breakdown, she thought hysterically. Maybe she was starting to hallucinate. Perhaps this was all a nightmare fabricated by her overwrought brain. But even as she questioned her sanity, she was walking toward the door, her hand lifting to accept Gryph's outstretched arm.

At the last second she shook off the odd compulsion she'd had to accept the mockery of gentlemanly assistance and brushed past him without taking his arm. She didn't look back, nor did she hesitate. She made straight for the huge carved doors at the end of the wide banking hall. She was aware that Gryph was following. When he caught up with her she ignored him. The small weight of the scarlet-toe on her shoulder was the only comfort she had. The lizard clung to the fabric of her dress with its tiny claws. She had the distinct impression the creature was jubilant about leaving Etion's office.

Gryph walked beside Sariana in silence. She refused to turn her head or speak to him, but she was suffocatingly aware of his presence. He was too tall, too strong, too big in every way. She felt smothered by his nearness. She wanted to flee from him and at the same time she wanted to scream at him. The mix of emotions left her feeling powerless. Sariana was not accustomed to handling such a dangerous combination of sensations.

Without a word she and Gryph made their way through the crowded streets. Neither of them paid much attention to the carriages or dragonponies and riders who tried to claim the thoroughfares. As if the drivers and riders sensed that these two were not playing the game today, they stayed out of the way.

By the time she was walking through the villa doors and

down the long gallery to her suite, Sariana was seething with frustrated rage. Gryph followed her silently into her room and she turned on him in fury.

"You are a bastard. A complete and utter bastard. You call yourself a gentleman. You claim to be a lord and that you are descended from a Prime Family but you lie. You must be lying. Either that or you are a disgrace to your clan. You have treated me abominably. No gentleman would have acted as you have acted."

"Sariana, I know you're angry and I guess you have a right to be, but—"

"Angry?" she blazed, backing toward the writing table. "Angry? You don't know the meaning of the word." She sought for and found some of the colorful phrases the locals used. "You are the arrogant, deceitful, lying spawn of a cloaksnake. With your degree of talent you should consider a career in dragonpony manure production. You have the sensitivity and understanding of a hawkbeetle. You are lower than the son of a needlerat. Worse than that. You must be the result of the mating of a pair of particularly slimey swamp toads. You have the sense of honor of a wharfsnake. I doubt your claim to a legitimate clan, do you hear me?"

"I hear you," Gryph said. "But let's leave my clan out of this." He stripped off his jacket and slung it over one shoulder. Then he stalked across the chamber to where a beautifully faceted wine carafe sat on a hospitality table. He picked up the carafe and splashed the contents into a tiny glass.

"By all means let's leave your clan out of this," Sariana snapped. "That sounds entirely reasonable considering the fact that there is apparently some question as to the origin of your entire social class." She couldn't think of a worse insult.

Gryph cocked one brow at her as he took a long swallow of wine. "Is that right? Who told you that? Rakken?"

"Yes, he did, as a matter of fact. He also told me about some totally ridiculous legend your people have managed to feed the rest of the westerners in order to win all sorts of special privileges."

"Rakken is surprisingly well-informed. Most easterners never hear much at all about the old legends concerning the Shields." Gryph poured himself another glass of wine. "What did he say about us?"

Sariana gripped the edge of her writing desk. She was trembling with the force of her emotions. Her voice shook with it. "He said you Shields have managed to concoct some crazy tale about not being members of the original social classes that arrived on board *The Serendipity*."

Gryph shrugged. "The tale is true."

"You expect me to believe that?"

"No. Not in your present mood. But one of these days you'll learn the whole story."

"I don't want to learn the whole story. Do you understand? I don't want any part of it. I don't want any part of you. I have enough problems in my life without getting involved in some idiotic local legend."

"If you had wanted to stay uninvolved with local legends," Gryph informed her with a strange smile, "you shouldn't have tried to play games with one."

Sariana gritted her teeth. "If you're talking about my using that hypnotic drug to try to make you a little more agreeable—"

"I am," he assured her and took another swallow of wine.

"I've explained about that. I was desperate."

"I suppose I should thank you for using the drug. If you hadn't tried that, I might never have found you. I wasn't looking for an eastern wife."

"You talk about hunting a wife the way you would hunt wild game!" Sariana almost lost her voice again.

"Wife hunting is more difficult. But it was time for me to try to find one. It's not easy for a Shield, you know. The right women are few and far between. Under the terms of the First Generation Pact, a Shield is allowed to search for a mate in any social class, but actually arranging to meet a lot of females from a lot of different classes is another problem. The population was so small back in the early days that it was relatively easy to locate a possible mate. The logistics of the situation have changed considerably since then. Clans have learned ways of keeping their daughters out of sight of a potential Shield husband. It's difficult to line up a number of women from which to choose. Social conventions have proven more formidable protection for young women than weapons and walls would have done."

Sariana's fingers closed around a hand-carved tray designed to hold stationery. "Now you speak of finding a wife the way you would talk of choosing fresh fish in the market!"

Gryph shook his head. "Shopping for fresh fish is simpler and more rewarding, believe me."

It was too much. Sariana lost the last shreds of her self-control. She hurled the stationery tray at Gryph's head.

He saw it coming but he didn't bother to duck. It was as if he took one look at its trajectory and knew it would miss him by a few centimeters. When it smashed against the wall behind him and fell harmlessly to the floor he took another swallow of wine.

"Get out of here," Sariana shouted, snatching up a writing instrument and flinging it at him. He reached out and casually snatched it out of midair.

"There are a few things I have to tell you first," Gryph said quietly.

"*I don't want to hear them.*" Her fingers touched another object and she lifted it unthinkingly. "Leave me alone."

Gryph eyed the sharp point on the message packet opener. "You and I are leaving at dawn tomorrow. Pack only the basics. We can't carry a lot of luggage."

"If you think I'm going anywhere with you you're out of your mind." She threw the packet opener, only realizing the potential danger of the blade after it had left her hand. Her eyes widened in horror as the knifelike utensil whipped across the room in the blink of an eye.

With a lazy movement that seemed to take place almost in slow motion, Gryph brought the jacket he'd slung over his shoulder down to a point just below his belt buckle. The packet opener slammed into the tough material of the jacket and lodged there. Gryph glanced down at where the blade would have struck had it not met the jacket first.

"I can see where a codpiece might be a useful fashion item on certain occasions," he observed.

Sariana was shocked by her own act of violence. It jolted her back to reality. "What have you done to me?" she asked in a dazed voice. "It's because of you I'm acting this way. I've lost my self-control."

"Relax, Sariana. Everyone does occasionally. It's nothing to get alarmed about."

She stumbled away from the desk and sank into the nearest chair. "Please leave," she said stiffly.

"Don't you want to know more about our trip?"

"I'm not going anywhere with you."

He ignored that and continued to lounge against the hospitality table while he swirled the wine in his glass. "As far as everyone else is concerned, it will be a traditional wedding journey. I'll be taking you home to introduce you to my clan. It's expected. No one will question it."

Something in his voice broke through Sariana's emotional daze. "You speak as if this stupid journey you're planning has another purpose besides ensuring my humiliation."

"It does. You and I are going to find the Avylyns' precious prisma cutter."

She looked up, startled.

Gryph smiled evenly. "I thought that might get your attention."

"Why do you continue to concern yourself with the cutter?"

Gryph finished the last of the wine and set the glass down. "As I told the Avylyns this morning, the cutter has become Shield business. It must be found."

"I don't understand you, Gryph."

"I know." He started toward the door. "And there is much about you that I don't understand. But we'll both have plenty of time to get to know each other on our wedding journey. Be ready at dawn, Sariana." He opened the door and closed it behind him.

Sariana plucked the scarlet-toe off her shoulder and cradled it gently in her palms. The lizard gazed up at her with its unwinking, jeweled eyes.

"If he thinks I'll tamely jump to his beck and call, he is in for a surprise," she informed the lizard. "You and I are indeed going on a journey tonight, but not with Gryph Chassyn. We are going to escape this madhouse."

Chapter
9

S ARIANA crouched behind a row of stacked wine casks in a dockside warehouse and decided she was learning far too much about fear lately. It seemed to her that she had been forced to deal with one overpowering wave of emotion after another during the past few hours. Life had become terrifyingly irrational and dangerous for a young woman who had always assumed she knew what she wanted and how she was going to get it. Nothing was certain any longer.

A tiny hissing sound in Sariana's ear warned her that the scarlet-toe was picking up on her anxiety. Automatically Sariana touched the lizard in a light, soothing gesture. The scarlet-toe hissed again, the sound so soft it didn't carry beyond the range of Sariana's hearing.

"It's your fault we're in here," Sariana muttered softly. It was true. It had been the lizard's insistent hissing that had first alerted her to the fact that she was being followed. She had assumed in the beginning that it was Gryph trailing her through the streets of Serendipity down to the wharf and she had been angered as well as nervous. She hated the feeling of being hunted.

But a few minutes ago she had realized her pursuer was not Gryph. She didn't know how she could be so certain of that but she was. She would *know* if it was Gryph closing in on her. There was another hunter on her trail tonight.

Sariana had left the Avylyn household an hour before dawn, carrying as many clothes and personal belongings as she could manage in two large travel pouches slung from her shoulders. The scarlet-toe had been perched on the shoulder of her cloak.

A lingering sense of duty had forced her to pause long enough to write out a series of instructions regarding the Avylyn household and business finances. She could only hope the Avylyns would have the sense to follow them in her absence.

Intent on making her way to the wharf where she would be able to book passage on one of the fast little windriggers that plied the coastal waters, Sariana had hurried through the dark streets.

The realization that someone was following her had hit just as she had reached the deserted warehouse area near the docks. The scarlet-toe had become increasingly agitated and Sariana, who had at first been furious that Gryph had followed her, had begun to feel a trickle of fear along her spine.

It was then she had decided that it couldn't be Gryph. She felt a lot of things around Chassyn, but she had never known that kind of fear.

She had quickened her pace until she was moving as fast as she could with the weight of the overloaded travel pouches. Anxiously she had glanced down the street, hoping to see an early rising sailor or dockworker or guard. There had been no one in sight.

There was no one visible behind her, either, but Sariana had no doubt the hunter was somewhere in the shadows.

Impulsively she had begun trying the warehouse doors she was passing. With each locked door she encountered, the fear crawling through her became stronger.

On the fifth try she had gotten lucky. The handle of a small side door had turned under her gloved fingers. Sariana hadn't hesitated. She had dashed inside and closed the door behind her.

She had found herself in a deep, looming darkness broken by the fitful light of a few, dim vapor lamps set in the walls.

Now she sat huddled in the deepest shadows she could find. She was sitting on a wine cask. Rank upon rank of barrels and casks were piled in front of her and behind her. The odor of wine was heavy in the air.

Sariana tried to decide how long she should stay in her hiding place. With any luck whoever had trailed her through the streets would grow weary of the search and seek other prey.

Then she heard the unmistakable sound of the side door opening and closing again. Sariana shuddered and squeezed her eyes shut briefly against the fear that threatened to overwhelm her. The scarlet-toe hissed its nearly silent hiss and clung tightly to the fabric of Sariana's cape.

Sariana opened her eyes and gazed out into the darkness. The beam of a small hand-held vapor lamp was reflected briefly from a far wall. Then it disappeared as whoever held it turned down another aisle. She could hear the scrape of boots on the warehouse floor. Whoever was hunting her was conducting a systematic search of the aisles. Sooner or later he would come down this aisle and she would be trapped.

Sariana came to a decision. She was not going to crouch there until the inevitable happened.

Stealthily she stood up and set down her travel pouches. Then she removed her cloak. The scarlet-toe scampered from the cloak to her arm and back up to her shoulder. There it sat poised and ready. The little creature seemed to have come to the same conclusion as Sariana. Anything was better than waiting to be discovered.

Sariana stepped softly out of her slippers and turned to confront the row of casks behind her. The barrels were stacked only four tiers high in the first row. It shouldn't be that difficult to climb to the top tier. Tentatively she searched for and found handholds and places for her stock-inged toes.

The climb proved harder than she had anticipated. By the time Sariana reached the top tier of casks she was breathing heavily and terrified that the searcher would hear her. Fortunately he was still moving systematically up and down the aisles. It would be a few minutes before he reached the aisle in which she'd left her travel pouches and cloak.

Sariana glanced around. There was a little more light from the vapor lamps up here. She could see the outlines of the casks on either side of her. Some of the barrels were smaller than others. She made her way cautiously along the curving ribs of the wine casks until she came to a tier of smaller containers that were stacked upright instead of on their sides.

Experimentally she tried nudging one of the small casks. It proved unexpectedly heavy. She would never be able to lift it, but she might be able to push it.

The beam of the vapor lamp turned the corner of Sariana's aisle. She froze, watching in horrified fascination as a figure made his way rapidly along the corridor of wine casks. In another moment he would see the travel pouches and Sariana's discarded cloak. Sariana held her breath and prepared to use all her strength on the barrel under her hands.

The man in the aisle gave a grunt of satisfaction when the vapor light picked out Sariana's possessions on the floor. He hurried forward, swinging the ray of light rapidly back and forth. He never once raised the light to examine the top rows of casks. It was obvious he assumed his quarry was huddled behind a wine barrel.

"You can come on out of hiding," the man urged, his voice oily with an attempt to coax his prey into the open. "I'm not going to hurt you. Come on now, little lady. It's all right. Come on out of your hiding place."

Sariana's fingers trembled on the rim of the upright wine

cask. She had to time this perfectly or she would be worse off than she already was.

Fortunately the searcher paused to examine the travel pouches. He bent over to open the clasps, intent on examining the contents. Sariana gathered herself, felt the scarlet-toe gather itself simultaneously, and then she shoved at the wine cask with all her might. Lucky hissed.

The man below jerked upright as he heard the scrape of wood on wood. The beam of his light caught the cask as it toppled downward and he cried out in startled anger.

Sariana watched, frozen in shock as the man tried to throw himself to one side. He was going to dodge the cask, she thought. Frantically she shoved at the next barrel in line and then the one stacked next to it.

A loud, groaning rumble filled the warehouse as half a dozen small casks of expensive wine went crashing down onto the hard floor. Somewhere in the midst of the noise a man's scream rose shrilly and then ended with heart-stopping suddenness. The vapor lamp winked out.

A moment later the last of the cascading barrels rolled to a halt and all was quiet.

Moving unsteadily, Sariana climbed down the large casks to the floor below. The scarlet-toe was hissing softly again.

Sariana tripped and nearly fell when her bare toe struck a fallen cask. Stifling an exclamation of pain, she scrambled through the maze of toppled casks, seeking her travel pouches.

She stumbled over the intruder's still form first and nearly screamed. But the man did not move. Sariana untangled herself from his short cape and frantically groped for her things. They were splashed with wine. She could smell it in the darkness and feel the dampness under her fingers.

Shoving her feet back into her slippers, she folded her travel cloak over one arm and grabbed up the pouches.

"Let's get out of here," she whispered to the scarlet-toe who signaled its agreement with a low grumble. Sariana was intent only on fleeing the warehouse. "This is all

Gryph's fault. I wouldn't be in this awful position if it wasn't for him. And since I am in this mess, you'd think the least he could do would be to come to my rescue. But no, I have to rescue myself. Typical of a man not to be around when you need him. They're more than ready to hop into bed with a woman but where are they when she's in trouble?"

She was chattering to the scarlet-toe out of anxiety, Sariana realized. It was ridiculous. It was a sign of how badly frayed her nerves were.

Finding the small warehouse door she let herself out onto the street where she struggled to balance her burdens.

"We should report this to the town guards," she muttered to the lizard. "But if we stop long enough to do that we'll never get away."

She hesitated, torn between civic duty and the need to escape. In the end the need to get out of town won. Sariana hurried down the empty street toward the wharf.

She reached the waterfront and heaved a sigh of relief. Dawn was still an hour away, but here and there vapor lamps provided enough light to see the outlines of the windriggers tied up to the docks. The sleek sailing ships creaked in the darkness and water slapped the pilings.

Sariana saw no one as she made her way toward the nearest windrigger. She wondered how long she would have to wait before she found a captain willing to let her book passage.

Sariana was making her way along a pier when the scarlet-toe hissed in her ear. She froze, aware that she was once more being stalked.

Sariana whirled around, dropping the travel pouches and her cloak. A man loomed up out of the darkness. He wasn't more than a few meters away from her. The wings of a short, hooded cape that shielded his features were pushed back over his shoulders, freeing his arms. In one hand he held an object Sariana knew must be a blade bow.

This time there was no place to hide and she could not outrun a blade bow. She was trapped.

"You have given us more trouble than we expected," the

man grated. "But it's over now. You will come with me, woman, or I will put a blade through your throat. Come here."

Sariana darted toward the edge of the pier, seeking the dubious safety of the black water below. Anything was better than facing a blade bow. She saw the man's hand lift higher as he swore viciously and took aim. She was never going to make it into the cold waters of the bay. She tried to scream, but no sound emerged from her tight throat.

But in the next instant someone else started to scream. The man aiming the blade bow jerked violently and the sound was choked off. He started to turn toward the dark alley that separated two warehouses but he never made it. He was already falling. He toppled over the edge of the pier, clutching at his chest. There was a moment of horrifying silence and then a soft splash announced his entry into the water.

Sariana swung her stunned gaze toward the alley just as Gryph stepped out into the pale glow of a vapor lamp. He was resealing the weapon kit as he strode toward her.

A dizzying sense of relief swept through Sariana. Without a second's hesitation she ran toward him.

"Gryph Chassyn! By the Storm, you bastard, it's about time you got here. This is all your fault, do you hear me? Twice I've nearly been robbed and murdered tonight. *Twice.* And it's all your damn fault."

Gryph opened his arms and she flung herself against him. He absorbed the impact easily, locking her tightly into his strength.

"I appreciate punctuality in a woman," he grated into her hair as she buried her face against his shirt. "But you didn't have to get to the wharf this early. We aren't scheduled to sail for another hour."

In that moment Sariana gave up. She was literally shaking with relief. She buried herself in Gryph's warmth, savoring his reassuring strength. There was no point running from him. A part of her would always be glancing back over her shoulder to see if he was following. She knew that with a deep certainty. For a long moment she clung to him and he held her without speaking, his arms hard and protective.

"It would appear half of Serendipity was following me tonight," Sariana finally muttered, pushing hair out of her eyes.

"If you hadn't convinced yourself that you had to try to escape me, you wouldn't have gotten yourself into this mess." Gryph took hold of her arm and started back along the pier to where she had dropped her travel pouches and cloak. "I want your word of honor you won't pull another stunt like this, Sariana. By the time I realized you had left the villa, it was almost too late."

A large portion of her initial relief gave way to the more familiar sense of frustration. "Why should I promise you anything?"

"Because I'm your husband and you owe me at least some measure of respect."

He picked up her travel pouches and handed her the cloak. The first tendrils of dawn lit his eyes as he looked down at her. Sariana saw his quietly implacable expression and wished she knew how to fight it. She was too tired to figure out what to do next. She had been through too much during the past few days.

"How many times do I have to explain to you that I don't consider myself married?" Sariana asked wearily as she put on her cloak. The scarlet-toe hopped around, adjusting itself until it was happily perched on the shoulder of the outer garment.

"You are married, Sariana. And I want your word that you won't run from me again."

"Why? Because you don't want to be put to the nuisance of coming after me?"

He shook his head. "No. Because it's too dangerous for you. I almost lost you tonight. As it was, things were much too close. I don't want to go through that again. By the way, when we're safely on board the ship you can tell me exactly what happened in that warehouse."

Sariana was violently aware of the morning chill in the air. "You found the first man?" she asked in a low whisper.

"I found him. I've been a few minutes behind you ever since you left the villa. Unfortunately, it took me a while to figure out which way you'd gone. By the time I did, those two clanless outlaws had picked up your trail. You'll never know how I felt when I discovered the first one."

"Was he dead?" Sariana was afraid of the answer.

"No. But he won't wake up for quite a while. Probably not until the warehouse manager finds him later on this morning. The assumption will be that he tried to steal a few casks of wine. That should get him locked up for a decent length of time. As for the other one . . ." Gryph finished the sentence with a careless shrug.

"What about him?" Sariana demanded as Gryph led her along the pier. "We should find a town guard and report this incident."

"None of this concerns the town guards. It's Shield business."

"Damn it, you keep saying that. What do the Shields care about a couple of street thieves?"

"The man who ended up in the bay tonight was the one who attacked me the night of the ball. He's probably the one who killed Brinton. As for the one whose head you dented with a wine cask, he was undoubtedly the accomplice who helped the murderer to escape the first time."

Sariana was dumbfounded. "You didn't tell me Brinton had been killed. You mean you think the two men who trailed me tonight were involved with the theft of the cutter?"

"Yes. But even if they had been just a random pair of thieves roaming the streets in search of easy prey, they would still be Shield business."

"Why is that?"

"Because they chose you to hunt down," Gryph explained. "And you are most definitely Shield property."

"I want to go home," Sariana said in a small voice. "I've had enough of this crazy place. I just want to go home."

"One of these days I'll take you to your new home. In the meantime, we have a journey to complete."

"Why must I accompany you?" she demanded.

"Because I can't take the risk of leaving you behind while I go after the cutter."

"You're afraid I'll run away from you?"

He shook his head. "That's the least of my concerns. I can always find you if you decide to run, Sariana. Remember that. Even if you go all the way back to Rendezvous I'd find you."

"But in Rendezvous you would no longer have any claim on me," she pointed out. "Under the laws of the eastern provinces I'm not married."

"My claim on you is not dependent on any law. I think, deep inside yourself, you know that. It's the real reason you tried to run from me this morning."

She ignored that because she was getting very tired of arguing the point. It was hard to argue with someone who arrogantly refused to see the logic or justice of his opponent's side. Sariana walked beside Gryph in silence for a few moments. With every step she felt increasingly trapped.

"You said you aren't afraid I'll run away if you leave me behind. So why are you afraid to take the risk of leaving me here?" she finally asked moodily.

"Whoever is responsible for stealing the prisma cutter has probably figured out what I'm doing on the scene. I think he's also learned that you are involved with me. That's why those two were after you. It wouldn't take much intelligence to decide to use you to stop me."

"Why would whoever it is make the assumption that I'm a vulnerable point for you?"

"Because you are a vulnerable point," he said simply. "You're my Shieldmate. Everyone in the western provinces understands how important a Shieldmate is to her lord and his clan."

"Everyone except me."

Gryph smiled crookedly. "But you're learning, aren't you?"

A typical summer dawn broke over the distant mountains a short time later. Sariana watched it from the deck of a windrigger in full sail. She gazed at the coastline slipping past and listened to the creak and snap of the skillfully designed sails. The ships of the western provinces were faster and more maneuverable than those of the east. Sailing was another area in which the experimentally inclined westerners excelled. The westerners were even working on a vapor fueled engine that might someday power their sleek ships.

Sariana was feeling resentful of clever westerners and just about everything else this morning. Life had not seemed very fair lately.

Soon she would have to go below to the cabin Gryph had booked. She had avoided it until now because she did not want to face the single bed she would find there. There was very little possibility that Gryph had booked himself into a separate cabin and she knew it. As far as he was concerned, he was a married man. Furthermore, he had decided she was in need of protection.

After what had happened in the dark hours before dawn, Sariana was forced to wonder if Gryph was right about that last detail. Two men were dead and she had almost been kidnapped. The search for the prisma cutter had turned into a far more serious affair than she had anticipated.

It was frightening the way things had a habit of getting out of control in the west. Sariana sighed. Just when she had thought she was making progress toward her ultimate goal of salvaging her future, everything had gone wrong.

The scarlet-toe hissed in sympathy and cuddled closer into the curve of Sariana's shoulder.

"What am I going to do now?" Sariana asked the scarlet-toe.

"Unpack," Gryph suggested as he came up behind her. He leaned one arm on the rail and looked down at her.

Sariana jumped and fixed him with a brief glare. Then she pretended to study the shoreline once more. "Gryph, we have got to talk about this situation. We've got to come to some sort of understanding."

"It all seems clear to me. What is it you don't understand?"

Sariana's hands tightened on the rail. "You simply are not going to be reasonable about this, are you?"

"You have no idea of how reasonable, patient and understanding I am being," he told her.

She bit off her useless protest and stood beside him in depressed silence.

Gryph was quiet for a while, too, but in the end he was the one who broke the charged silence with a weary groan. He leaned both of his arms on the rail and looked out to sea.

"You probably won't believe this, but I didn't intend things between us to become so complicated, Sariana. I swear I had every intention of going slowly. I told myself I would give you time and court you carefully. I knew you were unaccustomed to our ways and I wanted to introduce you to them gently. But the other night when I stupidly let myself get sliced by that blade, everything changed. I went to bed groggy from the painkiller the medic had given me and I woke up with a fever. When I saw you sitting in the chair beside my bed all I could think about was how much I wanted you. You wanted me, too. I knew that beyond a doubt. I decided I would explain all the details in the morning. But the next morning you were all business again, intent on keeping me at arm's length while you decided what to do next. You wouldn't even listen to me. It was as if nothing important had happened between us during the night."

"As far as I was concerned, the only thing that had occurred was a rather unpleasant attempt to start an affair with you. I should have known better. I can't understand what prompted me to even think about getting involved with you in that way. I must have been out of my mind."

Gryph winced. "I know it wasn't the most auspicious beginning for a relationship."

"It certainly was not," she shot back. "I'm still sore in places." Then she flushed and gritted her teeth as she realized what she had said.

"I've told you, I'm sorry about that. Please believe me, I had no idea the link would be that strong. Nobody warned me, either. But with practice we can both learn to control the crossover effects."

"I don't know what you're talking about," Sariana stormed, "but I do know that on top of everything else that happened that night you lied to me."

He stiffened and the humble apology went out of his voice. "I'm not accustomed to being labeled a liar. The fact that you're my Shieldmate does not give you any special privileges when it comes to making such accusations."

"Don't go all haughty and arrogant on me, Gryph. You lied to me and that's a fact."

"What, precisely, did I lie to you about?" he demanded icily.

"You said you were as inexperienced as I was!" She lifted her chin and waited for him to admit the falsehood.

Gryph relaxed slightly and turned back to the rail. "Oh, that."

"Yes, that."

"Well, it was true. I have never linked with any other woman."

"I'm not talking about linking, whatever that is. I'm talking about sex, damn it. Pure, simple, straightforward sex. You were no virgin, Gryph Chassyn," Sariana accused.

"I'm supposed to apologize for that, too?"

She glared at his profile, uncertain of his mood. "Are you laughing at me?"

He shook his head quickly. "No. I swear I'm not. I'm just realizing that there was a slight communication problem that night and you got the wrong impression. For that I apologize." He made a sweeping gesture with one hand. "Hell, I apologize for everything about the clumsy way I handled our first night together. If anything, my bungling should prove just how inexperienced I was. I wasn't any more prepared for the crossover effect than you were."

"What is all this nonsense about a crossover effect?" Sariana demanded.

"It's what happens when a Shield and his Shieldmate make love."

Sariana's eyes widened as she remembered the explosion of pain and passion and the way she had seemed to be absorbing everything he had been feeling that night as well as her own jumble of sensations.

"You're telling me I wasn't just hallucinating because of all that punch I drank?" she asked weakly.

"You weren't hallucinating," he assured her softly. "We were linked and you were picking up on my feelings as well as your own. Unfortunately, I wasn't in great shape that night. My shoulder hurt, I was running a fever and I was still recovering from the effects of the medic's anesthetic. To finish it off, there was the unavoidable discomfort that comes from tuning into the prisma the first time. Poor Sariana. You had enough new sensations of your own to deal with that night. I'm sorry you got hit with everything I was feeling and the prisma, too."

Sariana stared at him in openmouthed amazement. "You mean you go through that every time you make love to a woman?"

"Of course not," he said impatiently. "Haven't you been listening? It's only like that between a Shield and his Shieldmate. It doesn't happen with other women. And from what I've been told, it isn't supposed to be that bad between a Shield and his lady, either. What happened between us was very strong, Sariana. I'm not sure I understand all of it even though I've thought about it a lot since then. But I'm sure we can control it."

"Wait a minute. Are you telling me that you have been to bed with other women but it's never been like that with any of them?"

He smiled slightly. "I told you, you're my Shieldmate. There's been no other for me. I've never been married before. A Shield can't link with just any female, you see. Given several thousand women to choose from, a man would be very lucky to find even a few who had the potential of linking with a Shield. And even then there are likely to be other complications."

"Such as?" She couldn't believe she was hearing this, but Sariana couldn't bring herself to believe Gryph was lying, either. One thing was certain: He believed what he was saying. Westerners loved legends.

"Such as the fact that the woman in question might not be interested in going to bed with a Shield. Or she might be past childbearing age. Or she might already be married to a man from her own class in which case the Pact forbids the Shield from approaching her." Gryph's smile twisted wryly. "The First Generation colonists drove a shrewd bargain."

Sariana seized on the one point that applied to her. "You mean if the woman doesn't want to marry the Shield she's free to say no?"

"You weren't listening. As usual. For a bright woman, Sariana, you have an odd tendency to hear only what you want to hear. I said the woman is free to choose whether or not she wants to go to bed with the Shield. Once she's been to bed with him, she's married. Unless, for some reason, the link didn't work." His eyes grew very brilliant. "But there is no question of that in our case. We are linked, Sariana. One of these days you'll admit it to yourself and to me."

She instinctively took a step backward, even though he hadn't moved. "Why is it so important to . . . to link with a woman? You admitted you don't need to be linked in order to have a sexual relationship."

"There are two reasons why a Shield searches very hard for a woman with whom he can link," Gryph said evenly. "The first is that he cannot father a child with any woman except a true Shieldmate. All other unions are sterile. And even with a Shieldmate, he can only produce sons. No Shield has ever fathered a daughter. The future of every Shield clan is dependent on the sons finding mates among the descendants of the colonists of *The Serendipity*."

Sariana stared at him. "You're telling me the legend is true? Your class was not among those on board *The Serendipity*?"

Gryph lifted his head proudly. "My people were conveniently on hand when the lightstorm took *The Serendipity*. Without my ancestors, everyone on that ship would have died. We saved them. We saved them a second time on the ground. Someday I'll tell you the whole story. The important point is that the colonists repaid the Shields by negotiating the Pact. It binds us into their social system."

"This is all just a legend. A wild tale concocted by the people of the western provinces. I know it is."

"You know I'm not lying to you, Sariana. Look at me. I have never lied to you."

For a moment she was trapped by the truth in his eyes. She struggled to resist and became frantic when she could not. Without a word she spun around, seeking escape.

"Sariana."

She stopped but did not turn back to face him. She did not dare.

"You haven't heard the second reason why a Shield will go to any length to find a mate," Gryph said.

"What's the second reason?" But silently she was thinking that she did not want to hear it. The answer was already in her head. It had appeared there as if by magic.

"The second reason is that if he does not find a mate, a Shield will face a kind of loneliness no one else can even begin to comprehend. He'll know he has missed the special communication that comes through linking with a woman. He'll face it all the days of his life and when that life is over he will also face the knowledge that he has left nothing of himself to the future. Now do you see why I can't let you go, Sariana?"

Chapter
10

S EVERAL hours later Sariana lay alone in the large ship's bunk. She was wide awake and very thoughtful. It had been a long while since she had shared an early dinner with Gryph and the handful of other passengers on board the windrigger. She had retired to the cabin prepared to stage a determined battle when her so-called husband came to claim his marital rights.

But, as usual, Gryph had proven unpredictable. He had not come back to the cabin after dinner. It was almost midnight.

Sariana gave up trying to sleep and sat up against the pillows. A pale wash of moonlight bathed the cabin in a gentle glow. By western standards the room was quite restrained. Of course, she reflected half humorously, that still left a lot of leeway for artistic license. Some ship's designer had taken advantage of that leeway.

The cabinetry was beautifully finished with fine metal fittings and precision carving. The elaborately detailed bed on which she sat was solidly anchored to the deck, unlike most beds on shore. Presumably a suspended bed had been deemed too dangerous for shipboard use. There was a multi-paned window behind the bed through which the moonlight shone in a series of intricate prisms.

Prisms.

Sariana shied from the image. It reminded her of prisma crystal and the lock on her husband's weapon kit.

Damn it, he was *not* her husband, Sariana told herself for what must have been the millionth time.

Unfortunately local law and custom disagreed with her. Sariana was finally convinced that the only way out of the situation was to leave the western provinces and return to the eastern continent.

But she couldn't do that just yet. Her future in the east at this point was bleaker than the one she faced in the west. Her mouth curved faintly at the thought that at least here life held a certain amount of adventure and excitement. She would find neither at home.

Sariana swore softly and climbed out of bed. The fact that she could find something positive about such things as adventure and excitement was probably a sign that she had already been living in the west too long. It reminded her uncomfortably of how she had felt when Etion Rakken had made his businesslike marriage proposal. She had found herself thinking it would have been nice to have had a declaration of love and passion thrown in on the side. That had been a very western thought, too. No easterner in his right mind would have worried about the role of love and passion in a marriage that had everything else going for it.

Well, she had gotten a clear demonstration of passion, at least, from the man who had married her. Whatever else had happened on her wedding night, there had certainly been an element of passion involved. Gryph had wanted her with an intensity that had burned its way right into her soul. She had been vibrating with the aftershocks ever since she had left his bed.

This morning he had saved her life.

Tonight he had not tried to press his claim on her, even though he genuinely believed he was married to her.

Gryph Chassyn believed a lot of strange things, Sariana reflected. But, so did the other inhabitants of the western provinces. Their First Generation legends had taken some weird twists and turns. Which was understandable when one considered that *The Serendipity* had carried a whole class of storytellers and dramatists.

Sariana found her traveling cloak and slipped it around her shoulders. As long as she kept the front closed no one would know she was wearing only her sleeping chemise underneath. She stepped into her slippers.

At the cabin door she stopped, questioning her own actions. Then she opened the door and stepped into the corridor. There were things that had to be settled tonight. She had been floundering in a morass of emotions for far too long. The rule to follow when one found oneself in an untenable situation was to negotiate.

The scarlet-toe, nestled for the night on a glove Sariana had left on a nearby table, hissed questioningly. "Go back to sleep," Sariana told it. "I'll be back soon. I am finally thinking clearly again."

Gryph sensed her presence a second or two before he caught the sweep of her cloak out of the corner of his eye. He had been leaning against the rail, nursing a mug of ale and hoping the sea breeze would calm his restless, hungry senses to a point where he could sleep. Whatever progress he might have been making was undone completely when he realized Sariana had come looking for him.

He held the mug in both hands, his forearms resting on the railing, and turned his head to look at her. In the moonlight she looked very beautiful and infinitely compelling. The hood of the cloak framed her face, giving her a hint of feminine mystery. In the shadows he could see the mixture of caution and determination in her huge eyes. A few tantalizing tendrils of her unbound hair had escaped the confines of the hood. The long folds of the garment drifted around her slender figure, revealing even while concealing.

This was his wife, he told himself as he studied her in

the moonlight. This was his Shieldmate, whether she knew it yet or not. The realization still had the power to daze him. He wanted to reach out and take hold of her to ensure himself that she was real and solid. He restrained himself with difficulty.

She had sought him out of her own accord tonight. He would take that as a hopeful indication that she was beginning to accept the situation. He did not know all that much about women, but he decided this was probably not the moment to push her. He had been telling himself that bit of wisdom since dinner, though his body had raged against the decision. She deserved some time to herself, Gryph had determined. By the Lightstorm, she had been through a lot today. His stomach still twisted into a cold knot whenever he thought of her on the docks.

"The luck of the evening to you, Sariana," he said formally. He was afraid he'd send her running back to the cabin if he tried any other greeting. A kiss, for example. She'd probably turn and flee if he tried to kiss her. His hands tightened around the mug.

"And to you, Shield." She inclined her head regally.

Gryph's mouth twisted. She hadn't called him husband. She hadn't even called him by his name. She had addressed him by his social designation which was about as formal as a woman could get. "Can't you sleep?"

"No."

He nodded. "That's understandable, considering what you went through this morning."

"My life here has been one surprise after another."

He heard the dry note in her voice as she stood beside him at the rail and he felt a flicker of sympathetic amusement. "You adjust well, for the most part. We'll make a true westerner out of you yet."

"I thought your goal was to turn me into a true Shieldmate."

"You already are a true Shieldmate." He couldn't resist catching a tendril of her loose hair between two fingers. Its silkiness fascinated him. He looked down into her eyes. "I knew that for certain the night you came to my bed. You proved it again this morning when you saved yourself from the man who followed you into the warehouse. A woman who can link with a Shield is strong in many ways."

She searched his face for a long moment. Gryph wondered what she was thinking. He knew that he would be able to sense certain strong emotions from her at times of stress or passion, but the link between them was not true telepathy. They wouldn't be able to read each other's minds, although gradually, over time, they would become more aware of each other's thoughts. A few Shields and their mates who had been linked for years could almost read each other's minds at times. But that kind of communication took many years to forge and it was certainly not unique to Shields. Gryph had known other couples who had lived together for years who seemed able to second guess each other.

Nevertheless, there was something quite unique about the bonding that took place between a Shield and his mate. That bonding was at its strongest when there was an accompanying emotional intensity.

In other words, the link was at its most intense when they were in the grip of passion or danger. Gryph preferred the grip of passion. He recoiled at the idea of Sariana in danger.

"I did not come out here to discuss the strange customs and legends that lead you and people such as the Avylyns to assume I'm married to you," Sariana said quietly.

"Then why did you seek me out tonight, Sariana?"

She looked out over the moonlit sea. "I've finally had a chance to calm down and think."

He smiled faintly. "Translated, that means you've found a way to convince yourself you can turn the situation to your own advantage. I admire your resilience, Sariana. No matter how bad things get, you always manage to come out fighting. Tell me what you've been thinking. You have a way with logic that leaves a poor, humble male breathless."

His sarcasm annoyed her, but she ignored it. "I was educated to be practical and efficient in my thinking and decision making. For the past two days I have not been applying the benefits of that education. Instead I have been leaping irrationally from one emotional peak to another. It's a waste of energy, time and intelligence to operate in that manner. Tonight I've decided to take control of my own life again. I'm intelligent enough to know that, while I cannot always dictate the events of that life, I can certainly decide how I'll deal with those events."

"Ah, Sariana, I knew it. You do not disappoint me. Once again you are busy building a fortress made out of words."

"I am trying to deal rationally with an irrational situation," she retorted. "I've come to some conclusions and I have decided to offer you a working truce."

"We're not at war," he pointed out, curious in spite of himself.

"That's a matter of opinion, but never mind. My offer of a truce still stands."

"Why do we need this truce?"

"Because we both want the same thing. We want to find the prisma cutter. After the violence that has taken place, I'm inclined to believe that getting it back will be a far more dangerous task than I originally anticipated. Going to the guards is out because you and the Avylyns will not back me up. I would look like a crazy easterner making wild claims about a theft that everyone else would deny."

Gryph lifted one shoulder. "True."

"I want to get that cutter back as badly as you do. A great deal of my future success is tied to completing my contract with the Avylyns. They have convinced me that, as ridiculous as it seems and no matter how effectively I manage their business affairs, they cannot retain their preeminence in their social class without that tool."

"They're right."

"Very well, I accept the facts of the situation. The social and business position of the Avylyn Clan must be salvaged if I am to salvage my own future. That means the cutter must be retrieved. It is equally clear now that there is danger involved in getting it back. You're a man who is supposedly trained and equipped to handle danger. I'm a businesswoman, not a skilled fighter. I need your particular talents in this search and you have implied you are willing to help me retrieve the cutter, although I do not as yet understand your sudden insistence on completing the task."

"I think I'm beginning to see where your logic has led you, Sariana. You're an amazing creature."

"Therefore," Sariana pressed on vigorously, "as we share a common goal and are both committed to it, I see no reason why we shouldn't work together as two rational human beings."

"This is what you mean by a truce?" Gryph asked thoughtfully.

She turned to face him squarely, her eyes more mysterious than ever in the shadow of the hood. "Yes."

"What about my claim on you?" he asked bluntly.

She drew a deep breath, as if she were preparing to throw herself into the sea for a late night swim. "We will discuss that when we return to Serendipity with the cutter."

Gryph laughed. "It's all clear to me now. We will sidestep that issue while we're searching for the cutter. You'll pretend you aren't married to me and I will be gentlemanly enough not to bring up the subject. Once we're back in Serendipity with the cutter, you figure you'll be able to hop a rigger and return to the eastern provinces covered in glory. There you think you will be safe from western laws and customs, right?"

"As I said," Sariana stated demurely, "we can discuss the final resolution to our personal business when the cutter is safely back in Avylyn hands."

Gryph shook his head, still grinning. "And just what do you propose we do in the meantime?"

She tilted her head questioningly. "About what?"

The last of his amusement faded. "About that single bunk in our cabin. About the fact that I want you more than I want my next breath. About your curiosity to find out if there really is more to passion than a thousand screaming nerve endings."

"I am no longer particularly curious about such matters!"

"Sure you are. You're intelligent and you're educated and you know damn well that there must be more to sex than what you found the other night."

She looked up at him, not trying to deny such an obvious truth. "I think it would be better if I satisfied my curiosity with another man," she said seriously.

Gryph was so astonished he nearly dropped the mug. "Another man? After we have already lain together?" It took him an instant to recover himself. He could tell by the curious expression on her face that she had no real notion of the effort it took to master the wave of possessive rage her words had unleashed within him. He finished off the last of the ale in one long gulp.

"Gryph? Are you all right?"

"Do us both a favor, Sariana." His voice was strained with the tension of containing his anger. "Don't ever talk to me of going to another man's bed."

"I'm sorry, Gryph," she said very earnestly. "I can see it upsets you."

He lifted his eyes beseechingly toward the stars. "You have a talent for driving me to the edge. Be careful that you don't succeed in pushing me over one of these days."

"I said I'm sorry, but you must try to understand this situation from my point of view. I don't consider myself married. You cannot, in all good conscience, expect me to submit to the rules and customs established by western First Generation tales. I don't believe in all your legends."

"I could make you believe in them."

It was a warning and a declaration, but Sariana did not seem aware of either. For all her logic and her ability with words, his Shieldmate could be amazingly obtuse at times. Gryph was sure that obtuseness was deliberate. She used it when it served her purposes.

"As I said earlier, Gryph, it would be better if we don't discuss our personal situation until our mission is accomplished. I urge you to consider my offer of a working truce."

Gryph set down the mug, no longer able to resist putting

his hands on her. He clasped her shoulders, wondering if she would flinch away from him and oddly pleased when she did not. "If I am to accept a truce, then it will be in all things, not just in the matter of retrieving the cutter."

She gazed up at him with dawning relief and satisfaction. "You'll accept my offer to work together as a team?"

"As usual, Sariana, you have heard only what you want to hear. "I accept your offer of a truce, if that's what you want to call it. If you'd rather we didn't discuss our marriage until we return to Serendipity, I'll go along with that, too."

"Thank you, Gryph. This will all work out for the best. You'll see."

"But that still leaves us with a problem."

"What problem?"

"The matter of that single bunk in the cabin." His hand flexed on her shoulders.

"Gryph, I'm not sure how we should handle that problem."

"You were willing enough to start an affair with me the other night," he reminded her.

She touched the tip of her tongue to one corner of her lips. In the silvery moonlight her eyes were very deep and filled with unanswered questions. "Yes," she said with a simple honesty that took away his breath. "I thought an affair with you might be very . . . well, very interesting."

"Ah, there you go again. You have such a delicate way with language. Well, I suppose I should be glad you at least find me interesting." Gryph slid his hands inside the hood of her cloak, finding the slender column of her throat. He held her lightly, stroking his thumbs along the line of her jaw. "You've said that you can't bring yourself to admit you're married. Can you think of yourself as involved in an affair with me? For the duration of this truce of ours, can you have the affair you intended to start two nights ago?"

A tremor went through her. Gryph could feel the rising warmth in the silky skin of her throat. His fingers shook a little as he continued to stroke her skin.

"I don't know," she whispered. "I'm not sure what to

do. Nothing worked out as I thought it would, including that." She looked up at him with an aching longing tinged with deep wariness. "I thought it would be so different."

"It will be this time," he promised her recklessly. "That first time I was a clumsy, blundering idiot. I apologize again. I will apologize for that fiasco for the rest of my life, if that's what you want."

"Well, you weren't *that* bad," she offered consolingly.

He nearly choked on his laughter as he realized just how serious she was. "Thank you, Sariana. That's very generous of you." He urged her closer until the folds of her cloak brushed against him. Her unique fragrance filled his senses. Gryph forced himself to speak carefully. "I would like a second chance, Sariana. I want to show you how it should be. Spend the time of this truce having the affair you wanted to have with me. We'll let the future take care of itself."

She parted her lips to answer him. Gryph decided he didn't quite trust the response that hovered on the tip of her tongue. She was still poised on the brink, the passion in her at war with her practicality and reason. He needed to find a way for her to let the passion subdue her natural caution.

Carefully, lightly, restraining himself until his body throbbed with the effort, Gryph kissed her. He brushed his mouth against hers, demanding nothing, apologizing yet again for the way he had bungled their first time together, pleading for a second chance.

Intuitively he knew it was the humble plea that won the battle for him. Sariana, for all her strength, fortitude and will, was defenseless against his earnest, entreating approach. Gryph realized suddenly that she could not turn down his silent appeal any more than she had been able to refuse Luri's gift of the scarlet-toe. There was a deeply empathetic side to her nature. It was one of the things that made her a Shieldmate.

Sariana trembled again and then her arms emerged from the folds of the cloak and stole softly around his waist. Gryph's sense of relief and triumph was enough to make him shudder. Cautiously he deepened the kiss, tasting again the enticing warmth of her mouth. His hands slid farther into the cloak, seeking the small, delicate curves of her breasts. He froze when he realized he could feel her nipples very plainly beneath his palms.

"Hunter's hell, woman, you aren't dressed." He pulled back slightly, thoroughly outraged. "What do you mean by coming on deck wearing only your nightclothes? You haven't even got a robe on underneath your cloak."

She looked up at him, bemused by the passion that was just beginning to unfurl within her. She concentrated for a moment on his complaint and then smiled reassuringly. "No one can see how I'm dressed beneath my cloak."

"That's not the point. It's the principle of the thing. You're my—" He broke off just before calling her his Shieldmate. "You can't parade around in public wearing only a sleeping chemise and a traveling cloak. What if the wind catches the cloak? Sariana, it isn't like you to be so unconcerned about such things."

She studied him from beneath her lashes. "You're right. It isn't like me. You have a strange effect on me at times, Gryph."

He heard the return of wariness in her voice and cursed himself for having come very close to ruining everything a second time. Like the trained hunter he was he moved quickly to recover his position. He could scold her later for such lapses. There would be plenty of time in the future to teach her that his sense of possessiveness did not permit such immodest behavior on her part.

It was odd, Gryph thought fleetingly as he pulled her back against him. He had never been particularly concerned about a woman's modesty or lack of it before in his life. He was learning quickly that a man felt differently about such things when the woman in question was his wife.

He kissed her again, silently apologizing for the outburst. He seemed to be always apologizing to this woman. But it was worth it when he felt her begin to relax once more. Gryph held the kiss for a long while, luxuriating in the sweet, hot flavor of her. When the tip of her tongue touched his and followed it back into his own mouth Gryph stifled a groan and broke the kiss reluctantly. When she looked up at him with a thousand questions in her eyes he wrapped his arm around her. Without a word he led her toward the stairs that would take them down to their cabin. Sariana made no protest.

The scarlet-toe raised its sleek head and watched silently as Gryph led Sariana into the cabin. Then, apparently satisfied that all was as it should be, it went back to sleep.

Gryph ignored the small creature. His attention was centered on the woman in front of him. He was shaking with need and he hadn't even gotten her out of the cloak. He sought for self-control with all the skill at his command, determined not to bungle things this time.

Carefully he undid the fastenings of the cloak and eased it off Sariana's shoulders. It fell into a pool at her feet and in the moonlight he could see the shadows and curves of her body beneath the soft chemise.

He yanked impatiently at the laces of his shirt, flinging the garment heedlessly into the shadows. His fingers were on the buckle of his belt when he saw the direction of Sariana's wary gaze. She was eyeing the prisma lock of the weapon kit.

"Not this time, Sariana." He left his belt undone and reached out to catch her chin between his thumb and forefinger. He dropped a short, reassuring kiss on her parted lips. "We don't need it now. The link between us was forged that first time. We'll never need the prisma again."

She tilted her head questioningly, her eyes shimmering. "I don't understand."

"I know. It doesn't matter." He bit her very gently on her lower lip. "Just trust me, Sariana. This time it's going to be very good for you. I swear it. There is so much passion waiting to be discovered in you. I would have to be completely inept not to be able to help you find it this time."

She sighed softly and stepped closer under the gentle urging of his hand. Gryph slipped the chemise over her head and stared at her slender, graceful body with hungry fascination. Next to her he felt large and heavy and awkward. She was so soft and tantalizing. His fingers grazed lightly over the peaks of her breasts and he was rewarded when her sensitive flesh responded to his touch.

"You're so strong and hard," she breathed wonderingly as she spread her fingers across his chest. Her silver nails glimmered in the moonlight as she moved her hands to the broad curve of his shoulders.

Gryph thought he would go out of his mind. He brought her closer, sliding his fingers down under the sensual weight of her buttocks. He lifted her up against him, letting her feel his rigid manhood. She wrapped her arms around his neck and kissed him with a newfound boldness.

Gryph felt the first stirrings of the mental and emotional link that would soon leap to life between them. An intriguingly alien excitement raced through him. He was already starting to pick up on Sariana's sensations. Memories of that first night when he had experienced the shock of his own intrusion into her body even as she experienced it slammed into his head.

Gryph fought to control the crossover effects of the link this time. Sariana would not have the vaguest idea of how to channel and focus the devastatingly intimate contact. He had only a rough notion of how to do it himself, based on his training as a Shield.

It was freely acknowledged among Shields that however experienced a man was with prisma or with women, he was a novice when it came to establishing the permanent link with his Shieldmate. Each man struggled through the experience alone and unaided.

The task was made even more difficult, Gryph realized, because the woman involved had no training at all. No woman ever received Shield training.

In his case the whole event was further complicated by the fact that, in spite of having been through the initial linking, Sariana insisted on denying that anything out of the ordinary had taken place. He knew he would soon be getting the full impact of her reactions. She wouldn't know how to conceal them. Already he was being inundated with her rising passion.

The problem was that, for a man, there was no greater aphrodisiac in the universe than a woman's genuine passion. Gryph's desire was feeding hungrily on the rich feast it was being offered. The blaze within him was rapidly turning into a roaring fire.

With a stifled groan, he picked Sariana up and settled her in the middle of the wide bunk. He couldn't take his eyes off of her sleek, slender body while he jerked off his boots and stepped out of his trousers. She lay there devouring him with her eyes, one leg slightly drawn up to partially shadow the secrets between her thighs.

Gryph sat down on the edge of the bed and leaned over her, bracing himself with a hand on either side of her. When she touched his thigh inquisitively he groaned again and bent down to taste the tip of her breast with his tongue.

"You don't even know what you're doing to me," he whispered. "Here I am going through prisma fire trying to control myself and you're showering me with everything you've got."

She smiled up at him as her soft palm found his extended shaft. "Aren't you going to shower me with everything you've got?"

"On top of everything else, you're going to turn out to be a tease. I should have guessed." He felt her uncertain touch on his sensitive flesh and he shuddered again. She was going to drive him wild. He reached down to cover her hand with his own. "That's it, sweetheart. Pet me and stroke me and drive me out of my mind. I don't have much of a grasp left on it, anyway."

She looked up at him with genuine delight as she felt his physical reaction. He certainly wasn't going to bother trying to hide that part from her, Gryph decided. He couldn't have camouflaged his body's blunt, bold responses even if he had wanted to. It was hard enough trying to restrain his emotional reactions.

He pulsed under her touch and felt the thrill that went through her as she learned the extent of her own power over him. He didn't know whether to laugh or groan. He knew from past experience that Sariana was a woman who enjoyed exercising her strengths and abilities. When she discovered just how much talent she had for manipulating him, Gryph told himself, he was going to be in big trouble.

But a man could die happy in this kind of trouble.

"It's worth the risk," he told her, knowing she wouldn't understand the cryptic statement. "Besides, two can play at this game."

He flattened his palm on her stomach and swept his fingers through the triangle of hair below. She flinched when he unerringly found the nub that was the core of her sensations. Her fingers flexed on his leg and he felt the tips of her silvery nails digging into him.

Gryph stiffened in reaction and closed his eyes against the excitement that swept through him. For a few seconds he lost his grip on the control he was exerting. The power of his own emotions was too strong. They slipped from his grasp and poured into Sariana. She quivered beneath him, drawing back instinctively as his raging desire hit her mentally as well as physically. She let out a soft protest.

Gryph swore violently as he felt her trying to retreat. "No," he grated, anchoring her with one leg while he pushed her back into the pillows. "No, it's all right. I've got it now. Relax, Sariana, I'm in control. It's all right. Relax, my sweet. It's going to be okay. Don't be afraid. It's just that I want you so much." He rained small kisses across her breasts, his pulse thudding with the mental and physical effort he was exerting.

"I know," Sariana's voice was husky with the discovery she had just made. A thread of fear underlined her words. She clutched at him, her nails gripping his skin. "For a minute there I knew exactly how much you want me. It was like this the other night. I was so aware of how you felt. Gryph, what's happening between us?"

"Nothing that wasn't meant to happen." He hushed her with a kiss and rolled onto his back, taking her with him. He had to halt her agile mind from going down this path tonight. Now was not the time for her to acknowledge what was really happening. She might panic. He had to find a way to distract her.

He knew the exact instant passion reasserted its grip on her. It occurred when Sariana discovered herself astride him, his hot, throbbing manhood in her hands. She looked down at her prize and her thighs tightened convulsively around him. Her lashes were dark sweeps against her cheeks.

"There's so much power in you." She stroked him in wonder. "Everything about you is large and solid and beautiful in a way I can't quite explain."

He vibrated with the genuine pleasure she was taking in his masculinity. Gryph had to brace himself against the waves of desire beating at him. He locked his muscles, willing himself to take a step back from the edge of the climax that awaited him.

"Sariana, I keep telling you, you have a way with words."

He found the damp, hot flesh between her widely spread thighs and slowly slid a finger into her. She gasped and tightened around him. Gryph fought harder for his self-control. Slowly he withdrew his finger, his thumb gliding lightly over the small, secret bud of her desire in the process.

Sariana gave a tiny, choked cry. She rose to her knees in response to the new level of tension he was inducing. Gryph took advantage of the new position to trace the valley between her buttocks with his damp finger. Sariana quivered and inhaled deeply.

Gently he eased her back down until she was again sitting astride him. Her eyes were closed and he could see her tiny white teeth sinking into her lower lip. Her breasts were high and full with sexual tension. He could feel her reaching for the unknown conclusion to the exquisite torture and deliberately he stroked the fires within her with another slow insertion of his finger.

Again and again he repeated the slow, tantalizing caress, never filling her damp sheath as much as she craved, never removing his finger entirely. And always he finished the withdrawing stroke with a gentle circle around the beautifully sensitive nubbin sheltered in the triangular nest of hair.

Her climax hit her without warning. Gryph was taken as much by surprise as she was when it struck. One instant she was straining toward release, lost in the powerful new sensations that he was coaxing from her, and the next she was convulsing around his finger, crying out his name as her head tipped back and her eyes squeezed tightly shut.

The last of Gryph's self-control slipped from his grasp. The sudden onset of Sariana's intense climax pushed him into the heart of the storm he had been trying to manipulate and he was lost. He dug his fingers into her hips, lifting her and positioning her above him.

Then he pulled her down onto him with all his strength, sheathing himself in her tight, hot channel. Crying her name, he began to explode inside her almost at once.

Gryph could not shelter her from the force of his own release. It spilled into her, through her, over her just as his seed spilled deeply into her body.

His last coherent thought was that he could make Sariana pregnant. The knowledge filled him with joy.

Chapter
11

*P*REGNANT.

The word had seared its way into Sariana's mind at the climax of the lovemaking the night before and it seemed to be permanently implanted in her brain. She had been thinking about the implications most of the night. Her mind still reeled with them. She was fairly certain she was still in the safe zone of her monthly cycle, but every woman knew how unreliable such a method of contraception was.

As the anxious thoughts went through her head, Sariana was kneeling, fully dressed, on the cabin bunk. She was watching the activity on the docks of Little Chance through the multipaned window. The windrigger had just finished tying. Through the glass she could see laborers loading and unloading cargo from neighboring ships. In the distance she thought she could make out several rows of colorful pennants. Perhaps there was a fair going on in town.

"Little Chance looks like a busy place," Sariana remarked to Gryph as he moved purposefully about the cabin. He had bathed and shaved earlier and now he was intent on making preparations to go ashore.

"It is a busy place. Busiest port on the coast outside of Serendipity. Like most port towns, it's got its share of rough areas. That's why I want you to stay on board while I take care of my business. I'll only be gone a couple of hours."

"I can take care of myself, Gryph."

"The way you did yesterday morning in Serendipity when you tried to run from me?" He gave her an admonishing glance as he finished fastening his worn belt buckle. The buckle had definitely seen better days. The man carried a fortune in prisma in the form of a pouch lock but that appeared to be the sum total of his wealth. "Forget it. You stay right here and try not to get into any trouble. I'll have my plans made by the time I return. We might be taking a sled upriver. I'm not sure yet."

Sariana glanced over her shoulder. "What, exactly, are you going to do here?"

He sat down on the edge of the bunk, putting a sizable dent in the mattress, and tugged on his boots. "I'm going to see someone I know. An old friend. I want to discuss this matter of the cutter with him."

"He lives here? I thought Shields lived in the frontier towns. Little Chance is hardly a frontier town."

"Most Shields do live on the frontier. But not all. Delek chose to live in Little Chance because he no longer makes his living chasing bandits. And his lady prefers to live here. It's her home."

"Lucky woman. You mean your friend Delek actually gave her a choice?" Sariana didn't bother to hide the sarcasm.

Gryph raised one eyebrow at the tone of her voice but kept his own even. "Where they live isn't too critical in the case of Delek and his lady. They have no sons to be trained."

Sariana was suddenly very interested. "You mean the main reason Shields live out on the frontiers is because of the way they educate their children?"

"The main reason Shields prefer the frontier is because that's where the best employment opportunities are," Gryph muttered. "But educating sons is also a reason. It's difficult to train a young boy in the ways of the Shields while living in a city or town." Gryph stood up and reached for his jacket. "Too many distractions."

"Why doesn't Delek have any children?"

Gryph gave her a straight, blunt look as he fastened the plain buttons of his short jacket. "Delek and his lady, Alana, are not linked. She doesn't have the potential to be a Shieldmate, therefore the relationship is sterile."

Sariana stared at him in astonishment. "But Delek lives with her?"

"He's lived with her for years."

"You mean Shields sometimes get seriously involved with women with whom they don't believe they can, uh, link?"

"It's rare," Gryph said quietly, "but occasionally it happens. Sometimes a man just gives up the search for a Shieldmate. Sometimes a Shield loses his mate through death or adultery and he doesn't have the heart or interest to search for another, so he settles for a relationship that promises companionship or love. That's what Delek did."

"Love." Sariana went very still, her mind whirling as she absorbed this new information. "A Shield might fall in love with a woman even though she isn't a Shieldmate?"

Gryph smiled wryly. "Haven't you lived in Serendipity long enough to know that love doesn't always respect custom, law or social traditions?"

Sariana traced the intricate details of a massive reptilian head that had been carved into the bunk's headboard. "But if a Shield finds a mate with whom he thinks he can link—"

"It's not a question of thinking he can link with her," Gryph said impatiently. "He either can or can't. The link isn't a function of a man's imagination. It's very real. A Shield knows almost as soon as he meets a woman whether or not he can mate with her. One of these days you'll understand that."

Sariana focused her attention outside the window again and prepared to pursue her next question with quiet determination. She had to know the answer, she realized. "All right, I won't argue that right now."

"That's a relief."

Sariana lost her temper for a few seconds. "What I want to know is whether or not Shields ever marry for love. Or does this ... this linking eventually create love between a Shield and his mate?"

There was a heartbeat of silence behind her. Then Gryph answered coolly. "Do easterners ever marry for love?"

Sariana swallowed uncomfortably. "Rarely."

"They usually marry for business reasons, right?" Gryph persisted.

"Yes."

"Well, Shields marry for business reasons, too. In our case, the business is that of ensuring the survival of the next generation. Love is not an essential factor in that business. Sometimes it's present, sometimes it's not."

Sariana swung around to confront him. "But what about the passion that comes with this linking thing?"

"What about it?" Gryph replied offhandedly. "Linked sex is usually great sex for both people concerned. That kind of passion can form a strong bond between them. But that hasn't got anything to do with love. Don't tell me a sophisticated easterner like you doesn't know that passion can exist without love? An interesting, passionate relationship without the complications of love was exactly what you planned to have with me when you made the decision to start an affair, wasn't it?"

He was taunting her and Sariana was suddenly furious. It was all she could do to keep a grasp on her self-control. What she really longed to do was pick up her slipper and hurl it at him. For an instant the satisfying image of Gryph ducking the small projectile was very vivid in her head.

Gryph held up a hand. He gazed briefly at the slippers lying beside the bunk. When he lifted his eyes to her face again, they were glimmering with a cryptic satisfaction. "Please don't. I haven't got time this morning to use that slipper on your backside which is what I would feel obliged to do if you throw it at me."

Sariana glared at him. "Don't pretend you can read my mind. I know that's impossible. You just took an educated guess. It wouldn't be hard to figure out I'm annoyed with you and that slipper is the only convenient object at hand."

"And you do have a penchant for throwing things at me when you lose your temper," he concluded helpfully as he started toward the cabin door. "You're right, Sariana. It was just an educated guess. I'll see you early this afternoon. Try to stay out of trouble while I'm gone."

Sariana knelt upright on the bunk, her hands clenched. She stared at the door as it closed behind him. "And you, Gryph Chassyn," she informed the empty room, "have a penchant for giving orders. But I never agreed to obey them. We have a business arrangement. Just a mutually beneficial truce while we hunt for that cutter. That's all I agreed to last night. And I've got news for you, Lord Chassyn: when it comes to conducting business, I'm a thousand times faster and smarter than some dumb, arrogant, muscle-brained frontier lord who scrapes out a living hunting bandits."

She jumped off the bed and went to find her walking shoes. The scarlet-toe peeked over the edge of a cloak pocket where it had spent the night and hissed inquiringly.

"That's right, Lucky, we're busting out of here. There isn't a jail made that can hold us, pal. You and I are going to escape this joint for a few hours. Come on, let's go."

She picked up her cloak, settled the lizard onto her shoulder and made for the door.

She was involved in a business arrangement. She had that on good authority. The best. A Shield himself had told her so. Well, so be it.

The first order of business was to find a medic.

It wasn't hard to locate a female medic in Little Chance. An hour after she had left the windrigger, Sariana found herself talking bluntly with a competent, older woman who specialized in treating women. The medic wore the ancient

insignia of a serpent and staff which harked back to the
symbol of the medics who had been on board *The Serendipity.*

"Now, you're certain you understand how to dampen
and insert this little sponge?" the medic asked for the last
time.

Sariana nodded a little dubiously. "It seems simple
enough."

"It is. Effective, too. If it's used regularly. Don't think
you can skip a time or two. You must use it every time you
have sex."

"I understand."

The medic frowned. "Are you certain you don't want me
to give you something that your male friend can use also?
It would provide an extra margin of safety."

Sariana tried to imagine the reaction she would get from
Gryph if she presented him with a package of male contraceptives. "I don't think he would use anything."

The medic eyed her patient disapprovingly. "A woman
should think twice about getting involved with a man who
refuses to assume his share of the responsibility."

Sariana sighed. "I know. The problem is, he's a Shield
and I don't think he would—"

"A Shield!" The woman stared at her in astonishment.
"Then why are you worrying about contraceptives? There's
no danger of him getting you pregnant."

"Is that really true?" Sariana asked urgently. It was the
first reliable confirmation she'd had of what she had been
told. Surely a medic would not give credence to a legend
unless there was some genuine fact at the base of it.

"Of course it's true." The medic shook her head. "I keep
forgetting you easterners know very little about our ways
and you probably know nothing about Shields. To be honest, most of us don't talk about them too much to outsiders. I suppose we're a little in awe of them, even after
all these years of coexisting with them. But since you're
involved with one, you should know some facts. He can't
get you pregnant unless you're his Shieldmate, and if that's
the case, you can forget the contraceptives. He'll go

through prisma fire to get you pregnant. The last thing he would do is allow you to use anything. Not unless the pregnancy would endanger your life. And even in that rare situation I've heard of Shields and their mates taking a chance."

"Having children is so important to a Shield?"

The medic shrugged. "It's a matter of survival. As a class they are hanging on by their fingernails, one notch above extinction. Their birthrate is extremely low, even when the men manage to find mates. And they produce no female children. Without females of their own, Shields have a very shaky hold on reproduction. Each new generation of men must search for a mate among the other social classes, and the odds of finding a woman who can be a Shieldmate are not good. There's no way to test for the potential in a woman. Even if it were possible, I doubt that many respectable families would want their daughters tested."

"I think I can guess why," Sariana said dryly.

The medic shrugged. "A woman who marries a Shield leaves her clan and social class to join the Shield class. Practically speaking, that means she winds up living in some far-off mountain fortress town. Not too many women are anxious to give up their friends, family and the comforts of city life to keep house out on the frontier."

"I think I get the picture," Sariana said quietly. So part of what Gryph had told her was true. "After all these years of marrying non-Shield women, though, haven't their bloodlines become diluted?"

"They only care about the talent for working prisma. And that appears to be a dominant trait that is passed along by the males through certain receptive females. Just like their odd eye color. Neither eye color nor the skill with prisma shows any sign of weakening in successive generations. No medic pretends to understand the whole biological process, and Shields don't talk about it much to outsiders, but facts are facts. As long as a Shield can find a true mate, he can reproduce his own kind."

"But what kind is that?" Sariana asked in confusion. "What is this talk of working prisma?"

"You said you were involved in an affair with a Shield," the medic observed slowly.

"He tells me that under the law we're married," Sariana said ruefully.

The medic was startled. "You're his wife? A Shield-mate? Then I definitely think you should put your questions to him. I don't know enough to answer them completely for you, anyway. Furthermore, he probably would not take kindly to my attempting to educate you. Shields can be very difficult about matters they consider Shield business."

Sariana nodded in resignation. "Thank you, Medic Vallon."

"You're welcome." The medic eyed Sariana closely. "Are you really some Shield's mate?" she asked thoughtfully.

Sariana's hand closed around the package the medic had just given her. "He seems to think I am."

"And you intend to avoid getting pregnant?"

"It would ruin my whole future," Sariana whispered. "I'm not staying here, you see. Eventually I'll be going home to the eastern provinces. I was born and raised in Rendezvous. I'm only here for a year or two."

The medic shook her head uneasily. "This is the first time I have ever heard of a Shield finding a mate from the eastern provinces. Now that there is growing contact between us, this sort of situation may become more common. Unfortunately, no provision was made for it in the First Generation Pact the colonists made with the Shields."

Sariana didn't like the somber tone in the other woman's voice. "Why is it so unfortunate?"

Medic Vallon looked at her. "You can trust a Shield with your life. Everyone in the west knows that to a Shield, his word is his bond. They adhere rigidly to the terms of the Pact. But they are a desperate class who face extinction with each new generation. If they discover that they can find mates in the eastern provinces, you can be certain they will start searching for them there as well as here. But the people of the eastern continent have no pact with which to control them."

Sariana's mouth went dry. "Are they so very dangerous? It sounds like there are only a few of them."

"Any intelligent being facing extinction would probably become dangerous out of desperation. But in the case of the Shields, the business of being dangerous takes on new meaning. The luck of the day to you, Sariana Dayne. I'm beginning to think you will need it. A word of warning. If I were you, I would not let your Shield know about that little sponge I just gave you. If he does find out, I would consider it a great favor if you would avoid telling him who prescribed it for you."

There was a light, misty rain falling by the time Sariana reached the street. A disgusted hiss from Lucky made Sariana pause long enough to reach up and remove the lizard from her shoulder.

"So you don't like getting wet, hmm? Here you go. I hope that suits you." She popped the scarlet-toe into a pocket of her cloak and then pulled up the hood to cover her hair. The hissing stopped as the lizard settled down into the comfortable pocket. Sariana put the package she had gotten from the medic into another pocket.

If she hadn't gotten lost on the way back to the docks, she would never have stumbled onto the fair. It was being held at the edge of town and the array of brightly colored tents, awnings and flags stretched as far as Sariana could see. The misting rain did not seem to affect the enthusiasm of the crowds. The fairgrounds were thronged with brilliantly garbed people.

Sariana was fascinated. There was no equivalent to it in the eastern provinces. A few of the farming towns had annual festivals, but nothing on this scale. She found herself sucked into the crowds before she knew what had happened. The shouts of audiences and hucksters mingled with music and the screams of overexcited children. Warm, fragrant smells filled the air near the food booths and more acrid, earthy scents emanated from the animal stalls.

Sariana wandered for over an hour, taking in an exhibition of magic, staring in amused wonder at a muscleman who could lift an entire dragonpony off the ground, and listening to balladeers.

She turned a corner at one point and found herself in an aisle of craft booths. Idly she began studying the wares that were offered for sale. When she spotted a handsome metal belt buckle on display beneath a cheerful blue awning, she stopped.

The buckle was beautifully made. With an eye that had been trained for over a year in the Avylyn household, Sariana judged the craftsmanship and found it very satisfying. The motif was a finely executed head of a bird of prey. Its eyes were set with small, perfectly faceted stones that resembled prisma, although Sariana knew from the price of the object that the stones could not possibly be genuine crystal. The creature's black and gold feathers were fashioned in beautiful cloisonne work.

An image of Gryph's worn leather belt and scarred buckle flashed into Sariana's mind.

In that moment the vendor spotted her and rushed forward excitedly. "You have an eye for beauty, my lady. This is the finest piece in my collection. It was done by a member of my own clan. We're closely related to the Avylyns, you know. You've heard of them, of course?"

Sariana smiled faintly. It was not unusual for a provincial jewelers' clan to claim kinship with one of the Prime Families in the social class. The relationship was usually extremely distant if it existed at all. "As a matter of fact, I have. I have worked for the Avylyns in Serendipity for the past year."

The man's eyes widened in astonished pleasure. "By the Lightstorm! No wonder you picked out this buckle. You have been well trained. I will let you have it for a fraction of its true value. Clan discount, of course."

"That's very kind of you, but I'm really not certain I

want the buckle," Sariana said quickly. "I was just admiring it."

"Please," the vendor begged. "I want you to have it. It's you, my lady."

"Me? But it's a man's buckle . . . "

The man dismissed that with an extravagant wave of his hand. "It was made for you to give to a man. A husband, perhaps? A father? A brother? A lover? Who knows? It will be the perfect gift for some man who is important to you."

"I'm sure I couldn't possibly afford it, even with a clan discount. It's too beautifully made."

"Nonsense," the vendor said briskly, rubbing his hands. "I feel certain we can come to some agreement on the matter of price."

A few minutes later, Sariana, who had only been toying with the idea of buying the buckle, walked away from the booth with a package.

She was still wondering how a sophisticated businesswoman such as herself had gotten talked into buying something she really didn't need when she found herself passing a theater tent. It was the picture on the poster outside that drew her attention. The play that was about to be performed was a torrid bit of romantic adventure set in First Generation days. The story involved the Pact made between the Shields and the colonists.

Unable to resist finding out more about the western legend with which she had unwittingly become involved, Sariana let herself be caught up in the crowd pouring into the little theater. She wound up sitting next to a small boy named Keri who was obviously a great fan of First Generation tales. He had a krellcat draped over one shoulder. Keri took delight in telling Sariana what was going to happen onstage.

"How many times have you seen this play?" Sariana asked just as the play began.

"Five times this week," he whispered back proudly. "Look," he told her as the curtain rose, "the First Generation people are on board the ship. The explosions that nearly wrecked *The Serendipity* have just taken place. See all the blood and stuff?"

"Yes," Sariana said, surveying the realistic props. "I can see all the blood." With typical western theatrical abandon the stage was littered with a lot of red sauce and imitation body parts.

"Pretty soon the fire will break out," Keri went on importantly. Someone in the row behind him shushed him. He lowered his voice but he didn't stop talking. "Everybody thinks they're going to die."

Pandemonium reigned onstage as the embattled starship fought for its life. In spite of herself, Sariana got a lump in her throat. This part of the legend was not too different from the story in the surviving records of the First Generation of *The Rendezvous*. It didn't take much imagination to conjure up the panic and despair that had gripped the people aboard the ships. They had come so far and were so very near their destination and now they were threatened with annihilation.

"This is where *The Serendipity* loses track of *The Rendezvous* and everyone assumes *The Rendezvous* is destroyed," Keri said excitedly. Again he was shushed from the back row.

"Now what's happening?" Sariana asked in genuine confusion as a great light flashed on stage. It blinded both the audience and the actors for a few seconds.

"The Lightstorm," Keri explained in enthusiastic horror. "It's attacking the ship and everyone is going to die."

"What Lightstorm?"

"The one caused by the crystal ships," Keri whispered. "Don't you know anything?"

"There are times lately when I've wondered about that."

Bit by bit, with Keri's help, Sariana managed to put the tale together. According to the legend, *The Serendipity* had dealt with more than an explosion on board. She had also been faced with an indescribable storm of light that had deadened every piece of equipment on the ship. Unlike *The Rendezvous*, which had retained enough power to manage a controlled crash landing, *The Serendipity* had been utterly helpless. The ship had plummeted into the blazing storm of light.

"This is where the Shields arrive," Keri said excitedly. "Watch."

Sariana watched in astonishment as the legend took a bizarre twist. In a suspenseful sequence a strange ship materialized alongside *The Serendipity*. It was obviously caught in the grip of the Lightstorm, too, but it seemed able to control the descent of both itself and *The Serendipity* to some extent. It acted as a shield for the starship, leading the way through the storm of light. When it was through the storm, some of *The Serendipity*'s power was restored. She limped down through the atmosphere and made a landing similar to the one *The Rendezvous* had made. Fire had broken out immediately.

"The ship burned for days," Keri explained with relish. "The Shields helped fight it. But that wasn't the main problem."

"What was the main problem?" Sariana asked in fascination.

"The crew rebelled and tried to take control of all the other colonists. They had the only weapons on board and they threatened to kill everyone who didn't obey orders. See? There's one now. He's going to kill the captain who's trying to stop him."

Sariana was shocked as the poor starship captain died gallantly onstage in a very bloody fight. "How terrible." At least the people of *The Rendezvous* had been spared that particular trauma. The rigid lines of society had held firm throughout the chaos of the landing and its aftermath in the east. But they had apparently started crumbling right from the beginning here in the west.

"Oh, everything turned out okay. The Shields took care of the rebels. The Shields had weapons, too, and they used them against the outlaws. The bad members of the crew who weren't killed ran away and hid in the mountains. After that, the colonists found out about the prisma crystal ships. The one that had caused the Lightstorm was just one of many. There were lots more of them hidden in the mountains. Only the Shields knew how to neutralize the weapons on board."

"The Shields protected the colonists?"

"Sure. That's why we have the Pact. Don't you remember?"

"I'm not too familiar with the story," Sariana admitted cautiously.

"They brought *The Serendipity* safely through the Lightstorm and they protected the First Generation colonists from the rebels and the crystal ships. If they hadn't done that, none of us would be here now."

"I see. But, Keri, who are the Shields? Where did they come from?"

Keri shrugged. "They were here when we got here." He accepted that astounding piece of information with a youngster's unquestioning faith in legends. "I think my father once said they had come to hunt the crystal ships and got trapped here along with the First Generation colonists. They couldn't get back off the planet any more than we could."

Sariana was reeling with the ramifications of the tale. It couldn't be true, she told herself staunchly. Just another manifestation of the westerners' love of storytelling and drama.

But it was getting increasingly difficult to dismiss the tale of the Shields. Her own life was being turned upside down by a walking legend.

Sariana rose at intermission. She felt a sudden need to escape.

"Where are you going?" Keri asked. "Don't you want to see what happens when the Shields find out they can marry a few of the colonial women?"

"Not particularly. I need some fresh air."

Keri got up. "I don't blame you. The first half is the best part. The next act is kind of mushy." He trailed after Sariana, chatting happily.

"Where are your parents, Keri?" Sariana asked as they emerged into the mist.

"I don't have to meet them until lunchtime. How long are you going to be at the fair?"

"I can't stay long." Sariana checked the elaborate little timepiece the Avylyns had given her on her birthday. Gryph had said he would be returning to the windrigger in the early afternoon. It would probably be best if she were on board when he arrived, she decided wryly. The fewer explanations she was called upon to make to Gryph, the easier life would be. "I'm supposed to meet someone in an hour or so."

"You can't leave without seeing the House of Reflections," Keri said anxiously. "Come on, I'll show you. It's the best thing at the fair. Even better than the play about the First Generation colonists."

"How far away is it?" Sariana glanced around dubiously.

"It's at the far end of the fairgrounds, but I know a shortcut." He caught hold of Sariana's hand. "Let's go. It's a lot of fun."

Sariana smiled down at him, unable to resist his enthusiasm. Keri reminded her a bit of Luri, and she was surprised to realize she missed the youngest Avylyn. "All right. Let's go see this House of Reflections. Then I really must be going."

"It's great," Keri assured her as he pulled her into the crowds.

Sariana was totally disoriented by the time the boy stopped in front of a garishly decorated structure. Unlike the other booths, this was not a tent. The outer walls appeared quite solid and they were covered with intricately beveled reflective surfaces. It was gaudy enough beneath an overcast sky. In the full glare of a noonday sun, Sariana decided, it would be impossible to look directly at the thing because of the intense reflections.

"It's very large," she observed as she stood with her young escort and watched crowds of laughing people walk toward the entrance.

"Once you're inside, it looks like it goes on forever because of the way the mirrors and the prisms work. Wait'll you see it. I've been in there four times already and I'm going in again. I know my way around inside now. Come on, Sariana. I want to show it to you."

Sariana reluctantly bought two tickets and followed Keri through the mirrored doors. "I really should be getting back to the ship, Keri."

"We won't stay long," he promised.

An instant later they stepped into total darkness. Delighted screams of mock fright echoed in the blackness. Keri let go of Sariana's hand. She groped for him, glancing around uneasily and seeing absolutely nothing. The room was perfectly sealed. No outside light penetrated anywhere.

"Keri?"

"Over here, Sariana."

She tried to edge toward the sound of his voice, but the total darkness was confusing. She called out again.

This time there was no response.

"Keri? Where are you?"

Not only was there no answer from Keri, there was no longer a sense of anyone else being present either. The laughter and screams of delight had faded. She didn't brush up against anyone when she turned around in the inky dark. Sariana edged backward, seeking the door through which she had entered.

In that moment the room was suddenly flooded with light. Far too much of it. Bright, blazing, multi-colored light bounced off a thousand beveled surfaces and ricocheted from an endless corridor of mirrors. Countless pieces of prismatic glass dangled from a ceiling that appeared to have no permanent structure.

When she glanced up Sariana could see a million Sariana Daynes receding into the distance. When she looked down she had a wrenching attack of vertigo. She appeared to be suspended over a bottomless sea of reflective surfaces. Beneath her feet her own image was disrupted and reorganized in a kaleidoscopic array of color and light. She couldn't tell where the reflected images left off and her feet began. It was the most dizzying, disorienting sensation she had ever experienced.

The really unnerving part was that there was no sign of Keri or anyone else. She was alone in a hall full of endless reflections.

Sariana didn't begin to get nervous until she realized she couldn't find the exit.

Fear set in when she became aware that someone was stalking her through the maze of mirrors.

Chapter
12

SARIANA heard the laughter first. Stifled, malicious giggles and wildly excited bursts that were nervously cut off. Then the flapping edge of a cape filled the room, only to vanish an instant later as if the owner had retreated to some safe spot.

A low hiss from Sariana's cloak pocket announced the scarlet-toe's questioning concern.

"Hush," Sariana said soothingly. "I just need to find the door, that's all."

But she couldn't find the door. Every time she moved in a new direction the whole geography of the room shifted around her. It was like being in the center of a kaleidoscope. She tried closing her eyes and walking in a straight line, one hand extended in front of her, but that only led her into another dazzling room. This one was even worse than the last.

She thought she found a flight of mirrored steps, each tread a shifting maze of refracted light, but when she tried to climb them, they flattened beneath her and turned into a mirrored slide.

Sariana screamed as her feet went out from under her. She sat down hard on the slick surface and found herself sliding down an endless corridor. When she skidded to a halt she was in still another room.

"Are you all right, Lucky?" Anxiously she checked the cloak pocket. Her fingers touched the little lizard and she was reassured by the feel of her small companion. The scarlet-toe was not happy, however. Sariana felt a distinct nip on the tip of her finger. Not hard enough to draw blood, but sufficient to register the protest.

"I'm sorry," Sariana whispered. "I'll try yelling for help."

She sat in the middle of a room that was constantly shifting around her and screamed for assistance.

The only response was another malicious giggle.

Panic began to set in. On her hands and knees, figuring that was the best way to keep in touch with the only firm surface she could identify, Sariana began crawling in a straight line.

She might as well have been crawling through another dimension. After a while she began to wonder if she was really moving or if that, too, was an illusion. The countless copies of Sariana Dayne reflected around her seemed to move when she did, but they obviously weren't getting anywhere.

Sariana stopped, perplexed and thoroughly frightened. She took several deep breaths to control her fear and then tried to reason her way out of the dilemma. She badly needed to find some solid surface, if only for her peace of mind.

Kneeling on the bottomless floor, Sariana took off one shoe and rapped the heel smartly against the reflective surface. She was rewarded by a tiny fissure. But the crack only seemed to cause another set of disorienting reflections. Sariana struck the flooring again. The faceted mirror surface was tough. It had to be to stand up to thousands of pairs of fairgoers' feet.

Before she could try a third blow, the harsh giggles floated down the endless corridors again. Sariana froze and then scooted backward as a million booted feet suddenly appeared ahead of her. The boots were quickly withdrawn but Sariana knew they would return.

Frantically she glanced around, seeking some means of defense. She reached for what she thought was a dangling mirror, hoping to break it and secure a sharp piece of glass. But the mirror was just another illusion, the reflection of some other mirror. She groped wildly, but it was impossible to find the original.

The booted feet appeared again and so did the laughter. This time there was a voice. It sounded to Sariana like the voice of a teenaged male, but she couldn't be certain.

"She's in the next room, I tell you. She'll be terrified right out of her mind by now. Come on, let's close in."

"Not so fast." The second voice also sounded young and masculine. "The guy said we were to make sure she was good and scared first, remember? She isn't even screaming yet. Not really. I want to hear her scream."

"All right," the first boy said. "But let's at least get closer. We can't even see her yet. I want to see her face."

"Yeah," giggled a third voice, "let's get closer. Let's see how scared she gets."

The lizard hissed softly as Sariana inched backward. "I know, Lucky," Sariana muttered softly, "I'm not having an especially good time either. I hate to admit it, but I wish Gryph were here. He'd probably chew me up one side and down the other, but at least I wouldn't have to worry about those boys."

The realization that she was starting to chatter nervously made Sariana abruptly close her mouth. She kept retreating down a mirrored hall that seemed to vanish into the distance behind her. The worst part was that she wasn't even certain she was moving away from the voices and the booted feet. Given the crazy layout of the House of Reflections she might very well be heading straight into the clutches of the young males who were stalking her.

She scrambled on all fours around another turn in the

neverending hallway and barely stifled a shriek as she confronted a giant image of herself.

Sariana blinked, struggling to adjust to this new distortion. Sariana Dayne as a monster was an interesting sight. It was all a trick of mirrors and light, but the effect was uncanny. The huge Sariana seemed to be floating freely in the center of a small circular room. Sariana stared thoughtfully at the huge reflection of herself and wished very badly she really was that big and powerful. At the moment it would be quite useful.

"Come on," said a voice, "let's try this hall. I think I got a glimpse of her cape."

"Good thing we've been through this place a lot and know what to expect," one of the other teenagers observed with a nervous chuckle. "It's kind of spooky, even now."

"You shouldn't have offered to take this job if you were going to scare so easily," chided one of the others.

"I'm not scared, I just said it would be kind of weird trying to trail someone through here if you hadn't been through it a lot of times before."

"I think Holt really is getting scared," observed the first voice.

"Well, you're not exactly acting like a Shield, yourself," Holt retorted angrily. "Look at you. Your hands are shaking."

"They are not," the other boy shouted back, his voice much too high. "Shut up, Holt, or I swear, I'll smash you right into one of these dumb mirrors."

"Shut up, both of you," the third voice snapped. "You're going to ruin everything. Let's get going. I think it's time we closed in on her. That guy will be waiting."

Sariana moved into the center of the circular room and removed her cloak. Standing in the middle of the distorting chamber she no longer saw a giant version of herself. The image had disappeared when she moved into the heart of it. Lucky hissed softly as Sariana removed the lizard from her pocket. The crimson head swiveled quickly, jeweled eyes taking in the room, immediately dismissing the dazzling effect of light and mirrors.

"Good," Sariana murmured. "In some ways you're a lot smarter than a human. You know how to tell the real from the false, don't you?"

Lucky tasted Sariana's thumb with a tiny forked tongue. She placed the little lizard down on the mirrored floor and settled the edge of her cloak over it.

"I want you to stay right here, Lucky. Don't move. Do you understand?" Sariana swallowed a groan. "Of course you don't understand. How could you? But you're accustomed to my cloak so you shouldn't mind spending a few minutes under it."

The lizard moved its head back and forth a few times and hissed questioningly as the edge of the cloak was draped over it, but it stayed put, as if it understood.

"Good Lucky," Sariana murmured as she edged to the far side of the room. She stretched out the fabric of the cloak, keeping a grasp on one corner but leaving the opposite end over the scarlet-toe. She had barely positioned herself when she heard the excited voices of the boys.

"I'll bet she went this way. Come on, hurry. This is going to be fun."

There was another burst of nervous laughter and then a thousand teenage males filled the corridor that led into the distortion chamber. Sariana could see three distinct versions of the countless images. Three young toughs reflected into an army. They raced toward the room in which she crouched.

All three charged gleefully through the doorway. It was a tight fit.

Sariana yanked the cloak off of the scarlet-toe. The little lizard raised its head to see what all the commotion was about and then it opened its tiny mouth.

There were loud screams from the doorway as the young toughs confronted a giant image of Lucky Break. Sariana had a good idea of what the boys were seeing. The small, needle-sharp teeth of the lizard probably appeared as long as a man's arm under the effects of the distorting mirrors. The mouth was big enough to swallow that same man. Giant claws and a nasty, whipping tail would complete the image. And the shock of it all would be reinforced by huge crimson eyes.

The entire production was sufficient to send three already nervous and overly excited boys into a wild stampede back down the mirrored hall.

Sariana didn't hesitate. Given a few minutes to reconsider, all three were likely to come to the conclusion that they'd been had. She didn't want to be trapped in the mirrored room when that happened. Sariana scooped up Lucky and her cloak and headed down the same mirrored corridor the boys had just used. She could hear their boots on the floor as they raced for an exit.

"They seem to know their way out of here," Sariana told the scarlet-toe. "We'll try to follow them." Some of the crazy landscape was slightly familiar, she realized as she started to retrace her steps. She recognized certain distortions and optical effects that she had seen when she had been trying to flee from the boys.

Sariana was several meters down the corridor, feeling her way carefully so as not to run headlong into a sheet of mirrored glass, when she heard a new chorus of frightened teenage yells.

Wondering what had further alarmed her would-be stalkers, she slowed her pace and nearly stumbled over three huddled, jabbering youths as she rounded a mirrored curve and emerged into a large hall of brilliant lights and endless reflections.

It was easy to see what had reduced the teens to a state of abject terror. Under the circumstances, this set of images was probably even more intimidating than the giant version of Lucky.

The boys were confronting a thousand Shields, all of them ready for battle and all of them coldly, grimly angry.

Sariana took one look at the cascading images and nearly shouted her relief.

"Gryph."

Gryph had arrived at Delek's home on the outskirts of Little Chance soon after leaving the windrigger. He knew the way because he had visited the older man several times in the past. Delek was one of the men who had trained Gryph in the ways of prisma as well as the arts of bandit hunting. At the time Delek had lived in the same small frontier town as Gryph's family and had been married to a Shieldmate named Penela. There had been no sons.

Gryph had been young when Penela had died and remembered her only vaguely. What he did recall quite vividly was Delek's quiet acceptance of his wife's death. It had surprised Gryph at the time. He had assumed that the loss of a Shieldmate would be a devastating experience, especially when there had been no sons.

He had been as startled as everyone else when Delek, still a man in his prime, had made no effort to find another Shieldmate. Instead he had moved to Little Chance and found Alana, the daughter of a small textile design clan. There had been no marriage. Alana could not be accepted as a Shieldmate, and Delek was too proud to give up his own heritage in exchange for adoption into his lady's clan. The two had been living together so long that everyone had quietly accepted the situation.

Delek received his unexpected guest in a garden that was in full bloom. Gryph admired it as he sank into a carved wooden chair.

"It looks as though your hobby has turned into a full-time job, Delek."

The older man grinned in satisfaction and put aside the cane he used. "I keep busy. And I keep food on the table."

Gryph arched a brow. "Is there money in gardening?"

"Theoretically no, not unless you're a member of a horticulture clan," Delek admitted. "You know that as well as I do. But I've been doing some deals on the side with the Westelyn Clan. They grow flowers for the wholesale market. They've been paying good prices for some of my hybrid seeds. Between that and what Alana earns with her weaving designs we do all right. Fortunately. Since I took that bandit's blade in my knee two years ago, I haven't been fit for hunting or anything else. Amazing how hard it is to get along with a bad knee."

Alana emerged from the house, a good-looking, middle-aged woman with a stately carriage and soft eyes. She was carrying a tray of ale and crackers. "If I have anything to say about it, Delek won't ever accept another mercenary job or go back to fighting frontier bandits. I much prefer him working with flowers. This way the only thing I have to worry about is having him get stuck with a thorn or two."

Gryph smiled at her as he accepted the ale. "I can see there are some definite benefits to gardening."

Alana set the tray down, casting a shrewd glance at Gryph. "Correct me if I'm wrong, but I get the feeling this is not a routine visit to an old friend."

Gryph shrugged, unwilling to be rude, but anxious to get on with what he had come for. "I came to ask Delek's advice about certain matters."

"Ah, Shield business," Alana said knowingly. "I will leave you two to discuss it in private."

Delek frowned. "It's not necessary for you to leave us, my dear."

She shook her head, smiling slightly. "I think Gryph would be more comfortable if I went inside. I'll see you both later." She walked through the garden, the skirts of her yellow gown lightly brushing the heads of some of Delek's beautiful flowers.

Gryph saw the expression on Delek's face as Alana left. Love and pride and quiet satisfaction were clearly evident. Gryph raised his glass of ale.

"To your lady," he said formally.

"I'll drink to that." Delek took a long swallow from his own glass. "Now, let's get the business over with. Tell me what brings you so unexpectedly to Little Chance."

Gryph put his glass down and leaned forward, resting his elbows on his thighs. "I think someone has found a crystal ship, Delek."

Delek stared at him. "There hasn't been a ship found for over fifty years."

"I know. But someone has stolen a prisma cutter. Two men have died because of that cutter. One of those men was an informant I occasionally use in Serendipity. Before he died he told me there were rumors of the cutter being taken north to Little Chance. Little Chance is the last town before one heads into the region that contains the Gorge of Storms."

Delek sat forward, watching Gryph carefully. "The last few crystal ships were found in the gorge."

"I know."

"Shields searched the region thoroughly after they neutralized those ships to determine if there might be any more."

"That was over fifty years ago. It's possible a ship was missed."

Delek nodded slowly. "Possible. Not probable, but possible. The terrain of the gorge is tricky. The rock formations there can conceal prisma rays. Have you sent word to the frontier towns?"

"No. I haven't dared. For one thing, I don't think I have enough time to get a message to the borders and wait for the arrival of other Shields. For another, I'd have to trust the message to someone outside our class and I can't do that."

"Why not?"

Gryph sighed. "Because," he said carefully, "I think there's a rogue behind all this."

Delek stared at him. "Are you certain?"

"No. But my informant, the one who died, thought there was a Shield involved. Brinton's information was invariably accurate."

"I see your problem," Delek said. "This is truly Shield business, then. The possibility of another prisma crystal ship having been found is bad enough. But if a Shield has gone rogue, we're all in very serious trouble. Remember Targyn?"

"I remember." Gryph gazed at the flowers around him, remembering the tale he had once told Luri. "Luckily he's become pure legend."

"Had he lived, he would have been a very dangerous man," Delek said. "He had delusions of grandeur, I'm afraid. He dreamed of controlling prisma, you know. He wanted to test the old theories. He used to talk about it all the time. When no one supported his ideas he started spending more and more time alone in the mountains hunting bandits all by himself. He was crazy. No doubt about it. A real rogue Shield. Everyone was relieved when he met a glorious end. Saved us from having to send someone into the mountains to take care of him."

"Don't remind me," Gryph muttered. "I got the impression I might have been elected to do the job."

"Oh, no doubt about it," Delek assured him cheerfully. "There aren't many men who could have taken Targyn. You're one of the few who might have been able to do it. He was good. Damn good."

"Luckily for me Targyn passed into legend all by himself." Gryph paused, thinking. "Is there any other Shield in the area right now?"

"Not as far as I know. There haven't been many Shields through Little Chance during the past few months. No reason. Their work is out on the frontier and if they're looking for wives, they usually head for Serendipity or one of the bigger towns to the south."

"I couldn't find anyone in Serendipity and I haven't got time to search any other towns along the way."

"I'll come with you," Delek said flatly. "I may not be of much use because of this game leg, but it looks like I'm all you've got in the way of backup. I assume you're going into the gorge?"

"It's the only lead I've got. But I've given this some thought, Delek. I've decided it would be better if you took care of contacting the frontier clans. You know as well as I do that it has to be done in person. We can't take the risk of letting outsiders know a Shield may have gone rogue."

Delek nodded. "We'll have to take care of everything ourselves. I'll leave at once. It will take a few days, even with the fastest dragonponies."

"Good. We'll leave for the gorge this afternoon."

"We?" Delek asked quickly.

Gryph permitted himself a small, satisfied grin. He lifted

his glass. "Congratulate me, Delek. I've found a Shield-mate."

Delek smiled and raised his glass. "A cause for congrat-ulations, indeed. Your clan will be pleased. What is your wife's name?"

"Sariana Dayne. She's from the eastern provinces."

"Interesting," Delek mused. "I have not heard of any mates being found among the women of the east, but I suppose it's reasonable to assume there are some potential Shieldmates there. That should be good news to the clans."

"There are some complications with an eastern Shield-mate," Gryph admitted.

"Such as?"

"As far as she's concerned, the First Generation Pact between Shields and the colonists doesn't apply to her. After all, her people did not make any treaty with the Shields."

Delek gaped at him in amazement. "By the Lightstorm, Gryph, I hadn't thought about that. She's right." Delek grinned slowly, a very feral smile that reminded Gryph of the hunter Delek had once been. "But by the same token, she is not protected by the Pact."

"Nevertheless," Gryph stated proudly, "I followed the rules."

"But did she know the rules before you took her to bed?" Delek asked slyly.

"Things were rather confused that night," Gryph admit-ted. "There wasn't time or opportunity to give her an edu-cation on the history of Shields and colonists."

Delek roared with laughter and slapped his thigh. "I'll just bet there wasn't time. Did she open your kit the next morning?"

"Easily." Gryph smiled with pride. "As easily as if she were a Shield trained in working prisma and had her own kit. It was amazing."

"What does she think of this whole affair?"

Gryph shrugged and picked up his glass. "As I said, she refuses to concede that she's even married, let alone that anything unusual happened the night I linked with her. She insists she had a little too much to drink that evening."

"But she is with you now?"

Gryph opened one hand in a gesture. "Naturally. And she'll stay with me whether she likes it or not. I think someone has figured out she can be used to control me."

Delek met his gaze knowingly. "Another Shield would know that. But so would any westerner who is reasonably well-versed in Shield history. It's no secret that a Shield-mate is a very valuable commodity to a Shield, even if he would like to throttle her at times."

Gryph eyed Delek in surprise. "There have been one or two times already when I could willingly have taken my belt to Sariana's backside. She is willful, independent and smart. I'm learning that that is a dangerous combination in a woman."

Delek was amused. "True. What else is she?"

Gryph smiled. "She's also warm and gentle underneath her thorns, rather like one of your prize flowers, Delek. She has pride and strength. She's brave and gutsy, too. Back in Serendipity she nearly killed a man who was trying to assault her. Getting her to follow even the most reasonable of orders is proving to be a challenge, however."

Delek's grin broadened as he listened to the growing list of attributes. "A true Shieldmate for you, Gryph. You need a woman you can't intimidate."

"Intimidate! I don't intimidate women."

Delek laughed. "Your instinct is to dominate any situation in which you find yourself. It sounds as though you've found a woman who can deal with that aspect of your nature. You are indeed a lucky man. But I think you are also going to be a very busy man. You'll have your hands full trying to hold onto her unless she makes up her mind that she is married to you."

"Don't worry," Gryph stated. "She can kick and scream all she wants. I'm not going to let her get away." There was a short pause and then he said slowly, "Delek, I want to ask you something about linking."

Delek chuckled. "By now you already know the basics. Why would you need advice from an old hunter like me?"

Gryph forced back the mild embarrassment that threatened to redden his high cheekbones. "It's about the first time."

"What about it?"

"I want to know if there is really supposed to be so much pain," Gryph said quietly.

Delek appeared to realize just how serious Gryph was. "Pain? Well, there's the slight burning sensation both people get from the prisma, and there's the feeling of disorientation that occurs when each picks up on the other's emotions. If a woman has had little or no previous sexual experience, she might have some additional discomfort. The Shield might or might not feel some of that discomfort, depending on the strength of the link. But I wouldn't describe any of it as painful."

Gryph nodded. "That's what I thought, what I expected. Delek, it wasn't like that between Sariana and myself. The lock burned like a white-hot torch. We didn't get a sense of mild disorientation, we got a full load of each other's sensations. I had been wounded that night and she felt the pain of the wound as if she had taken the blade herself. I could feel everything she experienced when I took her. Her shock, her pain, her anger. I was running a fever and she also felt that. And the crossover seemed to magnify and reflect back. My wound hurt more than it had before the link. My fever felt several degrees hotter." He shook his head. "I can't explain it. I just know it was much more intense than I had been led to believe. I actually wondered if I had been told a few minor lies all these years."

"No, young Shields are not fed a pack of lies about linking or anything else. My first time with Penela wasn't anything like what you're describing. There was a lot of passion on both our parts and I was well aware of her excitement just as she was aware of mine, but that was about it. It sounds like you went through a very unusual linking, but I have no explanation for it."

Gryph sat back in his chair. "I was afraid of that. Do you miss Penela, Delek?"

Delek raised his eyebrows. "Penela was sexy as hell when we were linked. That woman could drive me out of my mind with lust. The rest of the time she was a complete pain in the ass. You're old enough to know that linking doesn't always mean loving. It doesn't even always imply a good friendship. You want the truth? The day I heard she had broken her fool neck on a wild dragonpony, I felt as if a part of me had been torn out. But there was also a sense of relief. I was free. Alana has more than filled up whatever emptiness my Shieldmate left behind in me."

"I understand." Gryph wondered if any woman, Shieldmate or lover, could fill up the empty place inside him that Sariana would create if she were to leave him now. It startled him to realize just how much a part of him she had become in such a short time.

A half hour later, their plans made, Gryph said good-bye to his friend and started back toward the windrigger.

He had passed the fairgrounds on his way to Delek's house. Now he found himself stopping on a whim. He really shouldn't waste any more time. There was much that had to be done by nightfall.

But it would only take a moment to choose a trinket for Sariana. She wasn't going to appreciate having been cooped up on the ship all day. Maybe he could win a smile or two from her. He browsed the craft aisles, searching for something that would suit her, something refined and simple in design.

He had just paid for an elegant cloak pin and was wondering if Sariana would give him one of her dazzling smiles when he presented it to her when his whole body tensed.

Sariana was nearby and she was in danger.

The sensation was so overpowering that Gryph didn't stop to question it. She was somewhere in the vicinity.

Prowling like a hunting cat through the crowds, Gryph homed in slowly on his goal.

He found himself standing in front of a large, eye-dazzling structure that he recognized as a familiar fair attraction, a House of Reflections. It appeared to be closed, but a small boy was standing at the entrance, trying to get the attention of a nearby adult.

"She's inside, I tell you. She didn't come out with the others. There's a lady still inside. You have to open the door," the boy wailed.

The attendant brushed aside the boy's clutching hand. "There's no one in there. Now get out of here. The House of Reflections is closed for repairs for the next hour or so. Go on, kid, get out of here."

Gryph stepped forward, his attention on the youngster. "Who's inside, boy? What does she look like?"

"I tell you there's no one in there." The attendant was reddening with rage.

"You're a Shield, aren't you?" the youngster said suddenly. "You're wearing a weapon kit. A real one."

Gryph crouched in front of the youngster. "I'm a Shield," he said softly. "Now tell me who's inside."

"Her name is Sariana. Are you going to get her out?"

"That's exactly what I'm going to do." Gryph rose and turned to confront the attendant only to find himself facing a fleeing back. He turned back to the boy. "It looks like we'll have to get her out by ourselves."

"You want me to help you rescue Sariana?" the youngster demanded, fascinated at the prospect.

"If you do, I will be in your debt," Gryph said gravely.

The boy's eyes widened. "In my debt? A real Shield would be in my debt?"

"Yes," said Gryph. "Who knows? Someday you may want me to return the favor you're doing me today. By my lock, I swear I will repay you." Gryph touched the prisma lock of his weapon kit as he swore the formal oath.

"Wow."

"What's your name, son?"

"Keri."

"I'll bet you've been inside this House of Reflections before, haven't you?"

"Yes, sir, lots of times, but this time it was different just inside the entrance. I got separated from Sariana and then the man who runs the house said everyone had to get out. But Sariana didn't come outside with the rest of us. She's still in there, but no one believes me."

"I believe you," Gryph said as another jolt of Sariana's fear went through him. Deliberately he shut it out so he could think more clearly. "Let's go find her."

He opened the weapon kit and withdrew a small metal instrument. The door to the House of Reflections shattered into a thousand glittering pieces when he slammed the tool into the glassy surface.

Keri led the way inside, but Gryph discovered he didn't need the boy's guidance. Already his awareness of Sariana was focusing in a certain direction. He moved down a kaleidoscopic hallway and found himself in a room that reflected his own image endlessly. Keri was on his heels.

Screams echoed from another hall that emptied into the same room. An instant later three teenage boys tumbled into the room, clearly in a panic. Sariana was right behind them.

"*Gryph!*" she shouted.

And then she was running straight into his arms. As he reached out to catch her he decided this was not the moment to point out how easily she had picked out the real Gryph Chassyn from among a thousand reflected images.

"What's going on here?" Gryph asked icily, his gaze on the cowering boys.

"These three young idiots were having a great time trying to terrorize me. To tell you the truth, they did a pretty good job."

"Wait outside with Keri," Gryph ordered. He put Sariana's hand in that of the boy's. "He knows the way out."

"But what about you?" she breathed.

"I'll be along shortly. First I'm going to have a talk with these three."

"Now, Gryph," she began dubiously.

"Sariana, once in a while you will do me the favor of following my orders," he stated flatly.

"I will?"

"Yes, you will. And this is one of those times. Go."

Sariana went.

Chapter
13

"WHAT did you do to those three boys?" Sariana demanded a short time later as Gryph steered her through the streets of Little Chance. He had emerged from the House of Reflections looking grim and thoughtful. That wasn't a particularly strange expression for Gryph, but she hadn't liked the grim expression in his eyes. He had said good-bye to Keri and thanked the boy in a surprisingly formal manner, and then he had taken Sariana's arm in a firm grip.

"I asked them a few questions."

"Gryph, that's not what I mean. What did you *do* to them?" Sariana demanded anxiously.

"Not as much as I had planned."

"What's that supposed to mean? What had you intended to do?" Sariana had to take occasional skips in order to keep up with Gryph as he towed her back to the windrigger.

"After I got the answers to my questions I decided to give them a taste of fear. I thought they ought to know how it felt to be on the receiving end." Gryph's eyes gleamed through his lashes as he glanced down into Sariana's face. "But I discovered that wasn't necessary. You and the scarlet-toe had already done a good job of terrorizing all three of them. That was an oversized image of Lucky they saw in one of the reflecting chambers, wasn't it?"

Sariana nodded, her spirits reviving rapidly. "I found the distortion chamber and hid Lucky under my cloak on the floor. When the boys stormed into the room I yanked the cover off and there Lucky was with a mouth big enough to swallow all three kids and enough teeth to do the job. The boys panicked." Sariana grinned in self-satisfaction. "Clever of Lucky and me, if I do say so myself."

"Not nearly as clever as staying on board the windrigger would have been. We'll get to your reasons for disobeying orders later. I'm sure they'll be intricate, detailed and fascinating. In the meantime, we've got things to do."

"You didn't tell me what questions you asked the boys or what answers you got," Sariana pointed out.

"I asked them who had paid them to corner you in the House of Reflections."

"Someone paid them to do that?" Sariana dug in her heels with sufficient force to slow Gryph momentarily. He paused long enough to yank her back into motion and then he nodded abruptly.

"That's right. Did you think it was all a coincidence that you got stranded in the fun house with three teenage monsters?"

"Well, I did wonder where everyone else had gone. I even lost track of little Keri."

"Someone bribed the attendant to close the place for a while, leaving you alone inside. Then that same someone sent those three kids in after you."

Sariana stared at Gryph in bewilderment. "But why?"

"The kids said they were told it was all a joke. That some man paid them to frighten you into the southwest corner of the House of Reflections."

"What was supposed to happen there?" Sariana groped for logic in an illogical situation.

"The boys said that the man who had paid them wanted to play hero. Something about wanting to impress you. He was supposed to appear at the last minute and grab you from their clutches."

"It doesn't make any sense."

"Yes it does," Gryph countered roughly. "It makes a lot of sense if you figure that what was really going on was another kidnapping attempt."

Sariana could have screamed with frustrated anger. She recalled the two men who had stalked her in Serendipity. "But why would anyone want me?"

Gryph shook his head at her obtuseness. "I've explained that. If someone gets hold of you, he's got hold of me."

"I don't understand."

Gryph halted without any warning and swung around to confront her. His face was a tightly controlled, unreadable mask. "You keep saying that but it's not true. You're smart and you're clever and you're educated. You do understand. At least you understand some of it. You just don't want to admit how involved with me you really are. And you have a bad habit of ignoring facts that don't happen to suit your version of events."

It was too much. Sariana decided she had been through enough that day. Her eyes narrowed. "It's not my fault if some stupid local has assumed we're married and that you'll do anything to keep your newfound breeding machine."

"It may not be your fault, but it's a fact," Gryph retorted heartlessly. It was obvious he, too, felt he'd suffered enough lately. He was in no mood to pacify his outraged wife.

Sariana felt her spirits plummet once more. The fight went out of her as Gryph steered her up the gangplank of the windrigger. "You're not even going to bother to deny it, are you?" she asked listlessly.

"Deny what?" Gryph was no longer paying close attention. He was scanning the deck for a member of the crew.

"That you think of me as nothing more than a breeding machine."

"Sariana, I haven't got time right now to soothe your feminine ego." He gave her a small push toward the entrance to the lower deck. "Go pack your things and mine, too. We're leaving the ship in a few minutes."

She started to demand an explanation for this latest irrational decision but it was too late. Gryph was already striding toward the captain's quarters. Sariana reached into her cloak pocket and touched the inquiring nose of the lizard.

"One of these days, Lucky, that man is going to find out that not everything functions according to his master plan. If I didn't want that cutter back as badly as he does I swear I'd walk off this ship this instant and disappear."

It was as she turned toward the cabin that it belatedly occurred to Sariana that disappearing might be exactly what she did if she got off the ship without Gryph's protection. The memories of the genuine scare she had received in the House of Reflections were still very vivid in her mind.

Late that afternoon Sariana found herself on a small craft called a river sled. It was another clever western invention, she was forced to concede as she sat in the bow and stared at the wide, lazy river unwinding in front of her. It required only one person to run the simple but efficient mechanism that propelled the small boat through the water with a system of meticulously designed blades. It came as no great surprise that Gryph knew how to manage the sled. Apparently there wasn't much he couldn't handle. Sariana felt a certain amount of resentment about that.

They had left Little Chance a couple of hours earlier, following the wide, meandering river that rolled lazily down from the distant mountains through farmland, plains and canyons. The last farm had been passed some time ago and Sariana had seen no further sign of civilization.

The flatlands and gently rolling hill country were giving way to more rugged scenes, but the river was still tame and manageable. Gryph appeared to be quite competent with the little boat. Sariana glanced back over her shoulder and saw that he was caught up in his own thoughts. There was an expression of concentration on his face.

The late afternoon sun painted the rough landscape a spectacular shade of yellow and mauve. Sariana began to relax for the first time that day. Idly she speculated on what sorts of convoluted, irrational, and no doubt cryptic thoughts a Shield might entertain while in the frame of mind Gryph was obviously in at the moment. The passing scenery lulled her into a passive mood. Almost casually she let her mind drift, opening herself to any stray thought that happened to float into it.

She nearly fell off the narrow bench on which she was sitting when an image of herself as seen from the rear formed in her mind. She was completely nude. Her back was gracefully straight, her head was held at an imperious angle, her waist looked small and her derriere . . . Sariana nearly choked as she realized that from this angle her rear end appeared to be quite lush and sensuously curved. Never in her life had she seen herself in this way.

And then it occurred to her that she wouldn't be viewing herself this way right now if it wasn't for the fact that someone else was seeing her this way. She resisted the urge to turn around. It was impossible. She refused to admit that the alien image of herself was coming straight from Gryph's head. Her imagination was running wild.

She blinked a few times to clear her befuddled brain and the disturbing image vanished. Experimentally she tried to recall it but it was gone for good. Sariana breathed a small sigh of relief and went back to studying the landscape.

The river was beginning to wind through small canyons now. Occasionally the water became rough for a short time, but under Gryph's expert handling the river sled bounced merrily through the light rapids and back into gentler waters without a protest.

The canyons became more frequent, their walls higher and more forbidding. Heavy shadows began to cloak the river.

"We'll stop here for the night," Gryph finally announced as he slowed the river sled and angled it into a serene cove.

It was the first time he had spoken in hours other than to issue curt commands relating to the boat.

Sariana lifted her chin. "I think you should know I have never camped out in my life."

"Somehow that doesn't surprise me. Don't worry, I'm an expert."

"That doesn't surprise *me*," she countered. She glanced around curiously. "At least it's warm and it's not raining."

"I'll build a fire ashore and we'll cook our evening meal there, but we'll sleep on board the sled. There are hawk-beetles in these canyons."

"What a pleasant thought." Sariana got to her feet and stretched. The scarlet-toe, which had been dozing on her shoulder, awakened and yawned. "I think I would like a bath before dinner. Are these waters safe?"

Gryph was rummaging around in the travel packs. "Safe enough here in the shallows. You can have your bath. I could use one, too."

"Good. I think I'll just trot around that little bend up ahead and find a nice, private spot." Sariana was feeling more cheerful as she contemplated her bath.

"You will stay right here in the cove," Gryph ordered without even bothering to glance at her. He was busy opening the food lockers. "I'm not letting you out of my sight again today."

"Now, Gryph," Sariana said soothingly, "there's no reason to overdo the protective bit. As long as I stay within shouting distance, what can go wrong?"

"You tell me. I'm afraid to guess. To be on the safe side you will stay within eyesight, not just shouting distance." He took off his boots and stepped over the edge of the flat sled. The clear waters lapped lazily at his bare feet.

"Do you know what your problem is, Gryph?"

"I've got all kinds of problems. Which one are you referring to?" He tossed a pack down onto the sandy beach and glanced back at her.

Sariana regarded him from the gently bobbing sled, her hands on her hips, her eyes militant. "Your problem is that you don't know how to deal with others on an equal basis.

You're arrogant and undiplomatic in the extreme. You're always giving orders. Especially to me."

"For all the good it does me." He studied her for a long moment. "Why did you leave the windrigger this morning, Sariana?"

Sariana eyed him warily. She had been hoping that he had forgotten about that piece of business. His silence on the subject during the river trip had convinced her he had decided not to reopen a sore subject. "I didn't feel like staying on board."

"You're lying."

"I am not lying!"

He regarded her closely. "All right, we'll compromise. You're not telling me the whole truth. How's that?"

"That sounds just fine to me," she retorted. She was beginning to feel cornered already and the knowledge made her angry.

"So what's the rest of the story? Why did you leave the windrigger? Was it just because I'd given you orders to stay on board? Are you so stubborn and temperamental and defiant that you'd disobey a reasonable request just to prove you don't have to take orders from me?"

"What do you think?" she challenged.

To her surprise, he appeared to consider the matter. "I think," Gryph finally said, "that you are independent and stubborn and irrational enough to do something like that just to provoke me, but I don't think that's why you disobeyed me this morning. I want to know why you went into town this morning, Sariana."

"Personal reasons." She sat down and began unlacing her walking boots in preparation for going ashore.

"What personal reasons?" Gryph waded back into the water and bounded onto the sled.

Sariana looked up and realized he had decided he wanted an answer and he wasn't going to leave her alone until he had it. "Why does it matter?"

"It just does, that's all. I've been thinking about it all afternoon and I've decided it definitely does matter." He put one bare foot on the low railing that went around the edge of the broad, flat sled and waited for her response.

Sariana dredged up a bright smile. "How about simple curiosity? I've never been to Little Chance before and I wanted to see what the place looked like."

He exhaled slowly, clearly doing his best to hang onto his patience. "Stop it, Sariana. Just tell me the truth. That's all I want. For the past few hours I've told myself it was your curiosity that took you ashore. Or else it was your desire to assert yourself. But something doesn't ring true about either one of those answers. That's why I want the whole story."

Sariana finished removing her second boot and sat quietly for a moment. "All right," she said at last. "It's simple enough. I went into town to find a medic."

"A medic?" Alarm flared in his eyes. "You didn't tell me you were ill."

"I'm not ill. I went to see a women's medic. One who could give me a contraceptive device. There. Does that answer your question?"

"You went into town to get something to use for birth control?" There was genuine shock in his tone.

Sariana stirred uneasily and rose to her feet. It didn't help much. He was a lot bigger than she was and they were very much alone out in the wilderness. "Why not?" she said bluntly. "I got the feeling you weren't going to do anything about it, and if it's true that for some reason you can . . . can make a baby with me then I have to protect myself, don't I?"

He didn't move, but Sariana had the impression that it was only an incredible willpower that kept him still. The image of him grasping her shoulders and shaking her was so strong that she was startled into wondering if it had seeped into her mind from his. It enraged her and frightened her to realize that such transference might really be possible between them. With all her heart she longed to deny the link and with each passing hour it became more difficult to do so.

"Sariana, I've warned you, you are going to push me too far one of these days."

Her temper exploded and she threw up her hands in a wild gesture. "What about me? I feel as though I've already been pushed too far. Don't my feelings count?"

"I know exactly what your feelings are when you lay in my arms and believe me, I take them into full account," he shot back. "You want me as much as I want you."

"All you really want is a good breeder," she snapped, "someone you can turn into a mother. How do you think that makes me feel?"

"It should make you feel needed and wanted and very important to me," he flung at her as his own control began to slip.

"Well, it doesn't. It makes me feel like a farm animal."

"That's ridiculous."

"You're telling me! And I'm tired of feeling ridiculous, do you hear me, Gryph Chassyn? I didn't think I could feel any more useless and ridiculous than I did the day I got word I had failed my academy entrance exams, but I was wrong. That was just a feeling of intellectual failure. You're trying to make me feel like a failure as a woman *and* a human being."

"Are you out of your mind?" he snarled, still not moving. "I'm more than willing to turn you into a success as a woman. It seems to me I'm offering you a better deal than any you'd get from a routine business marriage. At least with me your real talent as a woman will be fully appreciated."

"Having your babies is supposed to be a sign of my success?"

"You could do worse, lady."

"I could also do a whole lot better." Recklessly she took a step toward him, her eyes flashing with pride and outrage. "Do you hear me, Chassyn? I said I could do a whole lot better than you."

"How? By forming a marriage alliance with someone like that banker friend of yours? What do you think the chances are that you'd find any real passion in his arms?

What do you think the chances are of him bringing out the real woman in you?"

It was too much. Sariana went over some invisible edge. "What do you think the chances are that you can make me into a real woman when, from all accounts, you may not even be a real man yourself?"

Gryph stared at her disbelievingly. "What the hell are you saying?"

"I learned a lot about Shields from the medic this morning and I learned even more at the fair. There seems to be some question about whether or not you and your kind are even human! That severely diminishes your potential usefulness to me as a husband."

"Why you mouthy, bad-tempered, perverse little easterner. You really don't know when to shut up, do you? I'm as human as you are, lady, and tonight I'll prove it. What's more, you can damn well forget about using whatever contraceptive device that medic gave you. Is that clear?"

Sariana decided that he was right. She didn't seem to know when to shut up. She also didn't know when to quit. Her frustrated fury boiled over. Without any warning, not even a shout of anger, she launched herself at Gryph. Her spread hands caught him full on the chest and she shoved him backward with all her might.

Automatically Gryph tried to steady himself against the unexpected assault, but the low rail caught the back of his leg and he lost his balance. He didn't waste time trying to save himself after that. He simply wrapped one hand around Sariana's wrist and pulled her over with him.

The scarlet-toe wisely leaped from Sariana's shoulder to the safety of the sled rail.

Sariana gasped as she hit the water with a splash. The river was chilly but it wasn't freezing. She found herself floundering in water that only came up to her shoulders. Her skirts billowed out around her as she righted herself and surfaced. She pushed her hair back off her face and blinked away the water that was streaming into her eyes.

Gryph was surfacing a short distance away, his eyes glittering with a mixture of emotions that ran the gamut from fury to desire.

"So you've come to the conclusion I'm not a real man, Sariana?" Gryph started to glide slowly toward her through the water. "That's an interesting deduction. How do you define a real man?"

The plunge into the river was having a very sobering effect on Sariana's temper. "Calm down, Gryph. I was just feeling very provoked a few minutes ago. I'm sorry if I said anything to offend you." She retreated cautiously as he approached. She would have turned and tried to dash to shore, but she knew the weight of her clothes would hamper her too much. His sleek trousers and shirt were far less of a hindrance in the water. Gryph would catch her easily if she tried to escape.

"You're sorry for offending me? That's hard to believe. You seem to be making a career of offending me. You go out of your way to do it, in fact. It's going to take a lot more than an apology to calm me down this time." He began to close the distance between them. He did it with excruciating slowness, a hunter closing in on his prey. "Now tell me what your definition of a man is."

A shiver went through her that was not caused by the chill of the river water. "Gryph, this is hardly the time or place to discuss philosophy!"

"You're wrong. This is exactly the time and the place. What's more, I'm in the mood to discuss such matters."

"Well I'm not," she sputtered.

"Too bad. You started this, remember. As usual, your tendency to run off at the mouth has gotten you into trouble. Let's see how you get out of it. Tell me exactly where I fail to measure up to your standards for a man. I'll do my best to correct any problem areas."

Sariana eyed him warily. She was cold from the water. She was nervous about Gryph's intentions. She was still angry with him and she was determined not to let him win this battle. But into that chaotic mixture of emotions came another, familiar sensation of hungry excitement.

She could have fought that last feeling, Sariana realized.

She was more aware of it now. She could control an unwanted passion if that's all that was involved.

But as she watched Gryph coming toward her through the water she realized what the real problem was.

She was falling in love with the man. She had been falling in love with him since the night she had set out to coerce him into helping the Avylyns.

She was falling in love with him and she wasn't even sure now that he was wholly human.

"Gryph, stop this. I don't have to answer your foolish questions. You're just trying to make me nervous. Admit it."

"I'm not trying to make you nervous. You're already nervous. With good reason. Answer my question, Sariana. What does it take to make me a man in your eyes?"

"By the Lightstorm, you are a man! I've already apologized for implying otherwise. I told you, I was angry at the time. Stop tormenting me. Now let's get out of the water like sensible people. It's getting very cold."

"Don't worry, Shieldmate," he growled softly. "I'll warm you. I'll warm your backside so thoroughly you won't be able to sit down for the next few days. I think it's time you learned there are limits to my good nature. I'll teach you to imply I'm not a man. Your fast tongue has run away with you this time, Sariana. I'm going to help you learn to control it."

He swooped down on her, catching her up in his arms and lifting her high against his chest. Then he started wading toward shore.

"Gryph, put me down. Damn you, you're not going to have everything your own way."

"Neither are you." He set her on her feet in the sand and began stripping the wet clothing from her body.

"Then we've got a problem, don't we?" She shivered in the evening air.

"Nothing we can't resolve." Gryph let the last of her soaked garments fall to the sand. Then he reached for a blanket from his travel pouch and wrapped it around her. "Dry yourself," he ordered. "The last thing I need on this trip is for you to get sick." He went to work on his own clothes.

Sariana's temper rose once more. "Damn it, we certainly wouldn't want that to happen, would we? Mustn't interfere with the mysterious Shield's inscrutable plans by catching a little cold."

He dropped his shirt onto the sand and peeled off his wet trousers. "Sariana, if you have any sense you will close your mouth. You've said enough for one day."

"I haven't got any sense," she declared as she realized he was fully erect, his body hard with desire. So much for the lauded effects of a cold bath. Apparently it wasn't universally effective. "If I did, I wouldn't be here." Sariana clutched her blanket and watched as Gryph briskly rubbed himself dry.

"If I'd had any sense I would have left Serendipity the night you first sank your sharp little nails into me."

Sariana was unaccountably hurt. "What a terrible thing to say. I never sank my nails into you."

"The hell you didn't. You poisoned me and had me kidnapped. Then you tried to blackmail me into taking a job I didn't want. You've got a tongue like a razor and you've used it on me morning, noon and night. You won't follow simple, reasonable orders designed to keep you safe. You refuse to believe the legends I've tried to tell you." He finished drying himself and wrapped the blanket loosely around his waist. "And you are so damn stubborn you won't believe facts even when they hit you in the face. You hear only what you want to hear. The rest of the time you're talking so fast a man gets lost in the words. Maybe you'll think a little more clearly and behave a little more rationally after I've turned you over my knee."

An exhilarated sensation swept through Sariana as she realized that beneath the blanket Gryph was more aroused than ever. His temper was vying with his passion. The two made a very potent combination. Sariana could feel his sexual energy. It was lapping over her in waves.

"What makes you think I haven't still got my nails sunk into you?" she asked throatily.

Gryph, about to reach for a fresh shirt, paused at the new note in her voice. "What are you up to now, Sariana?"

"I think," she said musingly as she let her blanket slide slowly off her shoulders, "that I'm about to prove something."

"Are you?" He watched her intently as she walked slowly toward him across the sand. The blanket slid down a little farther. Now it only partially concealed the curve of Sariana's breasts and the dark triangle between her thighs. In the evening shadows she was all slender, graceful, feminine mystery.

A pleasantly euphoric sense of power began to blossom in Sariana. Gryph was bound to her and, as far as he was concerned, she was bound to him. So be it. She couldn't seem to fight that and she was reluctantly admitting she didn't want to fight it. But if she was going to continue in this bizarre situation she was determined to show Gryph that the dynamics of the relationship worked both ways.

"You're not going to use your belt on me and we both know it," Sariana murmured.

He scowled. "Is that right?"

"I think," she whispered as she paused in front of him, "that you need to learn what it feels like to be the one on the receiving end of all the orders."

A slow, curious smile edged Gryph's mouth as he looked down at her. He raised one hand and lightly grazed his palm across one gently shaped breast. "You've decided to teach me that lesson tonight?"

"Yes," she agreed thoughtfully, "I have."

"What makes you think you can, uh, drive the lesson home, so to speak?"

She reached out and pulled the blanket from his waist. His heavy, thrusting manhood leaped into her waiting hand. "Feminine intuition."

He sucked in his breath and his hands went to her shoulders. He started to pull her close. "You want me, don't you, lady? In spite of all your mouthy arguments and your temperamental ways, you want me."

"You're right. I want you. And you want me."

"Damn right." His fingers flexed on her shoulders. "I've wanted you from the first time I saw you. I've never denied it."

"I think it's time you learned that this relationship of ours is a two-way street. Tonight we'll do things my way."

He chuckled indulgently, the last of his temper dissolving into a blazing sensuality. "What is your way?"

"I'm going to tell you what to do and how to do it. And you, for once in your life, are going to follow orders. I'm going to teach you what it's like to be on the receiving end."

"What makes you think I'll follow orders?" He eased his hands down her back, removing the blanket entirely. As it fell to her feet he pulled her lower body into the cradle of his thighs.

She shook her head. "I don't know. Just a feeling." She nipped his shoulder lightly with her small, sharp teeth.

Gryph inhaled sharply. "Ah, a promising beginning. What's your first order, Lady Sariana?"

"Kiss me." She stood on tiptoe, twined her arms around his neck and lifted her lips invitingly.

"Gladly." He brushed his mouth teasingly across hers.

"Harder."

"No need to rush things," he murmured. "You'll enjoy it more if we take it slowly."

"I said," she responded, her tongue touching her parted lips, "that I want you to kiss me harder." She gathered herself and projected the image of a deep, passionate embrace blindly into the atmosphere around her. She wasn't at all certain what the reaction would be and the result took her by surprise, even though she had tried to prepare herself.

Gryph's mouth came down on hers with sudden, shattering hunger. He groaned deeply and his arms tightened fiercely. His fingers dug into her rounded buttocks as he pulled her to him. The hard, searching shaft of his manhood was like sleek iron against her soft stomach. His whole body vibrated with the intensity of his need.

Sariana realized he was reacting exactly the way she had

pictured him doing in the image of the embrace she had projected. In another moment she would be flat on her back and he would be on top of her, surging into her. Frantically she altered the image in her mind.

"Wait, not so hard," she gasped, wrenching her head aside. She sank her nails into his shoulders and shoved heavily.

Gryph didn't seem to hear her for a moment. When she finally got his attention he slowly raised his head and looked down at her with a confused expression in his glittering eyes.

"I thought that's what you wanted." His voice was a rasping whisper.

"Not quite." Sariana realized she was shaking. "Obviously I have to do some fine tuning here."

He watched her through dazed, narrowed eyes and raked a hand restlessly through his hair. "Sariana, what do you think you're doing?"

"I'm not sure yet." She gave him her most brilliant smile and sallied forth once more into the fray. She caught hold of his hand and put it against her breast. "Kiss me again. Not quite so fiercely. And this time I want you to touch me."

He swore softly but his fingers closed around her pert nipple as he lowered his mouth once more to hers. She painted a sensual picture in her head.

This time the kiss was just right.

"Exactly what I ordered," she said against his mouth.

He ignored that, too wrapped up in the embrace now to pay attention to her self-congratulations. Sariana could feel his vibrating excitement. His desire was a tangible force that reached out to engulf her. When she deliberately projected the sensation of his tongue tangling with hers, she immediately found her mouth invaded. Once again the assault was a little too forceful.

"Easy," she mumbled.

He backed off slightly. His tongue explored her softness while his hands kneaded the resilient flesh of her buttocks.

An image popped into Sariana's head. It was similar to

the picture of herself she had seen that afternoon on the sled, the view that seemed to linger on her backside. In this image the round cheeks of her buttocks were full and lightly flushed. The dark cleft that separated them was deep and shockingly mysterious. A familiar masculine hand was gliding around to explore the hidden valley.

Even as she realized what was happening, Sariana felt Gryph's fingers sliding into that secret place, seeking its mysteries with a boldness that made her tremble.

Sariana gasped for air and banished the picture with an act of will. This was her fantasy, not Gryph's. She would control it and control him in the process. He had a lesson coming and she knew now she could teach it.

Sariana won the battle to control his questing fingers but as she concentrated on that skirmish, she lost control of the kiss. It deepened quickly as his tongue slid between her teeth. Then she felt Gryph's blunt, hard shaft sliding along her stomach.

Sariana realized she had to control the sensual battle on all fronts. Gryph was too clever, too knowledgeable about her responses. He was too much the hunter, the one trained to take charge. And he'd figured out what she was trying to do.

Sariana replaced the graphic image she had just banished with one of her own. This was a much softer, more romantic picture of a woman lying on her back while a faceless man knelt beside her and gently touched her breasts.

"That's me, not some faceless fantasy," Gryph muttered, lowering Sariana to the blanket that had fallen onto the sand. "If you're going to draw pictures, get them right."

The unseen man kneeling beside the woman instantly assumed Gryph's features. And then Gryph himself was kneeling beside Sariana. He drew small circles around her dusky aureoles. The hard nipples grew even tauter. She arched upward, seeking a firmer touch.

"Is this what you want, Sariana?" He tugged gently at sensitized flesh.

"Yes," she managed. "Oh, yes, that's what I want." She

took his hand and raised it to her lips, kissing his rough palm. Then she pushed it slowly, firmly down her body.

When his fingers threaded through the dark hair between her thighs she moaned and lifted herself against him. She thought of the way he had touched her there the last time he had made love to her and deliberately she tried to project that image. Then he was touching her there.

His fingers grew wet with her natural dew and they moved more slickly over her. Sariana reached down urgently to guide his hand still lower.

Gryph sucked in his breath and obediently gave her the caress she sought. He slid two fingers just inside her throbbing passage and opened her slowly until she felt deliciously stretched and waiting.

"Do you like that?" he rasped thickly. "Is that what you want, little tyrant?"

"More," she pleaded imperiously. "I want more of you." She looked up at him and saw the stark hunger in his face.

"How much more?"

"Everything. Anything." She twisted restlessly under his hand and groped for him, trying to drag him down onto her. She was growing wild with her own desire and the knowledge that his passion was an inferno fed her responses. "Come here." An image of him lying on top of her, thrusting into her formed in her head. It was getting hard to think clearly enough to create such explicit pictures. This one was definitely fuzzy around the edges.

"Are you sure that's what you want?"

"What else is there?"

His eyes blazed down at her while his fingers continued a slow, achingly exciting motion. "Give the command and I'll show you."

She moved urgently. "Yes. Show me," she ordered.

"As my lady wishes." He moved then, but he didn't come down on top of her as she had thought he would. Instead he gently pried her thighs widely apart and knelt between them. Then he lowered his head to drop a startling, incredibly intimate kiss into her warmth.

Sariana jerked bolt upright in shock. "Gryph!"

"You don't like it?"

"I . . . I don't know," she hedged.

"Give it time." He eased her back down onto the blanket and once more treated her to the exquisite, worshipful caress.

"By the Lightstorm," Sariana whispered. She reached her hands down to push him away and found herself clutching at him and pressing him closer instead.

She could form no more coherent images. Her mind was consumed with a riot of colors and textures and heat. Sariana felt the tension coiling more and more tightly within her and she held Gryph firmly in place while she waited for the explosion.

Gryph didn't seem to mind the fierce grip she had on his tousled hair. He sipped at her warmth as if it were nectar. His fingers probed gently into her channel as he took the tiny bud of passion between his lips.

The sudden release of the sensual tension exploded out of nowhere, convulsing Sariana's entire body. She cried out and Gryph rode the storm as she arched upward and tightened her thighs around him.

When she sank slowly back to the ground, Gryph stretched out along her. His manhood poised at the vulnerable entrance of her body, his mouth still carrying the taste of her, he took her face between his hands and waited until she opened her eyes.

Sariana lay still for a long moment, vitally aware of him waiting for her to come back to her senses. She was tempted to let herself drift but there wasn't much point in that. Sooner or later she would have to open her eyes and she knew that no matter how long it would take he would be waiting. Silently she lifted her lashes.

An unspoken question throbbed in the air between them. But Sariana wasn't listening to silent questions. There was another image forming in her mind. She saw herself holding a babe with night-dark hair and blue-green eyes. The infant was smiling mischievously, its tiny fists grasping eagerly for whatever was within reach.

Gryph wanted that child. It represented life and the future to him.

Sariana realized she wanted to give him that babe.

She also knew in that moment that she wasn't falling in love with him. She was already in love with him.

Sariana thought about the contraceptive she had purchased from the medic that morning. Then she made her decision. She would not use it.

Wordlessly she pulled Gryph down onto her and into her. He took her with a low, hoarse groan of unremitting need, driving into her so deeply that Sariana knew instinctively she would never again be free of him.

Much later that night when she lay curled beside him on the gently rocking river sled, Sariana remembered the image of the babe that had formed in her mind.

She decided not to mention to Gryph that it had been a little baby girl.

Chapter
14

DAWN came late to the base of the river canyon. Gryph awakened in deep shadow. But he was stretched out on his back and when he looked straight up he could see the faint light in the strip of sky visible overhead. It was time to get moving. There was a lot of territory to cover.

But Sariana shifted slightly against him, her rounded hips nestling closer, and Gryph had several second thoughts about the virtues of rising early. He turned on his side and slid a hand under the rheenfeather quilt. It was cozy and warm underneath the lightweight quilt and the curve of Sariana's thigh was an invitation he couldn't resist. He was hard with his early morning arousal and the thought of sliding into Sariana's tight, clinging warmth was far more attractive than getting up and building a fire.

Sariana stirred at his touch and Gryph smiled in satisfaction. She knew and responded to him even in her sleep. Stealthily he eased apart her thighs and stroked the silky interior of her leg. She shifted delightfully but didn't waken.

Enjoying the game, Gryph gathered her closer. Her back was still turned toward him and she fit the natural curve of his body perfectly. When he explored further with his questing fingers he discovered she was warm and full and already slightly damp. He traced the outline of her body's entrance and she grew moister.

Gryph waited no longer. He was ready and so was she, whether she knew it or not. This was morning, a time for action, not a slow, lingering interlude. He positioned her hips and guided himself slowly between her legs from behind. When he entered her soft, feminine channel Sariana came awake with a rush.

"I think," she complained sleepily, "that you have just taken advantage of me."

"I'm only evening the score from last night." Gryph locked his hands around her hips, guiding her into the rhythm he wanted. "By the Lightstorm, you feel good first thing in the morning." He reached around to the front of her thighs and used his fingers to excite her further.

Sariana moaned and stopped complaining.

Lazy sensations of pleasure and gathering tension drifted in and out of Gryph's mind, mingling with his own driving urge. He no longer tried to hold back his own emotions. As far as he was concerned Sariana had surrendered her right to gentlemanly restraint on his part last night. Any woman who could turn into such an imperiously demanding, exciting creature of passion deserved to be hit with the full force of the response she invoked.

The memories of the night combined with the potent excitement of morning and Gryph's body drove into Sariana's one last, glorious time. His half stifled shout echoed from the canyon walls as he poured himself into her. Sariana's cry was much softer and more breathless but her climax seemed every bit as strong as his own. He could feel it subtly rippling through him even as his own swamped his senses for a long, sweet moment.

When it was finished Gryph inhaled deeply, feeling his

natural energy rush back into him. He grinned privately and sat up. Then he ruthlessly yanked the travel quilt off Sariana and slapped her bare thigh. He was enjoying the sensation of possessiveness, he realized.

"Up you go, woman. I'm waiting for my breakfast."

Sariana grabbed for the quilt and snuggled back under it. "What happens if I tell you to fix your own breakfast?"

"I pick you up and drop you into the river for a refreshing early morning dip."

"That's not much of a threat. I was going to bathe again this morning, anyway."

"Ah, but there are subtle differences between a delicate sponge bath at the shoreline using water heated over a fire and being dropped into a very chilly river," Gryph pointed out as he reached for his pants and boots.

"You are a cruel, heartless, ruthless man, Gryph Chassyn." Sariana sat up slowly.

"That's something I think we should talk about," Gryph announced, coming to a decision. He gazed thoughtfully at the scarlet-toe as it uncurled slowly from the depths of Sariana's cloak and began nibbling at the small pile of leaves that Sariana had put out for its breakfast.

Sariana followed his gaze to the scarlet-toe and then looked at Gryph questioningly. "You want to discuss your cruel, heartless and ruthless tendencies? This early in the morning?"

"No," said Gryph as he stepped over the side of the boat and waded toward shore. "I want to discuss the issue you raised so tactfully yesterday evening. The issue of my being a man."

He didn't bother to glance back as he went about building a fire and heating water for her morning bath. He couldn't tell what she was thinking. Nothing at all was seeping into his mind from her this morning.

Half an hour later, cloaked against the early morning chill, Sariana sat on the other side of the fire and sipped her laceleaf tea. She waited in silence for Gryph's explanations.

He lounged on a rock, warming his hands around his

mug and considered his intelligent, passionate, unpredictable wife. He searched for the words he needed.

"You said you learned something about Shields yesterday," he finally began.

"A few things," she admitted evasively.

"It was something that made you think I might not be as human as you are." He could feel his own grimness and wished he could control it better.

"I saw a portion of a play with Keri. It was a First Generation legend about the Shields saving the colonists on board *The Serendipity*."

"And you found yourself a chatty medic who implied a few things that also made you wonder who or what you had married." Gryph took a long swallow of tea. "Must have been a female medic," he muttered.

"It was, as a matter of fact."

Gryph gave her a level glance. "I told you last night that I'm as human as you are."

She returned his gaze. "Is it true the Shields weren't on board *The Serendipity* or is that just legend?"

"It's true."

"Then where did your people come from, Gryph?" she asked quietly.

"What your people don't know, Sariana, or else they've forgotten, is that their ancestors weren't part of the first wave of human colonists that left the home planets and scattered into the galaxy. There was another wave of colonization that took place a hundred years earlier. My people are descended from that first wave."

Sariana sat tensely, her tea unfinished in her hand. "I've never heard of a previous attempt at colonization."

"I know. Your people were lucky just to hang on to a distorted version of their own history. It's no wonder they've lost all record of a previous history of other colonists. Even if the records did exist, no one would pay them much attention. As far as my people are aware, no one on the home planets ever heard from that first wave again after the ships left the solar system. Most of the ships were headed into this sector of the galaxy because the scientists had determined there was a cluster of star systems here that would be able to support human life. The odds of finding new homes seemed reasonably good in this sector. Since *The Serendipity* and *The Rendezvous* were both sent in this direction, too, we can assume that at the time of the second wave the home system scientists were still of the same opinion about the usefulness of planets in this area."

"They were right," Sariana observed. "Windarra has been a very hospitable planet."

"That may have been true of the eastern continent, but the west was a deathtrap. Almost every other inhabitable planet in this sector was also a trap," Gryph informed her bluntly.

"What do you mean?"

"The main reason no one ever heard from the first wave of colonists was because most of them died in storms of light that consumed whole ships attempting to land on planets in the local star systems."

"There was a scene in the play yesterday," Sariana said softly, "a scene in which *The Serendipity* was nearly swallowed by such a storm."

Gryph nodded, wondering how to explain the rest of the tale. "The people on board my ancestors' colony ship were lucky. They escaped the storm that almost caught them when they attempted to land on the planet of their choice."

"Windarra?"

Gryph gave her a small smile. "No, not Windarra. A planet called Talis. It was located in a neighboring system." He saw the wonder in her eyes. He also saw the doubt. "It's true, Sariana. I swear it. My people have kept their own history all these years. We have not forgotten our origins."

"How did you come to Windarra?"

"We followed the trail of the crystal ships," he explained simply, then realized he had skipped over far too much. "I'll have to go back to the beginning. By pure luck my ancestors' ship escaped a lightstorm that awaited it on Talis. It backed off and went into a wide orbit around Talis' moon while the scientists and technologists on board tried to analyze what the storm was composed of and how to deal with the threat it represented." Gryph swallowed the last of his tea and set the mug down on the rock beside him. "They eventually found the answer."

"What was that answer?"

He still couldn't tell how she was taking any of this. It irritated him. It also made him wary. But he had gone too far now. He might as well finish. He got to his feet and strolled to the water's edge and stood looking out across the canyon floor.

"I told you I was as human as you are. But I am also different, Sariana."

"Tell me," she invited softly.

"The weapons that produce lightstorms are made of prisma crystal. The ships that contain the weapons are made of the same substance. My people named it prisma crystal because of its unique qualities. There is nothing else like it as far as we know. No one knows how, when or where it was created. But when we first arrived in this sector there were crystal ships full of weapons on nearly every planet. Some of the ships were huge. They were in orbit around the planets they protected. They reacted instantly to an alien ship attempting to land. It was those orbiting crystal ships that got most of the colonial starships."

"It was one of those orbiting ships that got *The Serendipity*?"

Gryph nodded. "And it was a side effect of a lightstorm that crippled *The Rendezvous*. Your people didn't get the full brunt of the explosion. *The Serendipity* did."

"But what about the Shields, Gryph? How did they happen to be here when *The Serendipity* arrived?"

Gryph reached down and scooped up a handful of pebbles. He sent two or three skipping across the placid river. This next part was going to be the hardest.

"My people were no slouches technologically. It didn't take them long to discover that the weapons that created the lightstorms could be controlled by certain men whose minds could be tuned chemically to the resonating frequencies of prisma crystal. The minds of those men could be made to function as shields against the energy the weapons produced. They could turn that energy back on itself and neutralize the prisma ships and their weapons. But not just any mind could be tuned. Only certain men had the potential. But to make a man into a Shield, the scientists first had to change him in certain ways. Permanent ways."

"I don't understand."

Gryph swung around to confront her. He knew he probably looked dangerous and aggressive and ready for battle in that moment. He couldn't help it. He was feeling exactly that way. This was the crunch. She had to accept what he told her next. If she didn't—He refused to let himself dwell on that. He wished he could read her mind right now. Truly read it.

"They injected men who showed a strong potential for tuning into prisma with a chemical that slightly altered their genes. The result is a man who has problems taking certain drugs because they disrupt his system. The result is a man who can't father a son unless he is fortunate enough to find a woman whose mind can resonate with his on at least a minimal level. He can't father daughters at all. The result is a man who can tune into prisma crystal and reverse its natural vibrations so that it jams and is rendered harmless."

"And you're one of those men."

"I'm one of them." He drew a deep, steadying breath. "The scientists and medics on board my ancestors' starship thought at first that the men they had altered genetically would be sterile. Obviously we aren't or there wouldn't be any of us left. But there aren't many women with whom we can mate."

"And you think I'm one of those women."

"You are. You're naturally empathic. You may be more than that. You may be slightly telepathic. I'm not sure and it doesn't matter. The important part is that your mind can link with mine on a fundamental level. Using the prisma I was able to tune you into my own mental vibrations. You proved the tuning had worked the morning you opened my weapon kit. Only another mind resonating on the same frequency as my own could have done it."

"I'm no telepath, Gryph. I've never had a telepathic experience in my life."

He smiled faintly. "Until you met me. Our linking is beyond the normal parameters, Sariana."

She flushed. "If you're talking about what happens between us when we make love—"

"It isn't just that. The link between us becomes strong in times of stress, too. How do you think I found you the night you slipped out of the Avylyn villa? And how do you think I found you yesterday at the fair?" He watched her deal with that for a moment. "And how do you think you got what you wanted from me last night?" he concluded softly. "Whatever you were before I met you, you're more than empathic now that you've been linked to me through prisma. And you're very strong. You can project and you can receive not only emotions felt during passion or danger, but you seem to be able to project and receive actual images."

"No, I don't think I do. It's just that I have a vivid imagination," she protested weakly.

He grinned in spite of himself. "That's a load of dragon-pony manure. Or maybe a vivid imagination is part of the whole thing. I don't know. All I know was that I was on the receiving end of what you were projecting last night and it wasn't my imagination that was going wild."

She got to her feet and walked down to the water's edge, not looking at him. "This is all very complicated."

"I know."

"How did your ancestors save *The Serendipity*? How did they even happen to be on Windarra when the starships arrived?"

"The original Shields cleaned up Talis and the planet was colonized. In the battle to survive on Talis, much of our technology was lost, including the secrets for producing more Shields and the secrets of interstellar travel. But a few Shields found mates and to everyone's shock, had sons. Fortunately, as it turned out. We never did rediscover the secret of creating more Shields. But when we got back into space we found out we still needed Shield talent. We were dependent on the ones who were descended from the original Shields."

"You did get back into space."

"Yes. We got back into space and when we did the Shields were needed once again to mop up the remaining planets of our solar system. And then faster, more sophisticated ships were designed. A decision was made to use the new technology to send exploration teams of Shields out beyond our star system to try to locate the source of the crystal ships. As long as they existed, they were a danger. My people decided they had to learn who or what had built them and where they came from. No trace of any living being has ever been found with the ships."

Sariana picked up a few pebbles and tossed them out over the water. Gryph could see that the arc was all wrong but he decided this wasn't the time to correct her pitching. The pebbles hit the water and sank without a single skip. She turned around to face him.

"Your ancestors, the ones who saved *The Serendipity*, formed one of the exploration teams, right?"

He nodded. "Right. They were tracking prisma to this planet when they picked up signals from *The Serendipity* and *The Rendezvous*. They didn't know the people inside the ships were human. Not at first. There was the distinct possibility that the beings in the new starships were the ones who had created the prisma weapons. So my ancestors stalked yours and wound up in orbit around Windarra. When the first lightstorms hit *The Serendipity* and *The Rendezvous*, someone realized you weren't the bad guys."

"So the Shields came to the rescue."

Gryph shrugged. "It was what Shields were created to do. But there was only one Shield ship. It couldn't protect both of the incoming colony ships. The Shield team chose the one that seemed damaged the most by the initial assault and rode the storm down with it." Gryph paused and then added soberly, "It was the worst lightstorm that had ever been encountered. Many Shields were killed and the ship was virtually destroyed. When it was all over, my ancestors were in the same shape as yours. Marooned on Windarra. No one on the home planet of Talis had any way of knowing where or how we had disappeared. As far as they were concerned we were missing in action. No one came looking for us."

"It seems to me," Sariana said softly, "that there was a major difference between the situation your ancestors faced and the one the colonists faced. The colonists, at least, had arrived at their intended destination. They had come here prepared to create a home world for themselves. Your people had no such intention. They were truly shipwrecked."

Gryph saw the understanding in her eyes and a rush of relief went through him. Her natural empathy was going to be his salvation. "Initially my ancestors assumed there would be no second generation of Shields. The odds were against finding suitable mates among this strange group of humans. They faced the fact that they would die in exile and there would be no offspring."

"But some of the stranded Shields found wives among the First Generation colonists."

"Yes. Your people were grateful to ours. But they were also bound by a very rigid social structure. If my people were to survive, they had to create a legitimate place for themselves within that structure."

"Hence the First Generation Pact was negotiated."

"And we have abided by the terms of the Pact," he stated proudly.

"Tell me something. What makes the Avylyns' precious cutter Shield business?" Sariana asked abruptly.

Startled by the change in subject, Gryph frowned. He wondered why she wasn't asking him more detailed questions about his people. "The cutter wasn't stolen by a rival jewelers' clan, Sariana. And if someone didn't need it to make prisma jewelry, there's only one other use for it."

"To cut prisma."

"Exactly. That means another crystal ship has been

found. But there is something else that bothers me even more than that."

She gave him a curious glance. "What is that?"

"Everyone in the western provinces knows the danger of the crystal ships. The last thing any sane or even any crazy westerner would do is try to get into one on his own." Gryph drew in a deep breath. "But it's just barely possible an insane Shield might attempt it."

Sariana's eyes widened. "Why?"

"Because a Shield is the only one who would know that it's theoretically possible to do something else besides jam the crystal frequencies and destroy the weapons on board the ships."

"What else can be done, Gryph?"

"Some of my people have speculated that it's just barely possible a Shield could manipulate the light frequencies of the crystal instead of jamming them. And if he could manipulate them, he might possibly be able to control the weapons."

Sariana stared at him. "He could use them? Turn them against others?"

"It's only a theory, Sariana. It's never been attempted, at least as far as we know. Certainly it hasn't been tried on Windarra. We Shields have been extremely careful to keep the theory to ourselves. No outsider has ever been told."

"I'm an outsider, aren't I?" she challenged.

"No," Gryph said. "Not any longer. You're a Shieldmate. My Shieldmate. You are entitled to know the secrets of my social class."

"Even if I'd rather not know them?" She looked wistfully out across the river.

"You're the kind of woman who ultimately prefers to face facts. You may waste a lot of energy trying to bend those facts to suit your fancy, but eventually you do face them. This secret I am telling you is a fact. And it's a fact that a rogue Shield may have stolen the cutter because he's discovered a crystal ship and has decided to see if he can get inside to control the power of the weapons for his own purposes."

"Why haven't you told anyone else about this?"

"I told Delek. He's sending for backup support from the frontier provinces, but it will be a long time coming. I'm not sure we have that much time. He and I decided I'd better start the search for the ship now and let the others catch up with me."

"You could ask for help from my people," she pointed out stubbornly.

"Sariana," he said as patiently as he could, "the other social classes must never know that such a thing as controlling the weapons is even theoretically possible for a Shield."

"Why not?"

"Use your head! My people are a very small minority among yours. We're tolerated because we have a history of having helped the colonists and because we're useful as mercenaries and bandit hunters. We are also tolerated because we've always abided by the terms of the Pact. People trust us."

"In other words, you have been tolerated because you are seen as loyal warriors, not a potential threat," she concluded.

"What do you think would happen if it became known that a Shield might be able to use the power of the crystal ships to control everyone on this planet?"

Sariana took a long time mulling that one over. "I see your point," she admitted finally. "You walk a narrow line, don't you, Gryph? You must keep people in awe of you if you are to maintain your secrets, yet you can't risk having the populace learn to fear you. If people knew how dangerous your kind could be, they might decide they would be safer without you around."

"The system has worked reasonably well since the First Generation. The last thing any Shield wants is war between our class and the other classes."

She nodded. "So now you have to hunt down this rogue Shield before he activates the crystal ship weapons you believe he's found."

"Or before some outsider discovers there is such a thing as a rogue Shield."

"You think the ship is somewhere in this gorge?" Sariana asked.

He rubbed the back of his neck and took a couple of steps closer to her. She was being a little too businesslike about this whole thing, he decided. He couldn't tell exactly how she was reacting behind that thoughtful facade. If she was experiencing any strong emotions she was rapidly learning how to conceal them from him. He wanted to pull her into his arms and prove to himself that she still wanted him in spite of everything he had just told her, but he had a hunch this wasn't the time.

"According to the records, the last weapon ships discovered were found around here. The Shields thought they had cleaned out the area but it's difficult to track prisma in this kind of country. Certain kinds of rock can get in the way of a Shield's ability to focus on the light radiation prisma produces. Today I start hunting."

"You've tracked weapon ships before?"

"No," he admitted. "Not real ones. I told you, the last ship was found before I was born. But I've been trained to work prisma."

"How do you do it?" she asked curiously.

He smiled wryly. "It's a little like the first link with a Shieldmate. Except that there's no passion involved. I use the lock on my weapon kit and sort of, well, tune myself, I guess you would say."

"I see. You had better get busy then, hadn't you?"

He narrowed his eyes and wondered again what the hell she was thinking. "Sariana?"

"Yes?" She turned toward him expectantly.

"Never mind. You're right. I'd better get busy."

He spent the afternoon seeking prisma as they cruised slowly through the awesome gorge. One hand on his lock, his mind concentrated to the point of pain, Gryph focused on the unique kind of disturbance a ship full of prisma weapons created. It wasn't easy finding one of the small crystal ships, he had been told by experts from his father's generation. It took time and patience.

The problem was he didn't have a lot of either.

"Maybe your weapon kit lock isn't strong enough to do the job under the kind of conditions you're encountering in this gorge," Sariana suggested that evening as they finished setting up camp.

"Maybe." Gryph sat gazing into the fire and wondered what he was going to do if he couldn't locate the weapon ship. "I wish I knew how much time I've got to track it. Whoever took that cutter could be getting into the ship right now. I should have brought Delek with me instead of sending him for help."

"Why?"

"Because two Shields could cover more territory than one working alone."

Sariana stroked the scarlet-toe curled in her lap. She was eyeing his weapon kit. "Something about that kit of yours has interested me from the beginning."

His mouth tilted. "I remember the night you took it off me. It fascinated you."

"I couldn't help myself. I wanted to examine it more closely. Unfortunately, you woke up before I could look inside."

"You wouldn't have been able to open it at that point. You had to be tuned to it by me. That's what happened the night we went to bed together the first time. The next morning you were able to open it and prove you were my—" he broke off before he said wife.

"And I haven't wanted to touch it since," she said wryly. "But I find I'm curious about it again tonight."

Gryph watched her closely for a long while. "You want to open the kit?"

She got up and put the lizard on her shoulder. Then she circled the fire and sat down beside him.

Gryph slowly unsnapped the kit and handed it to her. He felt an odd tingling sensation when she took it from him. She put the kit in her lap and examined it intently.

Gryph experienced another wave of the tingling sensation. He shook his head to clear it.

Sariana touched the lock, her silvered nails moving lightly over it.

Gryph was suddenly filled with a strange urgency. He was getting odd impressions in his head, the kind of filtered light he saw when he had first learned to work prisma.

Sariana stroked the lock with a lover's touch and Gryph drew a deep breath. He reached for her free hand.

"Think of light," he whispered. "Think of light in all its different colors. Think of a beam of white light broken out into a hundred million rays, each slightly different than the one next to it. Follow the spectrum into the range where the colors have no names. Look at the colors you can't see with your eyes. You can see them with your mind. Do you understand?"

"I don't know. I think so." Her voice shook.

"Now look for the colors in that range that have a certain pulse." Gryph realized he was holding onto Sariana with a savage grip.

Her eyes were closed and she had gone rigid with unnatural tension. Her fingers were frozen on the lock.

"Hold onto that pulsing light ray, Sariana. Follow it back to its source."

Gryph never knew what made him try for a working link. No woman had ever been able to work prisma according to the history he knew.

But he was desperate and Sariana was a most unpredictable female.

He touched the other side of the prisma lock and carefully tuned into it. Sariana was there. There was definitely another presence in tune with his lock and it was not a weak presence.

Gryph didn't stop to analyze what was happening. He cautiously reached out for other rays that would be generated by a crystal ship, the way he had been doing all afternoon.

Without any warning he found them.

The unseen vibrations of prisma light focused on the weapon kit lock and bounced through Gryph's head with such force that he nearly screamed.

He did hear a scream, but it wasn't his own. It was Sariana.

He wanted to reassure her but he wasn't given the chance. Unprepared to handle such an incredibly strong focus, Gryph's brain did the only sensible thing. It shut down temporarily and plunged him into unconsciousness.

Chapter
15

S ARIANA was shaking as she knelt beside Gryph. He was lying in the same unconscious sprawl he had been in the first time she had seen him. Frantically she sought for a pulse in his throat. Her own pulse was racing as if her bloodstream was attempting to dilute and drain away the impossible, unnamed rays of light that had filled her head for a split second.

"Gryph, wake up. Please wake up." Her trembling fingers found the steady beat in his throat and she told herself he was all right. "Come on, Gryph, open your eyes," she ordered tightly. Her whole being willed him to awaken. She almost collapsed when his dark lashes fluttered and lifted. He gazed up at her for a long moment.

"I always said you were an unpredictable woman, Sariana. But this time you've outdone yourself." Gryph swore softly as he sat up. Gingerly he reached for his weapon kit and reattached it to his belt.

"What happened?" she demanded, sitting back on her heels in the sand.

"You helped me work prisma," he told her simply. "We found the weapon ship. Or at least we found the beams it's putting out. I've never tuned in to live prisma crystal before, but I was told years ago that if I picked it up I would recognize it. The men who taught me that were right. It's very similar to neutralized prisma but it has a slightly different pulse. I'll be able to track it now." He leaned back against the rock from which he had toppled a few minutes earlier and gave her a strange smile. "It's supposed to be impossible, you know."

"What is?"

"No woman has ever worked prisma. The original Shield teams were all male and all their descendants are male."

"What about their Shieldmates?" Sariana asked. She was getting a distinctly uneasy feeling.

Gryph gazed up at the stars for a moment before answering. "Until now being a Shieldmate meant only that a woman had the ability to link with a Shield and, if all went well, give him a son. Sometimes, if everything went very well, there would eventually be two or three sons. Some experiments have been done through the years, but no woman has ever been able to work prisma beyond the point of being able to tune in to her lord's lock. We've always assumed the talent didn't go farther because the women had never undergone the original genetic alteration. They might have the potential, but without the chemical injection needed to strengthen that potential, women can't truly work prisma."

"Sounds like just the sort of conclusion a bunch of men would arrive at," Sariana said with a shaky smile.

"I have to tell you something, Sariana. I think that whatever happened between us that first time we linked was unusual, to say the least. It may well have been unique. You remember the way you felt? You picked up on the pain of my wound, my fever, and then there was the sensations of the link itself plus your own, uh, feminine reactions."

"You don't have to remind me," Sariana told him. "I

remember it all quite well. You said there might be some 'initial discomfort.' I believe that was the euphemism you used."

In the firelight Gryph's cheekbones seemed to darken to a dull red, but his eyes met hers steadily. "That's all I had ever been told to expect. But I talked to Delek about it and he said—"

Sariana was abruptly outraged. "You talked to Delek? Another man? About us? About what happened that first time? Gryph, how could you? Have you no respect for my feelings? My modesty? By the Lightstorm, what right did you have to discuss something that personal with someone I don't even know? I will die of embarrassment if I ever meet him. Of all the stupid, egotistical, unfeeling things to do."

He groaned and massaged his temples with both hands. "Please, Sariana, I could do without the cutting edge of your tongue tonight."

"You deserve it!"

"Maybe, but do me a favor and save it for later, all right? There are more important things to discuss at the moment."

"Ha!" But she said nothing more. She had the uncomfortable feeling he was right.

Gryph eyed her warily and then went on with his story. "As I was saying before you jumped all over me, I talked to Delek about our initial linking. He said it didn't sound normal to him. He said that I had been told the truth. There is supposed to be a faint burning sensation from the lock when the man tunes the woman to it. There is also generally a feeling of disorientation as the man and the woman catch traces of each other's feelings and emotions. There is a lot of powerful sexual energy being exchanged in such circumstances, and the sensation of picking up on your partner's passion can seem very strange until you get accustomed to it. Then it becomes very, uh, exciting. I've told you before, Shields and their mates have a strong bond between them. That bond starts with the sexual relationship. It's unique."

"You've already explained it doesn't necessarily lead to love," Sariana said stiffly.

"A Shield's first duty to his clan is to create a son. Love has nothing to do with that."

"It's always nice to feel needed," Sariana muttered.

Gryph held up a hand in protest. "You have chewed on me enough tonight. No more. Not now."

Sariana sighed. He was right. "Go on."

"I was just trying to explain to you that right from the start there was something different about our relationship. When you and I are in bed together we do much more than just pick up on each other's emotions. We practically pour our passion into each other along with whatever else we might be feeling at the time. And we seem to resonate with each other in a way that makes the original sensation stronger. We're like mirrors that both absorb, concentrate and reflect back sensation. When you felt my wound in your shoulder, the pain of it was more intense than the ache I was actually feeling. My fever made you feel hotter than I felt at the time. You transferred that heat back to me and I felt hotter. You see what I mean? Since that first time together we've both instinctively started figuring out how to control the reaction. We can tune out everything but the passion and the excitement, which is fortunate because otherwise we'd probably drive each other insane. But the interesting part is that we seem to have a bond so strong that it requires such internal control in the first place. We're communicating with each other on some very strange levels, Sariana."

"What else did this friend of yours say?" Sariana asked suspiciously.

"About us? Not much. I didn't tell him the link we have in bed seems to have already extended itself to other occasions. Normally the ability to sense when one's Shieldmate is in distress or exuberantly happy is an evolving process that takes years of living together to mature into anything that might be labeled telepathic. Even then it would be hard to distinguish it from the normal empathy that seems to develop between a man and a woman who live together for years. Except in bed, of course, where it stays unique. But with us it was there almost from the beginning. It's sporadic at this point, but it's also very strong. I think it's going to eventually grow even stronger."

Sariana thought of the image of her backside that had popped into her mind while she was on the river sled. She tugged on her lower lip and gazed into the fire while she considered it. Experimentally she tried projecting it toward Gryph, just as she had projected her passionate demands the night before. She glanced at Gryph.

"You see what I mean?" he said with an understanding expression.

"We would have no privacy at all," Sariana said in shock as she considered the ramifications.

He shook his head reassuringly. "I don't think it will work like that. I think we will have to be actively projecting in order to send anything even remotely comprehensible. Just like working prisma."

"Well, what about that—that lewd picture of myself that just appeared in my head yesterday?"

He grinned, showing his teeth in the firelight. "I was bored. For once you didn't seem inclined to talk so I decided to do a little experimenting. I just wanted to see what would happen if I tried projecting a scene into your mind. This is the first time you've admitted you picked up on it. Until now I had no way of knowing whether or not you had received it. Which should tell you something."

"What does it tell me?" Sariana asked automatically. Then she leaped to the obvious conclusion. "Oh, I see. I didn't send anything back to you so you had no way of knowing if I had gotten the message."

"Right. I'll admit I don't know much about telepathy. Shields and their mates have always just skirted the edges of anything that could be labeled genuine telepathy. But judging from what I've learned by working prisma,

I'd say it's not a passive process. It takes strength and a deliberate focus."

"And both factors come into play automatically under conditions of extreme stress, is that it?"

"And under conditions of passion," he added blandly. "Don't fret, Sariana, I can't read your mind any more than any other man can read a woman's mind."

"Well, that's a relief," she tried to say lightly. The truth was she was feeling extremely nervous about the whole matter. She rose and settled herself onto a convenient rock. "What are we going to do now?"

"That's my Sariana," he said approvingly. "Back to business when things get sticky. Now, thanks to you, I've got a fix on a large source of prisma somewhere in this gorge. Tomorrow morning I will stash you safely here in this cove and then I will see if I can track the beams to their point of origin."

She didn't like the casual way he said that. "Then what?"

Gryph shrugged in that gracefully negligent manner all westerners seemed to be born with. "Then I'll decide what to do about it. If I think there's enough time, I'll wait until Delek and the others arrive. If there isn't time, I'll try to neutralize the weapons on my own."

"Can one Shield neutralize a whole shipload of the prisma weapons?"

"If he's strong enough. And if the ship is a small one."

"How strong are you, Gryph?" Sariana asked quietly.

"I don't know," he told her. "No Shield learns the limits of his own strength until he actually confronts a weapon ship. I've never even seen a ship."

"Oh." She sat in silence for a while, thinking over what he had said. "If it turns out you aren't strong enough to neutralize the weapons and if you have no backup, what happens?"

"You worry too much, Sariana," he said calmly. He got to his feet and began banking the fire. "We have a lot to do tomorrow morning. I think we'd better get to bed."

Sariana started to demand an answer to her question,

but she stopped, realizing she could guess the answer from his evasive response. Whatever happened to a Shield who lacked sufficient strength to neutralize his target, it wasn't pleasant. Perhaps it meant death. Or insanity. Sariana shivered and folded her cloak more tightly about her.

The scarlet-toe on her shoulder yawned sleepily as Sariana reached up to pat it with the tip of her finger. Gryph moved around the fire, his actions efficient and economical as he made preparations for securing the campsite.

"How close do you think that ship is?" Sariana asked, glancing out into the night-shrouded canyon.

"Several kilometers away."

"What if this rogue Shield is watching for intruders into this gorge?"

"I've told you not to worry, haven't I?" Gryph asked with soft humor. "When are you going to learn to follow simple instructions?"

"But, Gryph—"

"If there is a rogue behind all this, my guess is he'll be sticking close to his prize. He's not out here prowling through the night. I'd know if he were. There is no prisma nearby other than my lock. It's not hard to estimate distance with prisma rays. You do it with a simple formula."

"I'm going to worry about you tomorrow," Sariana said bluntly.

Gryph took off his boots, crossed the sand toward her and handed her the boots. Then he swung her up into his arms. "I'm just selfish enough to admit I'm going to like having you worry about me. But you'll be safe, Shieldmate. I'll make certain of that before I leave you."

He waded out to the sled, lifted her over the low railing and set her on her feet. She clutched his boots while she waited for him to jump lightly on board the sled. The moon was directly overhead and a narrow strip of golden light managed to seep as far as the river canyon floor. It gilded the black depths of Gryph's hair and highlighted the arrogant planes of his harsh face. Sariana remembered the buckle she had purchased at the fair.

"I almost forgot," she murmured as she went over to her travel pouch and opened it. "I have a present for you." She smiled as she turned around to hand him the small package.

Gryph looked oddly startled. He stared at her in the moonlight and then his gaze dropped to the package in her hand. "For me?"

"Well, I don't know anyone else who needs this quite as much as you do," she teased. "Here. Open it."

His usually deft fingers fumbled slightly with the wrapping, but a moment later the exquisitely detailed buckle lay in his palm. Holding it in one hand, Gryph opened his weapon kit and withdrew a tiny vapor lamp. He thumbed a switch and a narrow beam of light revealed the intricacies of the buckle. Gryph studied it for a very long time, apparently fascinated. When he glanced up finally, it was difficult to read his shadowed gaze.

"It's beautiful." His voice was rough and strangely husky. "Thank you, Sariana."

"I bought it at the fair."

"I stopped there to buy something for you, too. That's how I happened to be close enough to realize you were in trouble. With so much going on yesterday and today, I forgot to give it to you." He reached into a pocket and withdrew a tiny package. "It's not much. After living with the Avylyns for a year you're probably accustomed to fancier jewelry."

She was amazed by his diffidence. It was so uncharacteristic of Gryph. Sariana was amazed too, by her own reaction to the gift he was handing her. She was thrilled. When she unwrapped the cloak pin she thought it was the most beautiful pin she had ever seen in her whole life.

"Thank you, Gryph. It's really very lovely." She thrust it at once into a fold of her cloak. The scarlet-toe peered over the edge of her shoulder and studied the pin with idle interest. Then it went back to dozing.

Gryph switched off the tiny vapor lamp and he and Sariana stood looking at each other in the moonlight.

"You'll be careful tomorrow?" Sariana asked.

"I'll be careful."

"Maybe I should come with you," she suggested.

"Absolutely out of the question. You've already been in too much danger because of this mess. I won't expose you to any more risk. I'm going to make certain you're well hidden tomorrow."

She heard the finality in his tone and knew this wasn't the time to argue. "What an arrogant man you are."

His smile was whimsical. "Does that mean you've decided I do qualify as a man, after all?"

She felt a pang of guilt as she realized he'd taken her provoking words seriously. "I only said those things because I was very, very annoyed with you."

"And because when you get annoyed you get even more mouthy than usual." He reached out to pull her closer. The soft night breeze wrapped her skirts around his legs. "Lucky for you I'm such an understanding man, hmm?"

"Lucky for me you're a man, period. Any kind of man at all," she whispered against his shirt.

He laughed softly into her hair. "Why is that?"

"Because I've fallen in love with you, Gryph."

He froze. Then his hands caught and held her face so that he could look down at her in the moonlight. His expression was stark and searching. "Sariana?"

"Let's not talk about it," she said, her fingertips sliding upward into his hair. "There is so little time before morning."

"But, Sariana—"

"Hold me, Gryph."

His arms enfolded her with an urgency that swamped everything else.

At dawn the next morning Gryph woke Sariana and gave her a few terse instructions. He told her she was safe in the shelter of the cove and if something happened to him, she could use the river sled to make her way back to Little Chance. There she was to go straight to Delek's house. Gryph made Sariana repeat the directions to his friend's home twice to make sure she had them.

"With any luck, I'll locate the ship this afternoon," he told her crisply as he finished checking his weapon kit. "I'll go in tonight for a closer look. Then I'll decide if I'll try to destroy it on my own or wait for Delek and the others. One way or another I'll be back tomorrow morning."

"I don't like it," Sariana said.

He smiled at that. "You rarely do approve of any of my suggestions, lady."

"You don't give suggestions. You give commands."

"I just want you to be as safe as possible."

"I know," she said with a cheeky grin. "The fact that I can sense your intentions are well meant is the only reason I even listen to you at times like this."

Gryph raised his eyes to the strip of dawn sky overhead. "Save me from empathic females." He picked up a blade bow and handed it to her. "Pay attention, Sariana. I'm going to leave this behind with you. It's a good, all-purpose weapon and it can also be a useful tool. See all these different blades?"

Sariana studied the small quiver of blades. Each was a slightly different shape. Many had attachments such as tiny ropes or nets that were cleverly bound to the shaft of the blade. The specialized attachments unfurled or uncoiled or snapped into position when the blade was fired.

"What about them?"

"You slide the one you want into firing position like this." Gryph demonstrated with cool precision. "You fire it by releasing this trigger."

"Clever," Sariana said dryly.

"Sure. That goes without saying. It was invented by a westerner."

He gave her one last, hard kiss and then he walked out of the cove without glancing back. He pushed all the hot memories of the previous night out of his mind, including Sariana's soft declaration of love. He had to keep his mind on his task or both of them and much of the populace of the western continent might wind up paying with their lives.

He would deal with the issue of love later.

Gryph made good time through the gorge. He walked swiftly along the river's edge. His fingers played on the prisma lock and in his mind he focused on the rays of light beyond the visible range that Sariana had helped him pick up last night. He kept a small portion of his awareness fixed on his surroundings. It would be stupid to become some hawkbeetle's dinner at this stage.

The pulsing beam of invisible light that was peculiar to live prisma was clear in his mind now. It was beyond the range of human eyesight, but through some poorly understood process, it could be channeled through another bit of prisma. When that happened, a receptive, tuned mind could pick it up.

Gryph had practiced long and hard as a boy learning how to focus, channel and control his awareness so that the strange prisma rays could be detected and tracked.

That had been only the initial part of his training. The other half had consisted of learning how to tune his mind to the frequency of the emitting beam of light and jam it.

The theoretical middle ground which no Shield had ever attempted as far as Gryph's people knew was to tune into the frequency of live prisma and resonate with it. It would be difficult to do, but once the frequency was under a man's control, he just might be able to stabilize it to the point where he could detonate the weapons in a deliberate, controlled manner.

It was far more likely such an experiment would result in wiping out everything and everyone in the vicinity, including the crazy Shield working the prisma.

By late afternoon Gryph had followed the pulsing beams to a point several kilometers from where he had left Sariana. He stopped when he realized how close to the source he was. All the hunting instincts and skills that had been bred and trained into him were fully alert.

The gorge had deepened. The walls rose dizzyingly high overhead, revealing only a tiny strip of sky. Evening shadows were already thick on the valley floor.

The river was a rough and tumble cascade now. White water foamed over boulders and squeezed through twists and turns in the narrowed riverbed channel.

Gryph used the shadows, although he was relatively certain he wouldn't be noticed, even if someone up ahead was watching. There was enough natural cover in the area to hide his movements. Even another Shield would be unable to sense his presence. The pulses of the live prisma were so strong Gryph was certain they masked everything, including the weaker pulse of the neutralized prisma in his lock.

The tricks he had learned fighting bandits in the frontier provinces were second nature to him. He used them without conscious thought while he fine-tuned his focus on the live prisma.

For a moment he was confused. The beams he had been following seemed to be emanating from overhead, not from a point farther along the gorge floor. He looked up, seeking a possible cave or ledge large enough to hold a ship. He used his mind link to narrow the search for the ship while he used other skills to hunt for signs of human beings.

Half an hour later, just as night threatened to overtake the gorge completely, Gryph found what he was looking for. A vapor lamp flared briefly high up on the canyon wall.

He hadn't been able to spot it from the base, but Gryph knew now there had to be an entrance into the rock up there somewhere. From the records he had studied as a young student, he knew that the ships on Windarra had frequently been hidden in small caves dug into such mountainsides as this one.

There had to be a way to climb to the place where he had caught the glimmer of a vapor lamp.

The canyon wall proved to be less sheer than it had looked from a distance. The climb toward his goal was easier than Gryph had originally thought it would be. In fact, it was more of a scramble over tumbled boulders and small landslides than a real rock climb.

A surprisingly short while after he had left the valley floor, Gryph was crouching within a few meters of his destination. From his vantage point it was easy to see the wide mouth that looked as if it had been gouged out of the canyon wall. A vapor lamp burned deep inside, but there was no sign of anyone around the lamp.

Nor was there any sign of a weapon ship. But the pulsing strength of the prisma rays focusing through his weapon kit lock and coalescing inside his brain was all the evidence Gryph needed of a ship's presence. The rays swamped the area, bathing it in invisible light. No single, cut piece of prisma could produce so much power.

For the first time in his life, Gryph thought, he was doing what he had been created to do. He had tracked a prisma ship to its lair.

This close to the source of live, uncut prisma, Gryph could not hope to isolate the small, delicate ray that would identify another Shield's lock. It was just as well. The masking effects of the stronger beams also concealed his own lock from anyone who might be monitoring the night for intruders.

Gryph watched the cave entrance for a while longer, willing someone to come fetch the vapor lamp. Whoever had put it there would surely want to retrieve it before long. It made no sense to leave the lamp burning with no one around.

Time slipped past with excruciating slowness and no one appeared. If it hadn't been for the burning lamp, Gryph wouldn't even have guessed there were humans in the vicinity. He was cold, cramped and bored. The best frontier training did not teach a man how to ignore the discomforts of a night watch. It just taught him how to endure them.

Gryph's patience was rewarded shortly before dawn.

The figure of a man appeared from the upper reaches of the gorge wall, following an unseen path that he must have found at the lip of the canyon. He carried a vapor lamp. The tiny light zigzagged slowly down the steep rock wall. Gryph watched it closely.

The man, who was draped in a stylish, knee-length cloak against the predawn chill, was only a dark shadow behind the lamp, but Gryph was ready for him. The figure passed no more than a couple of meters from Gryph's hiding place.

Gryph slipped silently out into the open, closing in on his target from behind. It would have been easy to kill the man, but that was the last thing Gryph intended in that moment. He needed answers, not the silence of death.

He took his victim around the throat, choking off any potential scream. The man flailed frantically as his airway was closed. The small vapor lamp he had been carrying dropped onto the rocks with a tiny clatter.

Gryph regretted the small noise, but there wasn't much he could do about it. He concentrated on subduing his quarry. He didn't want to spend any more time out in the open than necessary.

He was in the process of dragging his victim back into the shadows when a ball of fiery light and blazing pain burst inside his head.

Gryph had never experienced such agony in his life. It wasn't like the night he had first linked with Sariana and it wasn't like the silent explosion of light that had rendered him momentarily unconscious the previous night. He sensed vaguely that it was an effect of prisma, but it was nothing he had been trained to handle.

He fought back out of instinct. He held onto consciousness desperately, and rode the light rays in his mind the way he rode a normal prisma beam. There was something drastically abnormal about these rays, but he couldn't take time to analyze them.

Gryph groped for the frequency and locked onto it. His

fingers burned into his weapon kit lock as he fought to reverse the strangely pulsing rays.

The battle to force the blinding mental rays out of his mind was unlike any combat he had ever faced. He was learning as he went along. There was nothing like necessity to spur the educational process.

With a surge of effort he managed to tangle and jam the rays long enough to clear his mind. Gryph didn't hesitate. He sensed a second assault was already underway and he was too weak from the first battle to deal with it.

Mentally he studied the tangle of prisma beams he had just created, aware that it was already jamming and neutralizing itself. He knew he needed a barrier against the next slamming prisma ray. The only thing that could stop prisma was more prisma.

Not completely aware of how he was doing it, but driven by the need to survive, Gryph grabbed mentally at the disintegrating rays of the first assault. He touched his lock and deliberately tried to strengthen the retreating frequencies, sending them back toward their source with a positive rather than neutral force.

He had never tried anything like it before in his life, and the roar of anger that echoed in the canyon a moment later took him as much by surprise as anything else that had happened. It came from a figure who was even now staggering from the wide entrance of the cave.

"You bastard, you're almost as strong as I am and that's saying something."

Gryph opened his eyes, maintaining his fierce mental grip on the retreating frequencies. He was aware the rays he was trying to send back to their source had been halted by the other Shield. He also sensed that if he relaxed his grip for even a moment the other man would nail him.

It was a mental standoff, but it left Gryph physically helpless. It took every ounce of his energy and will to hold off the assault the other Shield was trying to send into his mind.

The cloaked figure Gryph had been about to drag off into the shadows coughed and sat up slowly. He looked at the two frozen Shields confronting each other and pushed back the hood of his cloak.

"Well," Etion Rakken said in a hoarse voice, "this is an interesting development. I always wondered what would happen if two Shields did battle with each other. I wonder what's going on inside your minds?"

"Get him in a twist," the other Shield grated through his teeth. "Hurry. He's far stronger than I would have guessed."

"Of course, Targyn," Rakken said soothingly. "I'll take care of everything. After all, we're partners, aren't we?"

Gryph was helpless to defend himself from Rakken as the banker deftly locked him in a twist, the device used on the frontier to chain bandits.

A few minutes later he was dragged into the cave and down a short corridor lined in a strange gray metal to a small chamber paneled in the same material.

When he was lying bound and helpless on the floor of the chamber the energy that had been beating at Gryph's mind finally relaxed.

Gryph looked up at the other Shield who was leaning against the door of the chamber and taking deep breaths to regain his strength.

"So much for a glorious death at the hands of bandits," Gryph remarked. "I hate to see a good legend ruined by reality, Targyn."

"The reality of what I am going to do with the prisma ship I have found in this mountain will create a legend that will last for a thousand years, Chassyn," Targyn said with grim satisfaction. He turned to Rakken. "Strip him."

Rakken glanced at Targyn. "Why? All we need is his weapon kit."

"You fool. Do you really think that all of a Shield's weapons are in his kit? A trained Shield can make a weapon out of almost anything. Strip him. He's safe enough while he's in that twist. When you're done I'll go through his clothing. Then you can give him back his trousers and his shirt. We'll leave him barefoot, however. A good pair of boots is a potential tool for a skilled man."

Etion Rakken hovered over his captive, loosening Gryph's clothing. Targyn went through everything carefully, removing a number of small nondescript strips of metal. When he was satisfied he flung the garments down on the floor. "Get dressed," he ordered.

Gryph slowly pulled on his clothes. The twist allowed very slow, very careful movements. His muscles felt weak and shaky from the mental battle he had fought earlier.

"That should take care of him for now," Targyn decided. He smiled humorlessly at his captive. "We'll have more to say to each other later, Chassyn." He picked up Gryph's weapon kit.

"Let me have that," Rakken said quickly. "I am very curious about these weapon kits. I would like to examine one more closely."

"What good will that do?" Targyn asked impatiently. "You can't possibly open it. Even I can't open another Shield's kit."

"Nevertheless, I would like to take a close look at it," Rakken insisted.

"As you wish, *partner*." Targyn slammed the door shut on the small chamber.

Gryph heard a standard western style lock click shut outside the room. If he could have gotten his hands on that lock, he could have probed its secrets in a matter of minutes.

But he could no more reach the lock through the door than he could reach the moon. Or Sariana.

Sariana.

Gryph wondered if she was already on her way back to Little Chance. The only hope now was that Delek would get back in time with enough Shields to deal with Targyn and the prisma ship.

Gryph wondered how many of his friends would die before they figured out how to fight another Shield who had learned the trick of turning prisma into a mind-to-mind weapon.

Chapter
16

THE harsh ball of light slammed into Sariana's head and burst into a thousand fragments.

It vanished in the next second.

Sariana awoke with a cry and jerked upright amid the folds of the travel quilt. She sat motionless on the gently rocking sled, her palms damp with sweat, her heart pounding. Lucky stuck its head out of a cloak pocket nearby and hissed inquiringly.

"It's all right," she whispered huskily to the lizard. "At least, I think it's all right. Just a nightmare."

Sariana waited for pieces of the dream to trickle back into her consciousness, but there was nothing. No lingering images or even people.

But she was filled with a sense of dread that no amount of rationalization could dispel. And as she calmed down she forced herself to acknowledge what she secretly feared: Something had happened to Gryph.

Sariana looked up at the narrow wedge of night sky

overhead. It would be dawn soon. She dared not wait any longer.

"Come on, Lucky. We'd better get moving."

The lizard sat on top of a storage locker and supervised Sariana's frantic preparations for departure.

"I wish I had paid more attention yesterday when Gryph showed me how to operate this thing," Sariana admitted to Lucky as she fumbled with the sled's propeller mechanism. The truth was she hadn't expected to have to run the boat on her own.

But her memory for detail stood her in good stead. Sariana pushed the sled farther out into the river, hopped back on board and settled herself on the bench Gryph had used. She took a firm hold on the hand grips and pulled back. With a soft slap of blades and fins hitting water, the river sled obediently leaped forward. The sled's cleverly designed system of gears, belts and pulleys created tremendous mechanical advantage that was translated into propulsion power. Another ingenious western invention, Sariana decided wryly. It was just as well her own people were so astute when it came to business and law. They were going to need whatever advantage they could get during the next few years to hold their own with the westerners.

There was barely enough starlight filtering down to the base of the canyon to enable Sariana to tell water from land. She aimed the craft deeper into the gorge. Lucky hopped onto Sariana's shoulder and settled there.

"I know he wanted us to go back to Little Chance," Sariana told the lizard, "but there isn't time. Something has happened. I have to get to him."

Sariana strained to see the dark river and wondered how angry Gryph would be when he discovered her latest act of disobedience.

"He can yell at me all he wants as soon as we find him, Lucky. And you can bet your tail he will yell. He seems to have been born with the odd notion that other people should always do what he tells them. I just hope that arrogance hasn't gotten him into real trouble this time."

She was chatting to calm herself again, Sariana realized. The truth was she was scared to death because she couldn't analyze the earlier explosion of light inside her head. There had been a sense of pain, but she had known it wasn't her own pain she was feeling. That meant it had to be Gryph's. But the sensation had vanished quickly along with the bursting beam of light.

She knew Gryph had to be a long distance away from her and it scared her to think of how devastating that light beam had been to have been reflected all the way from Gryph's mind to hers. Gryph had said the link between them was highly erratic and unpredictable. It worked best in moments of passion or moments of danger. Whatever had happened to Gryph, it definitely qualified as a moment of danger.

"What if he's dead, Lucky? What am I going to do?"

Sariana pulled harder on the blade handles. She would not allow herself to even think about that possibility again. Gryph wasn't dead. She would *know* if he were dead. That realization gave her comfort and energy. The blades and fins of the river sled sent the small craft skimming over the surface of the sluggish river.

The sled was a model of efficiency, but even so Sariana's arms ached by mid-morning. She switched to the foot pedals for a while and tried to estimate her progress. The sled was making good headway but the river was flowing more swiftly and powerfully now as the gorge narrowed. She glanced toward shore and wondered if she should tie the sled along the bank and go the rest of the way on foot.

One of the problems was that she didn't know exactly how far she had to go. She was counting on the odd sixth sense she seemed to have developed to let her know when she was getting close to Gryph. It had always worked best at short range, she reminded herself encouragingly. She had always been so acutely aware of him when he was near.

Absently she fingered the elegant pin on her cloak while she scanned the steep walls of the gorge. The water was definitely getting rough and the sled was slowing rapidly. The shoreline was not particularly inviting with its scrubby vegetation and rocky terrain, but Sariana knew it was time to get out of the sled. She decided she would tie up the craft somewhere around the next bend.

She heard the roar of the rapids a few seconds before she felt the sled begin to buck. Sariana grabbed the blade handles, steering desperately for the shore.

Putting the small craft at an angle to the strong current proved to be a mistake. It heaved once and then the whole right side lifted majestically up out of the water.

"Lucky!"

The lizard was already moving, darting into the safety of one of Sariana's cloak pockets. Sariana fought for control of the sled as it heaved again in the rough water. But she knew she did not have the expertise to save the boat. It was going to flip over and her biggest fear was getting trapped beneath the sled.

"Hang on," she muttered to the hapless lizard as she sealed the pocket of her cloak. "And hold your breath if you can." She bunched up the cloak and tied it around her shoulders so that it was out of the way. Then she grabbed the blade sling Gryph had entrusted to her and leaped out of the sled.

The water was cold, a shock to her system, but she had little time to think about it. Sariana's main concern was fighting through the rough current to get to shore. It wasn't that far away, she told herself, and the water wasn't that deep. She could make it.

But the driving power of the water was a force with which to reckon. It knocked the breath out of Sariana as it flung her carelessly against a boulder. She clung to the rock, gasping for air as she gazed longingly at the shoreline. Right now it seemed a hundred kilometers away. Lucky made anxious noises from deep inside the wet cloak.

Sariana glanced downstream and saw that the river sled had been driven against the bank. It was upside down. She decided that, on the whole, she would rather be where she was than underneath the sled. She sought for handholds on the rock and grimly fought her way out of the water.

Once seated on top of the precarious perch, Sariana ripped open the pocket of her cloak. The scarlet-toe blinked back at her. Lucky was clearly disgruntled but otherwise unhurt.

"Just hang on a little longer while I figure out how to use this gadget Gryph gave us," Sariana said bracingly to the skeptical looking lizard.

Sariana concentrated, remembering Gryph's terse instructions. She selected the blade with the thin cord wound around its shaft. Then she notched the blade, cocked the bow and aimed it at the dense foliage around the shoreline. Cautiously she released the tension in the small weapon.

The blade left the bow with a jolt that took Sariana by surprise. She held onto the rock to keep from falling into the raging current. Even as she made a grab for her balance the arrow was thudding into some unseen object in the foliage. The thin line it was trailing went taut in Sariana's fingers.

Sariana gingerly tested the line. It felt strong and tightly anchored. She pulled a little harder and it went abruptly slack in her hands as the blade dropped out of its target.

"Damn it to the Lightstorm!" Sariana's temper flared, overcoming her fear. Savagely she jerked at the limp line, pulling it back through the water.

A few minutes later she was holding a lapful of ungainly rope and a blade. She realized she had no idea how to recoil the line and rearm the bow.

"Of all the stupid, idiotic weapons," Sariana raged. "Dumb westerners and their gadgets. Arrogant Shields and their silly toys. I tell you, Lucky, I've about had it with the western provinces. Nothing is simple and straightforward around here. Nothing is logical and dependable. Do you think an easterner would have designed a crazy weapon like this? Or a useless sled that gets tipped over by the first wave it encounters? Never in a million years." She glared at the line spilling over her wet skirts.

It was a good, strong line. If one ignored the overly

clever bow and the useless blade, one was still left holding a strong length of rope.

"I think, Lucky, that the key here is simplicity, not clever gadgetry." Sariana picked up the end of the rope and reached down to loop it around the rock on which she was sitting. Water splashed over her hands and arms as she worked, but it proved relatively simple to tie a strong knot.

Sariana regarded her work dubiously for a few seconds and then tied a second knot just to be on the safe side.

"Ready Lucky? Don't feel bad. Neither am I." She re-sealed the lizard's pocket. Then, holding onto one end of the line, she coiled it around herself a couple of times. Cautiously she slipped down the side of the rock into the water.

The rushing river caught her, trying to yank her down-stream. It snapped the blade bow from her grasp. Sariana didn't try to hang on to it. She was too busy clinging to the line she had wrapped around herself. She paid it out slowly and deliberately. It proved stronger than the river. She was able to fight a controlled retreat out of the rough water into a calmer area.

Finally she felt the river's grip slacken. With renewed energy Sariana waded toward shore. A few minutes later she was sitting on the bank, the blade in her hand.

"I'm afraid that Gryph is just going to have to get an-other blade bow," Sariana told Lucky as she tossed aside the useless blade. The line to which it was attached was yanked back into the middle of the river by the force of the current and the blade disappeared into the water.

"Gadgets," Sariana muttered and started pulling off her soaked clothes.

Lucky scrambled out of the cloak pocket and headed for a nearby sun-warmed rock. Enroute he treated himself to several mouthfuls of leaves. Sariana looked wistfully at the sled which had snagged on the opposite side of the river and wondered if the food in the storage lockers had sur-vived. Given her present position, it didn't much matter. The wrecked sled might as well have been on the moon for all the good it did her.

Sariana left her chemise to dry on her body, picked up some of her wet garments and started forward. "Enough fun and games, Lucky. We've got to keep moving."

Her chemise dried fairly quickly. By mid-afternoon Sariana's cloak was also dry. The skirts of her traveling dress took longer, but she was finally able to put it on as the late afternoon shadows filled the gorge. When she was dressed once more she looked down at herself in wry disgust. Everything she had on showed evidence of its recent ordeal in the river. A few things, such as the bodice of the dress, appeared to have shrunk. Ahead of her was the dismal prospect of a night spent alone on shore with none of the recently maligned western gadgets to make herself more comfortable.

She wondered again just how far Gryph could have gotten the day before. The canyon walls loomed over her, rising to eerie heights and leaving very little sky visible as evening approached. Wearily she lowered herself to a rock and tried to figure out what to do next.

For the first time since she had deliberately compelled Gryph to make love to her, Sariana tried to use the freakish new sense of communication she had discovered within herself.

"It's probably just like every other western gadget," she informed the lizard as she sat on the rock and gazed out over the river. "A clever, intriguing toy that's ultimately useless—especially when you really need it."

She had just finished uttering the words when the tendril of awareness brushed her mind.

"Gryph!" She knew it was him. She was beginning to recognize the sensations of his mind. Those sensations were as unique and as identifiable to her as his physical features. He was somewhere nearby. She knew it.

Reenergized, Sariana floundered through the underbrush and over the tumbled boulders that lined the river. The roar of the rapids cut off all other sound now. Sariana struggled to hold on to a vague sense of direction she had picked up from the fleeting touch of Gryph's mind. She followed it blindly, heedless of the oncoming night, the rough terrain and the snagging undergrowth.

A few minutes later she came to a halt, aware that the sense of direction had changed. Gryph was no longer in front of her. She was certain of it. He was above her somewhere.

Sariana tipped back her head and scanned the dark walls of the canyon. He couldn't be up there, she thought. She must have misread the feeling of direction she had gotten. But he was close. He had to be somewhere near. She was certain of it.

Uneasily, Sariana eyed the boulders that had cascaded down the steep wall in front of her. Perhaps if she climbed higher she could get a clearer impression of where the stray thought had come from.

She was groping for toeholds in the darkness when the booted foot appeared above her on top of the boulder she had been about to climb.

Sariana screamed and jerked backward, nearly losing her balance. Lucky hissed inside the pocket.

"Only a very strongly linked Shieldmate would have come this far in search of her lord," the stranger said as he bent down and wrapped his fingers around her wrist. With seemingly little effort he pulled Sariana up the side of the boulder and stood her on her feet. Then he flipped on a small vapor lamp, revealing a scarred face. "Chassyn always did have the luck of the day. Until recently, that is. Come with me, Sariana. You are expected."

"Who are you?" she whispered, tugging her wrist free.

"I am Lord Targyn." A startlingly formal inclination of the head accompanied the introduction.

"You're a Shield." She glanced at the weapon kit hanging on his belt.

"The strongest one of all," Targyn murmured.

"I've always admired modesty. Let actions speak for themselves, I say. No need to brag." Tension seemed to be having its usual effect. Her ever-nimble tongue was gearing up for battle.

Targyn smiled strangely. "I, too, am a great believer in action. Are you ready?"

"Depends. Where are we going?"

"You have come to search for your lord, have you not?"

"If we're talking about Gryph, I should tell you I don't think of him as my lord."

Targyn frowned. "Chassyn is your husband, isn't he?"

"Actually, I don't think of him as either a lord or a husband. I think of him more as being a nuisance. But it's mutual. I'm sure he thinks of me precisely the same way."

"Enough of this nonsense. Come with me."

The scarlet-toe shifted slightly within Sariana's pocket but made no sound as Sariana bit down on her tongue. She had been around Gryph long enough to know that Shields tended to expect others to obey them.

"Arrogant bastards," Sariana mumbled as she started walking.

"What did you say?" The Shield moved up silently behind her.

"Nothing," she assured him. "You know, it's getting hard to see. Could you hold that vapor lamp steadier? A little professionalism would be appreciated."

Targyn appeared rather bemused by her display of annoyance. Without a word he moved closer and aimed the vapor lamp more carefully.

"Thank you," Sariana murmured dryly, then realized she was stepping over the last tumbled rock and into the wide mouth of a cave.

A large vapor lamp flared into life at the back of the cave and a figure moved forward. Sariana recognized the shape and carriage of the man before she saw his face in the glow of the lamp.

"Etion! What are you doing here?"

Rakken smiled his charming smile. "As it happens, I was just about to sit down to dinner. Will you join me?"

Sariana stared at him. "I'm sure you realize, Etion, that I've had a number of shocks recently. This is one of the biggest. As it happens, I'm starving. I will gladly join you for dinner under two conditions. The first is that you take me to Gryph. The second is that you promise to give me some explanation about what's going on here."

Etion nodded gravely. "Chassyn will be joining us for dinner, so that takes care of condition number one. As for condition number two, I think that can be dealt with also. Targyn? Will you join us?"

Targyn strode into the lamplight, scowling. "I don't think you should let Chassyn out of that chamber. He's dangerous."

"You assured me he was harmless enough as long as he was kept in the twist."

"That's true, but I still don't like having him out in the open."

"You'll be there to protect me if he somehow escapes the twist." Etion spoke soothingly, as if to a fractious child. "There is no doubt that you are the stronger Shield, is there?"

"None." Targyn lifted his head proudly and strode past Sariana and Rakken. "I'll get Chassyn."

Rakken sighed as the other man strode off. "Thick-headed bastard," he murmured under his breath.

Sariana drew a silent breath of relief. At least Gryph was alive and apparently unharmed if he could take a meal. She would take this one step at a time, feeling her way through the quagmire of events the same way she had felt her way through the House of Reflections.

The first task was to handle Etion Rakken. She couldn't begin to imagine what he was doing here, but if he had taken Gryph prisoner, it was clear he was on the wrong side in this mess.

"It would appear your journey upriver has been a little rough," Etion remarked as he graciously extended his arm and led Sariana down a corridor of gray metal. Once inside the corridor there were no vapor lamps. The illumination seemed to come from within the metal walls. Sariana gazed around in wonder as she spoke to Rakken.

"I lost the sled and had to swim to shore. I tell you, Etion, things like this never happened to me when I lived in Rendezvous."

Etion smiled faintly. "I'm well aware of how unexpected

life can be in the west." He paused in front of an opening carved in the corridor. "My humble chambers await." He bowed her into the room with a mocking flourish.

Sariana stepped inside and glanced around the odd room. It was a strange shape to her eyes, as if it were all just slightly out of proportion. The ceiling was a little too low for psychological comfort. It was lined with more of the metal she had noticed in the corridor. The glow of the illumination imbedded in the metal seemed vaguely wrong to her eyes. Instead of the soft, warm glow of vapor, it was a harsh light that jangled the senses.

"You get used to it," Etion said wryly.

"The light? Where does it come from?"

"I don't know." He shrugged. "I tried to take the ceiling apart a couple of months ago to find out, but I couldn't cut through that gray metal. The prisma cutter might do it, however. I'll give it a try one of these days. Sit down."

Sariana stepped slowly toward a round table that seemed a little too close to the floor. A bench of the same metal ringed the table. It was contoured in a slightly sloping fashion. When she sat down she felt uncomfortable.

"Etion, what is this place?"

"I wish I knew," Rakken said quietly as he went to the wall and pushed against it. A panel slid open revealing an assortment of familiar looking wines and ales. "A glass of wine, Sariana?"

"I could use it." She tried to speak calmly, as if everything that were happening was perfectly routine. Rakken handed her the wine. "Where's Gryph?"

There was a movement in the open doorway behind her.

"Right behind you," Gryph announced in a rough voice as he walked slowly and awkwardly into the room. Targyn followed. "I don't suppose there's any point asking you why you disobeyed my orders, is there, Sariana?"

"Of course not." Sariana jumped to her feet and went flying toward him. She stopped when she realized there was something wrong with the way he was standing. His hands were behind his back and he seemed to be having trouble staying on his feet.

"By the Lightstorm, what's wrong? What have they done to you?" she snapped, circling him to assess the damage.

Rakken chuckled. "Nothing yet. He's in a twist. Another witty little western invention designed by Shields to use on the bandits they take prisoner."

Sariana stared at the strange mechanism strapped to Gryph's waist at the back. Leather straps that appeared to be under extreme tension came from openings in a metal case. The straps were attached to Gryph's wrists and ankles.

"There's some give in the straps as long as he moves very slowly and cautiously," Rakken explained easily. "But if he makes any sudden moves—such as grabbing for my throat—the straps tighten and lock. He'll wind up flat on his back, possibly breaking an arm in the process. Here's your wine, my dear. Chassyn? What can I get for you?"

"Ale," Gryph said. His eyes were on Sariana's worried face. "What happened to you? You look like you swam the river."

"I did. I'll tell you all about it later."

An image of Lucky popped into her head but Gryph said nothing aloud. Sariana blinked, realizing he was projecting the question silently. Which meant he probably wanted a silent answer. She casually patted her cloak pocket. Lucky stayed silent.

"Targyn, take Lady Sariana's cloak, will you?" Rakken asked as he opened a bottle of ale. "And then tell Miscroft we're ready for dinner."

"Tell him yourself. You can take care of the woman's cloak, too. I don't take orders from you." Targyn strode across the room and snatched a bottle of ale from the cabinet in the wall. "I don't take orders from anyone," he added as he opened the bottle. "You have a bad habit of forgetting that, banker."

"My apologies, Lord Targyn. I'll tell Miscroft myself. Excuse me for a moment."

Sariana saw the anger in Rakken's eyes as he went past

her, but he was careful to keep it under control. It was obvious Etion did not want to push Targyn too much.

Targyn tipped the bottle of ale and downed several large swallows. Then he lowered the bottle and wiped his mouth on the back of his sleeve. He ignored Sariana but his eyes were feverishly alert as they scanned Gryph.

"I'm going to kill you," Targyn said. "Before this is all over, I'm going to kill you. There's a certain justice here, you know. I think you're the one the Council would have sent after me. Nervous fools. I'll use you for target practice. I've never killed another Shield. Should be interesting for both of us." He took another swallow of ale and chuckled. "Rakken wants to keep you alive for a while. He thinks we may need you. He's afraid I'll lose control of the prisma and detonate it accidentally if I don't have backup. But I'm a lot stronger than he thinks. When this is all over I'm going to get rid of you both. He's been useful up until now, but I don't need a banker for what I have in mind for the future."

"What do you have in mind?" Gryph crossed the room with painful slowness and finally dropped down onto the oddly contoured bench. His last movement was a little too quick and the twist locked for a few seconds. Gryph set his teeth against the obvious pain and waited until the straps loosened slightly.

Sariana hurried over to the cabinet and picked up the ale bottle Rakken had opened earlier for his prisoner. She brought it over to the low table and set it down in front of Gryph. She sensed the way he was focusing on Targyn and wondered at it. Gryph was concentrating much too hard on the other Shield, even though he was trying to hide the tense surveillance.

Sariana didn't pick up a sense of fear emanating from Gryph. It was more like a battle-ready tension. He clearly considered Targyn a dangerous opponent.

It came to Sariana in that moment that Targyn was somehow the source of that potentially lethal blast of light that had brought her awake in the early hours of the morning. And then she knew for certain that Gryph had been the target of that fireball. She shivered as she sat down near him. It didn't require any great intuitive powers to know Gryph had nearly been killed; that he still might be killed.

"What do I have in mind?" Targyn repeated as he lounged against the wall. "I'll tell you what I have in mind. I'm going to take control of the western provinces, Chassyn. I'm going to have access to all the potential Shield-mates I want and I'm going to produce sons who will someday run the eastern provinces as well as the west. I'm going to create a dynasty of Shields who will take their rightful place on this backwater world."

"The First Generation Pact establishes our role on this planet," Gryph pointed out calmly. He slowly and cautiously picked up the bottle of ale. "Nobody signed anything that puts us in charge."

"The First Generation Pact is an abomination. The Pact was made by sniveling cowards who thought they had to make an alliance with a bunch of stupid colonists who should have died in a lightstorm in the first place." Targyn moved away from the metal wall and waved his ale bottle in a gesture that took in the whole room. "Our brave forefathers were nothing but a herd of nervous keenshees, Chassyn. We got stranded on this planet with a bunch of fools who were involved in some sort of social experiment. We should have taken charge right from the beginning."

"There wasn't much point," Gryph observed mildly. "Once they realized they were stranded here, the Shields assumed there wouldn't be a second generation. It was a fluke that a handful of empathic females survived the crash and even more of a break that they were willing to mate with our ancestors."

Targyn swung around, his scarred face a taut mask of fury. "Those first Shields were cowards. They never assumed their rightful role. They were the strong ones. They should have dominated this continent. All of its resources should have been theirs. They should have ruled. Where are we instead? Living in isolated frontier towns, practicing the old ways of working prisma just in case a stray crystal ship shows up. In the meantime we earn our keep rooting out bandits and doing odd jobs for people who don't want to get their hands dirty. And each generation holds its breath hoping its sons will find a few usable females and that those females will be available under the terms of the damned Pact. Fools, idiots, cowards!" Targyn hurled his empty bottle against the wall. It shattered and fell onto the metal floor.

At that moment the door slid open. Etion Rakken walked in, ignoring the broken ale bottle as if nothing at all were out of the ordinary.

"Miscroft will bring us our meal in a few minutes. Another glass of wine, Sariana?" His gracious manner was intact.

"Yes," Sariana managed to get out in what she hoped was a reasonably calm voice. "I think I could use it."

Targyn glared at all of them. "I have no interest in this pretense of proper social behavior you all feel obliged to engage in. I've got more important things to do." He strode toward the door, indicating Gryph with his chin as he went out. "Watch him, Rakken. If he gets out of control it'll be your problem, not mine. If I find him running loose around here, I'll just kill him now and be done with it."

The door slid shut behind him.

Silence reigned for a short moment in the room. Then Gryph took a long swallow of his ale.

"He's insane, you know. Crazier than a keenshee in heat."

"I know," Rakken said calmly. "That's why I need you."

Sariana put her hands flat on the table. "Do you know what Targyn's planning to do?"

Rakken smiled grimly. "The man has delusions of grandeur."

"What about your delusions?" Gryph asked.

"Mine," Etion explained calmly, "are a lot more realistic. The biggest single find of prisma that has ever been made is sitting in a metal room not far from here. My plan was to use Targyn to neutralize it and then cut it up into marketable pieces. All of it. You see, unlike Targyn, I know what real power is and how it's achieved. One does not own a continent with weapons, although they may be useful as a threat from time to time." He smiled at Sariana. "I am an easterner at heart. I know that there is only one true source of power."

"Great wealth," Sariana concluded for him. She was awed in spite of herself at what he was proposing.

"Precisely, my dear." Rakken raised his glass of wine. "To a future filled with prisma."

Chapter
17

"SUPPOSE you give this to us in a straight line from the beginning, Rakken." Gryph examined the food being set in front of him as he spoke and decided his host probably wasn't going to poison him or Sariana. Not yet at any rate. He automatically reached for one of the eating implements left behind by the silent Miscroft and got his wrist jerked by the twist strap. It took a lot of effort to move with the slow deliberation required by the device. It was like having one's reflexes chained.

It wasn't the pain of the twist that was worrying him the most right now, although he detested being treated like a border bandit. His chief concern was Sariana.

He should have known she would follow him instead of heading back to Last Chance as ordered. Mentally he calculated the distance she had come. He didn't know for certain when she had left the cove, but he was willing to lay odds on the time having been shortly before dawn.

About the instant Targyn had sent that paralyzing blast of energy into his head.

She must have found him by the same means he had traced her at the Little Chance fair, using the strange link that shimmered erratically between them.

Gryph glanced at Sariana who was eating her food with all the fine manners she would use during a formal meal in the Avylyn household. From her calm, politely regal attitude a man would think she dined out in strange chambers lined with alien metal several times a month. She constantly amazed him.

He knew from the fact that she had obviously been drenched earlier in the day that the loss of the sled had been a harrowing ordeal. He could only speculate on what had happened to the blade bow. It had undoubtedly been lost when the sled capsized.

Ah, well, he chided himself. If it hadn't disappeared into the river, Targyn would have taken it from her when he had discovered her climbing the canyon wall. There was no point tormenting himself with thoughts of how useful the weapon would have been in their present situation. A man had to work with what he had.

Unfortunately, what he had at the moment was a very limited assortment of tools.

"From the beginning?" Rakken mused as he served himself from one of the platters Miscroft had left. He poured another glass of wine for himself while he was at it. "Well, that would take us back to a little over five years ago when I first accepted the reality of my circumstances. It was clear to me that I was going to have to live in exile for the rest of my days. An unfortunate scandal back home ensured my sentence. I determined then that my exile would be as comfortable as possible, however." He looked at Sariana with a faint smile. "For the past year I have urged you to accept the reality of your own exile, Sariana. But you insisted on clinging to your dreams of going home. If you had shown a realistic attitude, I would have taken you into my confidence much sooner. I have felt all along that you and I would make a good team. But you needed time to adjust to the notion of being stranded in the western provinces."

"She's not stranded," Gryph pointed out coolly. "Nor is she in exile. Not any longer. In case you've forgotten, she has recently married into a new social class. That class has a policy of looking after its own. That's something you would do well to keep in mind."

Rakken's mouth twisted slightly. "So you have become Shield business, Sariana. If you had shown some sense when I suggested a marriage alliance between the two of us you would not be in the situation you presently find yourself."

"What situation is that, Etion?" Sariana faced him with politely challenging inquiry. "Tell me exactly what is going on around here."

"Very well." Etion sat forward, his expression becoming more intense. He sipped wine, ignoring his food. "Five years ago I set out to make my fortune here in the west. The bank I established has proved quite profitable. The locals are shrewd in some ways but quite unsophisticated in others."

"Spoken like a typical easterner," Gryph muttered as he slowly put a wedge of bread into his mouth and chewed.

"I'm afraid it's true," Etion said mildly. "Westerners proved fairly easy to manipulate in business, although I'll admit they're learning. In any event, given the foreseeable future, I tried to make the best of matters. I learned as much as I could about western history, including the legend of the Shield class. It was, I soon found out, all bound up with the legend of the origin of prisma. I quickly discovered just how extremely valuable and rare prisma is. I decided that my goal would be to corner the market. But other than that which already exists as jewelry or weapon kit locks, the stuff is impossible to find. And then I learned that the only way to get more of it was to uncover something called a prisma crystal ship."

"I didn't even believe such ships existed until recently," Sariana put in.

Rakken nodded. "I know. The locals have a built-in tendency toward drama. They love a good story. For quite some time I was sure the tale of the ships and the Shields' ability to work prisma was just the stuff of legend. But I needed to know as much as possible about my subject, so I pursued that legend. I ran into other problems when I tried to find out the Shields' version of the story."

"Let me guess," Gryph said. "You couldn't get one to talk."

"You are an extremely closed-mouth lot as I found out when I finally made a journey to one of the frontier provinces. Strong, silent types. At least when it came to discussing your past. No cooperation at all. But I persevered."

"How did you root out Targyn?" Gryph asked with genuine curiosity. "He was supposed to have died gloriously fighting off a pack of bandits."

Sariana gave him a sidelong glance. "Apparently Shields like a good, rousing tale as much as everyone else around here does. You had no problem buying the legend of Targyn, I take it?"

Gryph shrugged and winced when the small action caused the twist's straps to jerk. "To tell you the truth, everyone was greatly relieved that Targyn had disappeared in a noble battle. He was becoming a problem."

Etion arched his eyebrows. "I can guess why. He's a rather obsessive individual, isn't he?"

"Nuttier than a rackle seed cake," Gryph agreed.

Etion nodded. "He's fanatically interested in Shield history."

"And in his own future?" Sariana asked dryly.

"Quite correct," Rakken said. "The man has apparently devoted a lifetime to exploring the possibilities of working prisma in unique ways. He obviously must have had some natural talent to begin with, but one must credit him with being willing to develop himself." Rakken looked directly at Gryph. "He is very strong when it comes to working prisma, I take it? Stronger than most Shields?"

"Most Shields don't attempt to turn prisma into a usable weapon," Gryph said with seeming carelessness. "It's dangerous enough as it is."

"Could you do what he plans to do?" Rakken insisted.

"Detonate prisma in a controlled manner?" Gryph shrugged. "I doubt it. Not without killing myself and everything else within a radius of several hundred kilometers. If you want my opinion, I doubt that Targyn can do it, either."

"He thinks he can."

"The man's insane," Gryph reminded him.

Rakken drummed his hands on the table. "I see. To be truthful, you relieve my mind somewhat. The last thing I want to do is blow up half the continent. I was almost sure Targyn couldn't manage to control the prisma he found, but one has to be cautious."

Gryph said nothing, but he caught a quick, questioning glance from Sariana. She was remembering the theoretical possibilities Gryph had mentioned to her when he had told her why the missing prisma cutter had become Shield business. Just because a theory had never been tested didn't mean it wasn't valid. There was little comfort in telling oneself that the theory might possibly be wrong.

"I only need Targyn to neutralize the material of the crystal ship we've found," Rakken was saying calmly. "Once that's done I understand the prisma will be in a usable state. Is that correct?"

"Essentially," said Gryph. "Who found the ship? Targyn?"

Rakken nodded. "He spent two years prospecting for it in this gorge after he faked his own death at the hands of the bandits. But when he found it, he discovered what every other prospector discovers. He needed money to excavate his claim. The ship, you see, was buried inside this cliff."

"So he went looking for a banker. Preferably one who could keep his mouth shut," Sariana said with an understanding nod. "He thought you fit the bill because you were an easterner and not likely to gossip about the find to the locals."

Gryph shot her a sidelong glance. "He also knew there wasn't much chance any western banker would help him.

A westerner would know immediately that what he was doing was illegal and incredibly dangerous. Any local banker would have contacted a respectable Shield clan and told them what was happening."

"But you saw the financial potential, right, Etion?" Sariana asked with what Gryph considered far too much professional admiration. The businesswoman in her was intrigued by what Rakken had done. Easterners had a definite problem when it came to putting financial matters into perspective.

Rakken was nodding genially over Sariana's comment. "I saw the financial potential at once, my dear."

"She's not your dear," Gryph said. "She's my wife."

Rakken raised his eyebrows at Sariana. "Not according to the laws of the eastern provinces, right Sariana?"

She carefully avoided looking at either man while she helped herself to more stew. "No, not according to the laws of the east. More stew, Gryph?" she asked brightly.

He paid no attention to the question which he sensed had been asked in order to sidetrack him. Sariana was trying to avoid violence at the dinner table. It was, no doubt, an ancient female custom.

"I have a few questions I'd like answered," Gryph said.

"By all means."

"Where did you get the hired help?"

"You mean Miscroft and the others? Oh, they're acquaintances of Targyn's," Rakken explained casually.

"Bandits he recruited?"

Rakken poured himself a little more wine. "I believe so. According to him the frontier bandits have always had a bad deal here. They are descended from the noble crew of *The Serendipity,* it seems."

"That's the same noble crew that mutinied right after the crash," Gryph advised him. "They killed a lot of people before they were driven off. They've been living on the frontiers ever since."

"Some would say they aren't much different than the Shields," Rakken murmured. "A bunch of outcasts who are barely surviving on the frontiers."

Genuine rage washed through Gryph at the insult. He controlled it with a fierce dose of willpower. "Shields are not outcasts and you damn well know it, Rakken. We are an honorable class. If you choose to do business with bandits and rogues, however, you had better watch your back."

"I always watch my back," Rakken told him. "I learned that lesson a long time ago. Before I came to the western continent. I don't need you to teach me that fundamental tactic."

Gryph studied him for a moment and then let the matter drop. "It was you who arranged to have the cutter stolen?"

Rakken relaxed slightly, pouring more wine for himself. "Targyn informed me we would need one to cut open the ship and whittle the prisma into manageable sizes."

"You're talking about a ship that's been neutralized. My guess is Targyn wants to try cutting into a live ship to see if he can manipulate the weapons individually. That's suicide, Rakken."

"I realize the time has come to get rid of Targyn. But until I found another Shield, I needed him."

"Wait a minute," Sariana said sharply. "This matter of the cutter interests me, Etion. You knew the Avylyns had one, didn't you? You asked me about it on a couple of occasions."

"I was aware of it, yes."

Gryph frowned as he realized the direction in which Sariana's astute reasoning powers were leading her. "Forget it, Sariana. We've got more important things to discuss."

She paid him no attention. She was scowling furiously at Rakken. "You used me, didn't you? You used the information I gave you to set up the theft of the cutter."

"I'll admit that having you in the Avylyn household was convenient," Rakken admitted without any show of remorse. "Don't look so upset, Sariana. It was just business."

Sariana inclined her head proudly. "I see. Business."

Gryph sensed her burning anger and deliberately tried to project a command to control herself. He knew he had been successful when she glanced at him, annoyed, and then went back to her meal.

"Who ordered my informant killed back in Serendipity?" Gryph demanded softly.

Rakken made a careless motion with his left hand. "We learned that Brinton had gotten too close to the truth. Targyn said we had to get rid of him. He gave the orders to the same two men who had already secured the cutter."

"And then you sent those two men after Sariana."

Rakken leaned forward, folding his elbows on the low table. "By then I realized Sariana had not only hired herself a Shield, she had, under local law, managed to get herself married to him. Targyn explained to me just what that meant. I knew by then that I was eventually going to have to get rid of Targyn. You seemed the obvious candidate to replace him."

"You figured you could use Sariana to control me," Gryph concluded.

Rakken smiled slightly. "She proved difficult to nab. The first try in Serendipity failed miserably. One of Targyn's men died and the other nearly drowned in wine."

Sariana drummed her fingers on the metal table. "Was the second try in Little Chance?"

Rakken nodded. "Ah, yes. The House of Reflections fiasco. I must admit, that was a last minute plan put together with local talent who proved most unreliable. But we couldn't just pick you up off the streets of Little Chance in broad daylight. When you headed for the fairgrounds we improvised. The attendant was paid well to look the other way while an elaborate joke was played on a visiting eastern tourist. It was easy to find three young toughs who were more than willing to terrorize said tourist. The goal was to frighten you witless and then drive you to a certain corner of the house. There's a hidden exit there. I had a man waiting to snatch you and bundle you off through the back gates of the fairgrounds. But once again you slipped through my fingers, Sariana."

"By then you knew we were on the trail of the cutter and you reasoned we would head for the gorge," Gryph said slowly.

"It was a logical assumption. Targyn and I decided that the easiest thing to do next was sit back and wait until you found us. Which you obligingly did very early this morning." Rakken peered intently at Gryph. "Tell me the truth. Can you kill Targyn?"

"Maybe. If I had my weapon kit."

Rakken looked thoughtful. "If you fail, he'll turn on me. Ours is a very precarious partnership, to say the least."

"What makes you think I won't turn on you if I'm successful?"

Rakken glanced at Sariana. "As long as I have her, you'll behave yourself."

Sariana spoke. "I think I'm getting a bit tired of being used by everyone concerned in this mess."

Rakken smiled thinly. "Don't worry, my dear. I am a reasonable man. Once Targyn is out of the way I will be more than willing to discuss the financial aspects of our new relationship."

Sariana tilted her head, her expression intently curious. "You're willing to cut us in on the prisma deal?"

"I would much rather do business with you than hold you hostage, Sariana." Rakken gave her a level glance. "I know you very well. More than that, I know your background. I was raised under similar circumstances. You have been trained to think in terms of finances and good business policy since you were in the cradle. One year of living in Serendipity hasn't changed you in that regard. I think you will be very interested in negotiating with me for your cut. Am I right?"

Sariana lifted one shoulder negligently and reached for her wine. "You're probably right, Etion."

Only the restraint of the twist kept Gryph from launching himself across the table at Rakken. The other man wasn't even bothering to seduce Sariana with promises of love and passion. Rakken was too shrewd for that. He was using the one thing guaranteed to make any easterner pay attention: The promise of big business profits.

Gryph was so full of anger that couldn't be released he almost didn't catch the stray, calming thought that wafted through his brain. Then he recognized the source of the soothing sensation. Sariana was telling him to relax.

"Well?" Rakken asked with quiet satisfaction as he scanned the faces of his prisoners. "Do we have an understanding? Gryph will take care of poor, unstable Targyn and then neutralize the ship. Afterward we will cut up the prisma, split it three ways and make our fortunes."

"What about Targyn's men?" Sariana asked. "Miscroft and the others?"

"There are only three," Rakken said. "And to be honest, none of them are very bright. They follow Targyn's orders because he has promised them great wealth. But with him out of the way they should be easy meat for a Shield."

Sariana stared at him. "You expect Gryph to kill all four of them? Targyn included?"

"Why not? It's what he's good at, isn't it?" Rakken asked blandly. "You forget, my dear, that Chassyn and the other Shields make their living fighting border bandits. Bandit disposal is their specialty, and I have it on good authority that they are very skilled at their job. You have only seen your quasi-husband in the sophisticated social context of a city. But that is not his natural habitat. Don't worry. Targyn is his only real problem. Taking care of Miscroft and the others will be nothing more than a mopping up operation for him. But if it makes you feel more secure, rest assured, I am not unarmed myself. I have a blade bow and I can use it. I'm not foolish enough to think I can take Targyn by surprise, but if Chassyn runs into trouble with any of the three bandits, I should be able to help him out."

The tension that gripped Sariana was almost palpable. Gryph could feel the violent anger and denial vibrating in her. But her voice was steady when she spoke to Rakken.

"Why haven't you killed Targyn yourself, Etion? You must have had plenty of opportunity."

Rakken chuckled but there was no humor in the sound. "If you believe a banker who has had no formal experience in hand-to-hand combat or any other kind of fighting can successfully take on a professionally armed Shield, you are very naive, Sariana. You still don't seem to realize just how skilled at violence these men are. Chassyn is every bit as dangerous to me as Targyn is. But at least with Chassyn I have some control."

"Me."

"You," he agreed. "And a business arrangement. It's said Shields honor their word. Sane Shields, at any rate. We'll leave poor Targyn out of this. One can't do business with an insane man."

"I suggest we get back to the main business at hand," Gryph said roughly. He wasn't picking up anything at all from Sariana now. She had shut down her mind as surely as if she had turned off a switch.

"Speaking of business," Rakken said easily, "there is one other point I would like to discuss before we conclude our little planning session."

"What?" Gryph asked.

"I would like Sariana to open your weapon kit for me."

Rakken got to his feet and walked across the room to open another hidden panel in the wall. Gryph's weapon kit sat on a shelf. Rakken picked it up and returned to the table. He placed the kit in front of Sariana who sat staring at it as if it were an alien bug.

Gryph ran through all the possibilities inherent in the situation in a split second and came to his decision. With all the power he could muster he sent the image of a palm blade in its sheath into Sariana's head.

Sariana trembled a little as she sat looking at the kit, but she didn't give any indication she had caught his silent message. She seemed lost in her own thoughts.

Gryph concentrated on projecting the message. Along with the image of the small, sharp blade, he sent a picture of how it could be picked up unnoticed and hidden in her palm. Sariana had no training in such things, but she just might be able to pull it off if Gryph provided some cover for her at the right moment. Rakken's heavy consumption of wine should have the effect of making the man less than keenly observant.

"I have become extremely interested in the contents of these kits," Rakken was saying as he fingered the prisma lock. "The prisma alone is worth a small fortune, yet Shields are not known for their wealth. Targyn, of course, guards his kit closely. He would not deign to show me the contents. But a Shieldmate is supposed to be able to open her husband's kit."

"I thought we agreed I wasn't married to Gryph," Sariana pointed out wryly.

"A matter of semantics, I'm afraid. Married or not, apparently he has given you the secret of unlocking his kit."

"And you want me to unlock it now?" Sariana stroked the snake cat leather pouch.

"I want to assess the technology of its contents," Rakken said quietly.

Sariana looked up sharply. "The technology? Why?"

"I want to see if it bears any resemblance to the technology of this room or the technology of the crystal ship. Do you realize that if the legends are even somewhat true then Shields are not like the rest of us, Sariana? They may be more closely related to the beings who built the prisma ships than they are to you and me. Those kits may hold the key to figuring out just who and what they are. I have tried very hard to open that one and I haven't put so much as a scratch on its surface. The lock is sealed, even to Targyn. Using you as a threat, I might be able to persuade Chassyn to open it, but it would probably be simpler if you did the job."

"All this talk of aliens makes me nervous," Sariana said with a faint shudder. But she didn't take her eyes off the kit.

"I agree," Rakken murmured. "But it is better to be prepared for anything. We are taking some grave risks, my dear. We need to know as much as possible about what's going on. The Shields keep entirely too many secrets. The weapon kits are one of those secrets. Open it."

Gryph watched Sariana slowly pull the bag toward herself. He concentrated on projecting the image of the small knife and how it could be palmed. At the same time he readied himself for whatever small disturbance he could cause. His fingers closed around his bottle of ale.

With a wary glance at Gryph, Sariana touched the prisma lock. Gryph could feel her concentrating. Opening the kit was still far from second nature to her. She was a little afraid of it.

Sariana licked her lower lip, touched the prisma once more very delicately and the kit yawned open under her fingers.

Gryph jerked his hand and the bottle of ale turned over with a loud clatter on the metal surface of the table. Automatically, Rakken glanced over at the toppled bottle. Simultaneously Lucky appeared from the folds of Sariana's skirts and skittered frantically around the table, small claws making tiny scratching sounds.

"In the name of the Lightstorm, where did that damn lizard come from?" Rakken made a grab for Lucky who nimbly hopped back into Sariana's lap and vanished into a pocket.

"It's okay, that's just Lucky, my pet scarlet-toe. You saw it once before in Serendipity, remember?" Sariana patted her pocket protectively. "Sorry about that. It usually stays in my pocket, but I think it's nervous right now. Lucky's been through a lot recently."

"Well, keep him or it out of the way," Rakken said grimly as he eagerly reached for the open kit and pulled it toward him.

"I'd be careful putting my hand in there if I were you," Gryph said in mild warning as he laboriously tried to mop up spilled ale.

Rakken looked up, startled at the thought of a trap. Then he pushed the kit toward Sariana. "Empty the contents onto the table," he commanded.

Sariana shrugged and turned the kit upside down. A variety of small gadgets fell out. Gryph studied them intently.

The palm blade was not among them. He allowed himself a measure of hope.

Rakken poked cautiously through the items on the table. He picked up the tiny vapor lamp and flicked it on, but he didn't figure out the second switch that ignited the blinding flare of vapor. Next he fiddled with a small gadget that opened without any warning and revealed a set of tiny disks. The edge of each disk was very sharp. Gryph felt some satisfaction when Rakken accidentally cut his finger on one.

"What are those damn things?" Rakken demanded in disgust as he quickly bound up his bleeding finger in a small scarf.

"Throwing blades," Gryph explained easily. "One of the metal working clans make them for us."

Rakken glared at him and went on to the next gadget. Carefully he experimented with one cleverly designed implement after another, but in the end he jumped to his feet in irritation and began pacing the room.

"There's nothing in that kit that couldn't have been made by local craftsmen," he complained.

"What did you expect?" Gryph asked calmly. "Local talent is all any of us have to work with. We're all stuck on this planet together, Rakken. That's something Targyn seems to have forgotten, but the rest of us haven't."

"Never mind," Rakken said as he strode back to the table. "I thought there might be something useful in there because you damn Shields are so protective of the kits. But the lock is the only oddity there. It's of no use to me. It looks like the mysteries of the weapon kits are just another idiotic legend."

Gryph kept his mouth shut. If the man didn't realize that the real value of the kit was in the prisma lock, far be it from Gryph to remind him.

"What next?" Sariana asked uneasily. She glanced from Rakken's face to Gryph's as she quietly scooped up the contents of the kit and dumped them back inside. Then she closed the pouch and released the lock.

"If I'm going to do anything about Targyn," Gryph

pointed out, "someone will have to let me out of this twist. What about it, Rakken? Have we got a deal?"

Rakken glowered at him. "Maybe. Maybe not. I'll decide in the morning. I want to talk to Sariana in private before I do anything drastic."

"I'll need the kit," Gryph said persuasively. With the kit in hand his limited set of options would broaden considerably.

But there was no chance to talk Rakken into putting the weapon kit within reach.

The three of them went still as a faint shushing sound announced the opening of the metal door. Targyn stood in the hall, a blade bow held casually in one hand.

"Something tells me dinner is over," Targyn said. He glanced at the weapon kit on the table. Then he looked at Rakken. "You're a fool, banker. The first thing Chassyn would do if he got hold of the kit is kill you. The fact that you're still around tells me he didn't get a chance to get his hands on it. Even in a twist he could do the job if he had access to some of the tools in that pouch. All things considered, that might not be such a bad idea. I'm not sure how useful you are anymore."

Rakken regarded Targyn with acute disdain. "I thought I would test the legend which states that a Shieldmate can open her husband's kit. Sariana was about to show me the truth of that tale."

Targyn grinned humorlessly. "Fool is not the word for you, banker. Stupid is a more appropriate term." He walked over to the low table and picked up the weapon kit. "I'll get rid of this so the banker won't be tempted to explore any of its secrets. Or tempted to give it back to you, Chassyn." He jerked the blade bow at Gryph. "Get up. I'm taking you back to your chamber."

Gryph started to rise, moving even more slowly and awkwardly than the twist required. He made a show of trying to extricate himself from the low bench and table arrangement and deliberately fell into a painful sprawl in the process.

"Keenshee guano," Targyn muttered, not moving. "Get

up, you clumsy bastard. Sariana," he added sharply as Sariana jumped to her feet and came to Gryph's assistance, "get away from him."

"How do you expect him to get to his feet wearing this awful contraption?" she retorted as she crouched beside Gryph and took his arm.

"I said get away from him," Targyn gritted. "If you don't I'll put a blade in him right now and be done with it."

Sariana nodded and stepped back quickly.

But not before Gryph felt the tiny palm knife slide into his hand. He kept it concealed in his own palm with a practiced movement as he turned slowly and moved toward the door. He didn't look back but he could feel Sariana's eyes on him as the door closed.

A stray, fleeting vision floated through his mind. It was a picture of an infant. He had seen that particular image before, on the night Sariana had seduced him beside the river.

This time he had the strangest impression that, although the infant was definitely his, it wasn't a boy. It was a little girl who looked up at him with blue-green eyes.

Chapter
18

"WHAT kind of deal did Rakken offer you to kill me?" Targyn asked in amusement as he thrust Gryph back into the small chamber.

Gryph tried to regain his balance but staggered again as the twist straps jerked in response to the quick movement. He wound up slamming against the cold metal wall. "About what you'd expect. My life and a cut of the prisma. Not bad, considering the alternative."

Targyn's eyes glittered as he lounged in the doorway. He touched Gryph's weapon kit. "Not a bad deal, true. Unfortunately, we both know you won't be able to keep your side of it. I'd like to keep you alive for a while, Chassyn. My goal now is to get one of the weapons out of the ship. I want to test the old theories. But when that's finished I'll want to practice on you."

"The minute you start playing with prisma the whole Shield class will be down on this gorge like the first snow of winter."

"Most will keep their distance rather than risk the destruction of whole towns. By then they will know I am fully capable of carrying out my threat. But there will be a few who will feel it their duty to try to stop me. That's why I must strengthen myself by practicing my mind skills on you. For some reason the skills are useless against untuned minds. The strongest blast of light goes unnoticed by a non-Shield. I know. I've experimented. But I'm sure I can devastate a tuned mind. I need to know precisely how strong I am before I take on the fools who will try to stop me."

"You can't escape all of them. Look how close I got to you," Gryph said, pushing himself cautiously away from the wall.

"You are here only because that idiot Rakken thinks he can use you and because I have a use for you. I've let Rakken have his way on several small matters because I needed him until recently. But soon I will no longer need him and then I'll get rid of him. He thinks he controls me, but the truth is just the opposite."

"How about letting Sariana out of the middle of this power struggle?" Gryph asked.

Targyn grinned. "Why should I let her go? You and I both know how hard it is to find potential Shieldmates. You've been able to link with her so I can assume she's a proven mate. Intelligent and educated, too. I think I'll link with her when this is all over. She can not only produce sons for me, she can replace Rakken as my business manager." Targyn laughed as Gryph stared at him expressionlessly. "Think about it, Chassyn. You won't be around to enjoy my good fortune, but your Shieldmate will. Take what comfort you can from that."

Gryph didn't move as the door slid shut. The lock outside clicked into place. He waited a long moment and then he fingered the palm blade in his hand.

It took some work, but the finely honed blade eventually sliced through the leather straps of the twist. When the last of the shackles had fallen away Gryph surveyed the door as he absently massaged his wrists.

Getting free of the twist was only the first step. Now he needed someone to open the door to his cell.

Having nothing better to do at the moment, Gryph closed his eyes and started groping mentally for Sariana. When he had successfully conveyed the image of the palm knife to her earlier he had learned something very interesting. It might not be possible to sort out the myriad prisma rays that were ricocheting through the mountain around him, but linking with Sariana was no trick at all now. The strange bond between them seemed to be growing stronger all the time.

In the chamber where the meal had been served, Sariana paced the floor and tried desperately to appear attentive to and interested in the plans Etion Rakken was outlining for her. But all she could think about was Gryph. She had to get to him.

"This is only a minor setback, Sariana," Rakken assured her. But his attempt at reassurance was hampered by the fact that he was very nervous himself. He poured himself some more wine in an apparent effort to soothe his anxiety. "Targyn walked in at a most inopportune moment, but there will be other chances to complete our plans."

"I'm not so sure about that." Sariana rubbed her palms up and down her forearms as she concentrated. "If you ask me, Targyn is nearly out of control. Who's to say he hasn't already killed Gryph?"

Rakken's hand shook. Wine slopped over the edge of the glass. "He wouldn't dare. Targyn knows I want Chassyn alive."

"Yes, but does Targyn care about your wishes? I got the impression he thinks he can complete his grand scheme without any further aid from you. He's dangerous, Etion."

Rakken's palm slapped the table. "I know he's dangerous. But I've been able to handle him until now. Damn it, he's just another hotheaded westerner. I can handle the locals."

"Don't count on it. I've been learning some lessons about the locals lately and I'm here to tell you they shouldn't be underestimated. Targyn's dangerous. He's needed you until now." Sariana stopped her pacing and gazed levelly at Rakken. "But does he really need you any longer?"

Rakken met her gaze for a few seconds and then looked away. "If he knows what's good for him—"

"The man is insane, Etion. Furthermore, as you just noted, he's a westerner," she added with a weak smile. "You can't count on him to apply logic or reason to the situation. If he's decided you're no longer useful to him as a businessman or partner, then I'd say he won't hesitate to get rid of you. But first he'll kill Gryph because he knows that of all of us, Gryph poses the only real danger to him."

Something crumpled inside Rakken. His growing anxiety blossomed visibly as he surged to his feet. It was as if he had suddenly given up trying to reassure himself that he was still in command of the situation.

"I'm not so sure Chassyn is much of a danger to him," Rakken announced morosely. "You didn't see the confrontation between the two of them that I witnessed early this morning. Targyn did something to Chassyn with his mind. Stopped him cold. I got the impression Chassyn barely survived the encounter. I wouldn't have believed it if I hadn't seen it with my own eyes. Targyn's been bragging about how 'strong' he's gotten since he's worked with the prisma hidden here, but I hadn't realized just what he meant. Damn it to the Lightstorm, Sariana, what are we going to do?"

"We have to set Gryph free so he can deal with Targyn before the man gets any stronger!" Sariana tried to keep her tone calm and forceful. This was a time for coolheaded, businesslike reasoning and persuasion. She didn't want to panic Rakken further, but at the same time she needed to push him in the direction she wanted him to go. Time was running out.

"What good is Chassyn going to be to us without that damn weapon kit?" Rakken muttered as he downed the remainder of his wine. "Even with the kit Targyn nearly killed him using some strange mental power. For some reason Targyn doesn't seem to be able to use his mind against normal people. At least not yet."

"We don't have much choice. Targyn might not be able to use his mind against us the way you say he did with Gryph, but you've admitted yourself that he's a trained warrior. What are chances of escaping without Gryph?"

"About zero," Rakken admitted. "Especially when you consider that there are three bandits working with Targyn. Miscroft might not be much of a problem. I've been talking to him on the side and we've almost decided to make a deal. He'd probably listen to reason. But the other two are definitely Targyn's men. Any one of the three is far more skilled with a blade bow or a knife than you or I could ever hope to be."

"All the more reason to find Gryph and set him free." Sariana paused as a familiar feeling tickled her mind. It was the sort of feeling she'd had earlier just before the image of the blade knife had slipped into her consciousness. This time there was a fleeting sense of urgency, an insistent command that she find Gryph. Then the image of a corridor flickered in her head.

"Sariana?" Rakken eyed her worriedly. "What is it?"

"We have to find Gryph. Now." She turned toward the door. At the last instant she stopped, remembering Lucky. She snatched up the cloak and headed back to the door.

"Sariana, wait! We have to talk about this further." Rakken leaped after her. "There might be a way for you and me to escape if we make some plans."

"There's no time left," Sariana said as she stepped into the metal corridor. "I have to get to Gryph."

"Damn that man. Sariana, you're putting far too much faith in him. He's useless to us without that weapon kit, and I no longer have it."

She whirled on him, her voice a tight whisper. "Please be quiet, Etion. One of Targyn's men might hear us. Do you know where Gryph is being held?"

Etion paused and then nodded bleakly toward a branching corridor. "Down that hall. There's a door on the left."

"Locked?"

"Of course it's locked. Do you think Targyn would keep Chassyn in an unlocked cell?"

"Let's go." Sariana hurried down the hall, scanning the blank walls for some sign of a door. Rakken, apparently unable to think of any other course of action, followed.

"There," he muttered, pointing to an intricate locking device affixed to a western style door. There was a grill at the top of the door. "Targyn said he might need a chamber for prisoners, but he couldn't figure out how to lock and unlock the metal doors in this place. This room didn't have a door so he had his men build this one and installed it in the opening."

"Targyn's got the only key, I suppose?"

Rakken nodded wordlessly.

"Sariana." Gryph's voice was a bare thread of sound from the other side of the grill.

Sariana's heart leaped. "Gryph! We're here, but the door's locked and Etion doesn't have a key."

"Then you'll just have to pick the lock, won't you?" Gryph asked mildly.

"Don't sound so damn casual," Sariana said tightly. "I have no more idea of how to pick a lock than I do of how to fly."

"No problem. I'll guide you through the whole process. All you have to do is pay attention and follow instructions. Got that cloak pin I gave you?"

Sariana blinked and glanced down. "I've got it. What about it?"

"Listen closely and do exactly as I say. I looked at the lock on the way in. It's pretty standard. Targyn probably didn't have time to have anything special made up. Take the pin and slide it along the seal that joins the two halves together."

Sariana pulled the pin from the cloak she was carrying and went to work. It was a tedious process and Gryph lost his patience more than once. He wasn't the only impatient male in the vicinity, Sariana noted. Rakken was pacing in a circle in the corridor behind her, muttering dire predictions of disaster.

"Damn it, Sariana," Gryph snapped at one point when she failed to probe the lock spring. "What's the matter with you? Can't you even follow a few simple orders?"

"Gryph, I'm trying. Explain the last sequence once more."

Rakken glanced at her, his eyes feverish with anxiety. "Hurry up, Sariana. If you can't do it, just say so and drop the whole thing. We might still be able to get out of here."

"Shut up," Sariana said absently as she frowned in concentration. "Both of you." She jiggled the cloak pin.

Gryph ran through the description of the next step, his voice taut and controlled.

Sariana tried again and failed to find the hidden spring. "Damn westerners," she mumbled under her breath, "too clever for their own good."

Rakken walked over to breathe down her neck. "Did you get it this time?"

"No, I didn't get it this time. Gryph, you'll have to describe it again. I can't find the spring."

"Sariana, any child could have released that spring by now," he said roughly.

"Then go find yourself a child," she retorted, losing patience. "Listen to me, both of you. In case either of you has failed to notice, I'm the only one doing any real work around here. I would appreciate a little quiet and some calm, rational behavior."

Rakken jerked away from her and resumed his pacing.

"All right, Sariana," Gryph said with barely concealed irritation. "We'll try this one more time. Now listen carefully."

Sariana listened carefully but still failed to find the spring on the next try. Her fingers were beginning to shake with the tension she was under.

"Gryph, I just can't find it. Maybe if we try it from a different angle?"

"There is no other angle! I told you, it's just a standard

locking device. There's no reason why you shouldn't be able to open it with that pin. You're just not listening!"

"I am listening, you arrogant Shield. This is all your fault. You're not explaining the process properly."

"What am I supposed to do from in here? Draw you a picture?"

There was a beat of silence as Sariana considered that. "Why don't you try?" she asked softly. "I got that image of the little knife clearly enough. Try drawing a picture inside my head, Gryph."

Gryph was silent for a few seconds. "I don't know if I can get anything this detailed across. But I'll try."

Sariana closed her eyes and concentrated on being totally receptive to the image appearing in her head. It was a meticulously detailed picture of the lock in her fingers. She watched a pin being slipped into a hidden slot at an oblique angle. The lock in her mind sprang open.

A few seconds later, so did the lock in her hands.

"I did it," Sariana said with a sense of elation shared by neither of the two men.

"Come on, let's get out of here," Rakken said. "Chassyn can cover us."

"Forget it," Gryph advised as he strode through the door. "You'll never make it. Targyn has traps set at the entrance. I saw them last night."

"What do you mean?" Rakken demanded furiously. "I gave no approval for any traps at the entrance."

"They're there. Take my word for it. They're the kind Shields and bandits use and you'll need my help to get past them. There's no point worrying about them now, though."

"Why not?" Rakken was enraged.

"Believe me, we can't get out of here without Targyn knowing. I have to get him before he gets us. It's as simple as that. Where's the crystal ship?"

"Why?" Rakken was suspicious.

"Because that's where I'll find Targyn, you fool." Gryph took a dangerous step toward the other man. "Now where is it?"

Rakken sighed and pointed down the corridor. "That

way. When you come to a branching point in the hall, turn left and then left again. The ship is sitting right where Targyn found it."

Gryph nodded once and turned to Sariana. "I want you to go back to that room where we had dinner. Stay there until I come for you."

"But, Gryph—"

He grasped her shoulders and gave her a slight shake. His eyes were gleaming as he looked down at her. "Do as I say, Shieldmate. I told you once there would be times when you would obey me. This is one of those times. This is Shield business and I know my business. Go."

She didn't try to argue against the implacable command she read in his face. "Yes, Gryph."

"Move."

She nodded and turned away, clutching her cloak and the pin she had used to open the lock. Rakken moved quickly to follow her. She stopped a few paces away and glanced back at Gryph. He was looking closely at the open lock.

"Gryph?" she whispered gently.

He didn't glance up from his study of the lock. "What is it, Sariana?"

"I love you."

That got his attention. His eyes gleamed in the unnatural corridor lighting. But Sariana didn't wait for a response. She smiled to herself and scurried back down the corridor with Etion Rakken at her heels.

Gryph might not realize it because he had a great deal on his mind at the moment, but he loved her. Sariana was sure of it. One of these days he'd figure it out for himself. He was a little thick at times, but he wasn't stupid.

Gryph waited only long enough to be sure Sariana was obeying his orders. When she and Rakken disappeared he pocketed the lock, then turned and started quickly down the corridor Rakken had indicated. There was no reason to think Rakken had lied. The man's nerve had gone. He was in no condition to lie.

The corridor was a long one, lit with the same internal

glow that characterized the rest of the cavern. A long time ago someone or something had excavated and built well. The metal looked almost new and the lighting system seemed strong even though it must have been functioning for centuries.

The significance of Targyn's discovery suddenly hit Gryph. According to the records only ships and weapons and a couple of prisma cutters had been found in the past. There had never been any indication of construction or habitation, and therefore no indication of what the creators of the prisma ships looked like.

But these corridors and rooms offered hints that whatever had set out to boobytrap this sector of the galaxy had a physical body that used such conveniences as benches. The beings also had at least some senses that were similar to those of humans. For example, they needed light in a familiar range of the spectrum to find their way around in the darkness.

But they had learned to do a great deal more with light than humans ever had, Gryph reminded himself as he turned left in the branching corridors. The beings who had built this installation and created the crystal ships had discovered how to turn light into a weapon that could be controlled by the mind.

And Targyn, a strong but mentally unstable Shield, had been living here, studying alien secrets for months.

Gryph slowed as he turned down the last corridor, his senses alert for that tingling awareness that indicated someone was approaching. It was a hunter's talent, not Shield talent he depended on now. Openings were scattered in the corridor walls. If he received sufficient warning of someone's approach, he should be able to duck out of sight for a few crucial minutes.

The warning that finally came was the faint rumble of voices from the other side of a bend in the corridor. Gryph sprinted to get to the safety of an open room. There was no time to slide the metal door shut behind him. The movement would have been obvious.

There also wasn't much point. Gryph decided it was

time to start whittling down the odds. Bandit hunting was familiar work. Lock in hand, he waited patiently just inside the chamber as the two men came down the hall.

The first man who spoke sounded disgruntled and a little scared.

"He's crazy I tell you," the man complained to his companion. "We should have known better than to make a deal with a Shield. All that talk of making our fortunes with prisma was just to get us to work harder for him. I don't think he ever intends to neutralize the stuff. He's going to continue fooling around with that live crystal."

"He'll kill us all in the process," the other man said bluntly. "So what do we do?"

"We can take him," the first man said softly. "He's good, I'll grant you that, but there's three of us and one of him. We'll have to get hold of Miscroft and explain just what's going on. Targyn can't use that crazy mind business on us because we're not Shields. It's just a case of three fighting men against one. We can handle those odds."

"Whatever we do it had better be quick. Since that other Shield arrived Targyn's been acting crazier than ever. He says he's going to prime the prisma, whatever that means."

"Let's find Miscroft. We'll make our move now. I think you're right. Targyn's mind is going fast and there's no telling what he'll do next."

Gryph listened to the conversation and decided there was an element of rationality to it. If the three bandits turned on Targyn they might just possibly take him. If they didn't succeed in that, they could at least distract him long enough for Gryph to do something permanent about Targyn's future. He lowered the arm he had raised in preparation for hurling the lock at a bandit head.

There was an old Shield saying to the effect that a little strategy went farther in the long run than a great deal of indiscriminate bandit bashing.

Unfortunately, strategy had its limitations. Even as Gryph made the decision to let the bandits pass down the corridor, he heard their choked yells.

"Targyn!" The first one sounded shaken. "Hey, wait a

minute. What's the matter with you? We were only going to—"

A faint whooshing noise filled the corridor, followed by a gargled scream. Gryph recognized both sounds. The first was the deadly vibration of a throwing disk. The second was the sound of death. Scratch one bandit as a potential ally.

Gryph heard the panicked, scrambling noises the second man was making as he tried to fire a blade bow. He got off one wild shot, but the next moment he too fell with an unmistakable thud.

This was as much of a distraction as he was likely to get, Gryph decided. He had to move now while Targyn was still resonating with the satisfaction of his kills. This was the point at which a hunter was most vulnerable.

Gryph pinpointed Targyn's position in the corridor as best he could based on the length of time it had taken for the hurled throwing blades to cut down the two bandits.

He launched himself out into the hall. A part of him objectively noted that he had approximated Targyn's position quite accurately. The other Shield stood a few meters away, facing Gryph. His burning eyes were surveying his victims who lay on the floor in widening pools of blood. In his hand he held a third throwing blade. Targyn was well-trained. He left little to chance.

Gryph sent the heavy metal lock hurling toward Targyn along a trajectory that would have caught the other man in the throat if all had gone well.

But it didn't. Targyn saw the flicker of movement an instant before Gryph appeared in the corridor. He reacted to it instinctively, throwing his lethal blade even as he whipped himself to one side.

The lock struck Targyn's shoulder instead of his throat. Targyn's blade whooshed down the corridor toward Gryph, who was no longer occupying the middle of it. It missed its target by scant centimeters.

As soon as he had launched his own poor weapon, Gryph had followed it toward its goal. He leaped the bodies of the bandits in the process and closed the gap between himself and Targyn swiftly. He had to reach the other Shield before Targyn could rearm himself.

But Targyn made no move to pull another weapon from his kit. Instead he slapped his fingers over the prisma lock. A deathly grin stretched his lips and an unnatural glitter lit his eyes.

Gryph sensed the mental blast of light a fraction of a second before it hit him. That small warning saved his life, but the blow stopped him cold. He went down beneath it as surely as if Targyn had struck him with a blade.

Instinctively he fought the slamming force of the light inside his head the same way he had fought it before. But this time he had no prisma to use as a focus tool.

Somehow he caught his mental balance and blocked the paralyzing rays before they could rip his mind to shreds. His whole body vibrated with the energy it was taking to adjust to the strange battle. He didn't know how he was managing the defense without his prisma lock, but he didn't question it. Gryph simply held on.

He opened his eyes and saw Targyn braced a short distance away. The other man's eyes widened and his grin broadened.

"This," Targyn said, "is going to be interesting."

Gryph's only consolation was that Targyn apparently had to exert as much physical energy in focusing the mind blast as Gryph was using to block it. At least the rogue Shield couldn't cut him to pieces with a blade while holding him pinned with the invisible light rays.

But Gryph knew he couldn't hold out for long. Already Targyn's mental weapon seemed to be gathering energy and strengthening itself. Targyn's fingers played on the prisma lock as if the man were searching for just the right wavelength.

Gryph closed his eyes, satisfied that his enemy was as physically immobilized as he was. For all the good that did. Then he started concentrating on feeling his way back along the wavelengths of painfully brilliant light that were trying to shatter him.

He had thought about this a lot during the past few

hours. He'd had little else to do but think about it while locked in the prison chamber.

His only hope lay in the suspicion that projecting the kind of mind violence Targyn was projecting couldn't be too dissimilar from projecting thoughts and images. The mechanics of the thing had to be the same, Gryph had reasoned. And he'd had plenty of experience lately projecting images into Sariana's head.

He concentrated the way he would if he had his lock under his fingers. The pulsing rays of light separated under his mental touch, just as they would if he were tracking prisma. Gryph found the ones he wanted and started the task of countering their rhythm, feeding the pattern back upon itself and projecting it.

The first indication he had of any success was when Targyn screamed in rage.

"You bastard! Do you think you can play this game? I'll show you how weak you are."

Gryph sensed the redoubling effort Targyn was making and he moved to counter it before the new blast could strike.

The battle was fought in an agonizing silence, the blood of the dead bandits trickling between Gryph's bare feet as he stood braced in the corridor.

Targyn screamed again, rage and hatred flaring out along the invisible beam of mental light.

Gryph caught the rage and hatred and sent it pulsing back along with the full force of the beam.

Targyn's control faltered for a moment. It resumed almost immediately, but Gryph had sensed the growing weakness in his opponent. He sent an image of that weakness back along with everything else he was trying to project.

Without any warning Targyn broke. The blast of mental light wavered and disappeared. Gryph was so overwhelmed by the sudden loss of a target that he staggered and slipped in the blood of one of the bandits.

He went down on one knee just as Targyn threw himself forward, knife in hand.

"I'll kill you anyway!" Targyn screamed. "You can't stop me. I'm stronger than you are. Stronger than any other Shield!"

Gryph scooped up the knife lying on the floor beside the fallen bandit. He brought the blade up in a short arc that ended in Targyn's chest.

Targyn collapsed across the body of the bandit he had killed earlier, his blood mingling with his victim's.

Gryph crouched warily beside him. A dying Shield was not an unarmed Shield.

"Targyn?"

Targyn's eyes opened, revealing a gaze that was already glazing over. He smiled grimly. "Too late, Chassyn. You're too damn late. It's already started."

"What's already started?"

"The reaction. Without me to control it, every weapon on the ship will detonate. It's going to take a big chunk out of this continent, Chassyn. There's enough power in those weapons to reach all the way to Little Chance. Maybe farther."

"How do I stop it?" Gryph demanded savagely.

"You're stronger than I thought, Chassyn. Maybe, just maybe, you could have done something if you had your lock or the aid of another Shield. But you have neither, do you? The storytellers will weave a hell of a legend out of all this, won't they?"

What was left of his life flowed out of Targyn before Gryph could figure out how to threaten a dying man.

Chapter
19

S ARIANA fell to the floor as the last of the painful energy vanished from her fevered mind. Lucky, perched on her shoulder, clung tightly and hissed anxiously. Sariana had been kneeling on the floor of the metal chamber, hugging herself while she endured the battle Gryph was fighting.

When she had picked up the echoes of the first blast that had struck Gryph she had known immediately that it was the same sort of attack that had caught him unaware yesterday morning. Now she knew its source. It wasn't hard to tell that Targyn was projecting a killing energy and that Gryph was fighting for his life.

She was powerless to do anything except watch mentally as the battle flared back and forth. But when the end came there was no sense of loss. She could still feel Gryph's presence somewhere in the corridors. He was alive. And she knew what that meant.

"Targyn's dead, Etion," she announced with weary relief. "He's gone."

Rakken, who was working his way through another bottle of wine, looked up with glazed hope in his eyes. "Dead? Are you certain? How can you know that?"

"I just know it." She stumbled to her feet, reaching up to soothe Lucky with a soothing stroke.

Rakken eyed her disbelievingly. "Even if you're right there are still those three bandits."

The door of the chamber shushed open. Sariana and Rakken both jumped. Gryph stood in the doorway. There was blood on his shirt and his face was etched with stark lines. "Make that one bandit. Targyn obligingly took care of the other two for us. But we've still got a big problem."

Rakken stood up so fast the wine bottle toppled over and shattered on the floor. His eyes were wide with excitement "What problem? All we have to do is cut up the prisma and we're rich!"

Gryph eyed him coldly. "Targyn did something to the prisma. Before he died he said it was primed to detonate. He claimed it's going to take a lot of the surrounding landscape with it, and I'm inclined to believe him. We can't run far enough or fast enough. We've got to try to stop it."

"We?" Sariana moved toward him, examining the blood on Gryph's shirt to make sure it wasn't his. She was so relieved to see him she could hardly stand. She longed to throw herself into his arms and just collapse.

"We." Gryph looked at her. "You and me, Sariana. I can't think of anything else to try. My weapon kit is gone and I can't use another Shield's prisma."

Sariana caught her breath at what he was proposing. "You think you can use me the way you would prisma?"

"I don't know." He reached for her hand. "But you're all I've got."

"It's so nice to feel needed," she muttered weakly as he pulled her into a run. It wasn't the first time she had made the sarcastic observation, but as usual Gryph wasn't paying any attention.

"Hey, wait," Rakken yelled behind them. "What do you think you're doing? What about the other bandit?"

Gryph ignored the man. He was too busy giving instructions to Sariana as he drew her down the hall. "When we reach the ship room I want you to just become passive. Think of yourself as a mirror. You'll catch the light I'm sending at you and reflect it back to me, but that's all. You don't have to try to focus or channel. I'll take care of that."

"I'm supposed to pretend I'm just a lifeless piece of prisma, right?"

"No," he retorted. "You're my new lock. You're tuned to me and I'm going to work the live prisma through you."

"Has anyone ever tried this before?" she asked breathlessly as she was pulled down another corridor.

"Not that I know of. But no Shield has ever had a Shieldmate like you before, either."

"How do you know?" Sariana demanded, not certain if the observation was a compliment or not.

"Take my word for it. If there had been a linking as strong as ours at some time in the past, there would be some legend or tale still circulating about it."

"You're probably right. Do you think we'll become legends someday, Gryph?"

"At the rate you're going it's not impossible." He turned another corner. "Don't look down," he ordered brusquely.

But of course she did and her punishment was a close view of three dead men. One of them was Targyn. Sariana tore her gaze from the terrible sight as Gryph yanked her quickly past them. She swallowed a few times in an effort to calm her queasy stomach, but before she could think of anything to say Gryph was turning another corner.

He stopped suddenly as the hallway opened onto a vast cavern. "By the Fire on board the Ship," he breathed in genuine awe.

Sariana knew exactly what he meant, but she couldn't even summon words. The sight that greeted her made her speechless.

The cavern was huge, lined with the same gray metal that lined the passageways and corridors behind them. But it wasn't the chamber that inspired awe and wonder. Awe and wonder were inspired by the strange ship that occupied most of the space inside the cavern.

The vehicle was roughly oval in shape with a sleek dome. It rested on its flat belly. But the alien shape of it wasn't nearly as fascinating as the material from which it was made. It was crystal clear and yet it wasn't. It glittered in the light, but the eye couldn't quite focus on that brightness. There was an impression of wide, flat, oval objects inside the ship, but one couldn't quite make out the details. The whole thing was lit from inside with a soft, pulsing glow.

Sariana peered at the ship for a long moment. "It's like looking into ice cubes," she finally announced.

"Living prisma crystal," Gryph said softly. "I've never seen prisma in this condition, although I've heard it described a thousand times in song and story." He strode farther into the room. "Targyn was right. This ship is much larger than any other ship found on this planet."

"Perhaps it was some sort of supply ship," Sariana suggested as she followed Gryph slowly into the room. "Perhaps it's bigger than all the others because it carried weapons to resupply the smaller ships."

Gryph nodded. "It's possible. Or perhaps it was designed for some major assault that was never launched."

"We'll never know." Sariana examined the vehicle more closely. "Something's moving inside it, Gryph!"

He followed her gaze and nodded. "Targyn said he had primed it. He had been experimenting. Somehow he started a reaction within the weapons. He thought he could control that reaction."

"What now, Gryph?"

"I'm not sure," he admitted.

"Somehow you being unsure about anything gives me cold chills."

"Sorry," he said with a wry smile. "I'll try to sound more in charge. Here, give me your hand."

Sariana held out her palm and he closed his fingers warmly around it.

"Remember that first night together?" Gryph asked as he tightened his hand on hers. "Remember how it felt when we touched the prisma lock together?"

"How can I ever forget? It was every woman's dream of a wedding night."

"This is no time for sarcasm," Gryph observed. "Save it for later. Concentrate on the sensation of linking with me."

Sariana closed her eyes and let the feeling of being linked sweep through her. It was easy to summon up that odd sense of awareness now. Almost immediately a wave of Gryph's emotions poured through her. She couldn't identify any single one, but she knew they were all from him.

The huge wave crested, broke and then coalesced. She felt Gryph testing himself against the image of a mirror she presented. Shafts of light in varying hues danced through her mind. Sariana flinched when the first ones arrived. The memories of the bright, lethal bursts of light Targyn had wielded were still fresh.

But after a moment it became clear that Gryph was in firm control of the energy he was using.

The lights in her head flared brighter. A rainbow of a million hues vibrated within her mind and bounced off the mirror she was creating.

In some manner, Sariana knew, Gryph was starting to take back the energy she was reflecting. It was stronger on the return trip, more concentrated.

Time became meaningless to Sariana. She stood perfectly still, her body poised, her mind alert but unfocused. Gryph's hand tightened on hers. Sariana's eyes were still closed so she didn't realize anything was happening to the ship until she felt the temperature in the cavern rise several degrees.

Her lashes lifted and she stared at the alien ship. It was no longer as clear as it had been. Portions of it were losing clarity, turning opaque. The change seemed to be starting from deep within the ship and working outward. The glow from the inside was fading.

"It's all right," Gryph whispered, his voice tight with the strain. "It's working. I've got it now."

She stared at the ship, concentrating harder as she tried to somehow free up more of her own mind energy for him to use. She didn't know what she was doing or how she was doing it, but she sensed the new strength within herself. She felt Gryph reach for that strength with the eagerness of a lover and then he was adding it to his own and projecting it toward the ship.

The crystal became more opaque, huge sections of it turning the familiar color of valuable prisma.

Slowly, methodically, Gryph worked the prisma through Sariana. She sensed the deliberate way he was projecting into the ship, finding the oval disks first and neutralizing them. Then he worked the structural material of the ship itself.

Suddenly it was all over. The ship in front of them was solid, gem quality prisma. The interior glow was gone. Sariana felt the weary rush of relief that seeped into her awareness and knew it was Gryph's reaction, not her own. She turned to look at him and found him staring at her, his features taut with the effort the task had taken. But he was grinning his familiar, slightly predatory grin. He pulled Sariana into his arms and hugged her as if he had just returned from a long trip.

"We did it! My sweet, unpredictable Sariana, we did it. Who would have guessed that you and I could work together like that? What legend spinner could have invented a tale this good? A whole ship full of weapons and we neutralized all of it, every last centimeter without the aid of a lock. By the Lightstorm, wait until they hear about this out on the frontier."

Sariana gave a shaky laugh, clinging tightly to him. "What makes you think they'll believe us?"

"They'll believe it. After all, they'll have the word of a Shield on it," Gryph stated with his familiar arrogance.

"Yes, of course. I almost forgot."

"Are you laughing at me, woman?"

She shook her head, her eyes full of euphoric relief. "I wouldn't dream of it."

"The hell you wouldn't." Gryph laughed, holding her as if he would never let go. "There is little you wouldn't dare,

Shieldmate. But we can discuss the matter later. I think it's time we found that cutter and got out of here."

"What about Rakken and that third bandit?"

"My guess is that the last bandit is long gone by now. He probably got a good look at the mess in the corridor outside and decided there were easier ways to make a living. As for Rakken." Gryph shrugged. "Who cares? The man is a nuisance. If he has any sense he'll stay out of my way."

They found the Avylyns' precious cutter near the entrance of the chamber that housed the alien ship. It had been left rather carelessly on a low worktable.

"It doesn't seem like the sort of thing that could cause all this trouble, does it?" Sariana asked as she picked up the tool.

The prisma cutter looked like nothing more than a thin, square box. One side of the square disappeared when a hidden spring was pushed. When that was done a smooth, rounded edge was exposed. The edge was not sharpened or serrated. A child could play with it and not cut himself. But when it was applied to prisma by a skilled craftsman using just the right pressure and angle, it cut through the crystal effortlessly. It was made of a metal that closely resembled the metal lining the surrounding corridors and chambers.

"Lately I've learned that trouble can come from some very unexpected sources," Gryph said as she handed the cutter to him. He also took Sariana's hand and started quickly for the corridor.

"What about your weapon kit?" Sariana thought to ask.

"I'll have to make another one. Targyn got rid of mine. No telling where it is."

"Can you make another one?" she asked in surprise. They were approaching the three bodies in the corridor.

"Sure," Gryph said as he paused beside Targyn's body. "I'll just take Targyn's kit. He won't be needing it any more and I've got better things to do than hunt down another snake cat. I'll need a new piece of prisma, but that won't be any problem, will it? There's a whole roomful of it back in that chamber."

"That brings up a very interesting question," Sariana said as the thought struck her. "Who owns the prisma?"

"By law it belongs to the Shields. To tell you the truth, it's been so long since any was found, I'm not sure what the procedure is for selling it to the jewelers and artisans who use it."

They made their way through the alien installation without any trouble. Gryph retrieved his boots on the way down one of the corridors. When they reached the entrance he examined the traps that had been set there for a few moments. He looked thoughtful but he said nothing.

Lucky appeared from a pocket as soon as Sariana stepped into the open. The lizard scrambled up to her shoulder and surveyed the world with satisfaction. Obviously it had not enjoyed the recent ventures.

As they started down the tumble of rocks and boulders that shielded the entrance to the cavern, Sariana remembered the river sled.

"I'm afraid it's going to be a long walk back to Little Chance, Gryph," she said unhappily.

"Ah, yes, your accident with the sled. Where did you leave it?"

"It left me a couple of kilometers downstream. I must say, it wasn't a very good river sled."

"Are you kidding?" Gryph asked. "It's the best there is. Cost me a small fortune to rent it."

"Well, it bounced all over the water when it hit the first few rapids."

"You tried to steer it through the rapids?" he demanded, glaring at her.

"What was I supposed to do? Get out and walk?"

"Damn right. Just as soon as the water turned rough. You've had no experience taking a sled through rapids. Why didn't you put the sled ashore and continue on foot?" Gryph blinked at his own words. "What am I saying? That's not the question I should be asking. The one that needs asking is why didn't you head straight back to Little Chance?"

Sariana lifted the hem of her skirt so it wouldn't get

caught in some thorny brush. "You know why I didn't go straight back to Little Chance, Gryph."

He was silent for a few seconds and then he stopped for a moment, wrapped his hand around her neck and tugged her close for a hard, possessive kiss. When he released her Sariana's lips felt slightly bruised. She looked up into his glittering eyes.

"I know why," Gryph admitted so softly Sariana could hardly hear the words. "You and I, we share something very special, don't we?"

"I've come to the conclusion that we do." Sariana smiled tremulously.

They found the sled a short time later. Gryph hauled it out of the water and proceeded to survey the damage. He grumbled a lot about inexperienced river sled pilots and made several comments on the nature of luck and women and then he got the craft running.

"You westerners are so clever," Sariana said with amused admiration as they floated into the middle of the river.

"I'm glad to see you're finally able to acknowledge a little of the local talent," Gryph muttered as he expertly set the sled skipping downstream.

When the late afternoon shadows descended, Gryph chose a small, protected cove in which to set up camp. He had become quieter and quieter as the day wore on. Sariana knew he was anxious to get back to Little Chance to see if Delek had returned with the other Shields.

The storage lockers of the small sled had survived the encounter with the rapids. The food supplies were intact, and as she set about fixing dinner over the fire Gryph had built, Sariana realized she was very hungry. She served the simple meal in silence.

Gryph accepted his plate with moody concentration. Sariana watched as he methodically ate his food. There was no flicker of awareness in her head. Whatever he was thinking, Gryph was obviously determined to keep it to himself.

A short time later, Sariana undressed down to her chemise and slid under the travel quilt Gryph had spread out on the deck. Gryph was already under it, his arms folded behind his head, his gaze fixed on the narrow patch of stars overhead. She reached out to touch him gently.

"Gryph? Is something wrong?"

"I've been thinking."

"Yes, I know," Sariana said gently. "But I don't know what you're thinking. I've been trying to read your mind all evening. It looks like you're right. The link doesn't work unless one of us is trying to project. It's very frustrating at times."

He continued to gaze resolutely at the stars. "I was thinking about us. You and me. Our marriage."

"Oh."

"You've been right all along." There was a note of grudging respect in his voice. "I've been very arrogant. It probably wasn't fair to marry you the way I did."

"An interesting admission for a Shield," Sariana said dryly. "What brought you to that conclusion?"

"I'm not sure," he said honestly. "But I've been thinking about it this afternoon and I've decided there's only one honorable thing for me to do."

Sariana held her breath. "What's that?"

He sat up without any warning. The quilt fell to his waist and faint starlight played on his broad shoulders. The same light also highlighted the proud planes of his face. "You have a right to choose, Sariana," he declared. "If you really want to go home to Rendezvous and become an executive in your clan's firm, I have no right to stop you."

Sariana probed silently for an accompanying mental image that would tell her he meant what he was saying. But it was useless. Gryph was definitely not projecting. It occurred to her that as they had both become more proficient at communicating, they also seemed to have learned some skills that guarded their privacy.

"I see," said Sariana, "that's certainly very noble and generous of you. I know how you westerners tend to assume that your ways are the only acceptable ways."

Gryph hesitated and then growled, "You easterners have the same problem, I believe."

"I suppose we do." She smiled her most brilliant smile.

Gryph glared at her. "Well?"

"Well what?" she countered.

He shot to his feet and paced to the bow of the sled. He was still wearing his trousers. "Are you going to take me up on my offer let you go back to Rendezvous?"

"Are you sure you mean it? I recall you once threatened to track me down and drag me back no matter how far I ran or where I hid. There's not much point of my accepting your generous offer if you're just going to chase after me."

Gryph sat down on a small storage locker, his palms spread wide on his thighs. He was tense and alert, a piece of prisma waiting to be detonated. "If I give you my word I won't chase after you—"

"Are you giving me your word?" Sariana asked with great interest.

"We'll get to that after you tell me what you want to do."

"Well, going home might be interesting. When I bring this cutter back to the Avylyns, it's going to put the seal on my success in the west. And if I can use that success to convince the academy to accept me, I could complete my education and take my rightful place in my clan's firm. It's certainly an interesting proposition."

Gryph lost the slender thread of his patience. "Stop throwing words at me! Just tell me what you want."

"And if I tell you, will you give it to me?" she asked softly.

"I'll try."

"Why?" she persisted.

"Because I love you," he roared. The words echoed between the canyon walls, filling the night. "Damn it, Sariana, I love you more than anything else on this planet. I finally realized that. The bond I feel with you isn't just based on physical passion. I know that now. I want you to be happy."

Lucky, curled in a cloak pocket, stuck its head out and hissed inquiringly.

Sariana smiled at Gryph as she got to her feet and walked over to him. "That's all I need to make me stay."

His hands caressed her shoulders. "Sariana, do you mean that?"

"I think I've been living in the west too long," she said with loving amusement. "I've fallen in love and I've developed the most illogical, unreasonable, unbusinesslike desire to be loved by you in return. I was fairly certain you did love me, but I'm glad to hear the words. Even with the mental link between us some things still need to be said in the old-fashioned way."

Gryph's relieved chuckle became a hoarse rumble of desire as Sariana rested her head against his bare shoulder. He slid his hands down Sariana's chemise to her waist, gripped her hard and lifted her high above him. He looked up at her, starlight in his eyes.

"I've lived in the west all my life, Sariana, but I didn't know what love was until I met you. My main concern was ensuring the future of my clan. Nothing was as important as that until I met you. I didn't even realize I was in love until I started thinking about doing the right thing and allowing you to choose your future, regardless of what that choice did to my own. You teach a rough lesson, lady."

"You see?" Sariana murmured as he let her slide sensually down the length of his hard body. "You westerners don't know everything, not even about love. You just think you do."

A long time later they lay together, saying nothing, just drifting in and out of each other's satisfaction. The intimacy of their link faded slowly to be replaced by the old-fashioned intimacy of lovers enjoying the sweet aftermath of joining.

Gryph reluctantly stirred to reach down and pull up the quilt.

"About that prisma," Sariana murmured sleepily, "I have an idea."

She never got the chance to finish. There was a faint movement on the shore and a soft hiss from Lucky. Sariana recoiled as Gryph rose to his feet, his hand reaching for an object in his trousers.

Sariana knew the intruder had to be the third bandit. Old business, she suddenly realized, should never be left unfinished.

Chapter
20

IT was over before Sariana could kick herself free of the quilt. She heard a choked yell from the attacker soon after Gryph's hand sliced through the air in a short, lethal motion. Something connected with the other man's throat.

The bandit crumpled and fell over the low railing into the water. Silence descended. Gryph walked to the edge of the sled and glanced over the side.

"He'll drown," Sariana said weakly.

"Probably." Gryph didn't seem overly interested in the matter. He reached over to unlock a storage locker and remove a small vapor lamp.

Sariana felt a chill go through her. She peered over the edge of the craft. "I think we ought to pull him out of the water, Gryph. It isn't right to just leave him there."

Gryph switched on the lamp and scanned the shoreline. He was obviously preoccupied. "He was trying to kill us in case you didn't notice."

"I noticed!" Irritated, Sariana started to climb over the edge of the railing. "What did you use on him?"

"The belt buckle you gave me. It was the closest thing available."

"Is everything you touch a potential weapon?" she demanded, seriously incensed. Reaction, she told herself. She was suffering from reaction.

"Not quite." He spoke absently, his attention still on the shoreline.

"Name one thing that isn't a weapon for you!"

"You." He turned to glance at her, frowning as he realized she was almost over the side. "Where do you think you're going?"

"I'm going to pull that bandit out of the water." She landed knee-deep in the black water and began fumbling for something that felt like a body. Her hand connected with a boot. She started hauling it toward the shore. "And don't tell me you can't turn me into a weapon just like you do everything else. What about the way you used me to neutralize that prisma ship?"

"Storm and light, Sariana, you really take things to extremes at times, don't you?" Gryph set down the lamp and vaulted over the side. Impatiently he jerked the half-conscious bandit from her grasp. "Here, give him to me. I don't know what the point of saving him is, but if it will make you happier—"

"That's one of the things I love about you, Gryph," she said in dulcet tones. "My happiness always comes first with you."

He glanced at her sharply and then shook his head with a rueful grin. "Mouthy wench."

"You love it. Tell me something, Gryph. Would you really have let me go home to Rendezvous?"

His teeth flashed in the shadows. "What do you think?"

She grinned back. "I think we're both very lucky we won't have to test the limits of your loving generosity."

"I think you're right. How could I have let you go, Sariana? You're part of me now. But don't I get some credit for at least trying to do the noble thing?"

"Of course, my love."

She watched him drag his victim to shore. The bandit sputtered and coughed and then proceeded to lose the contents of his stomach.

"Keenshee guano," Gryph muttered, yanking his bare foot out of the way. "This is my reward for humoring my wife. I'd like to know what you plan to do with this piece of garbage now that you've saved his neck."

"He should be taken back to Little Chance to stand trial," Sariana said stoutly.

Gryph just looked at her as if she weren't very bright. "We already know he's guilty of everything from dealing with live prisma to attempted murder."

"That's for a jury to determine."

"Sariana, have you gone mad? This man is Shield business. My business. In case you haven't figured it out yet, I am his judge and his jury."

"Well, you're not going to be his executioner," she told him forcefully. "I've been doing a lot of thinking lately and I've decided that one of your problems is that Shields have kept to themselves too much. They operate too independently of the rest of society. They're too secretive. There are too many mysteries surrounding them. They deliberately do things that keep people in awe of them. They take pride in their reputations as warriors. But the plain truth is they exist on the fringes of respectable society. That's a dangerous place to be in the long run. It not only makes you Shields vulnerable as a class, it also stunts your growth."

"What in the name of the Lightstorm are you talking about now?"

Sariana clambered back on board the sled. "I told you I've been doing some thinking about this, Gryph. I'm convinced that you Shields aren't going to last much longer as an important, respectable class unless you take steps to modernize yourselves. The people of this world are moving fast on both continents. You have to move with the times. You have to stop living solely on the frontiers. What are you going to do when there are no more bandits to fight?"

"There will always be bandits of one kind or another," Gryph said with certainty.

"Well, perhaps, but the people of the western provinces may decide they can form their own militia to control them, just as they've formed their own town guards."

"Sariana, this isn't exactly the time or the place to discuss social philosophy."

But Sariana was in full sail. She had some points to make and now seemed like an excellent time to make them.

"I'll tell you something else, Gryph. I bet it wouldn't be nearly as hard for Shields to find wives if they had easier access to the same society and opportunities the other classes have. Oh, sure, according to the Pact, you can look for a wife at any level of society, but as it stands, most respectable families keep their daughters quietly out of sight when they know there's a Shield in the vicinity. Who would want to lose a daughter to some stranger whose only job skills are throat cutting and working prisma? They know he'll sweep the poor girl away from home and family and society and take her to live in some remote frontier town. I'll tell you right now, most mothers will fight that tooth and nail. Most fathers probably will, too. No wonder you Shields have a hard time meeting potential Shield-mates. When was the last time anyone invited one of you to tea?"

"I can't remember," Gryph said dryly. He stood on the shore, his nude body poised and powerful above the retching, choking bandit at his feet and he stared at his wife. Gryph's expression in the reflected glow of the vapor lamp was an interesting mixture of amusement and exasperation.

"I'm telling you, Gryph, Shields have got to take a good look at the future and plan for it. Granted, your original role as a class was an important one, but times are changing. You have to integrate yourselves into mainstream society or you're going to find your whole class getting smaller and less important as the rest of the world grows. That would be a pity, and perhaps potentially lethal for the rest of us."

"I'm glad to know we'd be missed, but how do you figure our absence might prove lethal for everyone else?"

"Gryph, someday we're going to get back into space. With eastern financial wizardry and western technology that day probably isn't too far off. When we do we might very well find the beings who built those prisma ships waiting for us. Shields might come in very handy again at some point in the future."

"That's an easterner for you. Always planning ahead."

"I think your main problem is that your class is male dominated. Women only become members when they marry into it and there have been no daughters born into the clans. That means the males have made most of the policies and, to be perfectly blunt, males tend to be highly conservative by nature. You've stuck with the old ways because you didn't want to experiment with change. Yet all the other classes on both continents are changing rapidly. It's time for the Shields to start changing, too."

"What makes me think you have come up with some master plan for restructuring my entire social class?"

"I'll assume that's a rhetorical question. But as it happens, I've got some ideas I think you and the other Shields should consider."

"Somehow that doesn't surprise me."

Sariana was totally involved in her budding ideas. Absently she began to pace the deck of the sled. She was so enthralled in what she was planning that she didn't notice the chill of her wet chemise.

"The fundamental key to changing the Shields' role in society is to change their financial and business relationships with that society. You have to evolve out of your limited bandit hunting and find new financial niches for yourselves. What you need," she concluded triumphantly, "is a good business manager. Someone who can tackle the job of restructuring the economic position of an entire class."

"And as it happens," Gryph observed, "a very aggressive business manager has just recently married into my social class."

Sariana smiled her brilliant smile. "As it happens, you're right. This could be a lucky day for you and your entire class, Gryph."

He grinned. "Tell me something. Just how do you plan to change a whole class of frontier warriors into respectable craftsmen and business people?"

"That's easy," Sariana said smoothly. "All you need is a solid financial base and some shrewd investment advice. By a strange and interesting coincidence, you have recently come into possession of a cavern full of financial capital. In the past you Shields have obviously not handled the sale of your prisma with any great skill. There's a vast difference between selling your capital and investing it so that it continues to earn for you."

"And you're going to show us the difference, right?"

"As I said, this could be your lucky day."

Before Gryph could think of an appropriate response there was a crackle of underbrush behind him. Sariana jumped in startled surprise as Etion Rakken, looking quite tattered and unkempt, made his way slowly down to the shoreline. But Gryph greeted the banker's arrival with resignation.

"Hello, Rakken. I wondered how long it would take before you stumbled out into the open. When I realized you'd gotten past the traps back at the caverns, I figured you'd probably joined forces with Miscroft to escape. You have a nasty habit of working with inferior craftsmen." Gryph indicated the gasping bandit at his feet.

Rakken tried to straighten his clothing. Then he held up his hand in a placating gesture. "Sorry about that little scene on the sled just now. It was Miscroft's idea. He thought he could take you in your sleep and thus ensure that the Shields never find out about all that prisma. I told him it would never work, but who can reason with a bandit?" He turned to Sariana. "I've been listening to what you've been saying, Sariana. Do you think you could use some expert banking advice?"

Gryph swore softly as he watched the other two regard each other with intent interest. He scowled at his wife and then at Rakken. "I'll say one thing for you easterners, you never stop dealing."

The next day Gryph and his small party arrived in Little Chance to find a contingent of Shields waiting for them at Delek's house. Delek himself limped happily out to welcome his friend.

"I just got back with the others," he explained. "We were making preparations to set out after you."

Gryph displayed his teeth in a fierce, elated grin. "I'm very glad to see you, Delek. I have much to tell you. But I think that first I had better introduce you to my wife. She has a few suggestions to make on the subject of dealing prisma."

Delek cocked an eyebrow. "Do we have a lot of it to deal?"

Gryph slapped his friend on the back and reached for his wife's hand. "Let's go inside," he said to Delek. "I want to tell you the revised, updated version of the legend of Targyn the Bandit Hunter."

"You know me," Delek said easily, "I love a good story."

Seven months later Sariana looked up from a pile of papers on her desk and smiled brightly as her husband strode into her office. He had her winter cloak over his arm. Her warm, laughing, loving smile had no impact whatsoever on his forbidding expression. Gryph glanced pointedly at the timepiece on her desk.

"I thought we agreed that you would only work half days from now until the baby arrives, Sariana. Damn it, I have to watch you every minute. This pregnancy has been twice as much work for me as it has for you. I'm the one who has to remind you to take your tonic in the mornings. I'm the one who has to be responsible for getting you to your monthly checkups with the medic. I'm the one who had to make the appointment with the dressmaker so you'd have something to wear during these last few months. And I'm the one who has to make certain you don't work too hard."

"It's all right, Gryph, you're doing an excellent job on all accounts. You are very good at handling responsibility. You thrive on it, in fact." The lizard perched on her shoulder showed its teeth to Gryph in a taunting grin.

Gryph ignored Lucky. An understandable reaction as the lizard invariably sided with Sariana. Instead, he slung Sariana's cloak into a chair and walked across the chamber to plant both hands on the circular desk. "None of your sass, lady. It's lunchtime and you're supposed to stop work for the day. I'm taking you out to a meal."

Sariana surrendered to the inevitable and stood up. Her rounded stomach was elegantly draped in the folds of a yellow velvet business dress. At least, Gryph had told her it was a business gown. Sariana still had her doubts. The lace trimmings at the collar and on the cuffs of the gown were subdued by western standards, but still seemed quite decorative to Sariana's eyes, especially for an office setting.

But she could hardly complain. When the dressmaker had arrived for the fittings of the maternity gowns, Sariana had been too busy to take much time for making decisions about clothing. As a result, Gryph had ended up making most of the decisions. Sariana's new wardrobe was a great deal more colorful than her old one.

Gryph took her arm as she came out from behind the desk. His eyes strayed possessively over her pregnant figure. "How are you feeling?" he demanded tenderly as he wrapped her carefully in her winter cloak. Lucky scrambled to find a pocket. They left Sariana's office and headed toward the front door of the villa they had recently purchased.

"Just fine."

"How about your breasts? Still tender?"

Sariana blushed and glanced around quickly to see if any of the household attendants had overheard. "For the sake of the Ship, Gryph, keep your voice down."

He paid no attention. "I was worried after what happened last night. You should have told me they were tender."

She glared at him. "I enjoyed what happened last night. Now stop worrying about it."

"I hurt you."

"No you didn't."

Gryph rounded on her, his voice rising in volume. "Ha! Don't try to tell me I didn't hurt you when I kissed your breasts last night. I was there, remember? I *felt* it."

"You wouldn't have felt it if I'd had some warning," Sariana muttered. "You took me by surprise, that's all." It was the truth. She hadn't been prepared for the unexpected discomfort of her swollen breasts and had therefore been unable to stop herself from projecting it to Gryph along with everything else she was feeling at the time. Then she hid a small grin as she remembered the exquisitely tender lovemaking of the night.

She had been deliciously aroused, thoroughly involved in the emotional, mental and physical exchange of passion. Gryph had been trying very hard to be very gentle as he always was of late. When he had lowered his head to kiss her breasts, he had intended only the lightest of caresses.

But Sariana's taut, full breasts had proven almost unbearably sensitive. Gryph had lightly set his teeth around one tight nipple and Sariana had nearly gone through the roof.

And, of course, because they were intimately, passionately linked at the time, she had nearly taken Gryph with her.

Gryph's startled reaction had been much greater than her own as the sweet pain had translated itself into his mind. He'd yelped and leaped off the bed, sending it into a wide swing. Then he'd started making plans to call a medic in the middle of the night. Sariana had been laughing so hard she had nearly fallen out of the swinging bed. Gryph had not seen the humor in the situation.

When he'd finally climbed back into bed, his body still heavy with his arousal, he had made her pay for the earlier incident. He'd grinned wickedly and sprawled on his back, arms folded behind his head.

"We won't take any chances this time," he'd stated in a low, sexy voice. "You can do all the work. I'll just lie back and enjoy it."

Sariana had obliged with a willing, loving heart. Within minutes the lightstorm that always flared between them had reignited itself. Together they had hunted wild, flaming prisma, chasing colors and shades of light that had no names.

"What about your back?" Gryph asked as he opened the front door for her and guided her out onto the street. "Any aches? The medic warned me you might have some discomfort there."

"If I do you'll be the first to know," Sariana said with a teasing grin. "Just as you were the first to know when I started having morning sickness."

He winced. "Don't remind me. At least we're long past the morning sickness stage."

Sariana chuckled, remembering that unpleasant string of days just after she had realized she was pregnant. She had been miserable and on a few occasions she had been so ill she had unconsciously projected the queasiness to Gryph, who had borne it stoically. Sariana smiled at the memory and patted her tummy. "Junior is doing just fine, thank you. And so am I."

Gryph shook his head as he steered her toward a neighborhood cafe. There was still some snow on the ground, but not on the sidewalks. Last year one of the construction clans had developed a new device for keeping the pathways clear. The town council had adopted it at once. One of the eastern clans was negotiating to buy the invention.

"You've got to start taking it easy, Sariana. You've been working much too hard these past few months. I can see I'm going to have to be firmer with you. There will be plenty of time after the boy is born for you to implement your grand plans and schemes."

"It's just that they're all coming along so nicely and I'm so excited by them."

Gryph's mouth curved wryly. "You've turned the whole Shield class upside down. Not to mention what that process has done to the rest of the western classes."

"The wonderful thing about working with westerners is that they're so adaptable," Sariana said with satisfaction.

When she had made it known that the Shield class had recently discovered a sizable cache of prisma and would be putting it on the market in controlled amounts, the representatives of virtually all the jewelers' clans had shown up on her doorstep the following day. The Avylyns had, of course, been first in line.

Since then, Sariana had been systematically investing the profits on behalf of the entire Shield class. The members of the class had been highly skeptical about turning their business affairs over to a woman, and an easterner at that. No one remembered any Shield ever having done any sophisticated investing. Selling prisma had always been a simple, straightforward process, rather like killing bandits.

But the Shields had paid attention to Sariana. Her position as Gryph's wife guaranteed her a hearing and she had found plenty of support among the other wives. Most of them remembered well the pleasures of town living. Even the most devoted among them could see the advantages of increased contact with the more sophisticated world they had left behind. The wives were also very open to the notion of providing more career options for their sons than their husbands had had. Women married to warriors tended to worry a lot.

When Gryph and Sariana reached the cafe they hurried into the cherry warmth. The proprietor recognized them and greeted them enthusiastically.

"This way, my lord and lady. I have your usual table waiting. A bit chilly today, isn't it?"

"It is," Gryph agreed. "My wife will have some of the kalala fish stew, Myrig. The medic says it's very good for pregnant ladies. I'll have my usual."

Sariana, who had been thinking of having a salad and baked fish for a change, wrinkled her nose but made no protest. When it came to having babies, Gryph had decided he was an authority.

"How's business?" Sariana asked cheerfully as the cafe proprietor scurried off to place the orders with his cook.

Gryph lounged back in his suspended chair and smiled in satisfaction. "Business is booming, as you well know. It looks like I'll be hiring a couple more men next week."

"I told you there was a market for an agency specializing in private investigative services, security guards and escorts for people who need to travel to the frontier towns."

Gryph chuckled. "You were right."

"This kind of work is the perfect transition craft for a Shield. It allows him and his clan to live in town if he wishes. His sons can go to school with the children of other classes and learn to move comfortably in society. When the time comes, those same sons will have a much broader range of acquaintances from which to choose mates. And they'll also be a lot more acceptable as husbands to families who fear losing a daughter to the frontier. Eventually, as the Shields learn the ins and outs of investments, they'll make all kinds of social inroads. In the long run money is a lot more useful than a blade bow or a knife."

Gryph shrugged. "We'll see what happens. You've made one hell of a start on singlehandedly changing a whole social system, I'll say that for you."

"The whole social class system on both continents is undergoing a lot of change and restructuring. The old inflexible rules set down by the social philosophers who sent us here never did hold as well as those planners would have liked. Nothing stays static. Trust me. Things are going to be different around here in the coming years. I'm going to help make sure that our class doesn't get left behind in the dust."

"It isn't a question of trusting you, it's a question of keeping up with you, my love. Wait until your parents see what you've accomplished during your so-called exile here."

"We'll find out soon enough, won't we?" she retorted with a grin. "They're due to arrive next week."

"Worried about how they'll react to your new husband?"

"No." Sariana smiled. "My new husband is getting rich fast, and as I have tried to explain on countless occasions, easterners have a built-in respect for anyone who controls wealth."

"You certainly didn't have to worry about your welcome from my family, did you? When my folks took one look at you and realized you were pregnant, they adopted you instantly into the clan."

"I think both your parents and mine tend to be pragmatic about certain things. Oh, that reminds me," Sariana said, "would you mind very much if we had a little girl instead of a little boy?"

Gryph nearly dropped his fork: "Sariana, that's impossible. I've explained to you that Shields only produce male offspring."

"Yes, I know," she agreed soothingly, "but something tells me that's another thing that's going to start changing on Windarra."

Gryph shook his head, perplexed. "What makes you say that?"

"I don't know," she told him honestly. "Lately I haven't always understood how I know some of the things I know. But it's occurred to me that this planet may be changing all of us in small, subtle ways." She reached up to stroke the lizard on her shoulder. "Take this matter of women turning lizards into pets and krellcats having an affinity for human males. Even in the eastern provinces it's become fashionable in recent years for men and women to keep some odd pets. I never had one because I was always studying so hard, but I knew people who did have them. And there was something strange about the relationship, Gryph, just as there's something different about the relationship scarlet-toes and krellcats have with westerners. It's not a normal people-pet relationship."

"So scarlet-toes and krellcats are a little different. So what?"

"I'm not sure," Sariana said, frowning intently as their food arrived, "but I've been thinking about it and there are some other matters which seem to indicate slight changes taking place."

"Such as?"

"How about the matter of a Shield learning to use his mind as a weapon? Both you and Targyn achieved that dubious distinction. Is there any indication that any of your ancestors had that ability?"

"Well, no, but—"

"And what about you and me?" she continued forcefully. "You've said yourself that our link is unusual in many ways."

"Sariana," Gryph said grandly, "you would be an unusual wife on any planet in the universe. I strongly suspect you're totally unique. I don't know of another woman on the face of the planet who could have convinced me to let Etion Rakken's bank handle the prisma transactions."

"Don't change the subject. There are some other matters I've been thinking about."

"Such as?" Gryph leaned back, resigned.

"It has occurred to me that your ancestors were ordinary men who showed a slight potential for some form of mental ability. The scientists found a way to strengthen part of that potential by injecting those men with some chemical. Originally everyone assumed the result would be a sterile group of Shields."

"So?"

"I've wondered if all that really happened is that those scientists simply speeded up what might be a perfectly normal development process that's going on in humans already. It might be a long-range trend that would, under normal conditions, take thousands of years to impact an entire population. The scientists who worked on your ancestors concentrated on one small element of that potential, the element they could use as a shield against prisma rays. But who knows how far that basic potential can go? Maybe the environment of Windarra somehow encourages development of that kind of mental ability in human beings."

Gryph shook his head in indulgent amusement. "What makes you say that?"

"I've been wondering why that huge prisma ship was left here. You've said yourself there's no record of such a large one being found before."

"The records could be wrong, you know. Don't forget my people have been out of touch with their home world as long as yours have been from theirs. We don't know what's been happening with prisma elsewhere."

"True. But isn't it just possible Windarra was special in some way? Perhaps it made a particularly good storage planet for mind weapons because there's something in the environment here that favors that kind of development."

"Close your lovely mouth and eat your food, my love. Pregnancy is obviously affecting your usually admirable reasoning powers."

She tilted her head and looked at him. "Are you going to spend the rest of your life telling me to shut up?"

"Are you kidding? If I devoted my time to a job that size I'd never get anything else done. Now eat up, sweetheart. You need your nourishment."

"Yes, Gryph."

Two months later little Gryphina Chassyn was born and the entire Shield class went into shock. Births were always an important event, but the birth of a female Shield was unheard of. Sariana and her baby had so many visitors Gryph was forced to hire extra household attendants just to handle the flow.

Any doubts about the child's parentage on the paternal side were immediately put to rest when visitors got a good look at the infant. Gryphina had brilliant blue-green eyes; Shield eyes. She also had her father's dark hair.

Even if some had questioned the coincidence of hair and eye color, no one could doubt the strength of the bond between Gryph and Sariana. It was obvious to everyone that Gryph was claiming his daughter. He would have been just as certain of that even if she hadn't had his eyes and hair. He knew her mother too well and too intimately. The bond between Sariana and Gryph was stronger than prisma.

"I'm exhausted," Gryph had announced a few hours after the birth as he sat on his wife's bed, holding his new daughter. "I had no idea it was going to be that rough. And you deliberately blocked most of it from me, didn't you? I know you were fighting to keep from projecting. I told you to share it with me. As usual, you didn't follow orders very well."

"Yes, I know," Sariana admitted. "But some things a woman likes to do on her own. Didn't you get enough of a taste of it there toward the end?" she added with a tired but saucy grin. "By that point I had lost all my noble, womanly fortitude. I seem to recall thinking you deserved a sample of what it was like."

Gryph laughed. "You're right. That bit at the end was about all I could take. It was worth it though," he added as he played with one tiny little fist. "She's as beautiful as you are."

"I know it was sort of a shock for you, Gryph."

"That we have a little girl? I should have known you would prove as unpredictable in the matter of making babies as you have in everything else. But what does it mean? Why us? Why now? Maybe you were right when you said that this planet was making some changes in all of us."

Sariana smiled at him, love in her eyes. "It doesn't matter as long as we'll be together to face those changes."

"Oh, we'll be together," Gryph assured her with the arrogant, unswerving conviction of a Shield. "You can count on it."

"Word of a Shield?" she teased softly.

"The word of a Shield in love," he clarified as he bent down to kiss her with infinite tenderness.

GET
LOVESTRUCK!

AND GET STRIKING ROMANCES FROM POPULAR LIBRARY'S BELOVED AUTHORS

Watch for these exciting romances in the months to come:

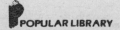

POPULAR LIBRARY